a domestic
bliss mystery

FALSE PREMISES

Leslie Caine

A DELL BOOK

FALSE PREMISES
A Dell Book / July 2005

Published by
Bantam Dell
A Division of Random House, Inc.
New York, New York

Dell is a registered trademark of Random House, Inc., and the colophon is a trademark of Random House, Inc.

ISBN 0-440-24176-6

Printed in the United States of America
Published simultaneously in Canada

www.bantamdell.com

(Printer's ID-tk) 10   9   8   7   6   5   4   3   2   1

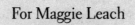
For Maggie Leach

FALSE
PREMISES

Chapter 1

For the second time in the past thirty minutes of our "girls' night out," the waitress arrived bearing drinks that Laura Smith and I hadn't ordered and didn't want. Within those same thirty minutes, we'd also been approached by two less-than-sober men asking if we were sisters. With Laura's drop-dead-gorgeous looks, that question was, at least, flattering to me, and, thankfully, Laura hadn't paled in horror. However, this latest drink offer was an unwanted interruption of a serious conversation.

Laura frowned slightly and asked the waitress, "Are these from the same guy as the last time?"

The baby-faced waitress, who had to be at least twenty-one in order to work in a bar in Colorado but looked all of fifteen, indicated with a jerk of her chin that the drink buyer was seated behind her at the brushed-aluminum bar. "Nope. A new one. And he has a buddy." She cocked her eyebrow and grinned. "They're both kind of cute, I gotta say."

Without so much as a curious glance in the men's direction, Laura replied, "Please tell them thanks, but no thanks . . . and that we're lesbians."

I hid my smile. The girl gave a slight nervous laugh, as if unsure of whether or not Laura was serious, murmured, "All righty, then," and turned away.

Laura and I were no more lesbians than we were sisters—just friends grabbing a quick bite and a glass of wine before we dashed off to hear a talk on home décor. After a dry spell, I had a new man in my life; and Laura was living with Dave Holland, a bespectacled, thirty-something man with a weak chin. Judging from the fortune that Dave had amassed, he must resemble Bill Gates in more ways than just physically. I'd met Dave and Laura nearly five months ago when Laura had hired me to decorate their gorgeous home in the foothills of the Rockies.

Come to think of it, my occupational habit of scanning my surroundings might have given the impression that I was scouting for men. In actuality, I'd merely been admiring the color scheme. The tomato-red wall behind the bar completed an eye-catching gradual transition from the lemon yellow of the opposite wall, through luscious hues of peach, apricot, orange, and pumpkin.

Laura leaned closer. "Getting back to our conversation, Erin, this was your *adoptive* mother who died, right?"

"Right. Just over two years ago from a congenital lung disease. How long ago did *your* mother pass away?" I asked.

"Fifteen years ago."

Because we were the same age, my mental math was automatic, and I cried, "So you were just twelve at the time. How awful!"

Laura merely nodded, so I continued, "She must have been fairly young. What happened to her? Was it a car accident?"

Laura turned away slightly and shook her head. She adjusted her Hermès silk scarf infinitesimally, drained the last of her Chablis, then answered quietly, "Murder."

I fought back a shudder. "She was *murdered*? My God."

Laura kept her eyes averted, but pain flickered across her face. "By my father. He killed my little brother, too. Then he took his own life."

"Good Lord. That's horrible! I'm so sorry." Reaching for the only possible positive spin, I said, "Thank God *you* were all right, though."

She gave me a sad smile and didn't respond. Then, in a near whisper, she said something that sounded like "I'm a slow bleeder."

"Pardon?"

She hooked a manicured finger in the knot of her gold and indigo scarf, slowly untied it, and revealed a pinkish-white line of skin that ran across the base of her neck. The puckered suture scars were also visible.

Her throat had once been slit.

A chill ran up my spine. In that instant, I vowed never again to feel sorry for myself and my lonely and, at times, difficult childhood. My heart ached at the unfathomable pain and horror that she'd somehow endured.

"Oh, my God," I murmured. "Laura, I'm so sorry."

In the light of her personal history, I was all the more impressed at how warm and welcoming she'd been to me from day one, when she'd hired me as her interior designer. Since that time, Laura had become more of a personal friend than a client. She'd been remarkably knowledgeable as we'd selected the million dollars' worth of antiques for her home. And yet, several weeks ago when she'd suggested that we go "bargain hunting" at a Denver flea market, she'd been every bit as comfortable and in her element while dickering over the asking price of a stained porcelain teacup as she was while selecting a handcrafted seventeenth-century armoire.

Now I understood the origin of the depth that I'd sensed in her and had found so compelling—the occasional sadness that passed over her features during quiet moments. She seemed to be unaware and unaffected by all the heads that turned her way whenever she walked by, and she noticed and found joy in the same details that I did—in the beauty of the sunlight catching an aubergine glass vase, the hue of purple-heart wood, the softness of the finest chenille, the amazing artistry and craftsmanship of Scalamandré wallpaper.

With her eyes downcast and the color rising in her cheeks, she retied her scarf.

"Do you want to tell me about it?" I asked impulsively, all the while thinking that if she said yes, I might have to signal the waitress and say that I'd changed my mind about accepting those drinks.

Laura sighed and fidgeted with a lock of her shoulder-length brown hair, a slight tremor in her fingers. "No, but thank you. Talking about it only brings back all those memories I try so hard to forget." She put her hand on top of mine on the table and, with forced gaiety, said, "Let's never mention it again, all right?"

"Of course."

She glanced at her watch. "Oh, shoot! We're late for your landlady's presentation!" She hopped to her feet and briefly insisted on leaving an overly generous tip, until she accepted my reminder that this evening was completely "my treat." The waitress benefited from Laura's and my exchange; I now felt compelled to give her the same over-sized tip.

"Actually, there's no rush," I told Laura as we left. "I've been to a couple of these events before, and Audrey's al-ways too busy signing autographs and chatting with her le-gions of fans to begin on time."

Audrey, my landlady, hosted a local television show three mornings a week entitled *Domestic Bliss with Audrey Munroe*. The name of her Martha Stewart–like show was more than a little ironic. Having shared Audrey's mansion on Maplewood Avenue for nearly six months now, I knew her to be indefatigable, irrepress-ible, and endlessly entertaining—but her domestic life was far from blissful. She allowed me to live there rent free, in exchange for the never-ending task of helping her to redecorate her home, which she did on frequent and breathtakingly rapid whims. (It took three months until she finally realized that it had been a mistake to turn the one bathtub in the house into a terrarium.) A former ballerina with the New York City Ballet, she was now in her mid-sixties, although she'd recently had a birthday and had informed me that she'd decided to welcome her birthdays by "awarding myself neg-ative numbers every year from here on out." I'd re-marked that some thirty years from now she was going to be a very old-looking thirty-five-year-old, indeed. She merely replied, with an index finger aloft, "But a wise one!"

It was a beautiful mid-April evening, and the crisp air lifted my spirits, and I didn't mind that the gentle breeze occasionally blew my auburn hair into my eyes. The sky was a rich indigo hue. The slightly deeper violet shapes of the mountains were just barely discernible in the distance. We meandered along the brick-paved pedestrian mall, window-shopping as we made the short journey to Paprika's. My relaxed mood evaporated when I realized that we were being followed: a bearded and dreadlocked man in Birkenstocks, grungy blue jeans, and a wrinkled, once-white long-sleeved shirt and sheepskin vest had left Rusty's Bar and Grill just moments after we had. Now he lingered behind us, matching our pace stride for stride.

In mock secret agent tones, I said to Laura, "Psst. Don't look now, but someone's close on our tail."

She immediately looked back. The man turned away as if waiting for someone to catch up to him.

"I wonder if that's our would-be drink purchaser, who now thinks we're lovers."

She laughed. "Oh, God. I hope not. I might have to ask you to kiss me." She again glanced back as we continued on our way. "Although by the looks of him, he'd probably be turned on."

"Oh, he looks harmless enough to me . . . though he's sure not your typical Rusty's patron." Rusty's had become the latest hot spot in Crestview; our midsize college town seemed especially prone to trendy hot spots.

"True. And he *really* doesn't look like the crystal-stemware, copper-pot type, so I'm sure we'll lose him when we go into Paprika's." She added as if in afterthought, "Not that I could blame him for not wanting to go inside. The personnel there isn't up to snuff."

"What makes you say that? I *love* the staff at Paprika's."

She gave me a warm smile as she opened the door for me. "That's only because *you* love everyone, Erin."

The man followed us inside the upscale kitchen store. Annoyed and slightly disconcerted, I whispered to Laura, "I'm going to confront him and ask why he's following us."

She touched my arm. "Let's just ignore him, okay?"

In the center of the first floor of the store, merchandise displays had been removed or shoved aside, and in their place, folding chairs had been set up to face the table where the illustrious Audrey Munroe was about to hold court. Only three chairs were empty, in the far corner of the two front rows. Audrey really had her fan club. As an interior designer, I too had been featured at a couple of these special "evening presentations," but hadn't drawn one quarter of this crowd.

We rounded the seats toward the two available chairs in the front row. From the back of the makeshift auditorium, Audrey was currently entertaining a large percentage of the customers, who were craning their necks to listen in as she joked with an elderly couple. She was wearing a chic two-piece black dress, perfectly tailored to flatter her trim, petite frame. She gave me a little wave. Beside her was Hannah Garrison, the manager of Paprika's. I could tell by Hannah's plastered-on smile that she'd been trying in vain to urge Audrey forward to begin her talk.

Hannah spotted me, grinned, and started to head over to say hello. But her smile faded midstep and mutated into a glare when she saw my companion. Puzzled, I glanced over my shoulder at Laura and caught her eyeing Hannah with a haughty smirk. Her expression seemed odd; I'd never seen Laura act the least bit haughty. Apparently Laura's dislike for the "personnel" included the store manager—and was mutual.

Hannah hesitated for a moment but soon joined us. She, like Laura and I, was in her late twenties. Tonight Hannah wore an ill-fitting skirt suit that wasn't flattering to her stubby, buxom frame. "Thank you so much for coming, Erin. It's always so great to see you." Her body

English hinted that she was trying hard to ignore Laura's presence on the other side of me.

The implication that it was *never* great for Hannah to see Laura hung in the air. I replied, "Likewise, Hannah. I love to come here."

"How are you, Hannah?" Laura asked pleasantly.

Although Hannah's smile was clearly forced, she replied, "Fine, Laura. And you?"

"Things couldn't be better. Thanks for asking."

As if it were a facial tic, Hannah's lip curled for just a split second, then she shifted her gaze to me. Hannah's arms were folded tightly across her chest, and Laura still wore the Cheshire cat grin. The tension was so palpable that I babbled, "You've got quite the crowd here tonight."

"Yes, we do," Hannah replied in hushed tones, "which is really good timing, because we've had a bit of trouble lately."

"Oh?"

"Paprika's has managed to become the target of a . . ." Her voice faded as she caught sight of the new patron in the second row, directly behind us. The bearded, scruffy man who'd followed us from the bar was apparently having some trouble getting comfortable. The front leg of his folding chair was missing its inch-tall base.

Hannah grimaced and said under her breath to us, "Speak of the devil." While Laura and I took our front-row seats, Hannah rounded our row and I heard her say quietly, "Please, sir. Not tonight. It isn't fair to Ms. Munroe, and there's no way she's going to mention you or your cause on her television show, no matter *how* big a scene you throw."

"Huh?" he muttered.

"Tell you what," Hannah said. Her tone had become patronizing. "Why don't you come to my office first thing tomorrow morning? You can air all of your grievances regarding Paprika's merchandise to me personally at that time."

Dreadlocks harrumphed and, again, seemed to deliberately turn his face when he felt Laura's gaze on him. "You don't *sell* these crappy chairs here, do you? 'Cuz someone's likely to fall off of one and break their neck."

"I'd be happy to get you a better chair, sir, in exchange for your promise that you'll listen quietly to the presentation. Please, just for tonight, keep your personal opinions about how we Americans should spend our money to yourself. Okay? Would that be too much to ask?"

I cleared my throat, hoping that I could catch Hannah's eye. She might want to let this all slide. The attention of the sixty or so people had shifted from Audrey to Hannah and Dreadlocks' conversation, which, to my mind, was defeating her purpose.

"*Look* at this!" As if to demonstrate his concern about the chair, he wobbled from side to side, the chair legs clanging against the tile floor. "This chair's totally *useless.*" He then hopped to his feet and bent down to examine the offending leg.

As he leaned over, the back of his shirt lifted a little, and I caught sight of an object tucked into his waistline. I stared in alarm as the man continued, "See? Here's the problem," he groused. "This one's busted."

Cupping my hand over my mouth so that only Laura could hear, I whispered, "Look! The guy's got a gun!"

Laura sprang to her feet. The sudden motion caught Dreadlocks' eye; he turned, and the two stared at each other. Laura gasped, then she yelled, "Get a grip on yourself! Stop hassling the poor woman! She made a perfectly reasonable request that you speak to her tomorrow!"

Why on earth was Laura so aggressive to an *armed* man? I shot a pleading look at Audrey, who cried, "Goodness! Look at the time!" and rushed forward. "Let's all take our seats—" With a nod to the still-standing dreadlocked man, she added, "Such as they are, and we'll begin talking about table settings."

As much as I wanted to set the tone by facing forward in my seat, Laura maintained her attempt to stare down the armed man. I stood up beside her. She and I had to get out of here right now; Dreadlocks wouldn't dare follow us with this many witnesses.

"Here," I said, offering him my chair. "Why don't you take this one, and—"

"You need to get out of here," Laura snarled at him. Her eyes were blazing. "Now!"

"Take it easy, miss. I'm just minding my own business, trying to learn about table settings. If *someone* could just *get* me a *freakin'* chair with four legs the same length, you *won't* hear another—"

He made a broad gesture and accidentally smacked Hannah in the chest. She gasped and stepped back.

Laura cried, "That does it!" She kicked her seat aside, grabbed the man's arm, and, in one swift motion, flipped him onto the floor, nearly upsetting a display of cutlery in the process.

The store patrons gasped and shrieked, riveted. I couldn't help but stare. The man's hair had shifted. As if merely checking his skull for injuries, he grabbed his head with both hands to center his wig. He struggled to his feet, and the weapon fell from his belt. A middle-aged woman in the seat next to his shrilled, "Oh, my God! He's got a gun!"

Everyone began to clamber to their feet. Already racing for the exit, Laura whipped out her cell phone and cried over her shoulder, "I'm calling the police! I'll be right back with them!"

Audrey's crowd also started to head for the exit. The man stuffed the gun into the back of his pants and shouted over the pandemonium, "Wait! It's okay, everyone! I'm an undercover cop!"

His words had an eye-of-the-hurricane effect on the crowd. The frantic commotion gradually quieted a little, and the two women closest to the exit hesitated and looked back at him tentatively.

"Ladies. Please! As an officer of the law, I have no intention of firing my gun, I assure you, and I'm not even on duty tonight." His voice was authoritative, even as he made placating gestures. "If everyone could please just take their seats . . ." He kept repeating this request, and eventually the edgy patrons began to shuffle back toward the chairs. The man glanced at Audrey. "Real sorry, ma'am. I'll get out of everyone's hair now." He left in the same direction that Laura had gone.

Audrey cleared her throat briskly and rang a small brass bell. "I hope everyone enjoyed my preshow entertainment, provided to you courtesy of the Free-for-All Players of Piedmont, Colorado. Be sure to check your local papers for their next performance. I hear their *Instant Shakespeare* is especially enjoyable. But right now, it's time to talk table settings."

Everyone chuckled with relief and began to reclaim their seats in earnest. There was no way I could simply sit down and listen to Audrey's presentation. Much as I wanted to believe that the wig-wearing man was truly a police officer, he hadn't shown his badge, he'd called attention to himself despite claiming to be undercover, and he was following Laura again.

I started to make my way toward the exit, past Hannah. She grabbed my elbow. "Erin. Are you all right?"

"Fine. But I'd better go check on my friend. Even though she's probably already on her way back here with a uniformed officer."

Hannah clicked her tongue and grumbled, "You obviously don't know Laura very well. There's no way she's coming back, let alone with a cop." She turned on her heel and stepped beside Audrey to introduce her to the audience.

I mouthed "Sorry" to Audrey and left. I trotted in the same direction Laura had headed and circled the entire pedestrian mall twice. Laura had vanished, as had the "undercover cop."

Worry niggled at me the next morning as I made the drive west toward Laura's sprawling mountain house, so I repeated to myself my personal mantra—confidence and optimism—which helped me to calm my nerves. Although I'd phoned Laura twice last night and left messages both times to "please call me back regardless of the hour," she hadn't returned my calls, and there'd been no answer when I tried again just an hour ago. If no one was home now, I decided, I could at least leave a note on the door.

I parked in the driveway of the two-story house, which, with its formidable white columns and arched windows, had a grand, *Gone with the Wind* aura despite its stucco exterior and mountain setting. I rang the doorbell and glanced around as I waited on the porch. The flowers were starting to bloom, after a late start. The climate in the mountains tends to delay Colorado's lower-elevation growing season by a good month or so.

Laura's boyfriend answered the door. Dave Holland had a case of bed head—the hair on the back of his head stuck straight up in the air like the flag on a mailbox—and he wasn't wearing his thick glasses. He gave me a goofy grin and queried cautiously, "Erin?"

"Yes. Hi, Dave."

"Well. Hello there. Long time no see."

"How've you been, Dave?"

"Good. Just got back from a long business trip to Atlanta late last night."

"Oh, dear. I hope I didn't wake you. I came over to see Laura. Is she home?"

"Yeah. She's in the john or something, but she'll be right out. Come on in."

"Thanks." I closed the door behind me as I entered the foyer. To my frustration, Dave, who was at least six foot two, was standing so close to me that he was blocking my view into the house.

He rocked on his heels a little and crossed and then re-crossed his arms. "I'd offer you something to drink, but it'd take me forever. My glasses seem to have disappeared. My *eye*glasses, I mean, not the drinking glasses. Anyway, point is, I'm as blind as a bat without them."

"Jeez. That's got to be really unpleasant. Don't you have any backup glasses, or contact lenses?"

"Yeah, but I seem to have misplaced *those,* as well. All I've got are my prescription sunglasses, but I feel like an idiot wearing those indoors. Anyway, I've been meaning to tell you, Laura's still loving all these hoity-toity old antiques you pulled together for us. Hardly a day goes by when she doesn't mention how much she likes this thing or the other." He stepped back and leaned against the doorjamb.

"That's great to hear. I'm always . . ." My voice drifted as my attention was captured by the Louis XV mirror in the foyer. Something was terribly wrong.

"You're always *what*?" Dave prompted.

Stunned into silence, I walked over to the giltwood

mirror and gently touched the frame. This was a cheap copy of the astonishing circa 1760 piece that I'd helped them purchase for twenty thousand dollars! And I'd had to dicker hard to get the antiques dealer to sell it at that price.

Dave squinted at me. "Is something the matter with the mirror? Or with your face?"

"The mirror was hanging a little crooked." Inwardly, I was shaking. Because Laura was my friend but I barely knew Dave, I wanted to discuss this with her first.

Had my clients been swindled? Had someone managed to swap this mirror with the expensive one that I'd installed? But how would that be possible? Laura's knowledge of antiques was comparable to my own. The inferiority of the scrollwork on the gold spray-painted frame was blatant.

I took a calming breath. Surely I was panicking over nothing. Dave or Laura must have simply decided that twenty grand for a mirror was too much, so they'd returned it.

"Grab a seat," Dave suggested as he ushered me into their front room. "I'll go see where she is."

My knees nearly buckled, but I managed to sputter "Thank you" as he wandered away to look for Laura. Though horror-struck, I remained standing. This room had been my personal masterpiece—my chance to work with an unlimited budget and a sophisticated client whose tastes mirrored my own. The results had been glorious, a radiant ensemble of unparalleled beauty in these irreplaceable handcrafted pieces that brought such serenity and warmth to the space, a household that conjured images of less-harried times when one-of-a-kind quality was celebrated and attention to detail mattered. Now just the dressings remained. The subtle peach hues on the ethereal lofted walls were the same, as were the vi-

brant window treatments, the to-die-for accessories, and
even the spectacular Oriental area rug with its rich classic
royal reds and blues. All unchanged. But the antiques, the
very heart and soul of the room and which I'd poured my
own heart and soul into to find, had been replaced with
fakes.

Reeling, I studied the chair by the door. Two months
ago, we had placed a Mary Washington chair from the
1800s in this very spot. Although the upholstery of the
two chairs was roughly the same cinnamon color, this
one's hand—that all-important feel of the fabric against
one's skin—was dreadful. The stretcher was now a plain
dowel, and the front legs had been lathed with modern
machinery.

My stomach in knots, I made my way to the writing
table. Pulling the drawer all the way out, I had to bite my
lip as I caught sight of the bottom. Cheap particleboard.
The joinery was crap—stapled together. The eighteenth-
century desk I'd selected and installed in this house had
been handcrafted with loving dovetail precision, mortise
and tenon legs. Sick at heart, I replaced the drawer.

I'd stepped into my own worst nightmare. Every stick
of furniture in sight had gone from a gorgeous antique
to a tacky reproduction. Anything beyond a cursory inspection would reveal that at once to any knowledgeable
eye.

What the hell was going on here?

Could someone have conned Laura and Dave into believing these fakes and frauds were the fortune in antiques
that they'd purchased? But that was impossible. Laura
would know instantly that these were fakes. And the au-
thentic pieces had been in place the last time I was in this
house, just two months earlier.

There was the slightest hitch in Laura's step as she
walked into the room and spotted me, and it broke my

heart. I'd come uninvited, and, obviously, she knew I would instantly realize that the furnishings had been switched.

"Erin," she said, that warm, Julia Roberts–like smile instantly on her face. "This is a surprise."

Chapter 2

Had Laura hidden Dave's glasses because she'd sold the antiques while he was on his business trip? Did she now plan to skip town with the profits? No, that was absurd. Nobody in their right mind would attempt such a thing. And Laura was a wonderful friend. I felt a pang of guilt for even thinking that she'd do something so rotten and underhanded.

I tried to calm myself. "I came over to make sure you were okay. I had visions of that guy you flipped to the floor last night tracking you down a second time. He left just a minute after you did."

"That's what *I* was afraid he'd do, too," Laura replied. "So I headed straight for my car while calling the police.

I'm sorry I didn't call you back and explain all that to you last night. But Dave had been gone a whole month and got home unexpectedly, and we had a lot of catching up to do."

"Did you recognize the guy with the dreadlocks or something?"

"Unfortunately. Though not at first . . . not underneath the beard and all that phony hair." She glanced over her shoulder, then said softly, "I don't know his name or anything, but he's been stalking me all over town."

"He *has*? Stalking you? Why?"

"I have no idea. He must have spotted me someplace and developed an infatuation." She combed her hair back from her face, her fingers trembling slightly. "What happened after I left?"

"He claimed he was an undercover cop, then he left, too."

Laura absently stroked her neck along the line of her cream-and-rose-tinted silk scarf. "He's no cop. I'm sure of at least *that* much."

Despite the serious subject matter, the duplicated furniture surrounding us pulled my attention like iron filings to a magnet. It was all I could do to keep my eyes focused on hers. I asked, "But you don't know where he lives or works? And why he suddenly donned a wig?"

"Exactly."

It was no use; my vision was drawn to the camelback sofa against the east wall. The seat cushions and back used to be covered in black woven horsehair, painstakingly blended with the original strands. The upholstery was now some sort of trashy-looking nylon-synthetic blend.

"It scares me half to death," Laura said, recapturing my full attention. "At least the police are on the lookout for the guy now, so maybe they'll catch him soon."

"I hope so. Plus, you showed him you're no pushover when you used him as your judo partner last night."

"*Judo* partner?" Dave repeated as he returned to the room.

Laura laughed lightly. "I was honing my self-defense skills last night with Erin." She pressed her chest against him in the process of giving him a little peck on the cheek and, in sugary tones, asked, "Sweetie, could you please go take care of that thing you were telling me about earlier?"

"What 'thing'?"

"The burned-out lightbulb in the basement that you promised you'd replace."

"Oh. Right. No problem." He gave me a small smile. "Nice to see you again, Erin." He added with a chuckle, "Even though you're mostly blurry."

"Good seeing you, too, Dave. And I hope you find your glasses very soon."

"One of these days you'll learn not to be so absent-minded," Laura said to him.

"Too late . . . that ship has sailed," he replied as he left the room, touching the wall as he cautiously rounded the corner.

The moment he was out of earshot, I demanded, "What's going on?"

"With our antiques?" Laura asked, her voice breezy. "Didn't I tell you about all that?"

"No."

"We're speculating . . . selling them, eventually, but we're holding on to them in safe storage for a couple of years until their value increases and we can find some really motivated buyers."

I stared at her, incredulous, yet she didn't blink. Prior to this moment, she hadn't mentioned one word about "speculating," and that would have influenced my furniture selections immeasurably. Also, why would they duplicate their antiques with cheap replicas? "And yet you didn't want to enjoy them yourselves in the meantime?"

She crinkled her nose. "Originally, that's what we'd planned to do." She sighed. "You've seen for yourself how Dave is, though. He's such a klutz even *with* his glasses that, sooner or later, he was bound to do some serious damage to something priceless."

My mind was in a whirl. Laura's explanation wasn't adding up; I needed to leave and sort through my thoughts. She continued, "He already managed to burn a hole clear through our new coffee table. He fell asleep with a lit cigarette on the edge of the ashtray."

"I didn't realize he smoked," I replied absently. Smoking habits was one of my standard questions whenever I met with new clients to design their rooms; that affected my decisions from furniture placement to fabric selection. Both Dave and Laura had said they were nonsmokers. *Why was my dear friend lying to me?* "Had you already swapped the table with a reproduction?"

"Yes, thank God."

I forced a smile, my stomach in knots. "Well, Laura, I'm glad to see that you're all right. I'd better get to my client's house now."

"Thanks so much for dropping by, Erin. Let me walk you to your car." She took my arm as we walked down the sandstone front steps. "I feel terrible about how our girls' night out yesterday got cut so short. But let me tell you how I'm making it up to you." She paused dramatically. "I've got a friend in Lyons who told me that she knows the owner of this gorgeous mansion up there, which, rumor has it, houses the nicest antiques west of the Mississippi. So, my friend is going to ask if you and I can take a private tour of the place sometime next week."

"Really? That sounds great." At least, it *would* have

sounded great fifteen minutes ago, before I'd spied her houseful of reproductions.

"You can say that again. But that is strictly *entre vous et moi*." She hesitated. "That is, if what I just said means 'between you and me' in French."

"It does."

"Oh, good." She grimaced. "It'd serve me right if I'd just accidentally told you to enter through my left nostril." Her laughter was infectious, as always, despite the circumstances. "Don't you just hate it when people throw French phrases into their speech? It is *so* pretentious!"

"Absolutely." I unlocked the door of my van. "I find it *trés ennuyeux, mon cher!*"

She laughed merrily. "I'll call you in a couple of days about Lyons. And, again, thank you for checking in on me. I'm really touched that you cared enough to come all the way out here."

She gave me a quick hug, and I told her honestly, "I'm just glad to see that you're all right, Laura. Let's talk soon, okay?"

She trotted toward the door, turned, flashed her glorious smile at me, and, as she ducked through her door, cried over her shoulder, "Brrr! I'm freezing my *derriere* off!" She winked. "That's French for 'sorry ass.'"

I mulled over our conversation as I drove away. I truly liked and admired Laura, and it would hurt me deeply to lose her friendship. There was surely a simple, innocent explanation for the smoking-versus-nonsmoking issue; Dave must be one of those people who quits smoking periodically but always believes that, this time, he'll kick the habit for good. But the cheap reproductions were harder to explain away. Why not place the speculative antique purchases directly into storage? Why duplicate everything, item for item? Most tellingly, if her actions were aboveboard, why hadn't she told me of her plans?

The mega-wealthy often wear paste jewelry copied from the phenomenally pricey jewelry that they keep locked in their personal vaults. Surely it wasn't unheard of to do the same thing with one's antique furniture. Which was not to say that I'd ever heard of such a thing. But surely there were *some* antiques collectors and dealers who put their items in storage and lived with the replicas.

It's just that, unfortunately, my every instinct was screaming at me that Laura Smith was not one of them.

Two hours later, I felt frustrated as I left my client's house. He was a wealthy widower who wanted to completely revamp his lifestyle and had hired an image consultant, who, in turn, had hired me. Although my client had denied it when I asked him point-blank, he seemed to be having serious second thoughts regarding our agreed-upon plans for his home makeover. If so, the sooner we got in sync the better. The design business is based on referrals, and I'd hoped that this job would lead to more work with the image consultant. That would never happen if my client was unhappy with the final results.

I felt myself easing up on the accelerator as I neared the café where I was supposed to meet my boyfriend, John Norton, for a lunch date. That wasn't a good sign. On the surface, John was the perfect match for me. It's just that I had the sinking suspicion that our relationship was heading down my typical path—even though he was wonderful in many ways, ultimately he was just not *the one*. We'd only been going out for two months, however—not long enough for me to come to a definitive conclusion. Besides, I could unconsciously be holding him accountable for something—and someone—he had no control over whatsoever.

I pulled into a space in the restaurant lot, shut off the engine, and sat in my van, staring through the windshield.

John was a terrific guy—nice-looking in that clichéd tall, dark, and handsome way. He was also intelligent and charming. He even had a professional interest in interior design; he managed a design center for one of the largest residential developers in the state and was in charge of furnishing showcase "demo" homes for his employers. It certainly wasn't *John's* fault that Steve Sullivan, of all people, had been the one to set up the two of us.

To John, Sullivan was an old friend. To me, Sullivan was a sometimes friend, sometimes professional rival. What Sullivan *always* was, though, was an enormous thorn in my side. With our downtown offices on the same street and separated by just three blocks, potential customers—especially the ones who were familiar with comic English operattas—sometimes got Gilbert versus Sullivan confused. In the two and a half years since I'd first moved to Crestview, both of us had been guilty of falsely accusing the other of deliberately taking advantage of our clients' confusion. A couple of months ago, just as our frayed feelings were finally on the mend, they'd unaccountably begun to unravel once again when John and I started dating.

The door to my van opened, and I jumped, my reverie abruptly shattered. John smiled at me, his dark eyes merry. "Oops. Sorry. Didn't mean to startle you. I spotted you through the window and figured you might be waiting for a personal escort, beautiful lady."

"I was just lost in thought." I returned his smile. "But I'll gladly accept an escort, kind sir."

He gave me a peck on the cheek as he helped me down from the van. "Client troubles?"

"Something like that."

He held the restaurant door for me. The female maître d'

gave him an appreciative once-over as she deposited us at our table. He and I chatted effortlessly, and I soon began to realize, as I always did whenever we were alone together, why it was that I was so drawn to him. John was excellent company and a really good guy. I was nuts to think that there was no magic between the two of us. I took a moment to silently admire his features. In his mid-thirties, John had the most wonderful laugh lines imaginable; when he smiled, they crinkled at the edges of his dark eyes, making them all the more appealing.

We ordered our lunch, and while we ate, I started to relate how I'd arrived at a client's house this morning and found her "myopic boyfriend" stumbling around the place and the antiques "downgraded to chintzy reproductions."

"Man, that's weird," John exclaimed. "So, what'd your client have to say for herself?"

"Well, the 'client' is my friend Laura . . . the one I went to Audrey's presentation with last night? She basically claims that she's keeping all of her pricey antiques under lock and key, while she and her boyfriend use the much less expensive replicas. She says they're simply speculating with the antiques and hope to sell them at a profit in another couple of years."

John's brow furrowed as he polished off the last bite of his chicken tetrazzini. "Her name's Laura?"

"Yeah. Laura Smith."

John nearly choked and had to grab for his water glass. He held up his palm as he struggled to regain his composure, as well as his air supply. "Sorry," he said after a moment. "I know a Laura Smith. I hope to God that's not the same woman. Describe her to me."

"She's roughly my size . . . five eight . . . about my weight, as well. Dark brown hair and eyes. Stunning.

Looks a lot like Angie Harmon from the TV show . . . the actress who married the football player."

To my increasing consternation, John was staring at me with his jaw agape. He cried, "Oh, shit, Erin! You're *friends* with this woman?"

"Yes. Why? Who *is* she?"

"Erin," he said, holding my gaze, "Laura *Smith*—or whatever her real last name is—is Steve Sullivan's infamous 'Laura.' "

"Oh, my God." If I'd been eating at that particular moment, I, too, would have nearly choked. "Oh, no. I can't . . . ! My friend Laura Smith is . . . the same woman who conned Steve and ran off with his former business partner?"

John nodded, the muscles in his jaw working. "The woman who ripped him off for all he was worth."

Stunned, I sat still and tried to fathom this revelation. There went my last shred of hope that there was an innocent explanation for the replaced antiques. My thoughts raced back through all the intimate personal details I'd shared with Laura while considering her a friend. I now knew a measure of what Steve must have felt; I, too, had been betrayed. "But . . . I thought she and Evan Cambridge had left the country, let alone the state of Colorado."

"They must have come back."

"Obviously. But *why*? Why come back to the same town where they can get thrown in jail?"

"They must be planning some sort of major con job. Could this 'boyfriend' of hers maybe be *Evan* in disguise?"

"No. I met Evan three or four times, and this is a different guy. Laura refers to Dave as her . . . life partner or something." This news was simply too bizarre to accept. "I can't believe that she . . . did this to me. Whatever 'this' is. She hasn't actually *done* anything yet."

"Makes you wonder. . . . If she was pulling off some sort of heist or con, why hire a designer who could catch her in the act?"

"She must've never intended to let me back into her house once her scam was under way. By using a professional designer and befriending me, I'd be an expert witness she could use if the insurance company questioned how valuable her belongings were. Meanwhile, her fakes are good enough to fool most everyone else, so she can . . . destroy her own home, supposedly with those priceless antiques still in place."

The more I thought about it, the angrier I became. "That little witch! No wonder she was so careful to document everything . . . getting certificates of authenticity from the antiques appraiser, taking photos of each piece. They live in the mountains, where there's always such a big risk of forest fires. They're probably going to torch the house and then quietly sell the antiques on the Internet!" I paused. "Or *she* is. Dave's seemingly clueless . . . there just to sign the checks. But that could be an act, for my benefit. Damn it all! *Now* I wish I'd asked Dave Holland about the missing antiques right away."

"So you're thinking this is an arson fraud in the offing."

"It's possible. She told me the household contents have been insured for a million dollars. Judging by the front room, they're now worth one-fiftieth that amount." I couldn't help but add under my breath, "She acted like we were getting to be such good friends."

"Are you finished eating?" John asked, his features grim.

I nodded at my half-full plate. "I've lost my appetite all of a sudden."

He signaled the waitress, pushed back his chair, and

dropped his red linen napkin on the table. "We'd better pay a visit to Sullivan . . . try to ease him into the news that Laura's back in town. If he's caught off guard, he'll do something crazy. Like wring her neck."

A deep, muffled voice was coming from the office as John cracked open the carved, custom-made oak door. Over his shoulder, he told me, "Sounds like he's with a client." I peered past him to see that Sullivan was alone and on the phone. He held a hand over the mouthpiece as John said, "Hey, Steve. I'm here with Erin. When you have a minute, we've got some business to discuss."

Sullivan gestured for us to come in. A designer's office is his first and best line of advertising, and this one was so effective that I had to prevent my brown eyes from turning green whenever I entered. Sullivan's taste was pure contemporary: clean lines, "less is more," nothing bulky, nothing that detracted from the sheer grace of the space. Though few, each furnishing he'd selected was exquisite. The texture of the wool Berber carpeting was sublime and augmented perfectly the grain of his knotty alder desk and cabinetry. His simple-but-astonishing sitting area in the back corner with its pair of posh, comfy club chairs and Sullivan-designed tiger-maple coffee table beckoned visitors to come peruse through his delectable portfolio. John and I, however, sat down in the two sleek, ultra-modern steel-gray chairs facing Sullivan's desk. The light fixtures suspended from the ceiling were formed from this same burnished steel. On the exposed brick wall behind him hung a single, unframed oil canvas—an iron-red horizon against a black background that looked like an emblazoned desert at nightfall.

Sullivan was wearing a white Arrow shirt, the sleeves rolled up. His light-brown hair was, as always, slightly in need of combing—a look that was surely calculated to make women yearn to run their fingers through it to straighten it for him. His hazel eyes were nothing short of gorgeous, but lately they were often angry in my presence. Even now there was a tightness to his handsome features.

Because it was infinitely safer, I shifted my admiring gaze to his marvelous desk. Its sexy lines with their gentle flair in the base and legs were so typical of a Sullivan design that he'd surely had this piece custom built. He completed his conversation, hung up, and said, "Hey, Erin, John. What's up?" He gave me only the briefest of glances before meeting John's gaze.

"Erin's got a new client who has a rocky personal history with you," John began.

"What do you mean by a 'rocky personal history'?" He finally looked at me. "Did I offend some client of yours somehow, Gilbert? If so, you'll have to fill me in from the top."

"It's nothing like that." Suddenly nervous and uncomfortable, I glanced at John, who nodded at me to go ahead. "John's talking about a friend of mine. At least, I *thought* she was a friend. She started out as my client four or five months ago. She acted so nice, and we seemed to have a lot of things in common and really hit it off. Maybe I should have thought twice, with her name being 'Laura' and all . . . but I didn't make the connection to you."

Steve's face paled, and I felt my own face growing warmer by the second. I continued, "You've never told me *your* Laura's last name. I dropped in on her unexpectedly today and found out she'd done this really odd thing with the antiques in her house . . . swapped them for reproductions. I happened to be telling John about it over lunch . . . and I mentioned her name."

Steve got to his feet. "Laura *Smith*?" he snarled, already in a rage. He leaned over his desk and shouted in my face, "Where is she? Where does she live? Give me her address, Erin! Now!"

"That's not a good idea," John said, rising, as well.

"Hey! This is *my* life we're talking about! Besides, I'm not going to do anything stupid. I just want to talk to that thief face-to-face."

I stood up. "Fine, Sullivan. I don't have any appointments scheduled for more than an hour. I'll drive you."

"You don't need to babysit me, for Christ's sake!"

"Maybe not, but unless I'm there, too, I'm not telling you her address or phone number," I replied firmly, trying not to flinch in the face of his fury. "If Laura's the major con artist everyone thinks she is, you might need a witness in case she tries to pull another fast one on you. So either I go with you, or you don't go at all."

Sullivan glared at me, no doubt on the verge of wanting to wring *my* neck. John interjected smoothly, "She's right, Steve. You confront Laura on your own, and she's liable to fake injuries and have you arrested for assault."

John gave Sullivan a moment to let this sink in. After a moment, Sullivan sighed. He raked both hands through his hair. "Guess you're right."

John glanced at his watch. "Listen, I was supposed to be back at work fifteen minutes ago, so I gotta run. Let me know how things pan out and what I can do to help." He gave me a quick kiss, then strode over to Sullivan and clapped his hand on his friend's shoulder. "Keep your head and play your cards right, dude. This could be your one and only chance to get your money back. So play it cool."

With the fury of a man so livid that he could mangle a steel bar with his bare hands, Sullivan retorted, "Yeah. Cool. No problem."

During the drive to Laura's home, Sullivan was so on edge he looked like a store mannequin whose joints couldn't bend far enough to let him fit in my passenger seat. I filled him in on Laura's and my encounter last night with the apparently phony "undercover cop," which made no more sense to Sullivan than it did to me. I then told him how Laura's boyfriend had "lost" his glasses. "John and I were thinking that Laura's probably pulling some kind of insurance scam. Maybe she's planning on burning down her house, then she'll sell off the real antiques."

Sullivan grumbled, "Sounds like something she'd do. You've met Evan, haven't you? Her boyfriend wouldn't be Evan in disguise, would he?"

"John asked me the same thing. But no way. They're different men. This guy's name is Dave Holland. Have you—"

"Holland? Shit! That's the guy she left a year and a half ago to take up with me. Or I should say, in order 'to take me,' period."

"Is he a con artist, too?"

"Not as far I know. But I don't make assumptions about people's innocence anymore. Not after what Laura and Evan did to me."

I clicked my tongue. "You can't mistrust *everyone* just because you ran into two bad apples, Sullivan!"

"I *don't.* I just mistrust my judgment of people."

"Which works out to be the same thing. You hold yourself back because you assume the worst."

"Yeah? Well, let's see how trusting and gregarious *you* feel, next time some client wants to stock their household in pricey furniture and become all chummy with you."

I fired back: "I'll take that risk, anytime."

"Sure," Sullivan scoffed. "But that's only because *you* didn't get your heart ripped out of your chest in the process."

Stung, I retorted: "It's not like you're the only person who's ever been hurt, Sullivan."

"True. But how many of us nearly lose their business and are driven to the verge of bankruptcy in the process?"

"That would depend upon how many ruthless divorce attorneys there are out there. It's not all that uncommon in messy divorce cases."

"You know what I mean, Gilbert. Laura lived with me for a year, pretending to love me. Then she stole all of my money!"

I negotiated a switchback as I neared Laura's mountain home. "Okay, I admit it . . . you were taken worse than anyone I know. But tell me something, Sullivan. Do you think that this hardship of yours means that you've won the right to be embittered for the rest of your life? Is it really worth trusting no one because one woman betrayed you?"

He said nothing for a minute or two, then, while staring straight ahead and not looking at me, he asked quietly, "Is Norton treating you right?"

"Yes. John's a great guy. Thanks for introducing us."

"That's the third or fourth time you've thanked me."

"Is it?" I was surprised. I hadn't thought we'd even *seen* each other three or four times since I'd started dating John.

"Yeah, but even so, you're running a distant second," Sullivan added. "Norton's thanked me a couple dozen times for introducing him to you."

"That's sweet." He truly was a great guy. And nice-looking. I should be thrilled that he was so interested in me.

Sullivan fidgeted with the door to my glove box, which was slightly askew ever since I'd bashed into it with my easel last month. "So, Gilbert. You in love with him?"

"We've only been dating for six weeks."

"It's been more than *eight* weeks."

That was true, actually, and I don't know why I'd said that it was only six. "Why are you keeping track?"

He frowned and didn't answer. I ground my teeth as I made the turn onto Laura's dead-end street. If he'd wanted to go out with me two months ago, he could have asked. At *that* time, I'd have said yes. Instead, he'd fixed me up with his buddy, as though I were a garish table-cloth that he couldn't wait to foist off on someone else. Now that he'd emptied out his linen closet, was he having second thoughts? If so, Sullivan was not only too late, but his behavior spoke volumes about his maturity level.

Fuming, I pulled into Laura's driveway and slammed on the brakes. Sullivan didn't even notice our unnecessarily abrupt stop. He was too busy staring at the stately two-story stucco house.

"So this is her place? Damn. Must be worth a cool million, easy. Not to mention that she's doubled the value with pricey furnishings. We should have brought the cops with us. Arrested her on the spot."

"For *what*? Suspicion of a fraud that hasn't even taken place yet?" I sighed, detesting how shrill my voice was. Something about Sullivan always brought out the worst in me, so maybe it was good that *one* of us had realized the wisdom in maintaining our distance. My ego would have preferred that particular discretion to have been mine, however. In softer tones, I asked, "Do you have any hard evidence whatsoever that she was in on Evan's scheme of stealing from you?"

"No," he said bleakly. "None that would stand up in a court of law, at any rate."

"That's what I was afraid of . . . it explains why she was willing to risk returning to Crestview."

I started to open my door, but Sullivan touched my thigh, then quickly jerked his hand away. "Do me a favor, Gilbert. When she comes to the door, pretend you're madly in love with me. Just for Laura's benefit, I mean."

"I can't."

"You *can't*?"

"It's too late for that. Women talk, you know. I told her all about John. She told me all about Dave."

"But you never mentioned *me*. Obviously." He got out of the van and slammed the door savagely.

"Obviously," I told him. "I doubt she even realized that you and I know each other. She probably just called Interiors by Gilbert at random."

He shook his head. "You're not getting it, Gilbert. The woman is a *professional* con artist. *Nothing* Laura does is 'at random.' Besides, she'd have known your name from me."

"But . . . we barely knew each other back when you two were together."

"Yeah, but I used to complain to her about Interiors by Gilbert moving into town just down the street from Sullivan Designs. She'd have thought she was hiring my archrival when she hooked up with you, and she'd have loved every minute of it."

"And yet look at us now," I said evenly, through a deliberately forced-looking smile. "Bosom buddies." We headed up the sandstone walkway, Sullivan maintaining such a purposeful march with his long legs that I had to trot to keep up with him. He pressed the doorbell so hard I half expected the button to crack into pieces.

A moment later, a positively radiant-looking Laura Smith threw open the door. Surprisingly, I felt a surge of anger at the sight of her that could easily be akin to hatred. Even more surprising—and frustrating—to me, tears stung my eyes.

Laura beamed at Sullivan as though she'd been expecting this visit, and squealed, "Oh, my gosh! Stevie! It's *so* good to see you!"

Chapter 3

Sullivan backed away, avoiding Laura's embrace. "Where's Evan?" he growled.

She donned a facial expression poised beautifully between hurt and perplexed. "Do you mean Evan *Cambridge*? Your slimy former partner?"

"Cambridge . . . Collins . . . whichever alias he was using while you two were working together!" Sullivan dragged his fingers through his tousled hair with both hands, as if to give them something to do other than strangle her.

"Evan and I have never worked together, and I honestly haven't got the faintest idea where he is."

"Bullshit!"

Her eyes welled with tears. She gave me a glance that managed to make her look both injured and confused, then returned her attention to Sullivan. Softly she said, "Stevie, why are you acting like this? What we once had was *special*. Just because things didn't work out doesn't mean you have to hate me."

"Cut the crap already! I'm totally on to you! You and Evan stole my money! You stole my car! I want it back! All of it!" He raised his hands and took a step closer, but then stopped himself from grabbing her shoulders. Instead he shouted into her face, "I want my *life* back, Laura!"

If Steve did take a swing at her, I wasn't sure I could blame him; I surely couldn't *stop* him. I glanced behind us, but there were only two houses with any view of this porch, and none of Laura's neighbors was outside. Dave, though, if he was still home, would surely be roused to join us any second now.

Laura started to cry openly. She searched Sullivan's eyes and said gently, "Oh, Steve. What's happened to you? And what kind of a monster do you think I am? I loved you once, and I thought you loved me, too. Can't you see? I had nothing to do with *anything* that Evan did to you."

Sullivan scoffed, "You're going to stand there and blame it all on Evan? Even though you knew about my getting ripped off . . . and *you* left town at the very same time!"

"Of course I *heard* about it . . . eventually." She swiped at her tears. "I asked around about you. When I moved back into town five months ago. Someone told me what Evan had done, and I felt terrible for you."

A chilly gust swept down the mountainside, knocking the three of us a little off balance with its force. The instant I'd regained my balance, my vision fell on the fake antique mirror behind Laura. I could see its shoddy craftsmanship, even at a distance. Resuming her Academy Award–caliber performance, Laura dried the last of her tears and said, "Why don't you both come inside? We'll try to unscramble this misunderstanding."

"No way!" Steve balled his fists. "I just want to know where Evan is . . . and where my money is. Then I want to get the hell away from you, forever! I did lots of detective work, Laura, and I know exactly how you two managed to scam me. Evan posed as me, and the two of you drove my Lexus to St. Louis and sold it. Then you bought two plane tickets and flew to Paris together from St. Louis."

Laura was shaking her head the entire time Sullivan was shouting his accusations at her. When he paused for air, she said emphatically, "No, Steve, you're wrong. I took a *taxi* to DIA, and my flight to Paris connected in St. Louis. I *did* happen to bump into Evan there, but that was just a strange coincidence."

"Jesus! I don't believe this!" Sullivan whacked his forehead with the heel of his hand.

As if thinking I was the only one rational enough to believe her, Laura turned to me. "There was a delay in St. Louis, so I went out to the ticketing area to see if I could switch flights. Evan and I happened to bump into each other there, and he claimed Steve had sent him to France to scope out some foreign suppliers for a major new client of theirs." She returned her attention to Sullivan. "I had no *possible* way of knowing that he'd stolen your money, Steve. You and I had just broken up, and I was heartbroken. I . . . needed a shoulder, so I waited in line with Evan, and we managed to get seats next to each other. We went our separate ways after we landed, and I never saw him again."

"My God, Laura!" Sullivan cried. "You don't actually expect anyone to believe that crock of shit, do you?"

Now Laura was finally starting to show some anger, though it was a mere fraction of his. "Yes! It happens to be the truth!" The wind was whipping her dark hair around, and she tucked it behind her ears and told him: "For what it's worth, I can certainly see how it must look to you. And that's precisely why I didn't call to tell you I was back in town. Once I heard what Evan had done . . . and knowing that I'd accidentally sat next to him on the flight . . . I was afraid you would assume the two of us were in league together." She sighed and glanced over her shoulder at the open doorway, as if longing to escape the cold. "Besides, I figured it was probably best left that way in the long run . . . you could go on blaming me for our breakup. *I* was willing to play the part of the bad guy, if that made things easier for you."

Sullivan let out a growl. To my dismay, he shifted his attention to me. "This . . . sugarcoated *poison* is what I swallowed for over a year. The thing is, *Laura*"—he jabbed a finger at her—"the police learned that a woman matching *your* description, who claimed to be my *wife*, sold *my* Lexus to a used-car dealer in St. Louis! She was *with* Evan Cambridge, who posed as me, and was armed with a forged driver's license."

She took in his accusations without so much as a blink of her beautiful brown eyes. "What can I say, Steve? Your information is wrong. I can prove precisely when I flew from Denver to St. Louis. In fact, I'm fairly certain that I still have my boarding pass. I used it as a bookmarker in some dreadful tome that I eventually gave up on. Do you want me to find it and show it to you?"

"That wouldn't prove anything," he shot back. "You flew to St. Louis while Evan drove out in my car. Then the two of you hocked my car and flew to Paris together."

"Wrong! I was only in St. Louis for three or four hours. I never left the airport. If you keep slandering me like this, *I'll* be forced to get the authorities to pull the records so that they can verify the times!"

"*Then* what would you do? Sue me? You've already ripped me off for every dime I ever earned!"

Laura said quietly, "You poor thing. You really can't accept that I simply chose to leave you."

Sullivan let out another growl and stepped toward her. Hastily, I thrust myself between them. I needed to calm him down before his temper completely exploded.

"Whoever the woman was that helped Evan steal your car, it wasn't *me*," Laura insisted. "She was probably a friend of Evan's in the St. Louis area. You know how easily Evan can hoodwink people. After all, he fooled both of us completely."

"But *you* took my title for the Lexus out of the desk in our bedroom, Laura! Evan wouldn't have known where to look for it."

"Or maybe, since you only had the *one* desk at home, he took an educated guess where it would be."

A black sports coupe pulled into the driveway and stopped behind my van. The driver shut off the engine and got out. It was Dave Holland; this time he wore sunglasses. "Hey," he shouted. "Laura? What's going on? Is everything okay?"

Steve sent a scalding glance in Dave's direction, then said firmly, "The police have a warrant for your arrest, Laura. Yours and Evan's."

Sullivan's bluff had no effect on Laura. She spread her arms. "That doesn't scare me in the least. I'll tell them the same thing I just told you, and they'll have to let me go, because I'm innocent."

Dave marched past us to Laura's side and threw his arm around her protectively. She buried her face in his jacket, whimpering, "Thank God you're finally home."

He hugged her and whispered, "It's all right, sweetie." Then he snapped at Steve, "Get it through your thick skull, asshole! It's over! She's never coming back to you! So get the hell out of here!"

"Dave," I cried, "we're just here to try to locate Evan Cambridge, Steve's old partner. You've obviously already heard what—"

"Yeah," he retorted. "I know exactly what Cambridge did to Sullivan. And we figured out that you'd think my Laura was involved. But she *wasn't*." He grimaced and wagged his finger in Steve's face. "Considering the way you treated her after you duped her into leaving me, you had—"

"Give me a break!" Steve fired back. "I never mistreated her!"

"Like hell you didn't!" Dave yelled, gently pushing Laura behind him until he was blocking her from Steve. "You think you need to use your fists on a woman to make you feel like a man, you coward!"

The men's anger was scaring me. "Steve—" I began.

"That's a crock!" Steve snarled. "She's lying to you, man! She's playing us against each other! She told me when she first left you for me that *you* beat *her*!"

Laura was tugging at Dave now, saying, "Come on inside, honey. He's making this all up to save his hide."

Steve took a step as if to follow them. Desperate, I once again blocked his path. "No, Steve! Don't!"

"It's the truth, Holland!" he hollered over my head. "Laura had a black eye when she moved in with me!"

The carved oak door slammed shut. Steve stood still. "Jesus! He believes her! He actually thinks I hit her!"

"Come on, Steve. Let's go."

Though I had to pull him by the arm at first, we made our way to my van. Dave's car—a rather ordinary-looking Toyota Camry in comparison to Laura's top-of-the-line BMW—was blocking my van. Sullivan sat in stony silence, staring out the front window while I maneuvered back and forth and finally managed to squeeze past the Toyota.

The moment we'd left the driveway, however, Sullivan pounded the fleshy parts of his fists on the dash and growled, "That miserable, lying bitch!"

"You're going to break your hands," I warned. "As well as my dashboard."

He sat back a little in the passenger seat. "*Now* you know why I hate women!"

I tightened my grip on the steering wheel but said evenly, "Evan Cambridge was in on the whole thing. He may well have been the mastermind. Do you hate all *men*, too?"

"We're going straight to the police, Gilbert. Right now. We're going to get them to drag that lying bitch out of her house in chains. We'll make her tell *them* her story, and all the lies she's told about me. I've never hit a woman in my life! I've never hit anyone!"

"I believe you, Steve. And yet now you've got bruised hands, and you're practically foaming at the mouth."

"So what? I'm pissed at her! Wouldn't *anybody* be?"

I took a curve a little too fast and inwardly chastised myself; I had to stay focused on my driving. I ached for Steve; his confrontation with Laura made me realize just how emotionally devastated he truly was by what she had done. I merely replied, "Yes, but that's not the point."

"What *is* your 'point,' Gilbert?"

His voice was sarcastic and ugly, and if he were a child, I would have pulled the car over and reprimanded him. As it was, I struggled not to lose my own temper and, after a moment, answered, "Sorry, Steve, but I'm not taking you to the police station when you're like this. You'd wind up spewing all this venom while you make your report, whereas Laura will be all calm and rational . . . batting her big brown eyes at the policemen. *You're* the one who's going to come off as the raving lunatic. It's going to look like you're just vengeful and trying to hurt her for leaving you. You've got to pull yourself together before you go to the police."

Steve opened his mouth as if to protest, but then shut it and turned to face forward. He remained silent for the next two miles. Then he said, "The funny thing is, Gilbert, she almost had me convinced. You believe that? Even now. Even after everything I know full well she did to me, I wanted to believe that she had nothing to do with Evan's treachery."

"She's a piece of work, all right. She nearly had me convinced, too. And now she has Dave under her spell."

After another pause, he muttered, "I don't hate all women, Gilbert. I just said that in anger."

"I realize that." Although, frankly, I still wasn't all that sure that he didn't hate *me*. There were times when he was nastier to me than he was to anyone else. We'd had some bad arguments in the two-plus years since we'd first met.

Forcing myself away from that line of thought, I said, "Here's the plan. I'm going to call Linda."

"Linda?"

"Officer Delgardio."

"Hey, that's right." Steve brightened a little. "You have an in with the cops."

"I prefer to think of her as a friend who happens to be a police officer."

"Whatever." He reached into his jacket pocket. "Want to use my cell phone?"

"No, thanks. I won't talk on the phone while driving. I'll call from my office, and I'll let you know what she says."

"Okay, but . . . we've got to move fast, Gilbert. Bet you

anything Laura's packing up to skip town, even as we speak."

"There'd be no point in her leaving town *now*, Sullivan. She can't rip off her insurance company when she knows we'd testify against her. And if she were worried about getting arrested, she wouldn't have returned to Crestview in the first place. She's obviously certain she can buffalo her way through this."

We'd arrived at Sullivan's office, and I pulled over to let him out. He grumbled, "If it comes down to it, I'll keep a watch on her place myself tonight."

"You're going to stake out her house?!"

"You bet I am!" Leaning down to my eye level, he explained, "The woman stole three hundred thousand dollars from me!"

"*That* much? Jeez!" I couldn't stay and help him to calm down; I was already late for an appointment with a client. I merely repeated, "I'll let you know what Linda says." Sullivan frowned and shut the door, and I drove off.

Was I giving him good advice? Maybe we *should* have driven straight to the police station. For one of the few times in my life, I felt hopelessly outmatched. All of the rules of normal human interactions were suddenly useless to me; they were based on the assumption that the other person had scruples. And yet Laura Smith was willing and able to lie about anything through those perfect teeth of hers. She had no compunction to play by the rules, whereas I didn't even know how to function without them.

I had a vision of Sullivan charging into his van and going back to confront her again the moment I was out of sight. That possibility frightened me to the bone. In Denver just a year or two ago a man had shot his neighbor's dog in the dog's own yard. When the neighbor stormed to the shooter's porch, he too was shot to death. The district attorney wouldn't bring the case to trial, because it fit the definition of the "make-my-day" self-defense law.

"Oh, Steve," I murmured, feeling helpless and confused. "Be wise."

Chapter 4

A centerpiece should be precisely that—an enticing and soul-centering piece of your household décor that captures the eye and draws you and your guests to your table, be it for a fancy feast or for a simple coffee break in an otherwise hectic day.

—Audrey Munroe

DOMESTIC BLISS

With Linda Delgardio unable to meet me until eight P.M. and Steve Sullivan merely keeping "a distant eye" on Laura's house—at least according to what he'd assured me on his cell phone— I rushed home after work, eager to unwind and tell my troubles to my cat, Hildi. My sleek black cat sometimes proved to be a better listener than Audrey Munroe, who could be so obsessed with preparing her show segments that she became oblivious to the fact that I, too, had a life.

For me, there was nothing quite as inspiring and soul-cheering as the walk I took from my street parking on Maplewood Avenue into Audrey's exquisite foyer. When designing this small, high-ceilinged entrance room, I'd angled the height of the chandelier so that, from Audrey's slate walkway, the illuminated crystals glittered and beckoned through the transom like bright, dangling diamonds.

I unlocked Audrey's ornate leaded-glass oak door and stepped inside, breathing in the sweet, warm air. In keeping with the Italianate design of this redbrick home, the floor was an Italian marble mosaic that made the footfalls of hard-soled shoes sound regal. The plaster walls were painted a light gray that Farrow & Ball had enticingly named "skylight." The paint gave such depth and substance to the walls that they instantly seemed to embrace me. From the carved dome ceiling, the crystal chandelier sparkled and bathed the room in shimmering light. Centered along one wall was a small square antique oak stand; on it, a stunning porcelain vase held a fresh-cut bouquet of white roses. On the opposite wall hung a mirror in a carved antique frame. Although lovely, that item now only reminded me of Laura's fake antique, and I averted my gaze.

I slowly removed my coat and hung it in the closet, where I also stashed my purse. In my current mood, I was in no hurry to enter the main living space. This foyer and the gorgeous kitchen were the only rooms that Audrey ever allowed to remain in pristine condition. There was never any way of telling just what awaited me, furniturewise, in the room on the other side of the French double doors.

Steeling myself, I opened the door and discovered that, indeed, Audrey was in the throes of one of her research projects for her show. She had shoved most of the furnishings against the walls and had spread out six tablecloths on the floor. Each cloth sported a centerpiece of varying size and composition. Audrey was seated in a semi-lotus position beside them, surveying the table arrangement directly in front of her. Hildi sat right next to her.

Hildi promptly meowed a greeting, feline, no doubt, for: *I had nothing to do with this mess.* She was no more fond of Audrey's frequent furniture rearranging than I was, although this particular project had given her so many accessible play toys that her suffering was minimal.

Without so much as a hello, Audrey asked, "What's your opinion on centerpieces, Erin?"

"You want my 'opinion,' singular? Such as if centerpieces work best on a table or on the floor?"

She didn't crack a smile. Instead, she grabbed the Tiffany notebook that she perpetually used to jot down ideas for Dom Bliss—her nickname for her highly rated TV show. "In terms of what their purpose and function should be."

"Ah. To decorate the table."

Again, she gave no reaction to my sarcasm. The woman could outstubborn me even at my most obstinate moments, so I might as well cooperate with her. I took a seat beside Audrey on the lush Oriental area rug. To pamper myself, I brushed my fingertips along the wool bristles, admiring the deep, rich, firebrick red, suitable for a king's robe, and the royal navy blue in their sometimes-geometric, sometimes-floral pattern. So much time, talent, and craftsmanship had gone into producing this one hand-knotted carpet.

With a sigh, I answered, "Personally, I consider centerpieces a must. When I'm revealing a newly done-up dining room or even a kitchen with a table, I always accessorize with a centerpiece. I make sure that it pulls in an accent color or echoes some of the room's lines." I paused and reconsidered my statement. "Actually, sometimes I just want the centerpiece to draw the eye to a particularly nice tabletop. I use a white centerpiece on a dark wood tabletop, or dark on light."

Audrey made a couple of swift notations, then surveyed the six tableclothes. "I've been trying these various centerpieces on the different shapes of tables . . . trying to decide if I like them better as symmetrical or asymmetrical, according to their table shape. What do you think?"

With regal grace, Hildi strode over and settled onto my lap. While stroking her soft fur, I answered Audrey. "For room designs, I'm a big believer in asymmetrical designs . . . but I like symmetrical centerpieces the best. I sort of like the idea of dinner guests being more or less equidistant from the centerpiece. That's really just a matter of personal taste, though. What *is* important is that the size of the centerpiece be in scale with the size of the table."

She nodded as she again took notes.

"You did a great job with the floating-candles one

here . . . particularly for not actually lighting them when Hildi is in the room to play with the flames," I added.

"That's my favorite centerpiece of the six." She peered at me over the frame of her reading glasses. "Any tips for the centerpiece composition itself?"

I gave a shrug. "You're more creative with this type of thing than I am. That simple arrangement you made last Christmas with the pine boughs and the small gold-spray-painted pumpkins and gourds was glorious."

She grinned at me. "Thank you!"

"But, in general, I love fresh-cut flowers, candles . . . the classics. I'm partial to crystal or porcelain bowls and vases. But ceramics can be wonderful, too. When it comes to everyday centerpieces, I like the old stand-bys . . . the bowl of fresh fruit for an everyday center-piece, the fresh-cut flowers in an attractive vase . . . one that doesn't tip over easily."

Audrey nodded, but she was still looking at me expectantly, so I continued. "If this is a dinner party where people don't necessarily know one another well, an un-usual centerpiece can be a nice conversation starter. The only type of centerpiece I truly hate is a big, tall con-traption where you have to crane your neck to see someone seated on the opposite side." I paused. "Or are you primarily interested in talking about centerpieces for special occasions?"

She winked. "That's okay, dear. Special occasions are *my* forte." Indeed, most of the arrangements that she'd done in this room were clearly intended for Easter. She'd used pastel colors for her flowers, dyed eggs, even some jelly beans. One especially nice arrangement incorporated a mirror base and a string of tiny white lights.

She closed her notebook. "Heard anything new from Wonder Woman?"

"Pardon?"

"Your guest from my presentation last night. The one who sent that odd-looking young man flying across the room. Did she ever call you back?" She rose and stretched. "And was she all right?"

"Physically, yes. In all other areas, the jury's still out."

"Have you eaten dinner already?" Audrey asked absently, glancing at her watch. Apparently she'd already lost interest in hearing about Laura.

"No, I have to—"

"You're in luck," she called as she left the room. "We had Chef Michael on today's show."

That cheered me up immediately. "Yum!" I said quietly to Hildi as she stepped off my lap to follow Audrey into the kitchen. "Dom-Bliss leftovers!"

The scents as I entered the kitchen made my mouth water. Even without the delectable aromas, this spacious room was utterly scrumptious, its colors, textures, and glittering surfaces making such a glorious feast for the eye. A red-to-yellow palette brought such warmth to the room—from the coppery-red hues of the maple floor and copper oven range hood to the creamy ivory walls above stately yellow-ocher ceramic tiles. Clear-glass-and-white-wood cabinet doors lovingly mimicked Audrey's eight-pane windows, giving such a clean, airy feel to the space. On the kitchen island, below the regal oval-shaped antique copper chandelier with its lovely alabaster ceramic candles, a Naples yellow bowl filled with Macintosh apples served as the centerpiece.

"What can I contribute?" I asked, heading toward the spotless stainless-steel refrigerator. "A spinach salad, maybe?"

Audrey removed a steaming dish from the oven and replied, "Absolutely." She set the dish on the Caledonia granite countertop near an indigo glass vase that brimmed with marigolds. "Plus all the details."

"Details?"

"About your enigmatic, judo-flipping friend." She turned to face me. "You didn't actually think I was going to let you off the hook with *that* skimpy story, did you?"

I had no good response to that question, so I merely gave her a sheepish smile, feeling my cheeks grow warm. Lately I seemed to be making a regular habit of misjudging people.

"Honestly, Erin! Do you think that Hildi is the only one around this joint with a little healthy curiosity?" She gestured for me to get going by drawing circles in the air with her poppy-patterned oven mitt. "Now, start at the beginning, and carry on from there."

Chapter 5

A little after eight P.M., I found a parking space on "the Hill," the typical college-town business area near the CU campus. Linda Delgardio had arranged to meet me at a local dive there. She was working a four-to-midnight shift all this month, so this was her dinner break. An hour earlier, I'd called Steve Sullivan's cell phone and tried to convince him to join us, but he remained intent on keeping watch over Laura's house, certain she was going to skip town, just as she had last year.

Linda was just finishing her burger and fries when I arrived at the noisy, greasy-smelling sandwich joint; I ordered a glass of water. Linda was having a bad day; her

partner had called in sick, and Linda looked more than a
little under the weather herself. Her nose was red, and her
normally sparkling dark eyes were dull. Her long black
hair was pinned up as usual whenever she was on duty, a
failed attempt—even despite her head-cold symptoms—
to make her nondescript within her masculine uniform.
We wasted little time with small talk before I asked, "Do
you know if there were any undercover police officers at
Paprika's last night?"

"I doubt it. Usually we just use undercover cops for
things like drug trafficking . . . a kitchenware store hardly
qualifies as a hot spot for drug deals."

"But maybe, since Audrey Munroe's a local celebrity
and was speaking, the police could have sent someone
to keep an eye out, in case someone wanted to harass
her."

Linda shook her head. "We'd just send a uniformed officer. It's possible a narc was there as part of some ongoing
investigation, I suppose, but he'd have kept a low profile.
You wouldn't have even known he was there. Why?
What's up?"

To the best of my ability, I related every detail of the
events of last night at Paprika's and my visit this morning
to Laura's home, as well as Sullivan's heated conversation
with Laura on her front porch. "My suspicion is that she's
either swindling Dave Holland out of his money or she's
setting up a big insurance fraud—planning to set the
house on fire and collect on the *lost* possessions . . . which
won't actually be lost at all."

"Sounds that way," Linda replied. She sneezed and
blew her nose. "You want me to question her?"

"As soon as possible."

"Okay. If nothing else, I want to ask her myself about
Evan Cambridge's whereabouts. That's bound to make
her think twice about trying to pull another scam anytime

soon. I'll let you know how it goes." She grabbed her pen and notepad. "What's the address?"

I hesitated. I didn't want to be cut out of the picture, and I was painfully aware of how important this whole thing was to Sullivan. "Actually, Steve Sullivan's already there, watching the house from a car down the street for fear she'll take off again. So . . . I was kind of hoping you'd let me come with you. Would that be possible?"

She raised an eyebrow and peered at me. "You want to ride out there and swear out a complaint against this woman in person?" She leaned back in her chair and added sarcastically, "Will you at least allow me to drive the squad car myself?"

I grinned in spite of myself. "Okay, point taken."

"Are things really that slow in the interior design business that you're desperate to go on police ride-alongs? Even if I *wanted* to take you with me tonight, Erin, I couldn't. Not till the proper paperwork's filed that says you won't sue us if you get shot, maimed . . . the usual drill."

"But if Steve and I happen to be waiting outside her house when you arrive, and Laura's willing to let us all in, *that* would be all right, wouldn't it?"

She rubbed her forehead and frowned.

I took a sip of water, feeling uncomfortable, hoping that I wouldn't have to explain myself. "This is important to me, Linda."

She regarded me for a moment. "Aren't you dating someone right now? Are you *more* than friends with this Sullivan character?"

I shook my head. "*Less* than friends. It's just that . . . I keep remembering how he shouted at Laura that he wants his life back. I get the feeling he means that almost literally . . . that she derailed him that completely. What she did to him was just so unfair, and so far she's gotten off scot-free. Sullivan was supportive when I blundered into that hideous ordeal back in December and needed help. I can't just turn my back on him now, when *he's* in need. It'll bug me forever."

"Some guy you're 'less than friends' with is going to haunt you forever?" She held my gaze.

I sighed. Linda seemed to be in investigating-officer mode. I wasn't sure myself how I felt about Sullivan. It was impossible to explain something that was purely emotional and not rational; all I knew was that, at the very least, I needed to balance things out with Sullivan—to know that he was back on an even keel in terms of his professional and his personal life—or I would never truly be able to give my relationship with his good friend John Norton a real chance. I chose to express none of that to Linda. Instead, I answered, "It sounds a little crazy, I know, because it *is* crazy, but . . . yes. I have to help Sullivan out, or everything will seem forever out of balance between us."

Linda blew her nose again. Although clearly none too happy, she grumbled, "Fine. I'll meet you there. Sarge will bust my butt if he finds out about this, though."

"Thanks, Linda. Can we go right away?"

She shook her head. "My schedule's already jam-packed. You or your 'less than a friend' can always just call this in . . . make a verbal complaint against her. But then the duty sergeant might assign someone else. Otherwise, I'll get there as soon as I can. Probably within the next hour or two, unless something urgent comes up in the meantime."

"I'd rather wait two hours and have *you* be the one who talks to her."

She shoved aside her pack of tissues and picked up her pen again. "So what's her address?"

If I hadn't known precisely where to look for Sullivan, I'd have driven right past the dark-colored sedan that he'd told me he'd borrowed. He was parked along a dead-end road in the mountainous subdivision, adjacent to Laura's cul-de-sac but a little farther down the main drag. Laura would be forced to drive past this intersection as she left the neighborhood. I parked my van several car lengths behind his, trotted to his car, waved, and waited for him to unlock my door, then slid into the passenger seat.

The interior reeked of old cigarette smoke. The ashtray was brimming with cigarette butts. The cheap plaid upholstery of my seat was ripped, and the plastic dashboard was cracked. "Nice wheels," I teased.

"Best I could do on such short notice. Belongs to a buddy of mine."

"Good thinking. Following Laura in a van marked 'Sullivan Designs' would have been something of a giveaway. It'd be like James Bond driving around in his tricked-up BMW with a big sign on the roof that read: 'Surveillance by Bond. *James* Bond.'"

Steve didn't even crack a smile. He continued to glower out the windshield as if his anger was necessary to maintain his vigilance. "No sign of her yet. Or of Holland. Just wish it hadn't taken me so long to borrow a car. She had more than two hours to clear out between the time we left her house and I got back up here. In retrospect, it would have been better to stick with the Sullivan Designs van and let her know full well that I was tailing her."

I held my tongue. In his mood, this was going to be a long wait, indeed. I reached for the dial of the radio to switch it on. "Radio's busted," Steve muttered.

"Perfect," I replied.

The time passed slowly. Sullivan was about as talkative as a sullen teenager. Mercifully, at ten after ten, Linda's squad car drove past us. Steve promptly followed it as far as the base of the driveway, parking on the street, and we walked the rest of the way. Linda waited for us by her black-and-white car. I gave her and Steve a cursory introduction but decided not to provoke her by saying much of anything else. Even so, she glared at me, her mood apparently having worsened since our meeting at the café.

"Like I said earlier, Erin, this totally goes against standard police procedure. I won't do anything to stop you two if you follow me to the front door, but I strongly suggest you let me do all the talking."

"No problem," Sullivan said. "Not a word from either of us."

Linda glanced at me, and I nodded, so she walked ahead of us toward the house. "Makes me nervous to have civilians trailing me like this." I resisted replying that it made *me* nervous to trail an armed police officer like this. She continued up the sandstone porch steps and rang the doorbell. She stepped to one side of the door, as if in habitual anticipation of a shotgun-blast greeting. Sullivan and I remained on the top step. If we *were* greeted with a shotgun blast, the two of us were dead ducks.

Dave opened the door, once again wearing his sunglasses. Linda introduced herself as Officer Delgardio and asked if he was Dave Holland.

He nodded grimly. "Is there some kind of trouble, Officer?" His face was red and damp with perspiration, and he seemed out of breath.

"I'd just like to ask Laura Smith some questions. Is she here?"

" 'Fraid not."

"She *isn't?*" Sullivan asked, bristling with alarm. "Are you *sure* about that?"

Dave retorted, "Check the garage if you don't believe me! Car's gone. Closet's cleared out . . . suitcases gone. Same as last time. I figured she was with *you*," he snarled at Sullivan.

"No way. I told you: I was just another of her patsies. If I were you, dude, I'd check the balance on all my savings and credit accounts."

"She wouldn't do that to me! After you *threatened* her this afternoon, she probably just got scared and ran. She'll be back, though. I'm sure of it."

"Did she leave a note?" Linda asked. There was a glint of annoyance in her voice, no doubt intended for Sullivan, who'd immediately broken his vow of silence.

"No, she just up and left."

"Right after Erin and I talked to her?" Sullivan again interjected.

"Sometime around then, yeah." Dave gave an angry shrug. "Like I said, you scared her. She must have panicked."

"Let me guess," Sullivan persisted nastily. "She sent you out on some dumb errand shortly after Erin and I left your place this afternoon, and she was gone by the time you got back."

In an obvious grudging consent that Sullivan's scenario was precisely what had occurred, Dave clenched his jaw and remained stubbornly silent. Linda asked, "Is there a reason you're wearing your sunglasses indoors at night, Mr. Holland?"

"Yeah. They're prescription. And I lost my glasses."

"Would you mind taking them off for me?" Her officious tone of voice made her words sound more like a direct order than a request.

He hesitated. "I'd rather not."

"Why?"

He frowned and didn't answer. When she continued to look at him without moving a muscle, he sighed and removed his glasses. I fought back a gasp of surprise. He was sporting a black eye.

"Were you in a fistfight recently, Mr. Holland?" Linda asked.

"No. Nothing like that." He touched his cheek gingerly, winced, then put on his sunglasses again. "I tripped on that stupid antique iron Ms. Gilbert got for us that Laura's been using as a doorstop." He touched his face a second time. "Clobbered myself right in the eye with the doorknob."

I said, "That 'antique iron' is now probably a fake, just like the rest of your furnishings, Dave."

Dave's jaw dropped. "Come again?"

"The antiques in your front room have been replaced with imitations. I noticed that this morning when I came here to speak with Laura."

"That's . . . not possible. That's the mirror you picked out for us, right there."

"It's a fake. Laura claimed that you were going to sell the antiques for a profit in a couple of years, and that you were keeping them safe in storage in the meantime."

"Mind if we come in?" Linda asked.

Dave ignored her. He went over to his faked twenty-thousand-dollar original Louis XV mirror, stammering, "But this is . . ." He lowered his sunglasses, then put them back in place, all the while studying in horror the bogus frame of the mirror. "There's no way. . . . This has to be some sort of mistake."

"That frame's only recently manufactured," Steve said as we stepped inside, taking advantage of Dave's confusion. "The carvings were made with power tools—you can see the marks where the bits were moved—and it's obviously been spray-painted gold."

In a total state of shock, Dave staggered through the doorway and into the front room. We followed. "Look at the drawer of the writing desk," I suggested. "The bottom piece was attached with staples. And the back piece was nailed."

He yanked the drawer all the way out, letting the papers inside flutter to the floor. "Jesus! Is everything in the whole house a fake?"

"I've only been in the foyer and front room," I replied, though I didn't have any doubts that the answer was yes.

Dave raised the drawer as if to hurl it to the floor, but then stopped himself as he looked in Linda's direction. He jammed the drawer back into place.

"Have you been out of town recently, Mr. Holland?" Linda asked.

"Yeah. For four weeks. Business trip. My technology company makes . . ." He shook his head. "Not important. Anyway, I just got back from Atlanta. Last night. I was supposed to be gone another week yet, but things went really well, and we finished up early." He grabbed his head with both hands, pressing on his temples with the heels of his hands as he added in a stunned voice, "Got in late last night. And my glasses suddenly disappeared this morning."

"Do you have any idea at all where Miss Smith could have gone?" Linda asked.

"All I know is that Laura's been really tense and upset about something lately. She said it was because she'd found out an old friend of hers has cancer. But . . . that was the same story she gave me the last time . . . said she was visiting an old friend with cancer when she was really seeing Sullivan here, on the sly."

Sullivan took a sharp breath, but to my relief, he said nothing.

"Were the antiques insured?" Linda asked. "And was your policy registered under your name or Laura's?"

"Both our names." He was growing steadily more pale, and I started to worry that he was going to faint at any moment. Poor Dave.

"Why don't we sit down for a couple of minutes and discuss this?" Linda asked gently, obviously worried about the same thing.

Dave shook his head. "No."

"Do you want me to take your statement?"

"Statement?" he repeated dully.

"A grand-larceny report."

"No. Not yet . . . anyway. I need to think."

"Do you want me to examine the rest of your furniture?" I asked, feeling deeply sorry for the man. Unless he was an even better actor than Laura was, he was utterly devastated to learn that his pricey furniture was gone. "I can help you make out a full report of every item that's missing or has been duplicated."

Again he shook his head, and sank into the nearest seat—the erstwhile black horsehair camelback sofa with hand-carved leaf filigrees on the front and back. The telltale squeak of springs, which hadn't even been invented at the time of the original's manufacture, made me wince. "Just go. Please. All of you." He sank his head into his hands. "This is the worst day of my life."

"Thank you for your time," Linda told him. "If you see Miss Smith, tell her I'd like to ask her a couple questions. I'm leaving my business card on the table."

We let ourselves out and walked toward Linda's squad car. "It'd be nice to get the name of whoever supplied her with these reproductions," I said. "She probably ordered them well in advance. She was always really specific about what pieces she wanted. Even if she saw fit to destroy the paperwork before she took off, it should be easy enough for us to call her bank and get a name, right?"

"Us?" Linda repeated in a near growl.

"*You*, I mean. The Crestview police."

"Erin, we can't investigate a theft until the owner reports it. Not unless he or Miss Smith puts in a claim against her insurance company." She opened the door of her squad car. "So *you* can't call her bank to get any names of furniture manufacturers, either."

"Understood." I gave her a warm smile. "Thanks so much for talking to Dave, Linda."

"Hey, no thanks are necessary. I smell a rat here, big time. I'd like nothing better than to get this Laura Smith put out of business permanently."

After she drove past us and out of sight, Sullivan and I walked down the driveway to his car. The night air felt frosty, but not nearly as ice-cold as my companion. "Damn it all!" he said. "I *knew* she'd run!"

"I'm sorry I discouraged you from going straight to the police."

He opened the passenger door for me. "Ah, hell. *That* didn't make much difference. She'd have been gone by the time the police arrived, too. It was *my* fault for not heading straight back up here with my van, instead of wasting all that time borrowing a car." We got into the car and he started the engine. He made a U-turn and drove the short distance to my van. He pulled up beside it, obviously waiting for me to leave.

"What are you going to do now?" I asked.

He shrugged. "Make a night of it, if I have to."

"What do you mean?"

"I'm staying put . . . waiting to see if Dave Holland makes any sudden midnight trips someplace."

"In other words, you think Dave's *lying* when he says he doesn't know where she is?"

"Nah. I think right about now he's digging through every receipt he can find till he finds a clue about her whereabouts. She's probably stored those antiques somewhere in the general area, where she can keep an eye on them."

"Oh, you're right. Of *course* she did." I shook my head, disappointed for not thinking of that myself.

Picking up on my body English, Sullivan gave me a second shrug. "Yeah. Well, don't forget: I've been in his shoes."

I put my hand on the door handle, but couldn't stand the thought of leaving Sullivan to sit alone in this miserable car, waiting for Dave to make a move. Stalling, I said, "You and Dave have obviously had some confrontations in the past."

"You could say that. He followed Laura one time to my place . . . one of those occasions when she claimed she was visiting the friend with cancer . . . and he burst in on us."

"Did you know then that she was living with another man?"

"Yeah. But she'd told *me* he was this violent monster that she was scared to death of . . . that he'd cut her throat the last time she tried to leave him. She—"

"Wait. She claimed it was *Dave* who cut her throat?" Had she deliberately played on my vulnerability over my mother's death? "She told *me* that she got that wound when her father killed her mother and her younger brother. Before he took his own life."

"No way. Her parents live in Indiana someplace. Or they used to, last time I spoke to them. When Laura took off with Evan for Europe, I called them, hoping they'd heard from her, but she never contacted them. They sound like nice, quiet people, unable to explain or control their wild daughter."

Lying to me about her scar felt like a much worse betrayal—more personal—than the fact that she'd used me as a pawn in a swindle. *That* was just business, whereas she'd used my mother's death to bond with me on a false pretense. I shook my head. "I don't believe Dave gave her that scar. He seems to be a decent, mellow person."

"Yeah. In retrospect, it's more likely she got it from some botched scam . . . that she chose the wrong mark one time and nearly paid the price with her life. But at the time, I hadn't even *met* Holland, and I believed her every word. She was all distraught when she showed up at my house that night, and she had a shiner . . . worse than the one Holland's got now. And he just barged into my house, screaming at Laura. Far as I was concerned, that was proof positive that the guy was an abusive maniac. So I threw him out, and Laura wound up moving in with me."

"Back then, why do you suppose she targeted you over him? It's so illogical. After all, *he's* the millionaire, not you." Still, the three hundred thousand dollars she'd stolen from Sullivan was a lot of money. . . .

"Not *then*, he wasn't. His company didn't hit the big time till a year or so ago, shortly *after* Laura moved in with me." He snorted. "For a while there, that was the only thing that cheered me up . . . the thought of how badly the timing of Dave's skyrocketing wealth must have rankled Laura." He frowned. "Figures she'd find a way to come back to Crestview and scarf up what she missed the first time."

My mind raced back through the troubling events of the last twenty-four hours. "I wonder what her relationship was with that gun-toting man in the dreadlocks wig last night. She might be running from him now, as much as from us. For all we know, *he* could be the guy who slit her throat."

Sullivan ignored this tangent and asked, "Need me to walk you to your car?"

"Actually, I'm going to wait with you, if that's all right."

"Why?"

Good question. Maybe I just needed to assuage my guilt for not believing him when he'd said that Laura would immediately run away. In any case, my instincts were telling me to stay. I shrugged. "To keep you out of trouble, I guess."

Chapter 6

We debated for quite a while about what Laura's connection might have been to last night's gun-toting, wig-wearing phony cop. We agreed that he was most likely tracking down Laura to bring her to justice for some previous scam. Because he'd proven to be singularly inept at keeping a low profile, my theory was that he was a scam victim himself, taking matters into his own hands. Steve thought it likeliest that he was "a P.I. who happens to be shitty at his job."

I argued, "But neither of those possibilities explains why he was harassing the store manager. Hannah Garrison says he's been targeting Paprika's for selling merchandise that he supposedly found offensive."

"Maybe the guy's Laura's new partner. Their tussle last night could have been staged."

"Yeah . . . but why? How on earth could their charade have helped them?"

"That's the million-dollar question," Steve muttered.

We sat in glum silence for several minutes, till I said, "I've got a personal stake in this. I spent days upon days selecting those pieces, dickering about their cost, assembling that magnificent collection of furnishings. Despite what Linda Delgardio told me about not poking around in police business myself, I'd really like to find whoever it was that duplicated Laura's antiques. That person could be in on this thing with Laura. Evan isn't an expert on antiques, is he?"

"No. Though he could've studied up on 'em."

"He wouldn't have the resources to manufacture a household of knockoffs himself, would he?"

"No way. And even if he *could*, that guy's not about to do anything resembling manual labor, such as building furniture. Evan's the sort to call a paramedic if he so much as gets a splinter in his pinky." Steve fought back a yawn.

Still determined that we could eventually hit on the answers if we kept theorizing, I suggested, "So maybe Evan and Laura parted company, and she teamed up with somebody who's making the fakes for her. Maybe this is just the start of a new operation of hers, and she's planning on repeating it at the next fall guy's house." Steve made no reply, so I added, "It's worth checking out, in any case."

He shrugged, and muttered, "I guess," obviously humoring me. He was probably too focused on his own predicament to care how extensive Laura's latest path of thievery might prove to be. Even in the dim lighting, Sullivan looked haggard, his features drawn. His quest to track down a professional con artist was a long shot.

Maybe I'd only made matters worse by volunteering to keep him company.

"Steve, there's been no sign of Evan here in Crestview. He's probably still in Europe. Even if we find Laura and manage to bring her to trial, I doubt if you'll be able to get your money back."

"Yeah, I know. But I'm not letting her get off scot-free again. Not a second time. Not without a fight."

To put a positive spin on matters, I said, "We can always hope that, once she gets arrested, she'll reveal Evan's location. And maybe you'll get your money back, after all."

"That'd be great." But his tone told me he held out no hope whatsoever for that possibility.

We fell into another silence, till Steve finally muttered, "I wish you'd brought some coffee with you, Laura. I could—"

I stiffened. Steve broke off abruptly as he realized what he'd just said. He flashed a sheepish smile at me. "Got a little tongue-tied, is all. I meant to say 'while we watch for Laura.' "

"So. I remind you of Laura?"

"No!" He raked his fingers through his hair, a frequent nervous gesture of his that I was beginning to think was what poker players call a "tell." "I was just . . . She's on my mind right now. You two are nothing alike. Other than a few . . . superficial similarities . . . maybe."

"Such as?"

He remained silent for a long time. Then he replied quietly, "You look a little similar, now that you mention it."

Laura was remarkably beautiful, so that was a compliment, but I'd designed too many bedrooms for recent divorcés to miss the underlying ramifications of Sullivan's equating the two of us. However lovely those bedrooms already were when I first arrived, the clients invariably wanted a radical change that would eradicate all reminders of their former spouses. "That's why you pushed me away, isn't it?"

"What do you mean?" Sullivan focused his perpetually angry eyes on me. "I never pushed you away."

"Oh, no? And what do you call fixing me up with your buddy John? A *bonding* experience? Just what do you think I am? Shag carpeting?"

"No, I . . . ." He gripped the steering wheel so tightly that I half expected it to crack into pieces. Through a clenched jaw and without looking at me, he said, "That's not how it was, Erin. I never said you should go out with him. *You're* the one who leapt at the chance to get all hooked up with a good friend of mine!"

"Your precise words to me when you introduced the two of us were: 'Erin, this is John Norton, who I think you should meet.' "

"I *meant* that you should meet him because he does demo homes for the residential developer he works for, and I thought you might want to *work* with him in the future."

"Uh-huh. And you're a designer, too, one who's fallen on hard times and needs all the work he can get."

"So what, Gilbert? Maybe I just . . . didn't want to have to ask a friend of mine for favors by hiring me! Did you ever think of that?"

Even while I silently wondered how this conversation had gone so wrong so fast, I heard myself snipe, "Or maybe you're being less than honest with me right now! Did *you* ever think of *that*?"

"You want honesty, do you? Fine! Go home! I *honestly* think I'd be better off waiting for Holland on my own!" He returned his gaze to the road ahead, as if too disgusted to continue to look at me.

I stared at him in profile and stayed put. If I did as he demanded, there wasn't a doubt in my mind that we would revert to the barely civil relationship that we'd had for my first two years in Crestview. He was going to have to say something else to me eventually, and his words would either repair or worsen this ever-deepening chasm between us.

"Anyway, he'd seen you before as you were leaving my office a couple days earlier and started bugging me for an introduction. I was hoping you wouldn't go for it, okay? But you practically threw yourself at him."

"So, in other words, you were testing me? Dangling your friend in front of me to see if I'd take the bait?"

"No! Jeez! Let's just drop it, Gilbert! Everything worked out for the best for all three of us. You and John are obviously all hot and heavy, so it's too late now. Besides, it's not as if—" He broke off as headlights emerged from the otherwise black void of the small cul-de-sac on the slope above us. "Holland's leaving! At nearly midnight! He's meeting her!"

We ducked down to avoid being seen in his headlights. Steve started the engine but left his own headlights off. This was such a small subdivision and seldom-traveled road that the trick would be to follow Holland's car from enough of a distance that he didn't realize he was being tailed, all the while not losing track of his car's taillights in the darkness. Once traffic picked up farther in town, we'd probably have to change strategies.

It was too dark to drive for long with no lights, though, and Sullivan soon relented and turned them on. Breaking the silence, I said quietly, "You're right. Everything did work out best for the three of us. You and I are like oil and water."

"Like cats and dogs."

"Exactly." Sullivan was a *dog*, all right.

We merged into the winding road that led to the canyon into downtown Crestview, just one car back from Dave Holland's. At length, Steve said, "As long as he stays on these two-lane roads, we won't have any trouble tailing him."

"Yeah. We'll be fine, as long as he doesn't get on the turnpike to Denver."

Minutes later, I groaned. The black coupe had turned onto the turnpike. We were doing our best to keep track of him, but despite the hour, there were dozens of cars on this section of the road. We soon lost track of which taillights were his when we got caught in a clot of traffic. Sullivan resorted to muttering four-letter words as we wove our way through the cars, failing to find Dave Holland's.

At the next exit, I spotted him passing under a street-lamp and pointed out his car by shouting, "There!"

Sullivan hit the brakes and made an abrupt exit, tailgating a truck, which blocked our vision of the road ahead. We'd lost Dave once again. Sullivan cursed and pounded the steering wheel. Just as we passed an intersection, I spotted Dave's car pulling away from a traffic light.

"That's him! He's going north. Turn around."

A couple of cars had boxed us in, and we had no choice but to continue to the next intersection.

"I know where he's going!" Sullivan cried as he finally managed to swing the car around. "He's heading toward the rental warehouse . . . U-Store. I'll bet that's where Laura's stashed the antiques."

He smacked the steering wheel again. "I should have realized this is where she'd keep the stuff! She knows all about U-Store. She always pumped me for information about my job. To think, I used to flatter myself into thinking she was interested in learning about my work."

"I've got a unit rented there right now." One of us should indeed have thought of the possibility that Laura had rented space at U-Store. Many, if not all, of the designers in Crestview used this facility. For large-scale jobs, a storage rental was a great convenience, well worth the expenditure. We could store the furniture as pieces were being shipped from different factories, allowing an entire project to be installed at the same time. U-Store gave us excellent discounts, and it was convenient, located partway to Denver, which was a hub for suppliers.

To our mutual horror, the gate was wide open at U-Store when we arrived. We drove inside. The place was a maze of buildings that were staggered to discourage speedsters. It also made it difficult to spot a particular parked car. We wove our way through the place, eating up precious time. It felt as though it had been at least twenty minutes since we'd lost track of Dave. All the while, I was horridly on edge, my intuition and sensibilities on red alert. At night, this place felt like a prison compound. I had an irrational fear that Dave's car had been a mirage to lure us here, where we'd be trapped forever.

Finally, our headlights glinted across the sleek silver surface of Laura's BMW. "There's her car!" I said, pointing.

"Nice. And she *owes* me a car," Steve grumbled.

We parked next to the BMW and got out. It was cold, quiet, and spooky, the ugly dark shapes of the cubical buildings looming all around us in this artless void. Although the complex was illuminated with overhead flood lamps, they were distantly spaced, and a couple of the bulbs were either burned out or broken. Sullivan mumbled that he needed to grab a flashlight, and he opened the car door and retrieved a small light from the backseat.

My heart raced. I shivered more from fear than from the cold. We were so isolated in this immense compound that we might as well have been in some deep, medieval forest. To quiet my nerves, I felt the need to talk and said, "I wonder how Dave got the gate open. And why security isn't already crawling all over the place."

No answer.

Walking shoulder to shoulder and concentrating on the small beam from Sullivan's flashlight against the asphalt, we crept farther from the main entrance and between the corrugated steel buildings.

"Someone's probably on the take," he finally replied. He cursed again. "Come to think of it, she probably didn't park all that close to her unit, in case someone figured out to look for her here. We'd have been better off continuing to hunt for *Dave's* car."

"True. *He* would know the exact unit number by now and would pull up right in front. Still, though, it can't be all *that* far away."

He snorted. "She's probably planning on holing herself up here overnight, living in the warehouse with the furniture till she can figure out where to go next. I can't wait to see the look on her face when we find her."

His words suddenly made me realize just how out-of-control this course of action really was. I grabbed his sleeve. "This is too risky, Sullivan. We should call Officer Delgardio before we look any further."

"No way! The police will insist that we clear out immediately. They might even threaten to arrest us for trespassing if we're still here by the time they arrive. I need to be the one to let Laura know that *this* time I was too quick for her. That I outsmarted her and caught her before she could bail."

"But what if Dave *is* in on this, too? He's got to be with her right now. They could be armed. Or she could have some other gun-toting partner. Like Mr. Dreadlocks. We could be waltzing into a trap."

"I'm not waltzing. I'm—"

Just then, tires squealed as a car sped around a corner and straight toward us. Its headlights were off.

I screamed, and Sullivan dived, tackling me, sending us both flying. The car zoomed past us as Sullivan and I crashed to the blacktop.

Stunned, embarrassed, and hurting, I cried out, "Jesus Christ! That car almost hit us!" Sullivan rolled off me, and I sprang to my feet, despite a searing pain that shot up my left leg.

More slowly, Sullivan rose, as well. "Are you all right?"

The heels of both hands hurt like mad, as did my left knee, which had slammed into the pavement. In short, I felt like I'd just been hit by a flying armoire.

"Yeah, sure. For the most part. Considering that we were playing tackle football on asphalt."

Sullivan retrieved the flashlight. Its narrow beam now felt like a target signal to allow the bad guys to locate *us*.

"Let's go back and get the car," I suggested. "We can see if Laura's car's still here, and, if it is, drive around till we find Dave's." I paused. "On second thought, we'd have heard the engine start behind us if Laura's car weren't still here. And the car that nearly ran us down was dark, like Dave's. The passenger seat was empty, but I didn't get a look at the driver at all."

"I could see it was a guy behind the wheel." Sullivan sighed. "You were right, Erin. Let's just go call the police right now."

I turned and started to limp back to the car. Sullivan promptly put his arm around me, helping me forward. If we lived through this night, I was going to soak in a hot bath for a week.

We rounded the corner. As I continued to walk, the pain in my leg eased, but I didn't mind Steve's arm around me and chose not to mention that I could walk fine on my own now. Just as we reached the car, he froze. "Wait. I smell smoke."

The scent had reached my nostrils, as well. "Smells like burning wood." I grabbed a handful of Steve's jacket to steady myself, my heart once again pounding. "Oh, dear God. Dave could have come here and set fire to his furniture."

"But why would he—"

"To spite Laura. She left him and stole the furniture, so he's making sure she can't turn a profit. Even though he'll be cutting off his own nose to spite his face."

"There was only one person in Dave's car. Laura must still be . . ." Steve's voice faded, and I felt the chill of fear at the implications. He thrust the car keys into my aching hands. "Get a cell phone. Call nine-one-one."

I threw open my door and snatched my cell phone from the compartment in my purse.

He was making his way toward the smoke. "Stay here," Steve yelled.

"No way! I'm coming with you!"

I raced after him as best I could, dialing the three digits as I did so. The dispatcher answered, and I reported the fire.

A thin rope of smoke was rising from the open door of a storage unit ahead. I gave the dispatcher the exact building and unit number, then hung up, unwilling to stay on the line. I slipped my phone into my pocket. Steve had already entered the building, holding the front of his jacket over the lower half of his face.

"Steve!" I cried from the doorway. "What the hell are you doing? Just wait for the fire department!"

"I've got to make sure Laura isn't in here."

With visions of having to drag him out of a burning warehouse, I followed him inside. It was a miniature trip into hell. Dozens of small fires rose from wadded-up newspaper scattered throughout, underneath, and alongside irreplaceable pieces of handcrafted wood items that had been lovingly preserved for generations. A makeshift pillow and a sleeping bag on top of a mattress had been stashed against the front wall. The mattress was now one of the smoldering objects but had not fully caught fire.

The room rapidly filled with choking smoke that took a stranglehold on my senses. I coughed, already barely able to get any air. Tears ran down my cheeks. It felt as though Tabasco sauce had been poured into my eyes. "Steve. We've got to get out of here!"

"Jesus," I heard him moan.

Oh, God. Was he hurt? Or had he found Laura? "Steve! What's wrong?"

No answer.

"Steve? Are you coming out?"

Silence. I couldn't see. The flames and furniture had made a deadly obstacle course. But Steve wasn't heading toward me and the exit. I had no choice but to go to him.

Blindly, I crept farther into the hellhole. "Steve?"

"Here."

I tried to follow his voice, but the smoke and heat had me disoriented.

I groped my way around a stacked wall of furniture. "Is it Laura?"

"I've got to get her out of here."

I spotted him. He was kneeling beside Laura, who lay in a pool of blood. Even with just the solitary beam of the flashlight on her, I could see the bloody stab wounds in her chest.

"She's dead," Steve said in a choked voice.

Chapter 7

Steve lifted Laura's body from the ash-and-debris-laden floor. Coughing, blinded, I groped for the exit. "This way," I yelled. Oily smoke was filling our already dark surroundings, making it impossible to see and difficult to breathe. I had to feel my way around—a macabre version of Blind Man's Bluff.

"Follow my voice," I instructed, and I called directions to Steve as I progressed.

The biting cold air was a welcome relief when we finally emerged. Still leading the way, I stopped at a safe distance from the burning building, but Steve carried Laura past me, then knelt and gently eased her body down near the base of a streetlamp.

Feeling helpless, I followed him. I glanced at Laura's body and hastily looked away. But the hideous image was already burned into my brain. Her clothes were drenched scarlet from the wounds in her chest. Her face was frozen in horror. Her omnipresent silk scarf was gone and her scar gleamed on the pale skin of her neck.

His voice thick with emotion, Steve said, "I can't stand to see her like this." He yanked off his jacket and draped it over her face. Tears were dampening Steve's cheeks— from the smoke or from his emotions, I didn't know.

I couldn't stand to see *him* like this. The flesh wounds on my hands stung and my left knee ached. My physical pain now felt like a betrayal, proof of my weak spirit that I continued to hurt from such superficial injuries in the face of Laura's mortal wounds.

A cloud of smoke wafting in our direction distracted me. Laura was beyond help, whereas the fire continued to burn. A short distance away, some of the most exquisite antiques I'd ever seen, utterly irreplaceable, were being destroyed.

Steve slumped to the ground near Laura's body. "I could have prevented this. If I'd just gotten in my van and driven straight up there again."

My heart ached for him. I said firmly, "She'd have seen you following her in your big van, while she was driving her sports car. Sooner or later, she'd have given you the slip."

He said nothing, his jaw and fists clenched. He was probably too upset right now for my words to have any impact. *I* was the one who'd prevented him from calling the police immediately; Laura's death was more my fault than his. Even so, for every second we spent here, pointlessly assessing blame and wallowing in guilt, the fire did even more damage.

I thrust my cell phone at him. "Steve. You need to call

nine-one-one again to tell them about Laura. Till the fire engines arrive, I want to keep the fire from spreading. Maybe I can save some of the furniture."

"*Furniture?*" he said accusingly, although he accepted the phone and started to dial.

His retort stung, but I trotted toward the fire nevertheless. *Both* of us couldn't desert her body, but I would have expected Steve Sullivan, of all people, to understand that one of us had to put some effort into firefighting.

Desperate to find the nearest container, I grabbed a drawer from a bureau just inside the door of Laura's rented space. I vaguely recalled seeing an outdoor spigot near my rental unit, which was only three units away, and soon located it.

I fought to douse the flames. It was painful and largely futile. One drawer full of water at a time, I limped back and forth between the tap and the storage unit. My efforts felt like a sick joke told by an idiot. It was as if I'd somehow become mired within a sadistic computer-animation game.

After what felt like an eternity, the firemen arrived. I gladly got out of their way and returned to Steve's side. He was slumped on the pavement, staring straight ahead, his face pale and his eyes black holes.

"Where the hell are the security people?" I cried out of sheer frustration. "The gate's supposed to be locked tight at night!"

"I have to contact Laura's parents. They moved from Indiana. I'm not sure how to reach them anymore."

"The police will locate them."

He rose but said nothing.

Thinking aloud, I said, "Dave must have started the fire. There's no other reasonable explanation. The fire hadn't been burning all that long before we arrived."

Steve remained silent.

"Maybe Dave started the fire from the back of the place and only discovered her body on his way out. Or do you think he killed her, then started the fire?"

Steve grumbled, "I don't want to talk."

"Fine. I won't say another word." Inwardly, though, my thoughts were a torrent of self-recriminations and defensive rebuttals. Maybe if I'd been smarter about Laura, had paid more attention, I could have recognized earlier that she wasn't playing straight with me. Should I have known she was a con artist? Insisted on swearing out some sort of complaint against her right away?

Who could have known that she was here, at an obscure storage facility in Northridge late at night, other than Dave? A partner in crime, maybe?

She'd been blessed with so much beauty, which our society holds so dear and rewards so greatly. Why had she opted to live her life by cheating the people who tried to get close to her? Had one of them killed her?

The police arrived shortly after the firefighters, and eventually Sullivan and I were driven by a patrol officer to the Northridge police station. Sullivan was taken to one room and I to another, where a female officer helped bandage my wounds, then interviewed me for what seemed like hours. At one point, when I'd been left alone briefly with the door open, I heard one officer mutter to another, "Sounds like a case of domestic violence." They obviously suspected Dave Holland of Laura's murder.

I answered the officers' questions, but my brain was feeling the effects of the late hour and the horror of finding the body of a woman I had believed was my friend. I went over my story a couple of times for two different officers. As time went on, my words seemed to be slurring of their own accord.

My third interviewer was a paunchy, middle-aged detective. He asked me, "You're sure it was Mr. Holland driving the car as you left Crestview?"

I hesitated. "I know that it was Dave Holland's *car*. . . . I saw him pull into his driveway in full daylight just this afternoon. And I could see that the driver was a man, and that his silhouette looked very much like Dave's . . . his basic size and shape, I mean. But it was too dark for me to know for certain that it was Dave."

"You didn't see the driver's face at all when the car nearly ran you down?"

"No. I was too busy trying to get out of the way."

He nodded and made a notation on his pad.

"Has anyone talked to Dave Holland yet?" I asked.

"I'm sure someone's working on that," the detective replied without looking up from his note-taking. When he'd finished, he met my eyes and gave me a pinched smile. "You and Mr. Sullivan were together tonight from eight P.M. on, right?"

"No, it was closer to nine. I met with Officer Delgardio at eight, while Sullivan was already keeping an eye on the house."

"I could have sworn you said . . ." He furrowed his brow and flipped back through his notes. "Huh. Mr. Sullivan's the one who said it was eight."

"If so, he was mistaken. It was nine."

"You're sure?"

"Positive. If he said it was eight, it was an innocent mistake, Detective. He certainly didn't kill Laura."

The detective held my gaze. "You understand the importance of the times, right, Miss Gilbert? It's not like the stuff you see on TV, where the coroner can establish the time of death to the minute."

"I understand. And I'm certain that I joined Steve in his car a few minutes before nine."

The detective nodded, impassive, and referred again to his notes. "The victim was a friend of yours?"

"I considered her a friend, yes."

"You mean . . . back before you learned she'd left the country with the contents of Mr. *Sullivan's* bank accounts?"

"Exactly." I'd answered quickly, but then it hit me that the detective had emphasized Steve's name. *Had I just implied he was guilty, after all?*

"Okay." He closed his notebook and stood, giving me another miserly smile. "Thanks for answering our questions. We'll have an officer drive you home now."

"Actually, I'd rather wait until Steve Sullivan can drive me. He can give me a ride to my car."

The detective narrowed his eyes. "And where *is* your car?"

"Near Laura Smith's house. In the mountains a few miles west of downtown Crestview. We drove Steve's car to the storage unit when we saw Dave Holland drive past us."

The detective held the door for me. "It'd be best if an officer escorted you, instead." He gave me a practiced smile and deposited me in the lobby. "I'll send an officer out who can drive you to your car. But if you think of anything else you need to tell me first, just have our dispatcher give me a buzz." He nodded at the woman wearing the headphones, pivoted, and left.

She winked at me while speaking into her phone. I felt like protesting Steve's and my innocence to her, even though she probably had not the slightest idea who either of us was or how much trouble we might be in.

It was nearly dawn by the time I got home. A patrol officer had driven me to my car, then followed me to my house. He must have been worried that I would immediately head right back up to Laura's and tamper with evidence. Or, perhaps, that I would warn Dave Holland or Steve Sullivan that they were prime suspects in a murder/arson investigation. In any case, I was very happy to reach the sanctity of my own bedroom, undetected by Audrey, who I hoped was blissfully asleep.

My alarm woke me at nine. Audrey, I knew, would have already left for work by then. I rescheduled my appointments for the day, then stumbled to bed again, but was unable to fall back to sleep. My bruised knee and hands were hurting again, and my heart was aching as well. Just two days ago, I'd been looking forward to spending the evening with my friend Laura Smith. Now she was dead. Our friendship had been exposed as a lie. My friendship with Steve Sullivan had probably been permanently derailed. Maybe life in general and the state of humanity in particular were every bit as dismal as Sullivan seemed to believe them to be.

Hildi squeezed through the doorway and sprang onto my bed, her yellow eyes smiling at me. "Morning, little one. People can be mean and nasty," I assured her as I stroked her soft black fur. "Cats are much nicer, aren't they?" She touched her pale pink nose to mine to signal the affirmative and rubbed her whiskers against my cheek.

Until Laura's murderer was behind bars, I would be a mass of raw nerves and unresolved hurts. People generally tended to open up to me, so if I asked around, I might be able to provide Linda Delgardio with some insider information. I sat up, my brain foggy and thrumming as though I'd spent the evening downing tequila instead of dousing flames. Paprika's would be open in less than an hour, and talking to Hannah Garrison seemed a logical first step. I needed to know more about the protestor-turned-pseudo-undercover-cop Laura had confronted that night. Also, Hannah and Laura had had a history that had left Hannah bitter and Laura furious. It would surely be enlightening to hear the story behind the two women's frayed relationship. Maybe I could find some way to extract a truth or two from the lies Laura had told to the various individuals in her life.

Paprika's was, as usual, doing a brisk business, at least in terms of the number of customers browsing the merchandise. Like me, others too enjoyed coming in simply to examine the displays and the new merchandise, with no intent of actually buying anything.

After a minute or two, I found Hannah. She was helping an overly perfumed woman who wore a dress in a garish, primary-colors floral pattern that would have worked better on lawn furniture. Hannah, too, was wearing a boldly patterned blouse, to go with her black slacks. From a distance, the short, buxom Hannah resembled a mini version of the customer—as though they were a pair of nestle dolls. Hannah turned and spotted me, and I held up my index finger to let her know I wanted to speak with her when she was free.

Now more than ever, I needed a reminder that there were still beautiful things in the world. I tried my best to focus my thoughts on Paprika's awesome array of salad bowl sets. There is something immensely appealing about the aesthetics of a finely crafted salad bowl, and my vision was drawn to an exquisite hand-carved mahogany salad bowl set. The rich color and dense grain of the wood were amazing. The asymmetrical bowls were so beautifully curved and balanced that they not only looked lovely but felt wonderful to hold—even in my still-tender hands.

Just as I was vacillating about whether or not my budget justified the purchase of yet another salad bowl set, Hannah joined me. Now that I wasn't with Laura Smith or being tailed by a gun-bearing Rastafarian imitator, she greeted me with her typical warmth, saying, "Good morning, Erin. Are you shopping, or just looking?"

"Just looking. And hoping to visit with you for a couple of minutes." I doubted that she had already heard the news of Laura's murder down in Northridge. Reluctantly, I returned the salad bowl to its spot on the shelf, then did a double take at Hannah's lips. She had what was either a slight injury or a cold sore that she was covering up beneath ruby-colored lipstick. "Can you take a coffee break with me?" I asked her.

"I was just about to suggest that myself. Come on back to the office, and we'll grab a cup."

With Hannah's typical arm-pumping, no-nonsense walk, she strode up to the counter, told the clerk that she'd be gone for a few minutes, and ushered me out of the immediate area.

She babbled to me about what "a delightful spring day" this was, and I responded with a few appreciative adjectives, although in truth, the weather this morning hadn't registered with me. We entered Hannah's "office," part of the storage room in the back of the store. Going from the brightly lit and colorful showroom to this dreary storage space with its stack of boxes and bare lightbulbs in the ceiling was like leaving a fabulous kitchen for an unfinished basement. Still chattering about how marvelous the climate in Colorado was, she emptied a Pyrex coffeepot into a pair of checkered aqua-and-dusty-rose mugs and handed me one. I did my best to settle into one of the two wooden slat-back chairs by Hannah's metal desk, although the seat was so uncomfortable that it was clearly designed for the function of keeping its occupant fully awake. I thanked her for my beverage, blew on the surface, and took a tentative sip. The coffee was half an hour or so shy of having been burned into sludge.

Choosing to omit the reason for my curiosity, I asked, "Did that man who claimed to be an undercover cop come back into the store yesterday?"

"No." She furrowed her brow. "I didn't want to upset everyone again by saying this at the time, but I can't believe for an instant that man was really a policeman. He'd been acting like a complete lunatic ever since he first walked into Paprika's."

"You mentioned that you'd had an encounter with him before . . . ?"

"Oh, it was way more than *one*." She took a sip and grimaced, either from the dreadful flavor or from her thoughts regarding the protestor. "I've had almost daily visits and the occasional picket sign from the jerk for a whole month now."

"Picket signs about *what*? 'Make charity donations, not household purchases'?"

She chuckled. "Essentially, yes. He claims a couple of the kitchen-products lines we carry have unethical practices . . . that the manufacturers use rain-forest woods, and so forth. As a matter of fact, that bowl you were examining was one of his hot points, yet the wood it's made from is forested in Florida. I tried to tell him that Paprika's would never sell rain-forest products. . . . In an earth-first town like Crestview, it would be professional suicide. I even double-checked . . . contacted the companies he complained about myself, and I gave him the results, which showed none of his claims are true."

"And that still didn't discourage him?"

She shook her head. "He just gabbled on about what he calls 'American gluttony' . . . how this country uses more resources per capita than any other country in the world. Like that's *my* fault?"

"So he's an anti-consumerism activist?"

"I guess that's what he calls himself." She snorted. "Apparently the guy's trying to save the world by impacting Paprika's sales revenues."

"Yeesh. That must be really frustrating for you."

"Mm-hmm." She frowned and took another sip of her coffee, then emptied a third packet of sugar into the murky liquid. "It's not winning me any popularity contests with Paprika's owners, I can tell you."

"What do they expect *you* to do about a kook?"

She shrugged. "Snap my fingers and make the nutcase disappear, I guess."

I paused, mulling over the protestor's objections. "We *do* use up too much of the world's resources in this country, for no purpose except to feather our own nests."

Hannah let out a bark of surprised laughter. "And this from an interior designer?"

My cheeks warmed a little, and I grinned at her. "I would never admit that to any of my clients, of course." But I *had* decided not to buy the salad bowls. Until someone invited me to their wedding. Or Christmas rolled around.

"Just like *I'll* never admit to my customers that I would never shop here myself if it weren't for the employee discount. Can't afford our merchandise. Not unless I win the lottery or get remarried to some millionaire. And this time, I'll make sure he doesn't hit the jackpot *after* our divorce."

"You're divorced?"

She gaped at me. "You didn't know?"

"Know *what*?"

She rolled her eyes. "Figures my ex and that little floozy would never see fit to mention my name to you. Even when she was flaunting the whole thing in front of me, right in my very own store."

Caught off guard, I set my cup down carefully on the corner of her desk, rather than risk spilling it on myself. "Are you talking about Dave Holland? Is *Dave* your ex-husband?"

"The one and only. He dumped me for Laura Smith." She smiled a little and added smugly, "Of course, just last year, he tried to get back with me. *After* she'd dumped him to take up with Steve Sullivan. Though that didn't last, either."

"You wouldn't take him back?"

"Hell, no. Dave and I nearly ripped each other to shreds while trying to reconcile. We wound up hating each other worse than ever. Like I was supposed to just forgive and forget. That bastard started having an affair with the little tramp less than three years after we got married. Then he used *my* ideas for his new company, and struck it rich."

She paused from her diatribe to study my face. "You looked so shocked, Erin. I guess he and Laura had you really fooled into thinking they were decent people."

"I got badly fooled, all right," I murmured.

"What did Laura have to say for herself after her scene with Jerry?"

"Jerry?"

"Jerry Stone. Our protestor turned phony 'undercover cop.' I figure she had to have known Jerry from someplace, or she'd never have sent him sprawling in front of everyone like that."

"She never told me who he was. Just that he'd been stalking her." I studied Hannah's eyes. She was normally so pleasant. Now she sounded bitter and almost hateful. "But you obviously haven't heard the terrible news, Hannah. Laura's dead. Someone stabbed her last night."

She set her cup down on her desk so fast that she

spilled a little. Drops spattered the beige metal panels of her desk. "My God! Are you serious?"

"Yes."

Hannah seemed to be sincerely surprised and paused as if to allow the news to register. "Huh. The tramp finally got what she deserved."

I winced, offended at her harshness.

She seemed to hear herself then, because she straightened her shoulders and held up a hand in apology. "I know *you* were taken in by her, so this must be hard on you. I'm sorry for your loss, Erin."

"Thanks," I muttered.

She grabbed her cup and took another sip. "Huh," she said for a second time, her brow furrowed. "Something about Laura seemed to attract violence. Like the mugging."

"Mugging?"

Hannah nodded. "Laura was attacked a couple years back when someone tried to grab her purse. That was how she got that awful scar on her neck . . . which she hid beneath those silk scarves of hers."

I sighed, feeling overwhelmed once again. "This is the third version I've heard in the last *two* days about how she got that scar. She told you it was from a mugging?"

"That's what she told *Dave*, who told me. Some thug down in Denver grabbed her purse and pulled a knife on her when she wouldn't release the strap. She thought he was going to cut the strap off, but he sliced her throat instead." She sighed. "When Dave moved out the first time, he tried to explain why he was so infatuated with Laura. According to him, *I* was capable of taking care of myself. Whereas precious *Laura* desperately needed him and his stability." She grimaced. "She *claimed* she was afraid to go places by herself at night, afraid of crowds. Made Dave feel like her big manly protector."

She clicked her tongue and met my gaze. "Come to think of it, she undoubtedly embellished the story. Or created it exclusively for Dave's sake. The scar could have been from a botched suicide, for all I know. That was Laura Smith for you . . . search out people's tender spots. Then drive an ice pick into them."

Chapter 8

After leaving Paprika's, I walked to my office, thinking that I could at least get some routine chores out of the way and perhaps shore up my spirits in the process. Wedged, as it were, between two trendy clothing stores, my office was on the second floor, the glass doors to Interiors by Gilbert opening to a narrow staircase. Bone weary and bewildered, I trudged up the steps.

Although my mother's Sheraton chair was on the visitor side of my desk, I shed my jacket and eagerly lowered myself into the seat. I've always been emotionally attached to certain pieces of furniture, and this family heirloom was my absolute favorite. Together my mother and I had reupholstered it, using her cross-stitched Victorian floral pattern on the back and the seat cushion. Six months ago, when I'd first moved in with Audrey, I'd felt too transient to place my beloved chair in her home, and since then I'd come to rely on the inspiration that I could draw from gazing at the chair when working up designs for my clients.

I ran my fingertips along the grooves in the mahogany armrests, remembering how often I'd seen my mother sitting in this chair when it was still in our old apartment in Albany, New York. I could picture her, seated in front of the drop-top corner desk, could almost smell the unique aroma when I was beside her in that one specific place— how her delicate perfume mingled with the trace of furniture polish and the tinge of burned dust from the brass floor lamp beside her.

Sitting here now, I liked to imagine that I could channel my mother. Our lives are surely a compilation of the thousands of little things that we do every day. Above all else, my mother had taught me that we need to find joy and love in this world, and that we need to have hope. After a few minutes in her chair, I could almost hear her voice—wonderfully melodic until her breath became ravaged from lung disease. She seemed to be telling me to keep going, to remember that there are many ways to make this so-imperfect world of ours a slightly better place; our surroundings are important to finding joy and keeping hold of hope.

I rose and rounded my desk to my practical, albeit less lovely, red-brown leather office chair. I dialed the number of a furniture manufacturer. A salesclerk, snapping her chewing gum at regular intervals, told me that my client's sectional sofa was complete and ready to be shipped tomorrow as planned. Just when I was about to hang up, she added, "Far as I know, this is the first time we've done this particular model in crimson Ultrasuede, but it looks kind of cool."

I double-checked my copy of the purchase order just in case I'd lost my mind. This order was a C.O.M.—customer's own material. Four weeks ago I'd brought the furniture manufacturer deep brown Ultrasuede fabric. "Are you sure we're talking about the same sofa? Ordered by Erin Gilbert for my client, Henry Toben?"

"Yep. That's the one."

"The Ultrasuede that I brought to you was chocolate brown, not crimson."

"Yep. Originally. But the next day, you put a stop on the order and swapped the brown for the red."

"I did no such thing!"

I heard some clicks of a computer keyboard to punctuate the gum-snapping sounds. "Yep, okay. Here it is. Henry Toben brought us the fabric. He came in himself."

"There must be some mistake. Let me call you back, after I talk to Mr. Toben."

"Sure thing. But I should probably warn you that if you want to switch back to the brown now, you'll, like, have to pay for the additional labor."

"I'll discuss this with my client and get back to you."

"Yep. Okay." There was a pause. "Henry Toben is 'Hammerin' Hank . . . who hammers out the best prices in town,' right? That guy who does all those obnoxious car ads on TV?"

"Yes, that's him."

"Tell me something." She lowered her voice, but not the noisy gum chewing. "Is he as obnoxious in person as he is on TV?"

"Oh, no, not at all." That was true, but only because Henry was much *more* obnoxious in person than on TV. No way would I bad-mouth a customer of mine, although in this particular case, it was actually the image consultant my client had hired to revamp his lifestyle who was paying my fee.

"Good to hear." Her gum made a wet smacking sound. "His commercials are just so . . . noisy. Figures he'd want his sofa *loud*, too." She unleashed a booming laugh into my ear.

The instant I got off the phone, I dialed Henry's cell phone. I gritted my teeth when he answered, "Howdy," in a Texas drawl. He must have been in front of some customers at one of his dealerships. "Hammerin' Hank," the TV personality, was from Houston, Texas. Henry Toben, however, was from a small town in Delaware.

"Hi, Henry. It's Erin."

"Hey, there, li'l darlin'. What-all can I do you for?"

"Did you go to the sectional-sofa manufacturer and supply them with red Ultrasuede instead of the brown that we'd agreed upon?"

There was a pause. Hammerin' Hank drawled, "Tell me somethin', missy. If'n I was to plead guilty, is the court likely to show a kindly ol' cowboy like myself some leniency?"

I counted to ten. Then to fifteen. I hadn't gotten enough sleep last night to suffer this pseudo-Texan fool gladly. Our communication was hampered by an even worse obstacle than Henry's on-again-off-again Texas accent; we had to reach through a layer of management. Henry's image consultant, Robert Pembrook, had hired me to design Henry's house, and both men, who were often at cross-purposes, had to approve my design. "The three of us went over this twice. Remember? With Robert Pembrook?"

"I do indeed, darlin', but as y'all might recall, I was on the fence at the time."

"Actually, Henry, I remember our conversation distinctly." I kept my voice even, despite my ever-increasing agitation. "When you said you wanted the red, Pembrook said it was 'too much,' and you said, 'Yes, you're absolutely right. Let's go with the Hershey's Kisses color.' " Henry had then gone on to say that he "might get lucky with the chocoholic babes," but if I continued to quote him, disgust was bound to creep into my voice. He'd said, "You betcha, darlin'," every time. And yet both of those conversations had taken place well *after* he'd already put a stop on the order and, unbeknownst to me, he had swapped our customer's-own-material at the manufacturers.

"The trouble is, Henry, I designed the entire room around the brown sectional, as the room's focal piece. Everything's already purchased, and almost all of it's been shipped to my storage unit." I fought back the image of Laura's oh-so-still body that the mention of the warehouse had invoked. "Tomorrow they're shipping the red sofa . . . and one full room's worth of surrounding furniture is now going to clash with it."

"Well, missy, what can I tell you? That dog just don't hunt."

"Pardon?"

In a slightly muffled voice, Henry said with a chuckle to someone in his vicinity, " 'Scuse me, y'all. I'll be back in three shakes of a coon-dog's tail."

While waiting for Henry to continue our decorating squabble in private, I silently reminded myself that when it came to interior design, the customer *was* always right; the interior of the owner's home had to be to his or her complete liking, not to mine. However, it was also my job to ensure that five years later, when fads change, the customer wasn't stuck with a white elephant. Henry could always reupholster his sofa at some point in the future. In the *present*, however, he was going to get a headache looking at red glaring against all the greens and violets I'd selected for accents and companion pieces.

"Back with you." Henry had switched to his Henry-from-Delaware voice. "I meant to tell you about that red. But I guess I've been so busy working my ass off at my dealerships, it just slipped my mind, honey. And, by the way, thanks for keeping me posted on where you got the cloth and everything. All I had to do was call the fabric store and buy the exact same thing, 'cept in a cherry lollipop color."

"But why didn't you tell me what you were doing? Or tell Robert?"

"I couldn't bring myself to tell him that I really, really wanted my couch to be red when he was sold on the brown."

"Why *couldn't* you? You're a major tycoon who owns three successful dealerships in Crestview County."

"Four, actually. But who's counting?"

"Surely you don't need assertiveness training."

"It's not that. It's just that this Pembrook gay sca—" He stopped abruptly and then corrected himself. "The guy scares me."

That had to be a Freudian slip; Henry must be uncomfortable around flamboyant, openly gay men, such as Robert Pembrook. "Remember that Robert works for *you*, not the other way around."

"It sure never feels like I'm the boss when he's telling me what I need to do with every last little thing in my life. In any case, I want *you* to handle this, Erin. That's part of what I'm paying you for. Just tell him that you agreed with me at the last minute, and we went with the red. Understand?"

"The thing is, Henry, *he* hired *me*. Technically, *he* is my boss. According to my contract with him, he has to sign off on my floor plans, or I don't get paid."

"That's a problem, all right, because I want the red."

I ruthlessly combed my fingers through my hair, desperate to keep a tight rein on my temper. "Henry, the three of us are going to have to sit down again and discuss this."

"No problem. Let's count on that. Matter of fact, this is super timing for the both of us. I'm already scheduled to meet him at two this afternoon, which I'm dreading. Bound to go better with you there."

"Why on earth are you continuing to employ someone you 'dread' seeing?"

"Ironic, ain't it? Bottom line is, I'm getting along with my employees much better ever since I took Pembrook's advice. I always let my wife deal with personnel matters. She was real patient, even with the perpetual whiners. See, I was the sales guru . . . she was the touchy-feely sort. Ever since she passed away, my workers are in and out of here so fast, I might as well install a revolving door. Till Pembrook taught me how to . . . I don't know . . . bring out my feminine side during business meetings. Plus, the guy's got me learning how to impress the ladies, big time, in the process."

This client still had a whole lot of learning to do as far as I was concerned. "That's great, Henry. But, getting back to the issue at hand, I've got a roomful of furniture and accessories that are going to be a disaster with a red sofa."

"That's why it's good that Pembrook brought me such an expert to pretty up my house. You'll think of something, honey."

Once again, I started to count, but hadn't made it to three before Henry added, "See you at two. Y'all take care, heah?" and hung up on me.

I grabbed a quick lunch, and calculating that I might as well show Robert Pembrook my recently completed plans for our client's home now, I collected them and stashed them in my van. I had a few minutes free and decided to check on Sullivan. Not surprisingly, his office was locked tight, so I called his house. The answering machine in his home clicked on, and although I identified myself, he didn't pick up. A little worried about him, I drove to his home—which would be directly on my way to Denver anyway—negotiated his slate walkway, and used his custom-made brass door knocker. The knocker was typical of a Sullivan design—elegant lines, sublimely suited to its function, but beautiful.

"It's open," I heard him call.

"Steve?" I said as I cautiously peeked inside. "It's me, Erin."

"I'm in the living room."

I rounded the corner and stopped. My eyes took a moment to adjust to the darkness; the blinds in the room were drawn. Sullivan lay sprawled on a chaise. Unshaven and rumpled-looking, he was barefoot, in jeans and a white shirt with half of the buttons left undone. The room was in the same shape it had been in the last time I'd seen it, several months ago. Although the few items he had in this room were exquisite, they were a trifle sparse. He had, at least, added a Windsor chair to accompany his chaise, sofa, and coffee table. Once he'd mentioned to me that he'd had to sell off some of his artwork and furniture to pay off his debts in the wake of Evan and Laura's disastrous betrayal.

"You're not answering your phone," I reproved gently.

"Didn't feel like it." He rubbed the back of his neck. "I'd offer you coffee or something, but you'll have to make it yourself."

"Do *you* want a cup?"

"Nah. But don't let that stop you."

"I'm fine. Thanks anyway."

He gestured for me to take a seat, and I dropped into

his cushy sofa. Upholstered in a neutral mushroom chenille, this heavenly sofa was as soft and cuddly as a kitten.

"What gives?" he asked. "Are you playing mother hen . . . checking in on me?"

Despite his sharp wording, my heart felt a pang. He looked so destitute alone in his shadowed room. "Should I claim that I was in the neighborhood and thought I'd stop by?"

He said nothing.

"You look like you've been lying there all night."

"Brilliant deduction." His eyes were so bloodshot that the sight of them almost made mine water. "That lady police officer you're friends with came here," he muttered. "I asked if they'd arrested Dave Holland yet. She said that he insisted he didn't even leave the house last night . . . that his brother was staying with him, and Dave let the brother borrow his car."

"That story's not going to carry much weight with Linda, or with *any* of the police, for that matter. Dave didn't mention his brother being there when the three of us were talking to him a few hours before we spotted the car leaving."

"Yeah. I asked her about that. Dave claimed his brother had gone for a late-night jog at the time."

"In pitch darkness? In the mountains?"

"Apparently his brother's backing up the story."

"Out of family loyalty, I'm sure."

"I should've done a better job tailing him last night. It should have been obvious to me where he was heading the moment he got on the turnpike . . . driven straight to the warehouse district and combed the place till I found her car. I lived with the woman for a year. I knew better than anybody how devious she was. I should have stayed a step ahead of her."

"It's not your fault, you know."

"Hmm?"

"What happened to Laura. It wasn't your fault."

"Yeah, it is. *Has* to be. She wouldn't have even *been* at U-Store if I hadn't confronted her."

"By that logic, *I'm* more culpable than you are. I'm the one who realized that she was switching out her expensive antiques for cheap imitations. And brought you to her place. And talked you out of going straight to the police. Do you think *I* should be feeling guilty?"

He merely grumbled, "I don't expect you to understand what I'm going through."

"Let me guess. You used to fantasize about wringing her neck. Now that someone *did* kill her, you think that your ill wishes somehow brought this all about."

"It's not like that at all, Gilbert."

"Then what *is* it like?"

He refused to answer. After a time he said, "The police suspect me."

"But you were with *me* from nine o'clock on. Which reminds me. Did you tell the police it was eight o'clock when I got to your car?"

"No . . . quarter of nine. Why?"

"Figures. The detective was trying to cross me up . . . see if I was certain about the times."

"See? There's your proof . . . I'm their chief suspect. They were trying to break my alibi. I had a motive and opportunity . . . there *would* have been enough time for me to have driven to her house, followed her to Northridge, and killed her, all before I borrowed the car from my buddy and arrived up there by eight forty-five, when you showed up."

"Even so, the police will canvass Laura's neighborhood. They'll be able to find someone who saw you parked up there all evening. As soon as they do, they'll have to cross you off their list of suspects."

He scowled at me fiercely, clearly unwilling to concede the logic of my argument. The man seemed determined to both blame himself for Laura's murder and get himself arrested for it. Why?

"I told the police I think Laura could have ripped off Evan and returned to Crestview, thinking he wouldn't follow her for fear of getting arrested. That she underestimated his determination, and he killed her."

"Is that possible?" I asked.

"Of *course* it's possible! Evan would do anything for money. If she ran off with his portion of the money they stole from me, he'd hunt her down and kill her. Or Evan could be in on the antiques scam. He could have camped out at the storage unit himself. Laura arrives, they argue, she winds up dead."

He's made Evan into the devil incarnate. I glanced discreetly at my watch. I had to get going. My visit wasn't doing Sullivan any good anyway; he seemed to be getting more depressed with each passing moment. My time would be better spent trying to resolve the situation with Robert Pembrook and Henry Toben. "Sorry, but I've got to get to a job down in Denver."

"In *Denver?*"

"We're just meeting there, actually. My client lives in Crestview. He's a recent widower."

"Huh."

Trying to throw Sullivan a bone in a last-ditch effort to cheer him up, I said, "Frankly, you'd probably have been a better choice of designers. My client's in his sixties, but he wants to make his place into something of a swinging bachelor pad. His image consultant was actually the one who hired me."

"An *image consultant* hired you?"

"As part of a package deal, apparently. He instructs his clients on how to interact with others and spiffs up their wardrobe, and he hires designers to do the same with their homes."

He swung his legs off the chaise and sat up to face me. Suddenly Sullivan was giving me his full attention. "What's his name?"

"Henry Toben. I'm sure you've seen his television ads—'Hankerin'' for a new car? Come see big Hammerin' Hank.'" Sullivan was staring at me with a furrowed brow, showing no sign of recognition, so I continued, "'I'll hammer out a deal for y'all.' Or something like that."

"No, I meant what's the image consultant's name, not your client's."

"Oh. Sorry. Robert Pembrook."

Sullivan sprang to his feet. "Something's up. That's another connection to Laura."

"*What* is? Did you and Laura both know Robert Pembrook?"

"I know *of* him." He started pacing, then stopped abruptly and commanded: "Tell me how you got this job. Had you already met the client . . . this Toben?"

Sullivan sounded just like Linda Delgardio, slipping into grilling-the-witness mode. Still, I decided not to let his interrogation irritate me. "No. Robert hired me to work with him. I didn't know who the client even *was* until all three of us got together about three months ago."

"So you met Pembrook first?"

"Essentially. He hired me over the phone . . . long distance. Four months ago. He was finishing up some job in Los Angeles and said that he'd heard good things about me, so, sight unseen, he hired me to work with Henry."

"Huh. Sounds like he hired you just a month or so after *Laura* moved back to Crestview. And had hired you to select her antiques."

"What's all this about, Sullivan?"

"Robert Pembrook was Evan Cambridge's boss. A couple of years ago. That's what Evan was doing when we met: interior makeovers for clients in Denver, while teamed up with an image consultant. Pembrook was moving his business to L.A. but Evan wanted to stay, and Pembrook gave him such a glowing recommendation that I agreed to hire Evan on a trial basis, then moved him into a partnership position."

"Did *Laura* ever mention the name Robert Pembrook to you?"

"No, but that doesn't mean anything. She was a con artist. I was her mark. She kept her past ties as secret as possible."

"Okay, so . . . Evan used to work for Robert in Denver, and now I'm working for Robert. You're thinking that, because Laura and Evan were partners in crime, *Robert's* somehow linked to Laura's murder in Crestview?" I paused. "Isn't that a pretty big leap?"

"Maybe. Maybe not. It's not much of a connection, but it's the only one I've got to Evan. Maybe he got in touch with his former boss recently." He jammed his hands into the pockets of his jeans and started pacing again. "I'm going to call Pembrook on some pretense . . . see if I can arrange to meet him."

I rose. "Clear your schedule and come with me to Denver right now. You can meet Robert and scope him out."

He peered at me. "Are you sure you want me to do that? I'm a prime suspect. You'd be better off not getting involved with me."

"Too late. I already *am* involved."

My statement, I promptly realized, could be misinterpreted. I blurted, "I'm getting paid a flat fee, so it won't make any difference to Robert if I tell him that I'm bringing an assistant on board."

"So I get to be your *assistant*?"

"Mm-hmm."

"Lucky me. I need a minute to get ready." He left the room, calling through the open door, "Good thing the unshaven look's in style now."

I called back, "You realize you're going to have to actually *work* as my assistant on this one job, or it'll look really bizarre . . . my having a new assistant who shows up for one meeting, then disappears."

"Good. That'll give me time to get to know the guy."

True to his word, in less than a minute we were ready to go. He'd donned a black suit jacket that had the nice lines of a pricey Italian tailor, shoes and socks, and he now looked annoyingly sexy in an arty, casual way.

"Just remember," I reminded him, "you're my assistant, so act completely subservient."

Steve grinned and held the door for me. "Sounds like fun. Lead on, O Master." He checked to make sure his front door was locked and asked me, "Has Pembrook left Los Angeles for good?"

"I doubt it. He's staying in this glam penthouse hotel room in Denver for the time being."

"Has he said what brought him back to Denver?"

"I think it was strictly to take this job for Henry Toben. As far as I know, anyway. There was probably some sort of Hollywood connection with all those local TV ads Henry does . . . maybe he got Robert's name from his producer or cameraman or something."

Sullivan grabbed my elbow and ushered me along his narrow walkway. "Do me a favor, Erin. When we meet Pembrook, not a word about Laura. From here on out, I'm treating everyone like they're guilty until proven innocent."

"I guess that's prudent, just so long as your everyone's-evil credo ends with the killer's arrest. You don't want to go through life being so worried about getting burned a second time that you freeze to death."

"Jeez, Gilbert! Enough with the damned advice!"

Hurt and affronted, I cried, "Hey! If that's the way you talk to your *superiors,* forget it! Don't come with me!"

"Oh, yeah? Well, if you want to be my—" He broke off abruptly. In a quieter voice, he said, "Guess we'd better take your van, since you're blocking mine in the garage."

I got behind the wheel. Though I momentarily considered driving off and leaving Sullivan to think twice before he snapped at me again, I unlocked the passenger door, and he slid in beside me.

"How'd your *boyfriend* take the news about Laura?" he asked as he reached for his seat belt.

"John! Oh, my God. I completely forgot to tell him!" I grabbed my purse to fetch my cell phone.

"That's okay. The police have probably contacted him by now."

Puzzled, I stared at him. "Why would they contact *John?*"

As though he'd gotten a sizable static electric shock, Sullivan's eyes widened and his lips parted. An instant later, a bland expression reclaimed his features. "I told them last night. Gave them the names of Laura's former associates. Laura and John knew each other. Through me. The three of us used to hang out sometimes."

"Damn it, Sullivan, what is it you're not telling me?"

"Ah, jeez, Gilbert. This is none of my business."

I gripped my cell phone in my fist and shook it in his face, fully prepared to bonk him on the head. "Out with it, Sullivan! Fess up!"

He mumbled, "I should've just kept my mouth shut."

He cursed under his breath, then said, "Better yet, *John* should've mentioned it during your lunch yesterday. When you found out from him who Laura was."

"Mentioned *what*?" I yelled.

"Laura and John used to date each other."

Chapter 9

I stared at Sullivan. "Laura dated *John*, too?" *Was there anyone in Crestview that woman* didn't *date?*

Sullivan repositioned his seat belt on his shoulder, no doubt wishing there were an eject button for my passenger seat. Damn it, the man was clearly embarrassed for me. "Just a few times. They were only together for a couple of months. Then Laura started seeing Dave Holland . . . and dumped Holland for me." He didn't need to add that she'd then gone back to Holland, after draining Sullivan's bank accounts.

I dumped my cell phone back into my purse. More than a little annoyed at John, I was no longer in any hurry to call him. Why hadn't he told me he'd dated Laura? I started the engine and pulled out of Sullivan's driveway. Laura had plied me for intimate details about myself and John Norton. Never once had she given me any sign that the two of them had once been an item. She was, after all, a professional con artist, but I expected better from John.

Sullivan cleared his throat. "Hey, Gilbert, I'm sure John didn't mention this to you simply because it was no big deal. He told me back then that he'd only gone out on a few dates with her and never really trusted her. *He* was smart enough to see through her."

"Bully for him," I growled.

We drove in silence. I was trying to get past my initial shock. When I thought back on yesterday's lunch conversation, I could see why John hadn't rushed into telling me that he, too, had dated Laura; after all, he hadn't really had all that much of an opportunity. We'd gotten so focused on the reason she was here and what that meant to Sullivan. The big question now, though, was where *I* fit into all of this. Had Sullivan introduced me to John as some sort of payback for John's having brought Laura into his life? If so, both men could go to hell. In any case, my life had certainly been a lot less complicated before I'd met either of them.

"Dave Holland divorced Hannah Garrison, who works at Paprika's, when he met Laura," I said. "So, does this mean that Laura was going out with *John* at the time? That she dumped John to go after a married man?"

Sullivan mumbled, "I'm not sure of the exact time frame."

I tightened my grip on the steering wheel. "It's just remarkable how you can discover that you're connected to this whole slew of people you've never even met."

Sullivan didn't reply, and remained silent for so long that I looked over to make sure his eyes were open. They were. Eventually, he said, "The headlights don't make sense."

I glanced at the oncoming cars, but none of them had their lights on. "*What* headlights?"

"They were off last night. The headlights. In Holland's car. Yet he'd had 'em *on* when he was driving *to* the warehouse, so it's not like he was trying to go unnoticed. Also, he was speeding . . . weaving through dimly lit buildings. Like he was so scared and anxious to get the hell out of there, it was all he could do just to start the engine. Just can't see him killing her, then starting the fire, *then* panicking and racing off, when he didn't even know anyone was following him."

"So you think he accidentally stumbled across her body while setting the fire, then panicked and took off?"

He nodded. "Exactly."

That was a good point, and the more I thought about it, the more it troubled me. If this tragedy turned out to be a case of "domestic violence," the police would quickly realize Sullivan was innocent; Laura would have met with her sordid end by virtue of trying to cheat her lover one too many times. But if the killer wasn't Dave, the murder investigation was bound to be intense for all of us who once thought we knew Laura Smith—only to have our hearts get stepped on like welcome mats.

We arrived in downtown Denver half an hour later, having multitasked and worked out a compatible schedule from here on out. In the parking lot, however, we argued about divvying up the proceeds from this assignment; Sullivan insisted that his time and services were "totally on the house," which was inane. The man had been all but bankrupted by Laura; he didn't have to work for me for free. I finally decided to let the matter slide until

Laura's murderer was behind bars. My hope was that Sullivan would then revert to the compassionate man that I knew was hiding beneath his current spate of bitterness — an ugly emotional slipcover, if ever there was one.

I allowed Sullivan to play his designated subservient role and carry my large, flat portfolio, plus walk a step behind me. I could easily get used to this treatment.

Henry Toben was pacing in the resplendent hotel lobby. Its black granite floor was polished to a dazzling sheen, the posh sectional sofa was so large that it would dwarf anyone who deigned to sit there, and glimmering brass bars blocked off an octagonal indoor garden lush with ferns and tropical flora. I half expected to see a toucan perched on the branch of the rubber tree.

"There you are," he growled to me the moment we neared. He was wearing silver cowboy boots, jeans, a Western-style butter-yellow silk shirt with black piping, and a bolo tie, but was sans his typical black ten-gallon hat.

Henry was stocky, but at just five foot seven or so, he was an inch or two shorter than I am. My theory was that he'd originally gone with "Hammerin' Hank" and his signature Western wear purely for the height-enhancing cowboy boots. His dark, even tan was so unnatural that the first time we'd met, I'd assumed it was stage makeup. Now I was sure it was some type of spray-on product. He had thick, snowy white hair, which I suspected was a toupee, perched atop his head like a dustcover. Despite his gruff greeting, his light-blue eyes twinkled, which I'd come to believe merely indicated that he was thinking about something raunchy.

Before I could introduce the two men, Henry stepped toward Steve with a proffered hand and bellowed, "Howdy, partner! Hank Toben."

While they shook hands vigorously, I said, "This is my assistant, Steve Sullivan."

Hank raised an eyebrow and visibly pulled away. Coldly, he said to me, "You never mentioned you had an assistant."

"It's a new role for me," Sullivan interjected. "I've been running my own interior design business in Crestview for four years now."

Henry rocked on his boot heels as he eyed Sullivan. "So you're an interior designer? Huh." He'd dropped the Texas accent. "I figured you were Erin's significant other." Chuckling, he clapped Sullivan on the shoulder. "Guess I was way off on that one, hey? Thing is, you don't really *act* like a fag." He turned and started to lead the way to the elevator, saying over his shoulder, "Well, you should get along real good with Robert Pembrook, then. He's gay as a jaybird."

Sullivan glowered, and I belatedly remembered that I'd neglected to mention to him that our client was a horse's ass.

Though Henry arrived at the elevator doors first, he waited for one of us to press the button, which Sullivan did. When the doors opened and we stepped inside the polished-silver elevator, I reached past Sullivan to press the button for the top floor. As the doors closed behind us, I explained to Sullivan, "Henry is uncomfortable around Robert Pembrook because of his sexual preference."

"Not just 'cuz of that. The man's got friends in high places, and I ain't just talking about the penthouse. He's done time."

"*Time?*" I repeated, incredulous. "As in prison?"

"You betcha. For embezzling. The man may be a fruit, but he's like one a them prickly pears." He wiggled his eyebrows at Sullivan. "You don't want to get too close to him, or you'd best watch your hide."

We got out on the top floor. The hallway was hotel chic—maroon and gold color palette—more upscale than most hotels, but too self-conscious for my own taste. In fairness, however, I don't design hotels and couldn't think off the top of my head of anything that would work all that much better. I knocked on Robert's door, and he swept it open with a typical flourish.

"Erin!" he cried. "What a marvelous surprise! I thought this was going to be just the boring ol' twosome with Henry today."

Henry paled, but I beamed at Robert as he said, "Hello, hello. Come in, come in." I loved the way the man had such unbridled enthusiasm that he said some words twice.

Robert had the same six-foot height and athletic body type as Steve Sullivan. They even had some facial characteristics in common—the strong chin and full head of tousled hair, although Robert's was mostly gray. Today he was impeccably dressed in a blue-gray turtleneck, tailored black slacks, and expensive black leather shoes. A white cable-knit sweater was draped over his shoulders, cape-like, to dashing effect. He also wore oversized black-framed glasses. My guess was that he wore bifocals, and the coaster-sized lenses probably spared him from having to crane his neck the way fashionably small glasses would have.

While Henry brushed past Robert and into the sitting room, I introduced Sullivan to Robert as my assistant. The two men shook hands. Then Robert fidgeted with his glasses as he continued to study Sullivan's handsome features. "Your name sounds familiar, but I can't quite place it, I'm afraid. And I *know* we haven't met. I never forget a face."

Instantly, I tensed. This was Steve's chance to learn about Robert's current ties with Laura's partner-in-crime,

Evan, and predictably, he leapt on it. He replied, "I was Evan Cambridge's business partner. In Crestview. After he stopped working for you."

"Oh, yes, yes, of course, of course. Steve Sullivan. *That's* where I know your name. That was a terrible ordeal he put you through."

"One that hasn't ended."

"Yes, yes. Indeed. I heard about how he ripped you off and then bolted overseas. I felt terrible about that, Steven."

"Steve."

"I had no idea Evan had something like that in him. He couldn't have been more trustworthy the entire time he worked for me." He glanced at me, sighed, then returned his attention thoughtfully to Sullivan. "And now you've apparently lost your business and are working for someone else."

"I treat Steve as a peer," I interjected hastily. "And he still has his own business. We just job-share sometimes."

"Have you heard from Evan lately?" Steve asked, his eyes locked on Robert.

"Nary a word, I'm afraid."

I glanced at Steve, hoping he would ask Robert if he'd known Laura as well, but he ignored me. I took that to mean that, as of yet, he could draw no conclusions about Robert's silk-thread-thin connection to Laura.

Robert ushered us farther into his hotel suite to join Henry. The suite was over-the-top opulent in its liberal use of shimmering gold satin textiles and marble surfaces and carvings. All told, it looked like a scaled-down version of Donald Trump's New York penthouse.

Robert urged us to "make yourselves comfortable," and he perched on the arm of the gold satin tuxedo-style sofa. "It is just amazing how morally bankrupt some people can be, isn't it?" he asked. "And all the while, it's people like me, in my role as 'image consultant' "—he sketched quotation marks in the air with his fingers—"who train them how to put up this slick, glittering front for the world."

"Face it, Pembrook: you have the perfect credentials for working with the 'morally bankrupt.' " Henry had slouched down in the overstuffed armchair and had spread out his legs as if to allow his annoying little body to take up as much space as possible.

Although the remark instantly set my teeth on edge, Robert merely chuckled. He looked at Sullivan and me and explained, "I had loose lips during one of our previous sessions and told Henry about my sordid past. Though it *is* the distant past . . . many, many years ago. I was arrested for embezzlement, did my time, and have been on the straight and narrow ever since." He paused. "Well, actually . . ." He winked and chuckled a second time. "Not so 'straight.' But 'on the *narrow*,' at any rate."

"I'm sure the vast majority of your clients are good people who just recognize that they need a little polish on their rough edges," I interjected.

"You are just too kind, Erin. But thank you." He sighed. "And you know what? That actually *used* to be true, while I was still working mostly with clients in Denver. But now that I'm in Hollywood . . ." He rolled his eyes. "Well, let's just say that you have no idea."

Rubbing his hands together, he hopped to his feet and once again gestured at Sullivan and me. "So. Sit, sit!" He eyed my portfolio case. "Are these the finished room plans?"

"Yes, indeed," I replied.

On cue, my new domestic slave, Sullivan, opened the portfolio and set up the easel.

"We're scheduled to receive the final shipment of furniture tomorrow," I told Robert.

"I can't wait!" he exclaimed. To my delight, he then

oohed and ahhed over my designs. Hanging over my head like a samurai sword, however, was the realization that, thanks to the cherry-lollipop sofa, the finished product was no longer going to match the *delightful* images on my design board. Also hanging over me was the fact that my "assistant" was really here to glean clues to Evan Cambridge's whereabouts.

At what I sensed was the opportune moment to bring up the topic, I announced, "One surprise is that Henry felt so strongly about the red Ultrasuede sofa that he changed the order on us."

Robert gasped and shifted his gaze to Henry. "You *didn't*!"

Henry shot me a glare, but then said to Robert, "I really preferred it to the brown. That's just so boring. You know?"

I said, "I only learned about the color switch a couple of hours ago and haven't had time to reflect that in my artwork. I'll be changing my accessories accordingly. This is probably going to affect my fee, I'm afraid."

"I would imagine so." Robert shook his head sorrowfully and clicked his tongue. "Henry, Henry. What can I say? You hire me to give you advice, but ultimately, *you're* the one who either takes or rejects it. For example, when was the last time you stood in front of a full-length mirror?"

"Just this morning!"

"And, at the time, had you already put on your dandy-cowboy duds?"

Henry spread his arms and looked down at his clothing as though he'd been doused with cold water. "Hey! This is still a workday for me! I need folks to recognize me from the TV ads!"

"Well, if it were up to me, you and Mr. Sullivan here would swap outfits." Robert gestured at Steve. "You see this look? *This*, Henry, is what I mean by casual chic for men—a black sports jacket; white, fashionably rumpled shirt with an open collar; jeans. See how sexy this is? Although at *your* age, you would want to tuck in the shirt. Then you would want to add a complementary pocket square to dress it up just a titch for commercials." He sat back down, openly studying Henry. "Furthermore, for heaven's sake, get yourself a less flamboyant pair of boots. Something in earth tones, matte finish, square toes." He chuckled and put his hands on his hips. "Should *I* really be the one telling *you* to be less flamboyant, Henry? Let's keep your big honkin' cowboy hat for transition purposes for the next commercial or two, then go without it. I'll take charge of your wardrobe during the taping of your next advertisement. Trust me. It'll be fabulous."

"But I already *tried* that. Shot a sample commercial while wearing a dark suit. I looked like a funeral director."

The mention of the word *funeral* gave me a pang for Laura's sake, but the men's conversation continued without a hitch. Robert sighed and shook his head at Sullivan and me. "Kind of makes you wonder what he's paying me all this hard-earned money for, doesn't it?"

"Hey," Henry said. "On the bright side, I haven't lost even one employee in the last two months! And a couple days ago, I met the perfect gal, exactly the type you've been nagging me to go out with."

"Fabulous," Robert replied. "Fabulous! So, in other words, you've finally stopped robbing the cradle?"

Henry grinned and sat up straight, giving his dustcover hair a reassuring pat. "This gal's *my* age . . . in other words, old enough to refuse to say how old she is. But I hear she had a birthday recently, and I do know she's at least sixty. We've got a lot in common, too. We're *both* local celebrities. Met her at the TV station where I was shooting my last commercial. She gave me her number, and we're going out Saturday."

I dug my fingers into the arms of my chair. Just the night before last, Audrey had mentioned that she'd agreed to go on a date next Saturday "with an obnoxious man, during a weak moment." I forced a smile and asked, "You're not talking about Audrey Munroe, are you?"

"As a matter of fact, I am." Henry beamed at me. "How'd you know that?"

"I rent a room from her, and she mentioned she was going out with someone new this Saturday."

"Well, now. How do you like that!" He reached over and patted my knee. My skin instantly prickled. "So you're my designer *and* my inside edge with my new lady. I'll have to be sure and stay on your good side, darlin'."

I fought back a smile at the thought of how swiftly Audrey would pound this joker into the turf if she ever heard him call her his *lady*. "Yes, you will." Not that he'd ever *been* on my good side.

"What other changes have you made to Erin's orders, Henry?" Robert asked.

Henry held up his palms. "That's it. Just the one sofa."

There was a plastic quality to Henry's facial expression that made me nervous, but if Robert noticed, he didn't reveal it. "Good, good," he said. "In that case, we're all set. Though, remember, *you* will ultimately be picking up the tab for Erin's having to increase her fee." He grabbed my hand and gave it a squeeze. "Erin, I'll be checking on your progress in Henry's home periodically." Grinning, he ran his eyes over Sullivan. "And, Steve, welcome to the team!"

"We'll need to double check Henry's new furniture that's been delivered to my storage unit," I said to Sullivan as we left the hotel parking lot.

"Yeah. He might have switched around half your orders. I don't trust that dime-store cowboy as far as a petting-park pony could throw him."

I chuckled at the image. "They're delivering the sectional tomorrow. Let's stop at U-Store now. Even if I trusted Henry, which I don't, I need to make sure there's no smoke damage. My unit's just three doors away from Laura's . . . too close for comfort." I shuddered.

Sullivan was silent. I knew he was even less fond than I was of the concept of going back to the scene of the recent, harrowing crime, but Henry's furniture needed to be examined. Sullivan muttered, "I don't trust Robert Pembrook any farther than that pony could throw him, either."

"You *don't*? I like the guy immensely!"

"Granted, he's infinitely more likable than Henry, but come on, Gilbert. He's a convicted criminal, and—"

"Which he's already paid his debt to society for."

"*And* he used to work with Evan Cambridge."

"You were partners with Evan!"

"Until the bastard *ripped me off*. Yet he *didn't* rip off his ex-con former boss. What does *that* tell you?"

"That Evan knew better than to cross someone who'd done jail time," I fired back.

"*Or* that Pembrook taught Evan everything he knew that *landed* him in jail in the first place."

I sighed, deeply annoyed. If only Sullivan could keep quiet, he'd be wonderful eye candy, but he insisted on opening his mouth and ruining the effect every time. "Robert came right out and told his client that he'd once been convicted of a white-collar crime. He isn't putting up any false fronts . . . quite the contrary. And if the government is willing to consider that his debt has been paid in full, it seems to me that *we* should be, too."

Sullivan said nothing, so I glanced over at him. His brow was deeply furrowed, and I was sorely tempted to tell him that if he didn't cut out all that frowning, his face was going to get stuck that way. He must have felt my eyes on him, because he said, "Two days ago, I might have agreed with you, Gilbert. Not now." He didn't have to explain that two days ago he hadn't known that Laura Smith was back in Crestview.

A horrid pang of guilt hit me. That one piece of information—the news that Laura had returned to town—could have been the catalyst to Laura's murder.

Our path to my storage unit took us past Laura's. The outer walls were blackened but still standing. It was cordoned off, but otherwise the place had its usual austere, giant-building-blocks appearance. The odor of charred wood hung in the air.

I started to unlock the door to my unit. Something immediately felt wrong with the lock. I felt a surge of panic as the knob moved freely before the key had fully clicked into place. "Oh, damn it! It's unlocked!" I cried to Sullivan. "I'm supposed to have the only key and I definitely locked it!" Terrified that there was going to be another dead body inside, I flung open the door and made a cursory inspection from the doorway. The contents seemed to be the same as when I'd last left it, the unit still about two-thirds full. "Things could have been stolen. We'll have to check off every item."

Sullivan started to brush past me to go inside, but I grabbed his jacket. "Wait. There could be evidence in here, fingerprints or something." Then I sighed. "Never mind. Too many people have been in here for fingerprints to matter."

"Could anyone else have the key?"

"Nobody but the U-Store manager. And our phantom

security guards. Damn it all! If anything's missing, I'm going to sue these idiots for all they're worth!"

"Which probably isn't much," Steve pointed out.

I dialed the U-Store central office on my cell phone, and they sent out a security guard and a manager in no time. Both were unable to say how or when someone had managed to break into my rented space, but they did give me plenty of obvious advice about making sure nothing was missing and reporting anything that was.

Glowering at the U-Store personnel as they left, Steve said to me, "I'm never using this place again. The security here is either inept or corrupt."

"Or both," I grumbled, and reached for my cell phone again. "I'm going to call our little cowboy on his cell phone to discuss this. And maybe play a hunch."

Henry answered, "Howdy, y'all. Hammerin' Hank speaking."

"This is Erin. I'm at the storage unit I rented to house your furniture, and I discovered that someone other than me has a key to the place."

"Is that right?"

"Yes. There were no signs of a break-in, yet the door was left unlocked. Did you pay off a U-Store employee to slip you a duplicate key, Henry?"

There was a pause. In his Henry-from-Delaware voice, he replied, "Technically, you realize, it's *my* storage unit. I'm the one picking up the tab. And everything inside it is mine."

"True, and you'll be very lucky if everything inside it is still here, since you forgot to lock the place!"

"Hey, now hold your horses, honey. It must have been one of my employees who did that. I always keep doors locked. You can't trust anybody anymore."

"No, you can't," I snarled. "But why on earth would

you give an *employee* access to a storage unit containing your *home* furniture?"

"Ah. Well, I had some furniture to move around in there. See, I needed to wait till after our meeting with Pembrook to tell you this, but I've made a few more adjustments to your design. No sense in my going head-to-head with a *convict* to get my own house the way I like it, you know? And you're so talented and creative, I'm sure you can fluff things over just fine."

Enraged, I reached for my confidence-and-optimism mantra *and* a quick count to ten. I was interrupted by a familiar voice from the doorway, saying, "Hey, guys."

I whirled around. It was John, looking handsome as always, but with a somewhat sheepish expression on his face. To Henry, I snapped, "I'll do my best. I've got to go. Bye," and hung up. "John," I said. "Hi. How did you know we were here?"

"I didn't. I'm setting up a couple of demo homes and have space rented here myself."

He seemed to sense that I didn't want him to greet me with a kiss, and to my relief, he hung back. "The police contacted me this morning, and I heard about Laura . . . and the fire. I was checking my furniture for smoke damage . . . happened to spot your van as I was about to head home."

John gave Steve a darting glance, then walked over to me, put his arm around me, and said quietly, "I'm so sorry about Laura. She had some severe shortcomings, but she sure didn't deserve *this*."

Not wanting to discuss his relationship with Laura, I merely nodded and asked, "Is all your stuff okay?"

"Yeah. Thanks. Is that what you're doing now, too? Checking for smoke damage?"

"Running inventory," Steve quickly interjected. "Haven't had a chance to start yet, though." He raised his eyebrow and gave me a look. Was he trying to signal me that he was considering *John* a possible suspect? No way! If he was going to consider his good friend a suspect, Sullivan was truly losing all perspective.

"Was *your* storage unit properly locked when you got here?" I asked John.

"Yeah. Why? Wasn't yours?"

"No. Someone left the place unlocked."

"Jeez." He took a moment to let the news sink in. "Let me help you take inventory. Where are your shipping lists?"

I retrieved one set of copies from the inside of the door, where I'd taped the plastic envelope for safekeeping, handed him a sheet, gave Sullivan a second, and kept the last one for myself.

A moment later, John shined the beam of his pocket flashlight through a hole in the box made from punchouts for handles and said, "Hmm." He opened the box. "What line of work is this client of yours in?" he asked me. "Leading African safaris?"

I stared at the ottoman in disbelief. The leopard-skin upholstery appeared to have been made of real fur. "That's *got* to be a mistake."

"You think the *factory* screwed this up?" Sullivan peered into a tall, thin box. "Huh. An African mask. Henry, or some lackey of his, must have swapped in all this circa-George-of-the-Jungle merchandise, then left the door unlocked."

"You've got to wonder why he'd bother," John said, peering into more boxes. "Seems so childish. Did he honestly think you'd never *notice* that the furniture wasn't what you ordered?"

"Beats me. I never know what's going on underneath that stupid cowboy hat of his."

Sullivan groaned. "A chartreuse velour beanbag!" he cried. "Henry must be channeling Elvis Presley."

"Huh. This is odd," John said.

"What is?" I asked, unable to see him behind a wall of furniture boxes.

"You've got some junky little side table back here. It's out of its packaging and all dinged up."

Steve and I exchanged puzzled glances and wove our way over to John. "I've never seen that table before."

"Could this be one of Laura's inexpensive reproductions, maybe?" Steve suggested.

"It's possible, I guess. But I can't think of any antiques I selected for her that looked anything like that piece. Her reproductions were duplicates of my purchases."

John was tugging on the side table's knob. "It's got a fake drawer front. Your basic seven dollars of materials with your seventy-dollar discount-store price tag. This knob's loose. That's weird. A slot's been sawed into the wood, to either side of the knob."

He gave the knob a quarter turn and tugged on it again. "Holy shit!" he cried. I watched in stunned silence as he removed a long, narrow blade from the interior of the table.

Chapter 10

Twenty minutes later, we were showing John's gruesome discovery to a pair of Northridge policemen—a young Hispanic who was handsome enough to be a TV cop and his pickle-barrel-shaped partner. Gripping the knife at the corner of the plastic bag in which he'd put it, the stout officer held it up to the light. "There's blood on it," he said to the Adonis. "See that?"

Adonis nodded and gazed in our direction; due to the cramped quarters, John, Steve, and I were huddled just inside the door. "We'll have to fingerprint all three of you to eliminate your prints for the lab's tests."

"I was the only one who touched the table or the knife," John said.

I explained, "Steve and I were going through the boxes. We didn't even notice the table till John called us over to look at it."

"So your prints will be on the table and the handle of the knife?" the barrel-like officer asked John.

He frowned and replied, "Maybe the blade, too."

"They wouldn't be on the blade," Sullivan told him. "You never touched that."

A corner of John's lips twitched, and he replied, "I think I might have touched it as I was setting it down, right while you were calling the police."

Sullivan scowled and gave me a worried glance. Annoyed, I pretended not to notice. No way was I going to let Sullivan's paranoia rub off on me! If John's fingerprints were on the blade, it happened as he set the knife down prior to the police arriving. End of story.

"What about the other contents of this shed?" the handsome cop asked me. "Can you give me a list of everyone who's been in this space since you first rented it?"

I shook my head. "That'd be nearly impossible. The merchandise has been shipped from more than six places, with various delivery personnel each time. We also had a couple of U-Store employees in here when we found the place unlocked."

"There's no sense dusting the storage room for prints, then," Adonis told his partner. "We'd be better off taking the table to the lab. We can fit it into the backseat, if not the trunk." He turned his attention to me. "You got any objections to our taking the table?"

"None. Like I said, the side table isn't mine or my client's. It shouldn't have been here in the first place."

"I'd better talk to your client, too," the second officer said.

I gave him Henry's address and phone number, then went into the story of how he'd swapped out my original purchases. After I'd spoken my piece, the rotund officer asked John and Sullivan if they had anything to add.

"Either the door was left unlocked by mistake by Erin's client, or the lock was picked," Sullivan said, stating the obvious. "I think Laura's killer stashed the table here to get rid of the evidence."

"Maybe he chose my storage area out of coincidence," I added, hoping to convince myself that was the case.

"What's strange is that there're other units closer to Laura's than yours," John remarked. He looked at the officers. "Why bother to carry the table that much farther? Unless he figured that'd make it less likely the murder weapon would be found right away." He turned his attention to Sullivan, who had his omnipresent scowl on his face. "But why move the table at all? If you set the place on fire, you'd want to burn up the weapon, too, not carry it some fifty yards and stash it someplace."

Another indication that the killer *hadn't* been the one to set the fire, but, unlike John or Sullivan, I didn't want to play cop in front of the real thing. It also occurred to me that, in the few minutes that Sullivan and I had lost sight of his car, Dave Holland would *not* have had the time to kill Laura, set the fire, return the knife to its camouflage as a harmless table knob, break into a storage unit a short distance away, stash the table toward the back of that unit, then speed away in his car—in the darkness, his headlights off.

As we stepped outside, John said, "I've got to get back to work in Crestview, if that's all right, Officers."

The handsome officer said, "You can come down to the station now or later today, so we can get those fingerprints. It'll just take a minute."

John grimaced, looked at his watch, then said, "I'd better follow your patrol car and get this over with now. I don't even know where your station is." He smiled at me, took both my hands, gave them a gentle squeeze, and, searching my eyes, said quietly, "I'll call you tonight."

I returned his smile and nodded, but saw Sullivan watching us, looking deeply concerned. I wanted to smack him. Sullivan had no right to rain on my relationships!

After fifteen or twenty minutes of taking inventory in, essentially, dead silence, Sullivan said, "You gotta wonder what your beau was thinking. Why speculate to the cops? It was like Norton was trying to get them to award him his Junior Detective Decoder Ring. Or was covering up for himself."

"What's *that* supposed to mean? *You're* the one who announced that the killer broke into my space and hid that table here. John was just getting his two cents in."

Sullivan's frown deepened. His jaw was clenched so tight, his teeth must be ready to crack.

I persisted. "And what do you mean that John may be 'covering up for himself'?"

He didn't look up from his work. "John's a good buddy. We like to hang out every so often . . . shoot some pool, that kind of thing. But we're not so close that I could predict how he'd react if he felt his neck was on the line . . . just don't know him well enough to say." He met my gaze for a moment, then went back to the inventory sheet. "And all I'm saying is, *you* don't know him well enough, either, Gilbert."

"In other words, trust no one. Live in fear."

He didn't reply, and I was too annoyed with him to strike up a new conversation. For the next half hour, we didn't exchange an unnecessary word. Afterward, I gave Sullivan a ride home. Our conversation was superficial and chilly, Sullivan thanking me as he got out of my van and telling me to "take care."

I headed straight to my office, eager to let my thoughts focus on something noncriminal for a change. Though I was loath to admit this to anyone, Henry Toben's misdeeds had given me a task that part of me—the immature daredevil part—relished. It's typically a pleasure when clients present me with some unusual furnishing to blend into a room design, such as when a client has an appreciation for the whimsical that doesn't necessarily match my own, or when a beloved relative has given them some bizarre item. This was the first time, however, that I'd been trapped into adding so many incongruous pieces at the eleventh hour. I wanted to see how well I could meet the challenge.

Once at my office, I spread my presentation boards around me in the center of the pine floor and diligently crossed out the dozen nice items now missing and noted their gaudy, tasteless equivalents. This was going to be a major challenge, indeed. It felt tantamount to a client suddenly announcing that I had all of two hours to find him a trained seal to juggle the exquisite Wedgwood china that I'd spent a month hand-selecting for him. As I stared at the fiasco in growing dismay, my cell phone bleated.

"Erin," John exclaimed, sounding almost boyish in his excitement, "I've been asking around, and I got a name for you."

"A name for what?"

"I found out who supplied the reproductions in Laura's house. I thought you might be curious."

"Definitely." I was already scrambling to my feet, snatching a notepad from a desk drawer.

"It was George Wong. Have you heard of him?"

"No. Have you?"

"I've worked with him a couple of times, getting some custom furniture for our showrooms. George has a national operation, mostly through the Internet. Guess where his home base is."

"Crestview?"

"Bingo. He's got a good-sized factory out in the boonies, northeast of the city limits."

Pen in hand, I dropped into my leather desk chair. "What's the address?"

He gave it to me, and I said, "I'll look into it. Thanks."

There was a pause. "Erin? When you say you'll 'look into it,' you mean through the police, right? Not that you'll look yourself."

"Right," I immediately replied, not sure if I meant that or not.

"Good, because I've had some dealings with this guy myself, and he's no pushover. From everything I've heard, Mr. Wong is nobody to trifle with."

"I won't trifle. Promise."

Silence.

"John?"

"Yeah. I was just . . ." He sighed. "Are we okay?" he asked.

Oh, God. I hate any and all where-is-our-relationship-heading conversations, even under the best of circumstances. These were about as far from good circumstances as one could get. "Fine. Why?" I stalled. "What do you mean?"

"You discovered the *body* of someone you knew, and who I knew, as well. Yet you didn't call me last night or this morning. Not even later in the day. Most women . . . most people, I mean, would have needed to talk to someone close to them, who they could trust."

I winced, realizing that if our situations were reversed, I, too, would worry about this same thing. "I was about to call you, when Sullivan told me about your having once dated Laura, and I . . . needed some time to let the news settle."

"Laura and I dated more than three years ago, and it only lasted a couple of months." He sounded defensive, and annoyed with me. Meanwhile, I couldn't help but do the simple math: he'd gone out with Laura for roughly as long as he and I had been dating.

"Sullivan told me that, too. And I've since realized that it would have been odd for you to have blurted it out to me during lunch yesterday: 'By the way, Erin, I dated her first, before she destroyed Sullivan.' It's just that . . . I tried to take today off, but everything immediately blew up in my face. Things keep snowballing on me. I hardly know which end is up right now, John."

"Let me help you, Erin. Let's get out of town for the weekend so you can forget about all this misery for a little while. We'll run off to some nice resort in Aspen, and I'll help you figure out which end's up."

I tightened my grip on the phone, unsettled at the unexpected suggestion. We'd certainly been moving toward sexual intimacy, but . . . "Um . . . I think I'd rather wait another week or two. I want to see when the funeral is, and . . . now's just not the time."

"That's okay. It was just a thought. I've got to get back to work." His tone was rife with disappointment.

We said our goodbyes, and I stashed my phone back in my purse. My spirits had plummeted once again. John's phone call had only reminded me how out of control my life had suddenly become. I sighed and returned the display boards to my portfolio case. There was no way I could concentrate on Henry Toben's design now. But I wasn't willing to sit around and mope about my waxing and waning feelings for John. What I *wanted* to do was something proactive that could let me regain some measure of control over my life and my confused feelings; I wanted to meet with George Wong.

I glanced at my watch. It was nearly six P.M., and the drive would take at least half an hour. If Mr. Wong had a storefront to his furniture workshop, it would surely be closed by the time I arrived. Even so, a nice drive through the countryside could help clear my head. . . .

I locked up and took off in my van.

Forty minutes later, as I pulled into the empty hard-packed dirt parking lot at the address John had given me, I was thinking that John had certainly been accurate in describing this building as "in the boonies." There was nothing nearby but cornfields. So much for the drive clearing my head; my brain still felt as cluttered as the average junk drawer.

An old-fashioned carved wood sign on the door read "Finest Furnishings," but there were no business hours listed. With little expectation, I tried the brass knob on the front door. It turned. And as I crossed the threshold, shutting the heavy oak door behind me, I found myself stepping back in time and into an absolutely stunning room. I felt giddy for a moment. This was like leaving a kid alone in an ice cream parlor with a big silver spoon in her hand.

The lighting, while electric, was housed in reproduction lamps that resembled gas lanterns. I strode into the shadowy center of the room and slowly turned a full 360 degrees. I drank in the vision of the adorable corner desk complete with a quill pen. Two fabulous Hepplewhite chairs upholstered in a crimson damask. A lovely cyan wingback with cabriole legs. Astonishing end tables, coffee table, and a long, gold sofa with astonishing mahogany leaf carvings. On the two narrow walls, matching gilded pier mirrors had been hung to brighten the space. A mahogany desk along the back wall was the only item that hinted at a more modern function; a receptionist was probably stationed there during the daytime. Wanting a closer look, I rounded the deserted receptionist's desk. A phone and an intercom were built into the desk and tucked beneath a hinged cover. A flat-panel display terminal was hidden from immediate view within a wooden handcrafted box.

This place tugged at my memory banks. I'd visited a very similar room before—some Founding Father's mansion that I'd seen during a school field trip; such excursions had been the highlight of my grade-school years. Livingston Manor perhaps? What a phenomenal re-creation this was! It could have been a drawing room straight out of an aristocrat's late-nineteenth-century home, and yet every stick of furniture appeared to be brand-new. The wallpaper was a rose-colored toile that would have been in high fashion in the late 1800s.

For all its glory, however, the furniture was out of balance. The matching mirror on one wall hung above a brilliantly crafted cabinet, but the mirror on the opposite wall hung above a blank spot. The pattern of the wallpaper there was slightly more intense. A large, rectangular piece of furniture had been removed recently. Perhaps it was being repaired.

This whole place seemed surreal to me. A master craftsman had built the nicest waiting room I'd ever seen, simply to serve as a storefront of a furniture workshop in the boonies of Colorado. Why? And what was to stop someone from wandering in and stealing this gorgeous furniture or the absent receptionist's computer? There had to be a hidden camera and a security man watching a closed-circuit TV; the camera was probably masked in a lighting fixture.

I tried the door behind the desk: locked. I tried the

other door. This one was unlocked. The hinge creaked as the door swung open, and the scent of fresh-cut lumber—an aroma I adore—greeted me. I called out, "Hello? Is anyone here?"

No answer.

Judging from the L-shape floor plan of this freestanding building, it was possible that the locked door behind the receptionist desk led to a private residence. As I entered this second, enormous room, I was abruptly pulled from nineteenth-century-America gentility and into a massive modern-day workshop. There were at least a dozen lathes, power saws, and other woodworking equipment. The stations were all shut down and deserted, but ahead of me was a half wall of cinder blocks with sliding glass partitions above the cinder blocks, and the fluorescent ceiling lights were all on.

As I made my way along an alley—so designated with yellow tape on the concrete floor—I could see into the office. A large man of Asian descent seated there saw me, too, and he gestured through the glass for me to come to the door. When I stepped into the office, he rose. I stifled a gasp. The man was enormous. It was difficult for me to guess his age, somewhere between forty and sixty, but in his youth, he definitely could have been a sumo wrestler. He said to me in careful diction, "May I help you?"

"I'm looking for George Wong."

"You found him. May I help you?" he repeated.

"I hope so. I wanted to discuss a mutual former client of ours. A woman named Laura Smith."

His expression did not change; no sign of recognition flickered in his dark eyes. "Yes?" he asked mildly.

"Um . . . my name is Erin Gilbert."

He initiated a handshake but said nothing, and my own hand had never felt so small. Afterward, he looked at me expectantly.

"May I sit down?" I asked.

"Yes."

We both took a seat. His was a substantial gray desk chair befitting his large frame, but mine was chrome and molded blue plastic, a style found in many school cafeterias. I suddenly realized this powerful-looking stranger and I might be the only two people in the building, way out in the middle of nowhere. Suddenly I wished I'd paid a little more attention to John's suggestion that I notify the police that this was a person they may want to interview, and stay out of their way myself. Really, though, what was George Wong going to do? Attack me just for asking him a few questions? That'd be one heck of a bad way to build up a client base. And even though we were off the beaten path, passing motorists would surely see my Interiors by Gilbert van, parked right near his unlocked Finest Furnishings door, where customers could enter at any given moment.

"I'm an interior designer," I began. "Five months ago, Laura Smith hired me to help decorate her home in expensive antiques. I visited her house again yesterday. That's when I discovered that all the wonderful pieces I'd purchased on her behalf had been replaced with reproductions."

"Yes?"

"I've since learned that those reproductions were supplied by your company."

"Yes?"

His laconic queries were making me feel more ridiculous by the moment, but I soldiered on. "I was wondering if you could tell me anything about how that came to pass."

He regarded me impassively, and I desperately tried to formulate a reasonable response to give if he asked me why I was asking. Keeping his hands pressed flat on the surface of his desk, he said, "Miss Smith asked me to duplicate her antiques as close as possible to the originals. She sent me digital photographs, and I sent pictures of my products back to her. I visited her house to see the furniture for myself only one time. We arranged to have her purchases delivered. She paid her bill."

He stopped, so I could only assume he felt that was all he had to say on the subject. I blundered on, "Did you hear that she was murdered last night?"

"No."

The news of her murder—if it *was* news—seemed to leave him untouched. He continued to hold my gaze. Now I felt totally idiotic. The man was definitely skilled at giving nothing away. I, on the other hand, was clearly no Miss Marple. I heard myself babbling, "I'm sure it's unrelated, but the whole business of the duplicated antiques was so puzzling to me that I wanted to find out what was going on."

"Yes?"

I squirmed in my prepubescent plastic chair. "Didn't *you* find it . . . puzzling?"

"It is not my job to ask why customers want the products that they purchase from me."

"Of course not, but still . . . didn't it seem odd? Have you ever had a customer ask you to duplicate their furniture before?"

"Miss Smith told me that she'd decided to keep the antiques locked away and sell them again in another ten years when they were even more valuable. Many people make a profit by reselling antiques."

"True, but not many people duplicate nearly every stick of furniture that they own."

He said nothing, merely sat there meeting my gaze, his palms still pressed flat on either side of his leather desk pad.

I cleared my throat, briefly mulling over the notion of pointing at the dingy, barren wall behind him and shrieking, "Oh, my God! What *is* that?" and bolting from the room when he turned. Instead, I replied, "One of my thoughts when I saw what she'd done was that she might have intended an insurance fraud . . . to burn down the house and then to sell off the antiques."

"Yes?"

I stared at his face, blank as an unadorned wall. Well, this little interview was not exactly turning into a Barbara Walters–style exposé. Then again, it couldn't get any worse. "Did you get to know Laura at all?"

"She was my customer."

"Was she a repeat customer?"

"Repeat?"

"Was this the second or third time that she bought furniture through your company?"

"No. Only the one time." He smiled. His expression reminded me of a dog baring its teeth before it attacks. "Is there anything else, Miss Gilbert?"

"No." I got to my feet. "Thank you for your time, Mr. Wong."

I headed for the door.

"It was nice to meet you, Miss Gilbert. Say hello to John Norton for me."

I froze, my heart in my throat. Telling myself to stay calm, I turned and asked, "You know John?"

He nodded. With his chilling grin, he replied, "John Norton's a repeat customer."

"And how did you know that *I* know him?"

"He said your name the last time he was here."

"When was that?" I tried to sound casual.

He flipped the pages of his desk calendar. "January. How time flies, as they say. Yes?"

I forced a smile. "It sure does. Nice meeting you, Mr. Wong."

"Yes, Miss Gilbert. And be sure to tell Mr. Norton that I said hello."

"I will. Bye." I let myself out of his office and crossed the cavernous room and forced myself to maintain a casual pace, certain that he was watching me through the glass.

John and I hadn't even met each other in January.

Chapter 11

> *Nothing establishes ambience faster than the way a room smells. For pet owners and the occasional less-than-vigilant cook, potpourri can cover a multitude of sins. After all, sometimes the nose only thinks it knows.*
>
> —Audrey Munroe

DOMESTIC BLISS

My stomach was still churning from anxiety by the time I arrived home. As I slipped through the French doors, I grimaced at the sight of the parlor, still in its future-square-dance motif, with the furniture rimming the walls and the center of the room bare. A lovely, sweet scent in the air distracted me from the visual chaos, however, and I followed my nose to the kitchen. There, Audrey was standing at the island and concocting a potpourri blend. She tended to have too much energy to spend much time sitting, which must have suited her well in her ballerina days.

The potpourri was in various stages of production—from fresh ingredients to final results. Arranged on her glorious black granite countertop were fresh-cut flowers yet to be sorted or dried, dried flowers with unpicked buds, ingredients to size that were yet to be measured, and blends in dozens of half-full jars that must have already been suitably aged.

"Oh, good," she said as she glanced up at me standing in the doorway. "A fresh pair of nostrils."

"Not the usual greeting after a rough day at the office. But I gather you want me to help you rate the aromas?"

"Good deduction. It's the subject of tomorrow's segment. And we're having fish tonight, so the potpourri is doing double duty." She winked at me. "Pull up a chair and prepare to breathe *deeply.*"

I grinned in spite of myself. At times like this, when Audrey's charm and her fascinating domestic projects allowed me a respite from my troubles, my good fortune at living in her home felt like nothing less than a gift from God. For the time being at least, my feeling of abject humiliation over my exchange with George Wong was forgotten. I'd called the Northridge lead detective and told him about Wong, but our conversation had made me feel even more like a dingbat. That, too, I decided, was now behind me.

"Okay," I said, eagerly perching on the elegant bar stool beside her at the kitchen island. "What's on the olfactory menu?"

"The completed concoctions are categorized according to the room they're to be placed in." She paused and grimaced. As if in a personal aside, she muttered, "I'm going to have to make a mental note *not* to say 'categorized completed concoctions' during my show. I'll sound like I'm coughing up a hair ball." She waved her hand over three sealed jars. "This first group, nearest you, is for closets. They're your basic walk-in-the-forest aromas . . . heavy on the pine boughs and cedar chips . . . using your more powerful crushed leaves and essential oils."

"Yep," I joshed her, "those oils *are* essential, all right."

She gave me her patient smile. "Actually, the *essential* ingredient in potpourri is the fixative to capture and retain the aromas. Otherwise you'll find yourself needing to replenish the stuff as fast as you can make it."

She waved her hand over the next set of three jars. "In the middle here are ingredients for sachets . . . to be used in bedrooms—the relaxing lavenders and sleep-conducive scents, the rosebuds and petals, the—"

I scanned the entire array before me and interrupted, "You collected *this* many flowers just from your garden?"

"Florist shops. I drive around town and ask for their discards, then I dry them." She indicated a third collection of potpourris. "What I'm working on right now is the final blend in the kitchen category of potpourri, which for obvious reasons leans more toward fruit peels and spices. And lastly, on the far side of the counter, we have our public-spaces scents. These are designed to lightly enhance the air, never to overwhelm. Your job, Erin, is to rank the blends within each category."

"Excellent. That's a task exactly up to my speed today." We hadn't seen or spoken to each other since yesterday. I swallowed hard, realizing that I had to tell her my horrible news.

She searched my eyes, then put her arm around my

shoulders and said quietly, "I heard about your friend, dear. I'm so terribly sorry. You must feel utterly traumatized."

"You could say that, yes." My throat tightened, and sensing I didn't want to talk about it now, she went back to her task of breaking off dried flower buds from their stems, without pursuing the topic. I, meanwhile, struggled to push the memories away and to concentrate on Audrey's pleasant assignment. John had said he'd call, and I had until then to avoid the subject of Wong's claiming that John had mentioned my name several weeks before we'd even met.

With fish-cooking odors on their way, I decided to start with the kitchen category, and ultimately selected the lemony one over the cinnamon-apple or minty ones. My favorite blend had an unusual and pleasing lemon-vanilla aroma. Audrey told me that she'd used gum benzion as the fixative, which was the vanilla scent that my nose had detected. I reasoned that it would be best to judge the more subtle aromas ahead of the stronger ones. As I moved on to the "public areas" collections, I asked, "Are you going to be keeping them in these containers?"

"Good heavens, no. I'll demonstrate how to make sachets and herb pillows, or how to make really attractive displays within open bowls, or lace-covered containers wherever there's the good possibility of the bowl getting tipped over."

The thought of bowls getting knocked over brought my bull-in-the-china-shop customer to mind. "By the way, through a strange coincidence, your Saturday night date is with one of my clients." I deliberately withheld the words *least favorite* from my description of Hammerin' Hank.

"Henry Toben is your client?"

"Yes. He doesn't exactly seem the sophisticated, distinguished type you normally go for."

"Don't remind me. When it comes to Mr. Toben, I'm definitely slumming. But this is only one evening out of my life, and sometimes these low-expectation dates can surprise you. I remember that I didn't especially want to go out with Walter."

"Husband number three?"

"Four."

"Audrey, I've gotta say, if you wind up being the second Mrs. Hammerin' Hank, I'll cry myself to sleep for weeks afterward."

"If that happens, you and I will be sharing Kleenex boxes, believe me." She dropped a rosebud into the bowl and its rich perfumes wafted toward me. "But don't worry, dear. Finding the fifth Mr. Audrey Munroe is nowhere on my list of things to do this year. And Hank is dead last on my list of eligible-bachelor candidates."

"Who's number one?"

She clutched her hands over her heart, beamed at me, and murmured wistfully, "Gregory Peck."

"He . . . died a couple years ago, Audrey."

Her face fell. "Did he? Oh, dear. That's dreadful news." She sighed and grabbed my arm as if for support. Under her breath, she added, "For one thing, this means that Hammerin' Hank just moved up a notch."

Audrey's Potpourri Recipe: Walk in the Woods

2 cups crushed leaves

2 cups crushed pinecones

1 cup pine needles

1 cup rose petals

½ cup violets

½ cup rosemary

6 drops pine oil

3 drops eucalyptus oil

1 cup cedar wood chips

1 cup mint leaves

5 tablespoons dried orris root

Chapter 12

Early the next morning, Sullivan came to my office to brainstorm about Henry's new purchases. I was already in a sour mood; I'd endured a rough night, unable to sleep as I ruminated on George Wong's passive-aggressive behavior. Plus, John hadn't called me despite saying he would, and it grew too late to place the call myself. So, when Sullivan remarked about it having been "awfully convenient that John claims he may have touched the blade just *yesterday*," it was all I could do not to light into Sullivan for introducing me to someone he now quite obviously believed capable of murder. Under the circumstances, I decided not to fuel Sullivan's fire and tell him about my confrontation with

Wong. And I certainly wouldn't tell him about Wong's parting line.

As for Sullivan's and my ability to work together on Henry's project, things started out well. We groused for a while about what a difficult client he was, though I pointed out that he *was* a recent widower. Sullivan agreed that the chartreuse velour beanbag chair would work best in a trash bin and that my vibrant violet and Kelly green to avocado accessories for the living room had to be returned and replaced with neutral hues. That was as far as our agreement could go. Like an old man with his one prized-but-hideous chair, Sullivan settled into and then clung to a ridiculous notion of creating an "African safari room," complete with the masks and various animal-skin products. He insisted we'd be better off sacrificing one entire room to the taste-challenged, whereas *I* was determined to minimize the impact of the tacky items and, at once, unify the home's interior by locating one piece of pseudo–African kitsch in each room.

"Here's the deal, Sullivan," I eventually proclaimed nastily, pulling rank. "This is my project, so I get the final say-so. But it's Henry's house, not mine. So. We'll each do a quick work-up of our respective ideas, and we'll let Henry decide."

"Fine." He rose, obviously eager to escape my company.

"Fine. And may the best designer win. Even though she might not."

He leveled his gaze at me. "*She?*"

I spread my arms. "If Henry had even one iota of good taste or judgment, he wouldn't have switched orders on me in the first place. So you've probably already got this silly competition in the Gucci handbag."

He made a derisive noise and growled, "Nice, Gilbert. Now if my design gets chosen, you can protect your ego and tell yourself that it's only because the customer is too unsophisticated."

"Only because that happens to be the truth."

"And it's *also* true that my solution for Toben's home is better than yours."

"No, it *isn't*, Sullivan!"

He glanced back at me, smirked, and replied, "Whatever you say. Keep up the good work, Gilbert." He descended the stairs.

"You too, Sullivan!" I called after him, livid. "Come to think of it, lumping all of a client's white elephants into one room is just freakin' *brilliant*! Why actually try to *incorporate* them into the overall *design* of his *living spaces*, when we can accept his money for treating an *entire room* of his like *one great big junk drawer*?"

Standing in the stairway below, he retorted, "Ask yourself this, Gilbert: If these were *real* white elephants, which would you prefer—having the herd isolated in one room, or spread throughout the entire household, wrecking everything in their path?"

The hinge creaked as he opened the door. Before it could shut behind him, I yelled, "I don't know and I don't care, because they *aren't* live elephants. Furthermore, your question proves that all those teachers who insist there's no such thing as a stupid question are *dead wrong*!"

"And so are *you*. Maybe you can all get together and form a club. See you later."

Unable to formulate a comeback, I grumbled to myself, "And, by the way, Mr. Sullivan, I *am* the best designer!" The door had already shut behind him.

The day dragged on. I had to admit that I'd been less than gracious to the deliverymen when I signed for the cherry-red sectional that morning. The fact that I *still* hadn't spoken to John about George Wong's insinuation was never far from my thoughts. Even so, I couldn't bring myself to pick up the phone and call him. If I did, I'd have to explain why I'd lied about not intending to visit with Wong myself and, worse, confront the doubts that had crept into my head and heart about John's innocence in Laura's murder. And that was something better discussed face-to-face.

It was nearly six P.M. by the time I was able to leave work, but before heading home to place the unavoidable phone call to John, I decided to stop by Paprika's. I wanted to offer to take Hannah to dinner so that we could chat about Jerry Stone, the activist cum undercover cop. I'd seen for myself that Laura had recognized Stone's face. Plus, although Hannah wasn't exactly a friend, she was at least a friendly acquaintance, so talking with her had to be a pleasant change of pace from police officers. Or from George Wong. Not to mention the oblivious, conniving, sour-visaged Steve Sullivan.

I entered the store and quickly spotted Hannah rearranging a display in the flatware section. She had a deep frown on her round face, and she appeared to be lost in thought. As I walked up beside her, I said, "Hi, Hannah."

She jumped and clenched a butter knife in her fist like a weapon as she whirled to face me. "Erin! You startled me." She didn't smile, let alone chuckle at her overreaction; she merely returned the butter knife to its designated slot.

So much for being friendly acquaintances. "Hannah, is everything all right?"

"Oh, sure."

"You look a little upset." *We designers are trained to notice subtle nuances,* I mused to myself.

She pursed her lips and resumed her task of micro-adjusting the alignment of every fork, spoon, and knife on the display table. "The owner's giving me a hard time about my handling of our little gang of thieves."

"Pardon?"

"We've been having a major problem with shoplifting all of a sudden."

"That's too bad. You've had one heck of a week . . . shoplifters plus getting berated by that activist. Jerry Stone, you said his name was?"

"Yeah. At least *he's* kept a low profile the last couple days. He hasn't shown his face here since Laura flipped him on his ass. Even so, if my downward spiral continues, I'm going to get fired."

"Oh, I'm sure that won't happen."

Hannah frowned and replied, "Just in case, I'd better figure out how to pry more money out of Dave."

"He's paying you alimony?"

She shrugged. "It's chicken feed, compared to what he earns." She finally turned away from the display, apparently satisfied. "So. What can I do for you?"

Turned off by her unpleasant mood, I had already changed my mind about asking her to dinner. The last thing I needed was to spend time with someone clearly as bitter as Steve Sullivan. "Nothing, really. Just thought I'd stop by before I went home . . . thought maybe Jerry Stone might have been hanging around in the last day or two. I'm hoping the police will be able to locate him and maybe find out how he knew Laura."

"Well, maybe they've already arrested him for loitering, or something. I'm sure they'll spot him easily enough. He's hard to miss, what with those dreadlocks and that beard."

"The dreadlocks were a wig. The beard might have been fake, as well."

Her eyes widened. "You're kidding. Why would anyone go to that kind of trouble . . . disguising himself like that?"

"To prevent Laura from recognizing him, I assume."

"But, if that was all there was to it, why would he be wearing the getup every day for, like, three or four weeks, and get in my face all that time about Paprika's merchandise? You'd think that if he was a stalker, he'd want to keep a low profile . . . not make a spectacle of himself. It's almost like he had a personal vendetta against both me *and* Laura at . . ."

Her voice faded, and her cheeks grew almost as red as Henry's new sofa.

Speculating aloud, I said, "Stalking one woman while publicly harassing another doesn't make much sense, unless it stemmed from the connection between you and Laura. Maybe he's linked with your ex-husband in some way."

She looked at me as though I'd just suggested she turn Paprika's into a bowling alley. "That isn't possible. Dave would never do anything underhanded like that."

"I didn't mean to suggest he had a direct hand in it . . . that he'd hired the guy to harass you, or something." Although, now that the possibility was out there, maybe that's exactly what Dave *had* done. Despite my growing doubts, I continued, "Dave might not even know about Jerry. Dave's business is obviously doing well. Corporations sometimes hire people to spy on their competitors. Maybe someone's investigating his personal connections . . . something like that."

Again, she shook her head. "That doesn't make sense." Without so much as glancing at her watch or noting that there were other customers in the store besides me, she snapped, "It's closing time. I'm afraid I'm going to have to ask you to leave, Erin."

"Of course. Sorry to have bothered you . . ."

She gave me a tight smile. "You didn't. And I'm sorry to be so abrupt. Just not having the best of days today, that's all." She took a few steps toward the door, in a not-subtle effort to usher me out of the store. "Stop in again sometime, and we'll talk."

"I'll do that. Good night, Hannah."

"Yes. Goodbye." She pivoted and walked toward the sales counter.

I stepped outside, into the brisk evening air. The darkening sky was a lovely indigo, but I was too puzzled by Hannah's behavior to admire my surroundings. Hannah had crossed the line from curtness into downright hostility. Why? And it was one thing to be "startled" and quite another to instantly be at the ready to physically defend yourself. Something had her spooked that went beyond apprehension regarding her job security. What? Or *who*?

I hesitated before returning to my office and my car. A man was skulking near Paprika's main entrance. He was wearing blue jeans and a plaid flannel shirt and was hugging himself to stay warm. He seemed to be hiding his face from me; he was turned toward the brick wall of a shop next door—not exactly the most natural-looking pose. I stared at his feet. He had on Birkenstock sandals and white socks. *Jerry Stone, sans the wig.* I promptly looked for any suspicious bulges in the small of his back. I didn't see any, so maybe this time he was unarmed.

What's he doing here? With my pulse racing, I strode purposefully around the corner, grabbed my cell phone, and called Linda Delgardio. She answered, and I said quickly in a hushed voice, "I found Jerry Stone, the guy Laura claimed was stalking her. He's on the downtown mall in front of Paprika's . . . Opal and Fourteenth. Can you get out here right away?"

"That's not far from where I am. I'll be right out. Describe him."

I described his clothing and basic body type, but his features had been hidden behind hair the only time I'd seen him face-to-face. Assuring Linda that I was going to "chat with the guy" and stall him until she could arrive in her squad car, I hung up and doubled back. Jerry had turned around and was shifting from foot to foot in an attempt to stay warm as he avidly watched Paprika's door.

The staff was leaving. Hannah lingered by the door as she let everyone and then herself out. Jerry made a show of hunkering over his cell phone, pretending to talk while he waited for Hannah. *Could he be stalking Hannah now?* I hesitated, hoping that Linda would arrive in time so that I wouldn't have to risk scaring him off by trying to stall him. Hannah began her usual brisk, choppy walk down the brown-brick pedestrian mall, and when she passed him, Jerry took off after her.

Keeping an eye out for a patrol car, I raced up to him before he could drift too far from Fourteenth Street for Linda to spot us both. "Jerry? Jerry Stone?"

He turned and gaped at me. Hannah kept walking. She rounded the next corner.

. Jerry took a step backward as though weighing the notion of running. Instead, however, he held his ground. "How'd you know my name?" His voice was—

"Hannah Garrison told me."

"Hannah Garrison?" Without his wig and beard, he was nondescript—neither handsome nor ugly, brown eyes, thin lips, a slightly bulbous nose that reminded me of Hildi's squeeze-toy mouse. He was clean-shaven, and roughly my age, with a deeply receding hairline that made him look older. "You mean the manager of that loathsome store?"

"Who you were *following* just now. Yes."

He at least had the decency to avert his eyes and show a little embarrassment at being caught. "Just trying to get through to the woman to mend her ways," he mumbled.

"By *stalking* her?"

He shrugged and took another step away. I had to soften my tone or he was sure to run off before Linda could arrive to question him about Laura. Casually, I said, "I was at Paprika's the other night, when you claimed to be there as an undercover cop."

"I remember. You were sitting in the front row."

"That's right. I'm curious, Jerry: Why did you claim to be a police officer?"

"Who says I'm *not?*"

"An *actual* Crestview police officer who's a friend of mine." *One who'd better be arriving any second now.*

"Yeah, well . . . I needed to keep everyone from panicking. Someone could've gotten trampled, running away from me like that. I wasn't out to hurt anybody. I just want everyone to be more respectful of Mother Earth."

"Why follow Hannah?"

"I *wasn't*," he said firmly. "I just wanted to talk to her, without making it look like I was waiting for her. I was going to accidentally on purpose bump into her at the next walk light."

That was marginally plausible. "And yet, Monday night, you followed my friend Laura Smith from Rusty's to Paprika's. Why?"

"Who's Laura Smith?"

"The woman who threw you to the floor. She told me you'd been stalking her all over town."

He shook his head. "Woman's whacked if she says that. It's *you* I've been following sometimes . . . you and a couple other designers." He wagged his finger in my face. "You people are the ringleaders for the destruction of the environment!"

"Oh, give me a break! You think we're ringleaders? Compared to oil companies? Compared to pipeline drillers in Alaska? To paper mills? Nuclear plants? Factories? You honestly believe that *those* operations are environmentally friendly, compared to a handful of interior designers in Crestview, Colorado?"

He shrugged. "Maybe I overstated my position. You suck less than the oil companies do. Make you feel better?"

I gritted my teeth. "I actually *do* consider the sustainability of products and materials before I make recommendations to my clients. I'm not irresponsible."

"Yeah, well, ain't that nice." He stuffed his hands in his pockets and resumed walking along the pedestrian mall in the same direction as Hannah had gone. Linda would only see us if she drove down Fifteenth Street. Unable to think up an excuse to detain him, I fell into step beside him. He continued, "There are children starving to death, you know. Every day. They don't have the money to keep themselves alive. I'm sure they appreciate all the thought you put into choosing wallpaper."

"And I'm sure the starving children *also* appreciate all the time you spend harassing me and Hannah. How exactly is *that* putting food on their tables?"

He spread his arms. "At least *I* try to get people to think twice about how they throw their money away."

We crossed Fifteenth, which was void of all police vehicles. *Damn it! Where was Linda?* We were already too far down the mall for her to find us quickly. I improvised desperately. "Listen, Jerry, can we talk about your opinions at length? How about if we meet for dinner tonight? You can choose the place and the time. I'll pick up the tab, of course."

"Sorry. I have plans. Some other time."

"Can I get your phone number . . . to schedule another time, then?"

"Don't have one."

"I saw you just a minute ago, speaking into your cell phone."

"That's just a prop. The thing doesn't work."

"Your address, then?"

He shot me an impatient glare. "If I had one of those, I'd probably have a phone number. I really gotta run." He picked up his pace.

"Wait, Jerry."

He said over his shoulder, "I gotta be someplace."

No time for tact. I called after him, "Laura Smith was murdered the night after you and she had your confrontation. Do you know anything about that?"

He froze. When he looked back at me, his face had gone pale. His thin lips were nearly white. "No. But I'm sorry."

I walked up to him once more. "*Are* you?" I asked.

"Sure. Whoever she was, I'm not wild about how she used judo on me for no reason. But I didn't want the woman dead."

"It would help the police investigation if you talked to them about that night."

"Yeah. Okay, Erin. I'll go in and talk to them."

"How did you know *my* name?"

"It's on your office door."

"Just my last name is. Not my first."

He resumed walking at a brisk pace. Keeping up with him and pleading with him was pointless. After a few strides, I stopped and watched him disappear around the corner. My heart sank.

I snatched my phone from my purse and called Linda Delgardio's cell. "Hi, Linda. It's Erin. I lost Jerry on Sixteenth Street, where he's heading south on foot."

"Thanks. I'm on Fourteenth, just a minute away. I should be able to spot him."

"I'll head down Sixteenth and see if I can help you find him."

"No, Erin." Her voice was stern. "You're getting overly involved . . . putting yourself in jeopardy. And I sure as hell don't want to wind up having to investigate *two* murders. For one thing, it'd be a total pain in the butt to have to try to find some other interior designer to replace you as my friend."

I chuckled and said, "It *would* be thoughtless of me to increase your things-to-do list like that."

"Right. I'll keep you posted, once we nab the killer. Gotta go."

She wasn't going to be pleased that I'd met George Wong last night, I thought as I put away my cell phone. She was bound to learn about that from the Northridge police detective I'd spoken to last night after my tense exchange with Mr. Wong.

Maybe I *was* getting a little overly involved. Patience and passivity have never been high on the list of my personality traits. Even so, I decided not to try to pursue Jerry Stone any further. Instead, I turned in the opposite direction to retrieve my van outside my office.

Hildi trotted up to greet me, but showed no interest in staying in the foyer with me. The place felt deserted, and indeed, I soon found a note on the kitchen counter:

E—Went to the movies. Back by eleven—A

I fixed myself a quick dinner of pasta and a salad. Halfway through my meal, the phone rang, and I answered.

"Hi, there," said a deep male voice—John.

"Hi." *Finally* he called.

"You sound tired."

"I must be even more tired than I feel if you can tell that from a single syllable."

"Your voice sounded deflated, actually."

"I had a long, difficult day." *And was not happy about having to discuss George Wong with John momentarily.*

"I wish I could perk you up, take you out to dinner tonight. But I have to meet with my boss. We've got to go over the final plans for the new showcase home out in Longmont."

"Oh?"

"Yeah. As a matter of fact, that's why I was calling. I was hoping to get your opinions on what I'm doing with the house. Not so much looking for a free consultation from you, you understand, as just . . . picking your brain a little."

"You want me to look at your drawings?"

"At the house itself, actually. I've got most of the furniture in place already, just need some help with accessorizing."

I brightened a little. "My favorite phase of room makeovers."

"I know. That's why I thought of you."

"I'd be happy to take a look."

"Great. Our lunch got cut short the other day. How 'bout if you stop by the showcase house at lunchtime tomorrow? We'll grab a bite to eat afterward."

Which would be the perfect chance for me to bring up George Wong's statement: "Be sure to tell John Norton I said hello." That topic was best handled face-to-face, but then again, it was burning on my mind right now.

As I jotted down the address, the doorbell rang. I said a hasty goodbye to John, assuring him that I'd meet him to-

morrow, then hung up. I trotted into the foyer and peered
through the sidelight. The hulking silhouette just outside
the wavy lead glass was unmistakable—George Wong.
Oh, my God! Why was he here?

I cursed under my breath. I didn't want to open my
door to him, but I also didn't want to give him the upper
hand and let him know that I was afraid of him. He knew
I was here; he would have heard my footsteps, seen my silhouette through the glass just as I'd seen his.

I straightened my back, took a deep breath, threw open
the door, and stepped out onto the porch, directly in front
of him. To my satisfaction, he took a step back.

He bowed his head at me. "Evening, Miss Gilbert."

"Mr. Wong. This is a surprise. How did you find out
where I live?"

"I asked some questions of our mutual associates. It is
not hard to locate someone in this town. As you have discovered for yourself."

"What do you mean?"

"You located me at my place of business, although *my*
number is unlisted."

Why would someone's *business* number be unlisted? I
wondered. "Well, sure, but I certainly don't know your
home address."

"They are one and the same. However, it is difficult
to catch *you* in your office. You are not there often, it
seems."

"I'm there by appointment only. And if you'd like
to make an appointment to discuss business, I'd be happy
to do that for you. But I don't bring my work home with
me."

He chuckled. "Yet now it seems as though the mountain has come to Muhammad."

"Why are you here, Mr. Wong?" I demanded.

"You have been talking to the police about me."

Though his voice remained dispassionate, I had a powerful urge to run for cover. "I . . . gave them your name as having supplied the reproductions in Laura Smith's house. She was *murdered*. The police need to investigate anyone who's had recent dealings with her."

"Yes, I've had recent dealings with Miss Smith. As you have. Everything I do in my business is legal."

"Good to know. So why are you here?"

"I hoped perhaps I might ask you to mind your own business. With a friend of yours dying, I would think that would be wise, yes?"

"Is that a threat, Mr. Wong?" A wave of fear was making my knees shake.

He gave me one of his unnervingly chilly smiles. "Of course not. It is a helpful suggestion, Miss Gilbert. I do not want to see you have the same kind of 'recent dealings' as Laura Smith."

A chill ran up my spine.

The icy smile never faded from George Wong's lips. He bowed his head a second time, turned, and made his way down the steps. I watched him leave, half expecting to see him get into the back of a black limo with smoke-black windows. He had driven himself, however, in what the dim lighting of the streetlamp revealed to be a cheerful-looking metallic spring-green VW Bug. As he let himself into his car and saw that I was watching him, he bobbed his head, then drove away.

The next day, I arrived at John's showcase home a few minutes early. No one answered the doorbell, and I couldn't tell if the bell was even working. I knocked, opened the door, and leaned inside. "John?"

No answer. I let myself in. As he'd described over the phone, the furniture on the main floor was in place, but the tables and walls were bare. I studied the room, imagining what I would do with accessories to warm the space and make this room feel personal and inviting.

The heavy, dark furniture needed vertical, lighter lines to counterbalance all the bold horizontal elements. Accessories would require elongated vertical lines. A slightly green tint of a clear vase on the side table. Lavender sprigs mixed with the dark jade of eucalyptus stalks, there. In the dark corner, a second vase of tall, regal ornamental grasses that would draw out the warm yellows in the room. In that cozy nook in the stairwell, some simple but dramatic arrangement of curly willows in an indigo vase would be stunning. On the coffee table, I would place a glass bowl containing nothing but clear marbles.

The artwork needed to be light in tone and texture. A watercolor above the sofa in blues and greens. On the short wall to the kitchen, a mirror in a simple, elegant frame. Opposite wall, a print of some kind—maybe a study in purples—a painting of violets, even. That would really pop against these too-typical ivory-colored walls.

After a minute or two of painting mental before-and-after pictures, I realized that I'd forgotten to locate John. I climbed the stairs and called his name again. He must have dashed off someplace with a coworker, because the company pickup truck that he normally drove was parked in the driveway. Even so, I wasn't sure it'd be all right for me to wander around the house by myself.

I went outside again to make sure that the pickup was really his, in which case I would simply wait in the living room for him to find me. I spotted something near the front tire of his truck. I knelt to get a closer look, my mind racing to deny what my eyes were seeing.

A scarf. Silk. Cream-colored, with rose highlights. The shimmery fabric to one side of the knot had been cut clear through. The same scarf that Laura had been wearing the last time I'd seen her alive.

There was dried blood on the fabric.

Chapter 13

I got to my feet unsteadily, my heart pounding, my thoughts whirling. The killer must have placed Laura's scarf here to frighten me off his or her trail. Which meant the killer knew I would recognize Laura's scarf and that I would see it on this particular driveway.

The killer must have followed my van; that was the only reasonable explanation. The other possibility—that John was a homicidal maniac and had set up a macabre and chilling warning to me—was *not* reasonable.

I gasped at the sound of the screen door creaking open behind me, and whirled around. John stood there, grinning at me. Suddenly his smile didn't seem quite so attractive.

"Erin. You're here."

In spite of myself, I flinched when he drew near. "Where were you just now?" My voice sounded distant to my own ear. "I called your name a couple of times. . . ."

He frowned, staring into my eyes. "I was in the garage, unpacking some furniture. What's wrong, Erin?"

"I found this." I stepped aside and pointed at the scarf by my feet. "It's Laura's. She was wearing it on the day she died. The killer had taken it . . . sliced it off her throat."

"Jesus!" John exclaimed. His fingers bit into my arm. "Erin. Who'd you tell that you were coming here today?"

"Nobody. I didn't tell anyone at all."

"Was it here when you first arrived?" He seemed to be every bit as stunned as I was.

I pulled my arm free, struggling to keep myself from panicking. "I don't think so. But it's possible I walked right past it. I'm not positive."

John snatched his cell phone out of a pocket in his khakis. "I'm calling the police." He scanned the deserted street and grabbed my arm again. "Let's get you inside. Someone must have followed you here." He softened his tone. "Everything's going to be fine, darling. Don't worry."

Though I despised it when someone told me not to worry about deeply upsetting things, I let him usher me inside. He kissed me gently on my temple and murmured some reassuring words. *This is nuts; I trust John. I'm not going to allow myself to get suspicious of everyone, like Sullivan is, damn it!*

To my severe disappointment, Linda Delgardio wasn't on duty yet. A uniformed male officer arrived, collected and bagged the scarf, and asked me predictable questions about the precise timing of my arrival and my discovery, and if I'd noticed any cars behind mine. He asked John the same questions, then explained ominously that the Crestview police department was working in tandem with the Northridge police on the homicide investigation, and that I "shouldn't be surprised" if they wanted me to come down to Northridge to answer some questions.

Afterward, I felt too agitated to discuss room designs with John and grudgingly agreed to take a long lunch at a quiet restaurant. We wound up in a booth at some Italian bistro on the eastern outskirts of Crestview. The décor was wonderfully old-family Italian—yellowed posters on the walls, red-and-white-checkered tablecloths, a partially melted candle in an empty wine bottle on every table.

We struggled to find topics of conversation. It was obvious that neither of us wanted to talk about my finding that scarf, yet anything else sounded trivial. As we picked at our entrées, John scanned our surroundings and asked, "Why do so many restaurants use red interiors?"

I peered at him. "You're humoring me, right?"

"No, I'm truly curious."

"Red's a complementary color for food . . . supposedly stimulating to appetites . . . and it's flattering to diners' complexions."

"Aha," he muttered.

"You honestly didn't know that? It's one of the first lessons on color selection in design schools."

"I got into the business through the construction side of things. Remember?"

"Oh, that's right." I sighed. "I'm sorry. I'm not being much of a conversationalist today. I'm still too distracted." Just then, there was a clatter behind me, and I gasped and spun around in my chair. A waiter had dropped a dish while trying to clear a table.

"You're downright jumpy, too," John observed as I turned back.

I was tempted to snap that anyone in my shoes would be equally "jumpy," but that remark didn't seem quite fair; only yesterday I'd found it suspicious that Hannah Garrison had been so easily startled by me when I went to Paprika's to ask about Jerry Stone.

Despite his tame assurances otherwise, Stone had stalked Laura: I'd also caught him in the act of following Hannah. Maybe he had killed Laura and was now stalking me, leaving her bloody scarf where I'd find it.

"Erin?" John said. "Maybe it'd help to talk about all of this."

Our eyes met. Once again there was something not so very attractive about his expression; a certain haughtiness, maybe? Surely I was just being paranoid. "I . . . went to talk to George Wong the night before last."

John squared his shoulders and glared at me. "You went to see Wong in person? Why? That guy's bad news! Didn't I *tell* you that? If I thought you'd do something so foolhardy, I never would have given you his name in the first place!"

Though annoyed mostly at myself—after all, I'd already paid for my mistake, with Wong's late-night visit—I snapped, "Where was the danger in just talking to him about Laura's furniture? It wasn't like I went storming into his office accusing him of murder . . . threatening that I was going to bring him down single-handedly. I'm not an idiot, John."

"I didn't say you were. I just think you took a foolish, unnecessary risk." He tried to put his hand atop mine on the table, but I pulled away.

So he didn't think I was a fool, just that I'd done a really, really stupid thing. Yippee! He'd made my ego soar like a neon-colored wind sock.

"You can't possibly argue the point, Erin. I mean, look

what's happened. Someone's tailing you now . . . obviously trying to mess with your head."

"Speaking of messing with my head," I replied evenly, "Mr. Wong said to say hello to you. When I asked how he knew that I knew you, he said you'd mentioned me when you saw him last, which he claimed was clear back in January."

"You and I didn't know each other in January."

"Yes, I realize that. That's my point." *Was it just me, just John, or were men forever pointing out the obvious to women?*

"That was a crazy thing for him to say. I saw him just three, four weeks ago. I must have mentioned your name then. In fact, I'm sure I did. He'd asked me about interior designers in Crestview . . . said it would help him to collect a list of business contacts."

"And you gave him my name?"

"Along with Steve's. Yeah."

"Yet you just said that the guy was 'bad news.' "

"Well, hey. I wouldn't want to run into him in a dark alley. He's great at what he does, though. You give Wong the dimensions and description of a shelf unit you want built, and he'll make it to your precise specifications."

I paused, trying to form a mental timeline. "When you last saw him, were you ordering furniture for today's showcase home, by any chance?"

John froze. Widening his eyes, he answered, "My God, you're right. I ordered an entertainment center. He shipped it just yesterday. So he knew *I'd* be there today. In fact, he's the only person who knew someone connected to Laura would be at that house. Maybe George Wong is the murderer!"

"But how could Wong have known that *you* knew Laura?"

He stared at me for a long moment, blinked, then said,

"Good point. He *couldn't* have. Even so, I'm going to tell the police about how Wong delivered furniture to that address just yesterday."

I mulled over telling John about Wong's unnerving visit to my home last night, but kept quiet. What good would another I-told-you-so tongue-lashing do for me? But I *would* tell Linda Delgardio about it.

"If I didn't know better, I'd think that someone was trying to frame *me*," John said. "First I find the murder weapon and get my fingerprints on the knife in the process. Then suddenly the scarf that Laura was wearing last is lying out in the open, right next to my truck. Not to mention having someone I barely know, George Wong, say 'tell John I said hello.' "

I averted my eyes, pretending to study my bland linguine. "You have a couple of weird coincidences going against you, all right."

"You can say that again." He chuckled and wiggled his eyebrows at me, leaning closer. "No wonder you're jumpy. You're having lunch with a prime suspect in a killing."

Offended, I fired back, "Laura was a friend of mine. Or at least, I thought she was. In any case, her death is not a joking matter."

His smile promptly faded. "Right. Sorry."

Everything I said to him from then on was like using expensive fabric to re-cover a chair that had a defective frame. John paid for our meals and we left, and he seemed lost in thought as he drove us back to the model home, where my van was still parked. He pulled into the driveway, set the parking brake, and asked, "Erin: Are you afraid of me?"

"Of course not!"

He held my gaze, as if trying to gauge my sincerity.

I sighed. "John, this has all been a nightmare, ever

since Laura and I went to Audrey's presentation on Monday night. The truth is, I'm not feeling very good about *anything* just now. All I want is for her killer to get arrested so I can stop feeling like I need to be looking over my shoulder. Ironically, if I *had* been watching through my rearview mirror more diligently today, maybe I'd have spotted the killer."

He glowered at me. "What if all of this had happened to Steve Sullivan instead of me? If *Steve* had found the knife in the table, if Wong had told you to say hello to Sullivan, and you'd found the scarf on the property of one of *Steve's* clients? Would you have acted this skittish around *him*?"

I hesitated. Then I said firmly, "Yes."

"I'm not sure that's true. And I've got to tell you honestly, Erin, it's a bit crowded in this relationship."

"I don't know what to say to that, John."

He got out of the truck. "Why don't you just say 'thanks for lunch'?" He slammed the door and let himself inside the house. I stayed seated for a minute or two, thinking. He might have made an excellent point just now, or he might have put up a subterfuge, deliberately distracting me by waving my unresolved feelings for Sullivan in front of me. Miserable, but unwilling to leave things this way between us, I followed him into the house.

John was pacing in the chef-style kitchen. In my sour mood, the upscale surroundings struck me as one more example of artifice. All the newer, fancier homes seemed to have these vast, mega-equipped kitchens nowadays, even though supposedly fewer and fewer homeowners were actually cooking. "I'm sorry I snapped at you, John."

He shrugged.

The wisest thing for us to do was probably to cool it for a couple of weeks, but he might only take that to mean I really believed he was guilty of this horrid crime. On the other hand, maybe I did believe that. Gently, I said, "I'm starting to get the feeling that the world is conspiring against us. Know what I mean?"

"I wish you'd met me first, instead of Steve." John refused to meet my gaze. "I doubt we'd be having this conversation today if we'd met sooner. Instead, you'd be telling me how suspicious Steve looks, with the woman who broke his heart and destroyed his life suddenly dying the very same night he finds out she's back in town."

"John, I'm not comfortable discussing Sullivan like this. It sounds like you're saying you suspect him. But he'd been with me for hours that night, *including* the period of time when the building was set on fire."

Now he stared into my eyes. "But you don't know how long Laura's body was lying there before the fire was set, do you?"

"No, but . . . Come on, John. This is Steve Sullivan we're talking about. You and he are good friends!"

"I'm just saying that it goes both ways. The other day he implied he didn't trust me when I said I might have touched the knife blade. Now he's obviously turned you against me."

"That's not true!" *Or was it?* My head ached. Was there anyone I trusted these days? "I have to go. I'm late for an appointment."

"Meeting Steve?"

"For work. Yes. Later this afternoon. We've got a batch of accessories to return. Thanks to Henry Toben's switcharoos, my living room purchases now clash."

My explanation was probably gibberish to him. I hadn't told him about Henry, but he nodded. "I'll call you soon."

He sounded sad, but then, he had a right to be; I was depressed, too. "Good. I'd like that. Take care, John." I let myself out. I could feel his eyes on me as I walked away, but I didn't look back.

Sullivan was supposed to meet me at U-Store. He was late. I separated out the items that needed to be exchanged and stacked them near the door. When Sullivan still hadn't arrived, I started marking the boxes for delivery to the rooms in Henry's house according to *my* floor plan and not Sullivan's. "You snooze, you lose," I muttered, working away in an increasingly foul temper.

Sullivan popped through the door a couple of minutes later. We exchanged frostily hellos, and he examined my work. Knowing he'd squawk any second now, I tried to distract him by saying, "I called my suppliers first thing this morning, and they all assure me that their fur upholstery is actual synthetic. And it's a good thing, too, because otherwise, I'd—"

"Whoa. The zebra-skin wall hanging goes in the den, not the back bedroom." He snatched the marker out of my hand.

"Hey! I'm lead designer. You're just my assistant. Remember?"

"*You're* the one with the faulty memory. We agreed to let Henry decide who designs the rooms."

"And we will. *After* he sees everything arranged my way."

"That's not what we agreed to *do*, Gilbert. We'll show him our plans and get his answer. *Then* we'll have the installers put everything in place accordingly. As your *assistant*, I already called and set up a meeting for both him and Pembrook to see the designs. Tomorrow afternoon at two."

"On a Saturday?" I protested.

"The day's going to be shot to hell, no matter what. Laura's funeral's at four."

For a minute there, I'd forgotten about Laura and all

the misery of her murder. Now it hit me like an ice-cold shower. I couldn't stop myself from taking my distress out on Sullivan, and griped, "It's a pretty lousy assistant who doesn't think to check with his supervisor before he makes a meeting for her."

Infuriatingly, Sullivan winked at me. "No problem. I can show Henry both designs by myself."

"So I won't be there to talk up my plan? Yeah, right! Like I'm really going to fall for that." I held out my hand. "Give me my marker back!"

"I don't think so. But I'll tell you what . . . after the meeting tomorrow, I'll mark the boxes myself."

Stretching the truth a little, I exclaimed, "But getting the boxes marked was the major reason we came down here today—to make sure our ducks were in a row and to get the shipment ready for the installers! Now we've both wasted a forty-minute round trip!"

"Seems that our ducks are a bit out of line, then. But don't worry. Like I said, I'll waddle on over here after our meeting tomorrow and make up for our lost time." He gave me a haughty smirk. "*And* I'll accept the shipment on the exchanges at the same time, which *was* the major reason we had to come down here today. The movers are charging Toben extra to deliver on a Saturday and for having to pick up the new merchandise from multiple stores, but he deserves as much. That's why I was a little late getting here. I was busy making the arrangements."

"Again, without checking with me first." *I* wanted to be the one to inspect the final purchases for *my* design, damn it all! "You're the world's worst assistant, Sullivan!" I shoved past him and out the door, wishing I was mean enough to lock him inside.

He poked his head out an instant later. "Yikes, Gilbert. Who shoved the bee up your bonnet?"

The question only infuriated me further, but he *did* at

least have the smarts to say *bonnet* instead of *butt*, or I might very well have changed my mind about locking him inside. "*You* did!"

He crossed his arms and retorted, "Come again?"

I stabbed my finger in his direction. "You're acting like the lead designer and undermining me! And, what's worse, you've been giving me signals that you suspect John of killing Laura. Naturally, today *I* wind up picking a fight with him. Partly because of your ugly, negative vibes toward him." I paused. My accusations were a sloppy paint job on the reality of the situation, and even if Sullivan didn't realize as much, *I* did. Under my breath, I added, "But mostly because I was so flipped out at finding Laura's scarf in front of John's showcase home."

Sullivan gaped at me. "You found her *scarf*? At the house *John's* working on?"

"He was *framed*! The killer's following me, making me scared of my own shadow!" *No way was I going to fuel Sullivan's fire by telling him about George Wong's remarks regarding John.*

Sullivan came forward and started to reach for me, as though to pull me into a hug. I whirled around to turn my shoulder to him . . . and throw an elbow, if necessary. A sudden wellspring of emotions threatened to make me dissolve into tears. *No way; not in front of Sullivan.* I cleared my throat and stated, "Everyone's relationships are getting destroyed. I'm feeling awkward around John now, and both of you are suspicious of each other."

"*John* suspects *me* of killing Laura?"

"No more than you do *him*."

Through clenched teeth, Sullivan said, "Great. That's just great."

"Well? He's just following *your* lead, Sullivan."

"Yeah? Laura's scarf didn't suddenly appear in front of

my workplace, now *did* it! Besides, the difference is, I know *I'm* not guilty."

"Which means, in effect, you think John Norton is capable of murder!"

He gave me no reply.

"I hate this!" I stormed past him and locked my storage unit. "Everyone's suspicious of everyone else. It's like living in a prison. I'm going home. I'll see you later, Sullivan."

Though I hoped he would stop me—that he would say something wise or encouraging to cast this all in a better light—he remained stone silent.

Chapter 14

When shopping for furniture, never settle for something you don't like. If finances are tight, buy used and fix up the purchase till it's good as new. After all, your furnishings are not mere furnishings. They're a statement of who you are, what you value, and how you choose to live your life.

—Audrey Munroe

DOMESTIC BLISS

Already discouraged and exhausted when I got home, at the sight of the parlor I longed to curl into the fetal position. Audrey must have hired a moving man to assist her in her newest Domestic Bliss research project, because the large room was crammed wall to wall with eight sofas and eight cocktail tables.

"Erin?" she called, peering around the doorway to the dining room. "Before you get busy with other things, I need your advice on these sofa and coffee table pairings."

I forced a smile. "Sure. My advice is: there are eight times too many sofas and coffee tables

in here. Keep the fabulous sage sofa that was in here before, and get rid of the other seven."

She released a dramatic sigh. "We're in *that* kind of
mood, are we?"

"No, *we* aren't. Just *me*." I began to shimmy across the
room in the hopes of grabbing myself a glass of wine.
"There is no dignified way to get through this obstacle
course. If there were a fire in the kitchen, we'd both burn
to a crisp trying to escape." My unthinking remark
brought the memory of the fire and Laura's murder to
the forefront of my conscience, blackening my spirits
even further.

"If there *were* a fire in the kitchen," Audrey replied
serenely, "we would act like Hildi and walk *over* the furniture and straight out the front door."

"So *this* is your attempt to force us all to live like
cats?" I gestured at the surroundings that I was knee-
deep in.

"No, simply to consider how to go about matching
coffee tables to sofas for an upcoming Dom Bliss segment. I've obviously caught you at a bad time. However,
bear this in mind: the sooner you help me, the sooner I
get the movers back over here to remove the excess furniture."

"Well, put in *those* terms, now is the perfect time for a
Dom Bliss chat."

I regarded all those tables and sofas in the parlor for
a moment or two, formulating my answer. "Audrey, I don't
agree with your general premise. Matching a table to a
sofa isn't really the first thing you think about when you

select one or the other item. Granted, I *do* typically start with the sofa when I'm designing a room, simply because that's a large, front-and-center type of item. But tons of things go into choosing the coffee table. I don't concentrate on pairing it with the sofa, but rather with the homeowners . . . how sturdy it needs to be; how this room and this table will be utilized; ages of their children; pets, if any; do they eat on this sofa; do the kids race around the room and wrestle; and so forth. Then you look at all the other lines and shapes in the room, not just at the sofa.

"In fact, it's the exact reverse of a sofa being the first furnishing I select. The coffee table tends to be the very last piece, just because it *is* so central to any design; it's directly in front of what's arguably the most important piece of furniture in the room. There's almost an art to the process. I tend to look at a hundred or more different coffee tables and mentally picture them in the room, until I almost magically know that, out of the immense selection, this one table is the perfect choice."

Audrey was staring at me with a peculiar expression on her face when I turned and met her eyes. She said, "Goodness, Erin. I don't know if I've ever heard you string so many words together in so short a time." While I was still formulating a response, she added, "And the most extraordinary thing is, nary a *one* of your words was of any help to me whatsoever."

I had to resist the temptation to roll my eyes. She

continued firmly, "Like it or not, Erin, my show segment is about *matching coffee tables with sofas*. Period."

She stood there, arms akimbo, blocking my path to the kitchen. She was smaller and older than I was. Odds were, I could take her. But, of course, that was the very last of my intentions. I massaged my neck and looked once again at the wall-to-wall rows of sofas and tables. I glanced behind Audrey at the dining room and saw that it, and no doubt the den and the living room, had acquired the overflow of the original parlor furnishings. "Does this mean you'll be keeping the house like it is now till you've got your segment planned?"

She spread her arms. "What choice do I have?"

I bit back a snide answer and, instead, took a calming breath and ran through a couple of silent confidence-and-optimism mantra repetitions for good measure. Come to think of it, there actually *was* plenty to consider when strictly focusing on pairing a coffee table with a particular sofa—the hues of the sofa fabric compared to the table material, the size of each item, the height and bulk of each, their shapes . . .

"Okay, Audrey." I gave her a wan smile. "You win. Let's break out the booze, and I'll tell you all about how to match coffee tables with sofas."

"Wonderful." She turned on a heel, marched into the kitchen, and said, "Pinot Noir or Chardonnay?"

"Semillon," I replied, just to be difficult. I'd never known her to have any of that blended type of white wine on hand and, truth be told, I had never as much as tasted that particular vintage.

To my surprise, I heard her open the basement door that led to the wine cellar. "Coming right up," she called.

Chapter 15

The next day, Henry let out a low whistle of appreciation as he looked at Sullivan's "safari room" floor plan for his den. Robert Pembrook, however, clicked his tongue. Robert had informed us that he had business in town that day, and so we'd converged in Henry's comfortable-but-vanillaish temporary quarters—a Courtyard Hotel suite in Crestview—until we'd finished decorating his house. Still studying the design board and ignoring his consultant's reaction, Henry grinned and decreed, "I like this one even better. My *wife* would've hated it, though." I was squarely in his late wife's corner. He'd only just now finished raving about how much he liked *my* "new and improved" plans for his house.

"Here's the reason we should go with our first idea, Henry, instead of this one . . . despite our second idea's merits," I attempted.

Sullivan kept a bland expression but combed his hand through his hair. Robert, meanwhile, arched an eyebrow. He'd clearly seen through our ploy of "these are our two equally effective plans," now that I was speaking up in defense of mine.

"The furnishings that you selected all feature bold colors and designs inspired by exotic locales." Both Pembrook and Sullivan, I knew, recognized my double-speak for "gaudy" and "pseudo-safari," but I soldiered on. "By spreading them out, as we do in our first plan, we can use them as a unifying thread throughout your home. Also, you're obviously especially fond of those particular items, or you wouldn't have gone to such lengths to order them." *You miserable, arrogant little toad, you.* "*This* way, you'll have at least one of your favorite purchases in each and every room of your home." With a Vanna White smile and hand gestures, I indicated my own furniture plan.

"True, but . . ." Henry looked longingly at Sullivan's safari room.

"As they say on the TV ads, Henry, 'Just do it,' " Robert interposed. "This is the very least you can do for Erin after your devious modus operandi has caused the poor girl so much extra work. Trust me, dear boy."

Henry forced a thin smile but said nothing. With his head of phony white hair and his old-man short-sleeve button-down shirt, too-short trousers, white socks, and black wingtips, he looked about as far from a "dear boy" as humanly possible. This was the first time I'd seen him in casual weekend attire, and I was amazed to discover that I preferred his dime-store cowboy look. In fact, when Robert had first arrived and saw his client's pathetic attire, he had gasped and declared, "You make me want to weep." On the other hand, last night Audrey and I had caught a new Hammerin' Hank commercial produced under Robert's tutelage, and if I hadn't known better, I would think that "Hank" was a charming, trustworthy man who sincerely wanted to sell me a good car.

"Okay," Henry said reluctantly. "We'll go with Erin's plan." But it was with obvious reluctance that he peeled his eyes away from Sullivan's drawing.

"Good," I said with a big smile. We all knew, however, that two minutes after we completed the job and parted company, Henry Toben would be rearranging the furniture to enact Sullivan's plan. I was not about to give Sullivan the satisfaction of hearing me admit that aloud, however.

I watched Sullivan put away the presentation boards in my portfolio case. Our eyes met, and I tossed him the key to my storage unit. His smug smile promptly faded. "We've got to take off," I said, gathering my things. "Steve has to go to our storage unit and mark the boxes for the moving men to use on Monday, then we have a funeral to attend this afternoon."

"Oh, dear. So do I." Robert reached over and gave my shoulder a squeeze. "You must have known Laura, too."

So he *had* known Laura! "Yes. She was a friend. And she used to live with Steve."

"*You* knew Laura Smith?" Sullivan asked Robert. His attempt to make the question sound casual fell far short of the mark.

Robert gave a theatrical sigh. "The woman was one of my first clients, more than a dozen years ago. She was just a young teenager then . . . thirteen or fourteen. Her guardians had brought her to me because, frankly, the child was such a mess . . . so insecure and scared of people, she could barely function."

"Guardians?" I repeated.

"Where was this?" Steve interrupted, his muscles so tense and his posture so guarded that I half expected him to pop Robert in the jaw if he said the wrong thing.

"Chicago."

"*Laura* was insecure around people?" I asked, remembering how self-assured she was.

"I was working in tandem with her therapist, helping her to gain some self-confidence." Robert met my incredulous gaze and explained, "Oh, darling. Didn't she tell you about her tragic upbringing? She got a terrible injury when her father slit her throat. Then he killed himself."

"But . . . the Smiths . . . Richard and Ethel . . ." Steve stammered. "I spoke to them several times. They used to call her when she was living with me. They said *they* were her parents."

Robert nodded solemnly. "You mean Laura's aunt and uncle. After her parents' death, they raised her as their own." To me he said, "I didn't even realize she'd changed her name to theirs, until I heard about her murder on the news. Dreadful. Just dreadful. Back then, she went by her birth name—Laura Montgomery."

Sullivan gave me an anxious look. The wheels were obviously turning in his head. Now he would want to research old news stories in the Chicago newspapers, looking for the murder-suicide of the Montgomery family. He asked Robert, "Were you aware that she was in league with Evan Cambridge when they stole from my business?"

Robert peered at him. "Are you sure about that? When I knew her, she was one of the sweetest girls I'd ever met."

"She grew jaded over time, then."

"Dear, dear," Robert murmured sadly. "Laura was so . . . special. Her tragic past must have done her in, in spite of everything she had going for her."

Sullivan said nothing, his vision riveted on Robert's face.

Robert hesitated and resettled his large glasses on his nose. "Laura had been *living* with you? So do you mean that she pretended to be an item with you, and then stole from you?"

"Yeah, that's exactly what she did."

Robert clicked his tongue. "You poor thing! That would have made everything that Evan did to you three times worse!"

A vein in Sullivan's neck was bulging and his fists were so tightly balled that his knuckles were white.

"When was the last time you saw Laura, Robert?" I asked.

"Oh, gosh. It must have been nine or ten years ago, before I moved to Denver. She was doing much better by then."

"So she was just eighteen or so?"

He nodded. "She'd learned her lessons well by then. I taught her how to dress and handle herself in public. She was bright . . . a very fast study. And, of course, absolutely gorgeous to look at." He looked at Henry from head to foot. The latter had been listening to all of this in silence, sprawled in the tan overstuffed chair. "I wish all of my clients listened half as well to my instructions as *she* did."

Sullivan's brow was furrowed, indicating that he wasn't necessarily buying Robert's story. Even *I* had to admit that the thin connection between Robert and Laura had suddenly strengthened considerably. And Henry was sure being uncharacteristically quiet, for some reason. To Robert, I said in all honesty, "She was one of the most charismatic people I've ever met."

"Yes. She was. She was, indeed." He heaved a sigh. "Although, apparently, she used her charisma and natural beauty to become a con artist." He shook his head. "What a waste."

At quarter of four, I was apparently the first mourner to arrive at the small funeral home in downtown Crestview. The interior walls were identical to the blond brick exterior. I made my way down the central aisle between the charcoal-gray upholstered pews. Directly ahead of me, the arched stained-glass windows were generic and yet vaguely Christian, designed not to offend, I surmised. I took a seat in the fifth row. A minute or two later, I glanced behind me and spotted Linda Delgardio, wearing a forest-green blouse and dark jacket, sitting in the back corner. She gave me a slight nod of greeting, which I returned.

Soft and somber instrumental music was being piped into the room, but otherwise, it was completely silent. As time passed and no one else arrived, I began to squirm. Finally, Robert Pembrook arrived, looking splendid in a black Italian suit. Unlike his more casual look at Henry's a couple of hours earlier, he had buttoned his black shirt and was now wearing a thin purple tie with a matching pocket square. He took a seat on the opposite side of the aisle, a couple of rows back from mine, giving me a grimace while spreading his fingers on both hands, pantomiming: *Where is everybody?*

A minute later, Sullivan arrived and muttered, "Hey," then sat down next to me. Due, no doubt, to our surroundings, his greeting made me think of my mother, who would always retort, "Hay is for horses." One time I'd compounded my verbal miscue by wisecracking, "And 'High' is for drugheads." In the wake of the riot act she read to me, I was careful to greet her exclusively with "hello" for the next few weeks.

Dave Holland and a second man, who looked so similar the two men could only be brothers, took a seat in the front row, directly ahead of us. Apparently Bill Gates had *two* look-alikes in Crestview, Colorado. Dave turned toward me. He was wearing his prescription sunglasses, but even so, the grief portrayed in his features was instantly apparent. I wondered if his black eye had healed.

I glanced back a second time, hoping the room had filled. A half dozen people in their thirties or so had arrived. I didn't recognize any of them, but they seemed to know one another, and I had the feeling they were Dave's employees. George Wong now sat alone in the back corner, opposite Linda Delgardio's seat.

"I'm surprised Wong is here," I whispered to Sullivan.

"Who?"

"George Wong. He made Laura's reproductions. He insisted he barely knew her . . . that she was just a customer." I realized then that I'd done a grossly inadequate job of keeping Sullivan informed about the snippets of information I was gathering about Laura. I peered at Sullivan's face. His eyes looked glassy. Maybe it was best for me to keep things this way. "I'm sure this is hard on you."

He shrugged. "I'm fine." His voice was way too casual.

John Norton entered the room just then, handsome in his black suit with an open collar. He started to head down the aisle, then got a hitch in his step as he spotted Sullivan beside me. "Let's move over a little so John can join us," I said to Sullivan, who rose.

"Actually," Sullivan told me, "I'm going to go sit back by the door. I've got a rush job this evening and need to get going the moment this is over."

The men exchanged a "hey," and John took Sullivan's vacated seat. "Sorry I'm late," he whispered, putting his arm around me. A few seconds later, he glanced over his shoulder. "I didn't mean to drive Steve clear out of the place."

"He's just sitting in the back."

"No, he left."

Surprised, I turned. Sullivan indeed was gone. A short, plump, gray-haired couple was coming down the aisle—to the family members' section. At a glance, it was clear that these were not Laura's biological parents.

The service was brief, with the eulogist disguising as best he could that he'd never met Laura Smith. He mentioned repeatedly how beautiful she was, so at the very least he'd seen a photograph of her. He announced that there would be a reception afterward in the basement. My heart sank. A reception would make the pitiful turnout all the more acute, I thought.

George Wong and Linda Delgardio had already left by the time John took my arm and we made our way down the aisle. Maybe that was because Linda was keeping an eye on George. Perhaps she was already interrogating him. John whispered, "I wish I'd realized this few people would come to Laura's service. I'd have dragged some people here from work."

"I feel so bad for her parents. For her aunt and uncle, rather."

Dave Holland was standing by the stairwell, and though his eyes were hidden behind his shades, his body English told me that he was waiting for me. "I'm sorry for your loss, Dave."

"Yeah. Thanks, uh, Erin. Can I . . . speak to you for a sec?"

John said gently in my ear, "I'll wait for you downstairs." He gave me a reassuring smile and descended the stairs.

The moment he was out of earshot, Dave blurted out, "The police in Northridge seem to think I'm the prime suspect. I didn't kill her. I was nowhere near the place."

I held my tongue.

"I know what you've been telling 'em . . . about following my car to the warehouse that night. But you're wrong. You followed my brother, Alan."

"What was your *brother* doing, driving to Laura's storage unit?"

"I don't know. But neither of us killed Laura."

There was an awkward pause. It struck me how radically different this service would feel to me if I'd never gone to Laura's house Tuesday morning. Then I could have held on to the wonderful, but false, image that she'd so carefully presented to me. "Are you going to the reception?"

"No." He pressed against his temples with the heels of his hands and stared at his shoes. "Laura once told me if she died first, she'd want me to go out on the town and celebrate her life, not sit around in a black suit mourning her death." He straightened. "So that's what Alan and I are going to go do. He's waiting in the car. Besides, her parents are here. I'm sure they suspect me. I just wanted *you* to know I'm innocent."

"Okay. Take care, Dave."

"Yeah. You too."

Shoulders sagging, he turned and left. I went downstairs to the reception. I believed Dave about not killing Laura, but was still certain he'd set the fire.

Loudspeakers were playing the same piped-in orchestra music as upstairs. This low-ceilinged room had roughly the same square footage as the chapel. At the opposite wall, a row of rectangular tables dressed in royal blue tablecloths held enough platters of finger food to feed fifty. Six circular tables with eight chairs apiece were evenly placed on the remaining floor space. One table was occupied by all six of the mourners who were unfamiliar to me. At the silver coffee urn, Robert Pembrook was bending John's ear. The two men's posture and bearing indicated that they didn't know each other, but had no one else to talk to. Laura's adoptive parents, looking lost and despairing, sat at a round table nearby.

I walked over to them. "Mr. and Mrs. Smith? I'm Erin Gilbert, a friend of Laura's."

Although her husband didn't acknowledge me, Mrs. Smith looked up at me with vacant eyes. "Won't you sit down?"

I murmured my thanks and slipped into the chair next to hers.

"Kind of you to come," she said on a sigh. "Not many did."

"Laura hadn't been back in Crestview very long. Not long enough to get to know many people."

Mrs. Smith frowned and said softly, "It would have been the same story if we'd held the service in our new home in Kansas. Or in South Bend, where we moved from. Laura had a hard time getting close to people. Whenever she did . . . well, she was afraid she'd come to love them, only to lose them, you see. She told you about what happened to her birth parents?"

"Yes, she did. I'm sure that was unfathomably difficult for her to handle."

Mrs. Smith nodded with pursed lips and dabbed at her brimming eyes. Angry red splotches were forming on Mr. Smith's cheeks, meanwhile, and he was studiously avoiding my gaze.

"I was adopted, too," I said. "Not under anything like Laura's circumstances, though, of course."

"He was my brother. Her father was, I mean," Mrs. Smith replied. "We tried our best to raise her right."

"You did everything you could for her," I replied. "You got her into therapy. And you even took her to see Robert Pembrook."

"Who?" she asked.

At the mention of the name, her husband regarded me with fierce, bright eyes, but said nothing.

"The image consultant. He's right . . ." I glanced behind me to point him out. John was now speaking to the eulogist, and the two of them were the only people in the room other than those of us at the two tables. "He must have left. He was at the service."

"Oh, yes. Robert Pembrook. In the black shirt and purple tie. I'd forgotten his name. Laura did that on her own." Her voice and expression were inscrutable.

"You mean she smartened up her self-image on her own, or that she chose to see Mr. Pembrook on her own?"

"That queer ruined my daughter's life, you ask me," Laura's father said with a snarl.

"Well, nobody *did* ask you!" his wife fired back.

"Are you some sort of undercover cop?" he demanded, glaring at me.

"No. Like I said, I was a friend of Laura's."

"Yeah? Well, you were sitting right next to her killer."

"Oh, Richard . . ." his wife moaned.

Shocked, I asked, "You don't mean John Norton, do you?"

"I mean the bastard you were sitting with first. The one who took off before I could confront him."

"Richard! Stop! You don't even know that that was the same man! You just have that one photograph that Laura sent us last year, back when they were living together."

"Steve Sullivan?" I had to struggle to keep my voice down.

"*That's* the one," Mr. Smith promptly replied over his

wife's protests. "He kept calling us, demanding to know where she was, making all kinds of ridiculous accusations. I warned her. When she told us she'd moved back to Crestview, I told her it was a big mistake. That she was going to wind up dead at that crazy man's hand. But she wouldn't listen to me."

"Steve didn't kill her, Mr. Smith," I said firmly.

"Yeah?" He rose. "That's just what my wife said about her brother. For the longest time. Kept insisting some stranger had broken into the house, done all those murders. Didn't matter how many expert witnesses they called in to look at the evidence or Laura's testimony about what her own father had done." He shoved his chair in with such force that the whole table shook. "You women . . . you listen with your damn heart. There's a reason our ears are right next to our brains, you know! *That's* the way it's supposed to be. We're supposed to listen to what our *brain's* telling us!"

"But I was *with* Steve that night, and I *know* he's innocent," I insisted, on the verge of tears. Mrs. Smith lost the battle with her own emotions and began to sob.

As though he hadn't heard me, he snarled, "That little girl didn't stand a chance. Soon as she was old enough to take off, she stayed way away from us. We just reminded her of her terrible past. Begged me, she did, to stay away, to let her live her own life. I kept hoping she'd come back home to us. But who knows what it would have taken to get her back there? I figure if she'd been given the choice between our family farm and prison, she'd have opted for prison." He crossed behind my chair as if to leave, but then rounded and stopped long enough to wag his finger in my face. "Your friend, Mr. Sullivan, *he's* the one who belongs behind bars!" He stormed out the door, still grumbling to himself.

I shot a glance at the other occupied table. Everyone

was staring agape at us. Mrs. Smith said through her tears, "Don't mind my husband. He's grief-struck. We couldn't have kids ourselves. But Laura was so beautiful. Somebody killed our baby. Our beautiful baby."

I gave her a quick hug around the shoulders and whispered, "I'm so sorry."

John crossed the room. He bent a little at the waist and said gently, "Mrs. Smith? I'm John Norton. I'm sorry for your loss. Laura was a beautiful person."

She showed no signs of recognizing John's name. She hiccuped a couple of times, then dried her tears and said, "Thank you."

"Is there anything I can do for you?" he asked. "Can I get you something to eat or drink? Do you and your husband need a ride back to your hotel or anything?"

At his solicitous offer, she squared her shoulders. "No, but why don't you take your lady friend someplace nice now?" She got unsteadily to her feet, waving off his attempts to help her rise. "Richard and I are used to being alone."

She shuffled out of the room in the direction her husband had gone. "Oh, dear God," I murmured. I felt heartbroken for the woman.

"Should we leave?" John asked quietly.

I nodded and rose. John took my hand. We left by way of the opposite exit. Although the sky was a beautiful azure and the air felt crisp, I remained on the edge of tears. "This is about as depressing as a day can get," John said under his breath.

"Knock wood," I muttered.

"Guess I can't blame Steve for not being able to take it. And I suppose seeing me was the last straw. If he honestly thinks I had anything to do with her death, though, he's gone off the deep end."

I felt myself tense. I couldn't stand this; even while we

were leaving Laura's service, John was telling me that Sullivan was crazy to suspect him. Although Steve had bolted without a word, I felt compelled to defend him. "I'm sure your arrival just gave him the excuse to stand up, and once he did, he fled."

I stopped walking, only then realizing we were heading away from my van. John's bright red Audi was in the second, small parking lot, straight ahead of us. "I'm parked on the other side of the building."

He turned toward me and took both my hands in his, lacing his fingers through mine. "I've got to get back to work. We have an open house next week, so I'm working all weekend. Otherwise, I'd offer to take you out for drinks. Like Mrs. Smith said, we *should* go someplace nice. We haven't seen much of each other lately."

I nodded and said, "So I've noticed." He gave me a smile, kissed me softly, then we parted company, muttering vague salvos about things getting better soon.

When would they get better? How? All this animosity and cross-accusation was hard to bear. If this murder wasn't solved very soon, I was going to lose my mind.

As I rounded the building, I spotted Hannah Garrison standing near my car. "Hannah. Hi." I glanced back at the funeral home. "Were you waiting for Dave?"

"Originally. But he already left."

So who's she waiting for now? Me?

She frowned. "He didn't even see me, I don't think. He looked terrible. I felt sorry for him . . . even though he's feeling this way due to the" —she drew finger quotes in the air and continued— "*other woman.*"

I sighed, determined to rid my immediate thoughts of the pain of Laura's adoptive parents. Hannah obviously needed someone to chat with, so, just to be kind,

I suggested, "Want to go get a cup of coffee or something?"

"That'd be nice," she replied with a smile.

Minutes later, as we sipped our coffee, I tried to let the quiet, stately ambience of the restaurant restore me. Hannah said, "You know what, Erin? Even though I would never actually go through with it myself, there were times when I would pray for Laura to die a hideous, mutilating death."

That statement was a major ambience killer if ever there was one. "Are you still in love with Dave?" I asked impulsively.

"No, but I'm no longer in *hate* with him, so that's good. It took me a while to forgive him. Really, he's just this sweet guy that Laura led around by the nose."

"You couldn't have thought so kindly of him when you were still 'in hate' with him."

She peered at me over the rim of her scuffed-up white ceramic cup, then set it down in its saucer. "I'm sure that he felt like he'd hit the jackpot when Laura came on to him." She motioned as though she were displaying a banner headline in the air and continued, " 'The Geek Lands the Sexpot.' I'm sure he knew Laura just wanted him for his money, but he didn't care. And what chance did *I* have . . . his equally geeky high school sweetheart."

And yet, according to what Sullivan had told me, Dave and Laura had originally linked up *before* Dave had struck gold in the business world. Pointing out that discrepancy to Hannah would be like pouring salt in her wounds, so I merely asked, "You two were sweethearts back in high school?"

She nodded. "And while we were both going to college at CU."

"Steve Sullivan told me that when he first met Laura, she convinced him that Dave was physically abusive to her."

She furrowed her brow. "That was a ridiculous lie. Dave and I had some doozies of fights, believe me. Especially when our marriage was breaking up," she added bitterly, "thanks to Laura. But, even so, he never once raised a hand to me."

"Did you notice his black eye?"

"Dave's got a black eye?"

"Hidden behind his dark glasses."

"Laura must have clobbered him."

"He claims he tripped."

She scoffed, "Even if she came at him with a baseball bat, he'd kill himself before he'd have harmed a hair on her head. He worshiped the ground that conniving bitch walked upon. He was too love-blind to see what she was, so in love with herself that there was no room in her shriveled heart for anyone else."

I frowned, but held my tongue. In spite of Laura's extreme shortcomings, I resented Hannah's speaking so scathingly of her on the day of her funeral. Hannah took another sip of coffee, then said, "Actually, I'm kind of sorry she's dead. In a weird, sick way, I *owe* her. Laura Smith gave me a reason to get up in the morning. I wanted to prove that I was somebody, too, that Dave had made a terrible mistake in leaving me."

"You once said he tried to win you back, when Laura dumped him for Steve Sullivan."

She raised her chin and perked up a little. "He tried to, yes, but I wouldn't take him back. I might have, eventually, but I made it clear he had to prove that he was home for good. And, of course, he went crawling back to Laura the moment she returned to town."

She looked at her watch and sprang to her feet. "Oh,

dear. I should have been at work ages ago." She swept up her purse, which she'd hooked on her chair, then rounded the table, patting my shoulder just as she headed for the door. "Sorry, but I've got to run. Thanks for the coffee, Erin."

"You're welcome. Take care."

Maybe I'd been hanging around Sullivan too long, but I, too, was starting to become skeptical. Hannah's tale of rejecting her husband struck me as false. A weird theory popped unbidden into my head: *What if Hannah had conspired with Laura to rip off her ex-husband?*

My thoughts were in turmoil as I made the short drive home. To shore up my flagging spirits, I told myself to take in the soul-warming grace of Audrey's home as I made my way up the walkway.

That instruction to myself backfired. There was nothing soul warming about what I was seeing as I neared the house. I kept thinking my eyes were deceiving me. By the time I'd reached the front steps, there was no denying the sight.

A knife had been stabbed with tremendous force into the center of Audrey's oak door.

Chapter 16

Audrey seemed unable to stop pacing as Linda Delgardio and her partner interviewed us. Three months ago, Audrey had told me that she wanted an "old-world Italian feel" to this room, and I'd applied sunny yellow Venetian plaster to the walls, replaced the ugly parquet floor with terra-cotta tiles, stained the wood trim a deep, rich brown, and installed filigreed crown molding and a matching ceiling medallion, from which I'd hung an elegant chandelier. We both loved the results, but then she'd told me that she wanted to select the furniture herself. She had yet to do so. Instead of "old-world Italian," we now had a time-traveling, continent-hopping hodgepodge—

the kind of interior space that a tactful designer terms "eclectic."

Officer Mansfield, Linda's partner, kept making gentle suggestions that Audrey "might be more comfortable" if she took a seat. Linda had met Audrey a couple of times: she already knew that Audrey did precisely what she wanted to do.

"You always use the back door when you come and go?" Linda asked her.

"Yes. There's a one-car garage back there. It used to be the carriage house, when the home was first built."

"You didn't ever open the front door today?"

"No." She continued her path from the west wall to the east and back again.

"Not even to get the mail?" Mansfield asked.

"No. There's a slot for mail next to the sidelight. Although I would *think* that if the knife had been there at the time of delivery, the mailman would have rung my doorbell and asked whether or not I had intentionally stabbed a six-inch knife into my front door."

He made a notation in his notepad. "Yeah. That's probably a safe bet, but we'd better locate your carrier and ask him straight-out, just in case."

"The mail's always here between two and two-thirty. And before you ask, nobody came to the door today and, no, I didn't hear any suspicious noises or notice anything out of the ordinary."

"No strange cars idling their engines, or suspicious-looking passersby?"

"That would fit into the general category of 'out of the ordinary,'" she said, donning her patient smile, which was actually an indication she was *losing* her patience.

Linda rose, and her partner followed suit. "The lab will examine the knife. And we've already put in a call for CSI to dust the door for prints. We'll let you know what we find out."

"Thanks, Linda," I said.

"You *do* realize that this is a not-too-subtle message to Erin that her life is in jeopardy, don't you?" Audrey asked them.

"We'll do our best to catch whoever's done this, Ms. Munroe," Mansfield responded.

"We're going to canvass the neighborhood now," Linda said. "Maybe we'll get lucky and find an eyewitness."

"Keep us posted," Audrey replied as she ushered them out the marred door. That too-patient smile was back on her lips, but had faded by the time she returned to the room.

I massaged my neck and tried to make my escape. "What a long, horrendous day this has been! I'm going to turn in early and—"

"It's quarter after seven. Not even infants or nuns go to bed this early." She snatched off the ottoman cum coffee table the small loose-leaf notebook she used for grocery lists and, finally, took a seat in the sleek, black-leather-and-chrome Barcelona chair across from my mahogany-and-velvet Martha Washington chair. "I want the name of each and every person you've met who is even remotely connected to Laura Smith."

"Why? The police are—"

"We'll give your police-gal friend the list later, if there are any surprises on it. In the meantime, I'm not taking any more chances with your well-being, and you shouldn't, either."

"But what good would a—"

"What's the name of the man she was living with?"

I gave myself another self-massage. Now I really *did* have a pain in my neck—both literally and figuratively. "Dave Holland."

She wrote that down, then looked at me expectantly.

"Hannah Garrison. She's Dave's ex-wife." Audrey raised her eyebrows in surprise at this—she, too, knew Hannah from Paprika's—but diligently jotted down the name. "Robert Pembrook, who was once Laura's image consultant and who recently subcontracted me for a redecorating job. George Wong, who made Laura's reproductions. And Jerry Stone. That's the name of the dreadlocks guy Laura threw to the floor during your presentation." The name "John Norton" popped into my brain, but I didn't want to tell Audrey that my boyfriend had connections to Laura Smith. "That's everyone."

She peered at me. "You're omitting someone, Erin."

"John only dated her a few times, years ago," I protested. "It's not fair to put him on the same list as those others."

"You mean John *Norton* used to date her? The man you're currently seeing?"

I felt my cheeks grow warm, giving Audrey her answer.

"My goodness, but that woman got around!" She shook her head and sighed, returning her attention to compiling the list. "That makes *two* names you left off our list. You *also* failed to mention Steve Sullivan." She rose and tore the sheet out of her notebook. "You're going to be careful around everyone on this list. I'll post it on the refrigerator, in case you forget." She wagged her finger. "One of these people is trying to warn you that they're willing to put a knife in your back, missy, and that ain't happening. Not on my watch."

She strode out of the room, and an instant later, I heard her slap a magnet onto her stainless-steel refrigerator. I sighed and tried to fight off the chill that crept up my spine. *Thanks, Audrey. I feel safer already.*

"At least *one* good thing is going to come from this insanity," she called to me from her post in the kitchen. "I'm phoning Henry Toben and telling him that tonight's date is hereby canceled. I'm not leaving you home alone for one instant."

Sunday provided a much-needed break for me, and Audrey and I stayed home all day and played gin rummy and Boggle, basically pretending that nothing out of the ordinary had happened. She had ignored, however, my not-too-subtle hints that we *could* be restoring the parlor to a human—as opposed to a feline—abode by ridding ourselves of the excess sofas and tables.

Monday morning, Sullivan and I met at Henry's house. Though it was petty of me, I decided that I wasn't going to tell Sullivan about the knife in Audrey's door unless and until he said something to me about his abrupt departure from Laura's service, and he seemed to be in no hurry to do so. The movers arrived right on schedule. As the lead designer, I banished Sullivan to the second floor with gleeful relish, while I oversaw the main floor.

I vastly prefer that homeowners *not* be present while I install their rooms, but against my express wishes, Henry had taken the day off from work and was "here to help." Ironically, that meant that while Audrey had deftly escaped spending time in Henry's presence, I was boxed into spending time with both him *and* Sullivan. My client seemed to be on edge about something, trying to be the first to peer into every carton that the movers unloaded and, in the process, getting in the way and slowing us down. Thankfully, he finally said he needed to "grab a smoke" but was out of cigarettes, and he left us to our work.

I heard a noise outside and looked out the dining room window. A man darted around the corner of Henry's property. I gasped. Could that be Jerry Stone? What the heck could he be doing here? I raced into the kitchen and peered out those windows, but couldn't get a second look at him.

"Miss?" one of the moving men called as he tromped into the room, followed by his partner. "We got the heavy stuff unloaded . . . just need to make sure everything's exactly where it's s'posed to be. Your boss told us to start downstairs."

"Actually, you got our roles backward; I'm *Mr. Sullivan's* boss."

"Okay. Sorry."

I eyed him and his muscular partner. These men could crack the reedlike Jerry Stone in two. "I think it'd be easiest if you helped install the bedrooms first."

"Suit yourself," he replied with a shrug.

Both men thumped up the stairs. I weighed the risk of confronting a prowler against the possibility of gleaning valuable insight into Laura's murder. The slightest peep from me would bring up to three men instantly dashing to my aid. Though scared, I slid open the kitchen door, slipped outside, and crept around the corner. The trespasser was shading his eyes, trying to spy through the dining room window. "Jerry!"

He jumped and clutched at his chest as he pivoted to face me. He flattened himself against the side of the house. His cheeks were flushed and his forehead was dotted with perspiration. His clothing reeked of sweat and cigarette smoke.

"What are you doing here? And how did you get here?" There were no other cars on Henry's cul-de-sac besides Sullivan's and mine.

"I snuck into the moving van. Just before those steroid abusers you hired took off from your storage unit."

"*Why?* And how did you know to be watching for them at some storage unit in Northridge?"

"I've been following you, actually."

I thought about the mattress and sleeping bag in Laura's storage unit. "You haven't been living at the U-Store facility, by any chance, have you, Jerry?"

"No. And anyways, that's all irrelevant. You've got to quit this job, Erin."

"Why?"

"Because you bullshitted me about your use of environmentally responsible materials."

He must have seen the zebra-hide wall hanging. And the leopard-skin ottoman. "With this particular client, I've had to compromise on a couple of items, but—"

"A couple of items?!" he cried. "How do you *sleep* at night?!"

That was more than a little overstated, but I held my tongue. Even though I didn't believe that he was telling me the whole truth about his motives for following Laura and Hannah, I *did* believe that he was truly a conservationist, and I respected that.

He gestured at Henry's house. "This . . . this . . . reprehensible, death-bounty merchandise represents everything I've devoted my life to working against!"

"Um, Jerry, I was assured that the leopard skin is a clever fake, and the . . ." I stopped, and sighed. He was staring at me in horror, as though I'd drowned a puppy in front of his eyes. "Why me, Jerry? Out of all the designers and all the home-goods stores selling merchandise that use fur or leather, why have you zeroed in on *me*?"

"Paprika's made me realize how offensive consumerism really is. One night, when I didn't have anyplace to stay, I walked by their window display. I'm seeing all this . . . useless nonsense that costs more bucks than I'm likely to make in a lifetime. I targeted *them*, not you. But your office is close to Paprika's."

Lucky me, I thought sourly. Steve Sullivan's office was

nearby, too. Why couldn't *Sullivan* have gained his own personal activist? "How were you planning on getting back downtown, Jerry? Were you hoping to sneak unnoticed into an *empty* delivery van?"

He shrugged. "Hadn't thought that far ahead. I just knew I had to do whatever it takes to convince you to quit this job. Have you looked in all the boxes? Seen all the animal blood that's on your hands?"

"What are you talking about? I told you, the fur is *synthetic*."

"You think that *ashtray* is a fake?"

"*What* ashtray?"

He shook his head and grumbled, "I don't know how you can sleep at night."

That was the second time he'd made the comment, and I'd had enough. "I sleep just fine, Jerry. Safe and comfy, under a roof that I'm helping to pay for." *More or less.*

"Yeah. Great. By working for people like Henry Toben," he sneered. "And before you ask, I read his name on the shipping labels." He spat on the ground in my direction, then eyed me with disgust. "You know what? You deserve what you're getting, lady. I give up." He turned on a heel.

"What do you mean 'what you're getting'? What are you talking about?"

He called, "You're a gorilla killer!"

"Pardon?" I'd been called many things, but never *that*.

He continued to storm down the hill, then turned and shouted, "I'd like to see how you'd feel if someone were to do that to your cat!"

I shouted after him, "How did you know I have a cat, Jerry?"

He turned away and resumed his path down the sidewalk, making a rude gesture at me over his shoulder.

What on earth was he talking about? What ashtray?

What gorilla? I mulled over chasing after him, but didn't want to risk it. For all I knew, he could be the knife-wielding maniac who'd killed Laura. Maybe he saw Hildi yesterday, when he was thrusting a knife into Audrey's front door.

I walked up the ramp and into the van to investigate. As the movers had reported, only small boxes and loose items intended to accessorize Henry's home remained. Within moments, I spotted the cause of Jerry's diatribe. A gorilla's paw, amputated at the wrist, that had been turned into an ashtray.

The sight made me sick to my stomach. Unwilling to touch the thing, I left it where it was and stormed back into the house and up the stairs, wanting to put my fist in Henry's face, if only he were there right now.

The men were putting together the bed frame in the guest room, the zebra hide that was to hang above it currently on the floor nearby. I examined it with renewed disgust; I should never have allowed Henry to include it with purchases made in my name.

"Thanks, gentlemen," I told the movers. "Change in plans. We're done here."

"But . . . we haven't placed the dining room table for you or—"

"The homeowner can do that himself, once he returns."

Sullivan glared at me. "Gilbert? What's going on?"

"I can't do this. Jerry's right."

"Jerry who?"

"Jerry Stone. I'll explain in a moment."

One of the moving men thundered, "We still have a batch of stuff on the driveway and in the garage that we—"

"Again, the homeowner can take care of it. You've done an excellent job. Thank you."

The one mover looked at the other, then glanced back at me. "Suit yourself, lady. Guess we'll just empty the rest of the van on the driveway and take off."

"Fine. Thanks for all your work."

He scoffed a little as he thumped down the stairs. "Yeah. No problem."

"What happened?" Sullivan asked me gently. "Does this have something to do with Laura?"

"No, with Henry's disgusting taste. I'm putting my foot down." Unable to get the hideous image of the ashtray out of my mind, I muttered, "If it were up to Henry, he'd lop off *my* foot and turn it into a doorstop."

"What are—"

A door banged downstairs and Henry called, "Darlin'? The moving men are leaving. I thought you said they'd do the installation, too, but there's still—"

I tromped down the stairs and snarled, "Good, you're back. Now you can explain to my face how you thought I'd agree to placing illegal and reprehensible contraband in one of my designs!"

"Contraband? What? You mean *drugs*?"

"No! The gorilla's paw!" I pointed at the door. "Go look outside, wherever the movers have dumped the rest of your things!"

Henry stared at me, then at Sullivan, now standing on the stairs behind me. "I'll do that." Crimson splotches had formed on his cheeks, but I was quite certain they were from the embarrassment of getting caught in the act. Indignant, he stormed out the door.

"Henry bought a gorilla's paw?" Sullivan asked me. "What a jerk."

"I'd call him a lot stronger names than *that*. Come on. We're leaving."

Sullivan, however, stayed put. Just as I was about to protest, Henry came puffing back inside, carrying the grotesque ashtray. "This isn't mine, honey. Someone must have made a mistake."

I didn't believe him for a second. "Give me the shipping order. It's got to be among the things the ashtray came with, or it couldn't have been delivered. I'll call the store and double-check the order."

Henry winced, looked at me, then said meekly, "Okay, you got me, darlin'. It *is* mine, but I told them specifically to ship it directly to the house next week, so you wouldn't see it. The store loused up my order. I *knew* they'd do that, the idiots!"

I wasn't sure how or when he'd sneaked this particular delivery past me; it certainly hadn't been there when Sullivan and I checked everything less than a week ago. For now, there was a more important matter to resolve. "I need to know where you bought that horrible thing, Henry. A gorilla's paw is illegal to import. Whoever did so needs to be turned in to the authorities and have their operation shut down for good."

"Uh, well . . ." Henry tugged on his white dustcover of a toupee. "I got it from an independent source. Don't even remember the guy's name. *He* approached *me*. He was just another customer in that furniture store on the mall. He had a catalogue of stuff like this, and he handled everything." He looked up at Sullivan, still standing on the stairs. "He was a real scruffy-looking guy. Maybe even homeless, for all I know. I guess I shouldn't have trusted him."

The description made me uneasy. "What did he look like exactly?"

"I dunno. White guy with a beard. Average height. Thin."

"His name wasn't Jerry Stone, was it?"

"He never told me his name. The company's name was African Trading Company, though."

"There was a man wearing grungy jeans and a ratty-looking gray sweater who left here just a couple of minutes before you arrived. He was hitchhiking back to downtown Crestview. Did you see him on your way home just now?"

Henry shook his head. "There wasn't anyone out there hitchhiking."

"He must have already gotten a ride."

"I only passed one car on the main road. A beat-up Chevy. I didn't see any passengers in it."

I rubbed my forehead, frustrated. Could Jerry have lied about how he'd gotten here? Had he simply tailed the delivery van? "Someone *butchered* a gorilla to make your ashtray, Henry. How could you buy such a thing?"

He spread his arms. "Because it's . . . comical. Like you said when you were designing the place . . . it's whimsical. You're the one who told me you like a touch of whimsy in your design."

"Then wallpaper a bathroom with funny pages! But don't buy from some poacher who would kill a gorilla just to amuse some heartless American businessman who wants to snuff out his cigarettes in some poor primate's foot!"

Henry threw up his hands and said, "Okay, okay! If it bothers you that much, I'll send it back."

"Good," Sullivan interrupted. "You do that. Immediately. Or else the authorities are going to hold *you* personally responsible." He touched my shoulder and said, "Let's get back to work, Gilbert. I've got the whole master bedroom to install yet, and now there's just the two of us."

Enraged, I gaped at him. "I'll do no such thing! Don't patronize me, Sullivan!"

"Henry said he'd send the ashtray back. There's nothing more he can do at this point. It's not like he can go to Africa and sew the gorilla's paw back on."

"But what about the zebra and the leopard? Henry assured me they were from a company that only sells fakes, and I believed him! He duped me into supporting the slaughter of animals!"

"And just where do you think the leather comes from for the recliner in the living room, Gilbert?" Sullivan fired back. "You're wearing leather shoes! Where do you draw the line between what kind of animal you'll allow to be killed to produce the goods that you yourself use?"

"There's a big line between using cowhide products and knowingly supporting poachers, Sullivan, and you know it!"

He averted his gaze and said nothing.

I stormed outside, shouting, "I need to get some fresh air and clear my head!"

"I'll get *your* work done for you in the meantime," Sullivan shot back.

I paced next to my van. Furious, I repeated to myself: " 'It's not like he can go sew the gorilla's paw back on.' " I kicked a pebble. "What a jerk!" To think that I was trying so hard to *help* Sullivan! *John Norton is a terrific guy and the absolute perfect match for me. John was right, damn it all!* If only I'd met the two men in reverse order, I could well have been in love with John by now, instead of harboring a stupid crush on his stupid surly friend, who was, in turn, harboring a stupid grudge against all womankind simply because he'd stupidly fallen for a deeply disturbed woman. Stupid! Stupid! Stupid!

It took me nearly twenty minutes on the phone until I was satisfied that a wildlife inspector from the Denver office of the Fish and Wildlife Service would drag the full information out of Henry and try to shut down this "African Trading Company" black-market business. By then I had calmed down enough to suspect that Sullivan was simply playing devil's advocate and befriending Henry so that he could continue to pry information from him. Which was not to say that I would forgive Sullivan, only that I could understand where he was coming from.

Resolved, I returned to the house, and saw that Henry was arranging the dining room on his own. "Hello, darlin'. I've got the ashtray all packaged back up and ready to be returned. You over your hissy fit yet?"

"I *was*, up until this moment. For your information, Mr. Toben, that was *not* a 'hissy fit,' that was *rage* at having been duped into supporting the import of illegal contraband from poachers. I could have lost my business license if I'd knowingly purchased such an item." I wasn't actually sure if that was true, but it certainly *should* be. "I've already contacted the proper authorities. They'll be in touch with you soon."

Henry paled. "I just thought it was a gag item. You know . . . a joke."

"Where's Steve?"

"In the garage."

"No, he isn't. I walked right past the open doorway."

"He's in the storage area above the garage. He could probably use some help, in fact. That's where we stashed the few items from my original household that you allowed me to keep."

I decided not to quibble with Henry's wording; I didn't wield sufficient power to control which new items I purchased on his behalf, let alone "allow" him to keep only a few old ones. I went to the garage. A flight of pull-down attic stairs was just ahead of me. "Sullivan?" I called.

"Yeah?" He started to come down the stairs, carrying a chair, and I waited, telling myself not to haul him over the coals, but rather to see things from his perspective. After all, he'd had to absorb a lot of heavy personal defeats in the past year.

Just as he put his weight on the next step, it gave way. I screamed, and watched helplessly as he crashed to the concrete floor.

Chapter 17

I shoved the chair Steve had been carrying out of my way and rushed to his side. He was writhing in pain, clutching his leg.

"Steve? Oh, my God. Are you okay?"

"Cripes! Does it *look* like I'm okay?"

My heart was pounding. I didn't know what to do. He tried to get up, but dropped back down and again grabbed his leg at the knee. "Shit! My leg. Broken," he managed, obviously in too much pain to say more.

Henry appeared, panting, in the doorway. "What happened?"

"Stair broke," Steve gasped. He was attempting to rise on his good leg, and I helped him up.

"His leg's broken." My throat was tightening.

Unexpectedly, Henry took charge. "Let's get you to the hospital. Get out of the way, Erin." Calculating that he probably was a little stronger than I was, I let him take my place and allow Sullivan to lean on him.

The stair must have been on the verge of giving way and only cracked through as he stepped on it a second time with the added weight of the chair. I looked at the stair and cried, "No wonder you fell! The stair didn't break; it was partially sawed through!"

Henry and Steve looked at the sabotaged stair. Steve cursed under his breath at the sight.

"Let's get him to my van," I growled at Henry, not trusting him behind the wheel. "I'll drive to the emergency room."

Steve continued to stare at the sawed stair as if transfixed. "Jeez! Look at that! Somebody was trying to kill me!"

"Or *me*. As the original designer, I was probably the likeliest person to be climbing up and down those stairs."

"This trap was obviously set for me," Henry protested. "Whoever sawed through those steps was gunning for me, not some designer, for cryin' out loud."

The next morning as I let myself into my office, I had the unshakable sensation that I was being followed. In fact, I'd been feeling that way ever since leaving the emergency room the night before to drive Sullivan to his home. With his tongue loosened by the trauma of his bad fall, he'd admitted that he, too, had been horrified by the ashtray, yet had hoped that he could "buddy up to Hammerin' Hank" and get more information from him about Robert Pembrook. Sullivan suspected him of Laura's murder. I'd asked if he'd gotten any information out of Henry yet, and he grumbled, "Nope. Just a broken leg."

Steve was, at least, going to be able to walk in his cast in a couple of days. He had a break in his tibia.

Now, as I stepped through the doorway, I noticed a manila envelope had been slid under my office door. I swept it up, assuming it was from a client, but began to worry a little when I flipped it over and saw that it was unmarked. I opened the envelope as I climbed the steps.

As I reached the top step, the contents chilled me—a black-and-white photograph of a middle-aged man kissing a much younger woman in front of the door to what looked like a motel room. The second photograph showed their faces in profile. The man was Henry Toben—with thinning dark hair—and the woman was a very young-looking Laura Smith. A third photograph clearly revealed that Henry was groping Laura under her skirt. She, meanwhile, was smirking directly at the camera.

When these photographs were taken—and I was guessing that was roughly ten years ago—it would have been bad news for Henry Toben. His wife would still have been alive.

I had an hourlong meeting with a supplier, then locked my office and headed straight for Steve Sullivan's home; I'd already called and told him about the photos, and he told me to let myself in. Nevertheless, I knocked, cracked open the door, and said, "It's just me."

"Come on in," he called.

He lay on his chaise longue in his underfurnished living room. It had been less than twenty-four hours since I'd seen him, but his face looked drawn. His hair was in need of a combing, and I longed to straighten it for him. He was wearing jogging shorts, and despite the cast from the knee down, it was hard not to stare at his sexy, muscular thighs.

Totally unnerved, I took a seat on his mushroom-colored sofa. The sight of him convalescing was bringing out the nursing instincts in me, and I had to battle ludicrous fantasies about how I could distract him from his pain. I focused on the envelope in my hand, determined not to act flustered. "Look at this." I handed him the pictures of Henry and Laura.

"Someone just shoved this under your office door?"

"Yes."

He made a derisive noise. "You should have someone look at that door of yours, you know. Install a weather strip, at least. You're wasting energy without one."

With forced sweet tones, I replied, "I'll take that into consideration. Thanks." The good thing about his smug nit-picking was that Sullivan had already managed to wring the mothering instinct right out of me.

He studied the three photos, then returned them to the envelope. "This could be a setup of some kind. Maybe Laura's killer just wants to throw light on another possible suspect. So he or she had some dirt on Henry, and is using it to full effect."

"But if that's the case, why not send the photos to the police? Why give them to me?"

"Good question. Did you tell your policewoman friend about this?"

Her name's Linda. How hard is that to remember? "Not yet."

Steve handed the envelope back to me. "When you do, you'd better explain that you assumed whoever sent them wore gloves and didn't get fingerprints on the photos and envelope. We've both been handling them and have probably smudged any of the sender's prints."

I peered at him in dismay. Though I managed to keep the comment to myself, I considered saying: *Maybe you should check the label of your pain medication and see if "tendency to behave like a pretentious know-it-all" is a known side effect of the drug.*

"Granted, Sullivan, I should have been more careful handling the envelope and its contents. Till I opened it and saw the photographs, I'd assumed a client had just slipped an innocuous letter under my door when they happened to be downtown."

Sullivan was drumming his fingers on the arm of his chaise, lost in thought. "Knowing Laura, she probably hired the photographer and set up Toben for blackmail. He's been broadcasting his TV ads ever since I moved to the Denver area to start college—some twelve years ago— so we know that he was wealthy back whenever this liaison took place. Plus, he was married and in the public eye. My hunch is he paid big bucks to keep this away from his wife."

"Probably so."

Steve stared at me without comment.

"Are you okay?" I finally asked.

"Sure." He shifted his position but continued to study my features.

"Why are you staring at me?"

Again, he said nothing.

I rose. "I should go. I'll make copies for us and take these straight to the police . . . maybe see what Henry has to say for himself."

"Gilbert. You shouldn't mess with this. It's *my* problem. And somebody knows we're getting personally involved with the investigation. I'm sure of it." He tapped his cast. "That's how I wound up with a busted leg."

And how I discovered a knife embedded in the front door of my home. I hadn't told Sullivan about that yet. Now I'd missed my chance; he would just drive me nuts with his demands that I desert his quest to find Laura's killer, and there was no way I was willing to do that.

I said, "You know, Henry made a good point as we were leaving for the hospital. It makes sense that he was the intended target, not either of us."

"Yeah, unless *Henry* rigged the whole thing, sawing through the one stair himself."

"But what would he have to gain?"

"Maybe he knows we're poking around in the murder investigation, and he hoped to put one of us out of commission. You need to back off, Gilbert. Give those photos to the police and stay the hell away from Toben. Don't tell him about the pictures, whatever you do."

He was sure being fast and loose with the unsolicited advice all of a sudden, but, again, I decided not to bicker with him. "Right. Straight to the police." I headed to the door. "Take it easy, Sullivan. Let me know if there's anything I can do for you."

"Actually, there is." He gave me a sheepish grin as I turned back to face him. "You can stay and keep me company," he said softly.

I gaped at him in surprise. The painkillers must be talking; Sullivan would never suggest that I "keep him company" of his own volition. "I would, but I have a full workday ahead of me. I'm sorry."

He studied my features. "Not at Henry's house, though, right?"

"Is *that* why you said you want me to stay? Because you assume I'll run right over to Henry's place?"

He gave me a slight shrug.

"I'm not an idiot, you know. There's no need for

you to do a Neanderthal protect-the-little-lady number on me."

"Get real, Gilbert. Just how many Neanderthal men do you think pursue a career in interior design?"

I grinned. "Can't say as I know enough Neanderthals to say. For all we know, that could have been the root of those first cave drawings, as in: 'Dang it, Thor! Pay attention to your color wheel. Draw those woolly mammoths using reds and oranges, not cerulean blue! For God's sake, this is a *cave*! Warm the place up a bit!' "

"Right." Steve chuckled and gestured theatrically. " 'And that twig-and-sheepskin bed you bought positively *screams* Mesozoic! *All* the upscale, modern caves in town have switched to saber-tooth bedding! Get with the times!' "

I laughed, but had to look away when our eyes met. Even though John had obviously picked up on my signals that we needed to cool things for a while, *he* was the one I was dating, not Sullivan. To my horror, I felt my cheeks grow warm. Still avoiding Sullivan's intoxicating hazel eyes, I stated, "I'd better run." I waved the manila envelope. "I'll drop this off at the police station on my way." I opened the door.

"Gilbert, seriously, I . . ." He let his voice fade.

"Yes?"

"I appreciate your coming over."

"No problem, Sullivan. I'll give you a call tomorrow. Bye."

I let myself out, trotted to my van, and started the engine. Tomorrow I would have to break the news to Sullivan that I fully intended to complete Henry's install myself now. But I *wasn't* going to tell Sullivan that I also intended to confront Henry with photocopies of these pictures today, after giving the originals to the police. It was

not within my nature to sit back and wait. I was too enraged at the possibility that Henry had indeed jerry-rigged
his own stair.

I drove to the nearest copy shop, called Henry's cell
phone, and said that I had something important to show
him and was on my way. He'd taken a second day off from
work and was at his house.

Henry looked like a trapped white-coiffed rat as he studied the grainy photocopies. "Where did you get these?"

"Like I told you, someone anonymously slid them under my office door. I've already given the originals to the
police. And I told them I was coming here now to see
you." The last line was, of course, a fib to discourage
Henry from doing anything rash.

The muscles in his jaw were working. "I knew these
damn things would surface, sooner or later."

"Laura blackmailed you?"

"It would have destroyed my marriage . . . broken my
wife's heart. Not to mention that Laura was jailbait . . .
not even sixteen. She looked so much older, but then she
showed me her high school ID card. For ten thousand
dollars, she claimed I'd get the film, the only copies, and
never see her again." He snorted. "One out of three. I *did*
get the film."

Her high school ID was probably a fake, knowing
Laura. "Who was the photographer she was working
with?" I asked.

Henry gave me an angry shrug. "I never found out." He
thrust the photocopies back to me. "You can do whatever
you want with these. They can't hurt me now. My wife's
gone. If someone thought they were going to blackmail
me again over this past history, they're barkin' up the
wrong sassafras tree."

Henry was convincing. And I'd seen enough of his ads on TV to know the man couldn't act worth packaging peanuts. "Is this the first time you've seen the photos again in the years since Laura first blackmailed you?"

"Yeah. Good thing it was you showing them to me. Anybody else, I'd have ripped their head off. *You*, I gotta be nice to."

"Because your home isn't finished yet, you mean?"

He wiggled his eyebrows. "Because of the rain check I've got on the date with your landlady. I still need you to talk me up to her. She's a great ol' gal, that Audrey."

And wouldn't Audrey hate to be called a "great ol' gal." I grinned. "You should tell her that, Henry. Exactly like you just told me."

He did a double take. "If I didn't know better, I'd think you were deliberately giving me some bad advice."

I lifted my palms. "Dating advice is not my territory. But fortunately for you, you've got Robert Pembrook for that."

"True enough. So long as I don't discuss specifics with that fruitcake."

I bit back my ungenerous response.

I started for the door, photocopies in hand. "Have a good day, Henry."

"But . . . my house isn't finished yet. Like you said yourself. I don't know where to hang the pictures or put the pillows, or anything."

"I'll get to it as soon as I can. *After* you show me some proof that you've taken that ashtray to the folks at the Fish and Wildlife Service and filed a full report."

"How 'bout just the master bedroom, then?" He winked at me. "You never know, tonight might be the night Audrey says yes to the date, and I might get lucky."

"Actually, I *do* —" I managed to stop myself from saying that I *knew* that Audrey would never let him "get lucky" on a first date. Needing a tactful way to complete the sentence, I said, "—have a few minutes free before I have to go."

"Super. Everything's already in the room. Y'all just have to put together the final touches . . . to make my bedroom look all sexy, like you said you would."

"I said I would make it *romantic*, Henry. There's a difference."

He chuckled. "Yeah. To *women*, maybe. Anyway, I need to make sure my bedroom's ready for Hammerin' Hank, if you know what I mean."

"I'm trying to ignore the fact that I *do* know what you mean. You need more than an image change, Henry. You need an *attitude* change. Audrey Munroe is *way* out of your league." I clenched my teeth. I was never this sharp with customers. My nerves must be unraveling. Again, I started to head for the door.

"I was just kidding around," Henry exclaimed. "I really want to have my bedroom put together today, just so's I can start to feeling at home. I don't know where things should go, an' I don't want to louse up your pretty design any more than I already have."

The man was as close to sincere as he was capable of being. He'd already installed some of the rooms by himself, which was decidedly not what was normally demanded of my clients. I relented. "Okay, Henry. I'll take care of that now. I'll only have time for the master bedroom. Everything else will have to wait."

Almost all of the small, breakable items in Henry's bedroom were still in their packaging. The room install proceeded nicely, until I cut my finger on a sharp edge of a picture frame while I removed it from its box. I wrapped my finger in a tissue and continued to work, having to struggle to hang the damned picture without cutting my hand a second time.

Thirty minutes later, I began to feel hideously sick. My throat was burning, my head was pounding, and my vision swimming. I absolutely *had* to knock off for the day. I muttered a few words to Henry and left. I was practically staggering as I made my way to my van. To my utter surprise, Jerry Stone was sitting on the sidewalk in front of Henry's property.

"What are you doing here?" I asked.

"I followed your van." He rose and brushed off his filthy jeans.

"In *what*? Where's your car?"

"Near the main entrance to the neighborhood." He stared at my injured finger. "Were . . . you hanging pictures on the wall just now? Stuff like that?"

"Yes. Why?"

He kept his eye riveted to my finger. "Did you hurt yourself?"

"I scratched my finger on a picture frame. It's nothing."

He cursed under his breath.

"Look, Jerry, I'd love to talk to you, but I'm tired right now and—"

"Feel achy?" he interrupted. "Like you're coming down with the flu?"

"I s'pose."

"We've got to get you to the hospital."

"But . . . it's just a minor cut—"

"Come on." He grabbed me by the elbow and yanked the keys from my hand. "We've got to hurry. You're starting to slur your words."

Was I? I felt half-asleep on my feet.

He unlocked the passenger door. "Get in. I'm driving."

I had a hard time getting onto the seat, but managed.

As I fumbled with my seat belt, I saw that he was already behind the wheel. He started the engine. He looked tense, his thin lips set in a white line. "Jerry. Did you slip some photographs under my office door last night or early this morning?"

"Photographs? No. Wasn't me."

I didn't believe him. Barely able to keep my eyes open, I asked, "But you sabotaged the picture frame? Put poison on a jagged edge of the frame?"

"Only because I was following . . . my heart. Trying to stop you from destroying Mother Earth. Back when I put the stuff on it, I didn't even know you. We hadn't met. Don't take it personal."

I shut my eyes. "The poison . . . am I going to die?"

"There's an antidote. You'll be fine."

I nodded—and then nodded out. Next thing I knew, Jerry was half carrying, half dragging me through the front door of Crestview Hospital. I heard him say, "Just tell the doctors that . . ."

Maybe he said more, but I didn't hear him. He dropped me into a seat and set my purse on my lap. I was having a hard time staying awake. I nodded out again, and next thing I knew, he was fastening a sticky-pad sheet to the back of my hand. Just then a nurse was approaching, demanding to know what was going on.

"Nurse," Jerry said, "this woman needs help. Right away. She was babbling something about being poisoned."

My legs felt heavy, too heavy to move, and there was a strange taste in my mouth. Jerry whispered into my ear, "If I stay with you, they'll bust me. You'll be fine. I'll park your van near your home."

He turned, said something to the nurse, then bolted for the door just as I blacked out once more.

The next hours passed in a throbbing-headed, wavery blur. I was dimly aware that Audrey was there, and I was able to grasp that I "was out of danger" but that the doctors wanted to keep me hospitalized overnight for observation.

When I awoke the next morning, it felt as though I had been drinking shots of tequila all night and now had the world's worst hangover. I forced myself to sit up a little and looked around. This sterile, pea-green room was simply miserable. Surely they could make some effort to make the horrid place a bit less dreary. I spotted an elderly man skulking by the door, and at first thought he was visiting the patient in the bed next to me, a very old woman who was asleep most of the time. Then I got a look at his face just as he turned to leave.

"Jerry? What are you doing here?"

He gave me a sheepish smile. "If anyone asks, I'm your mother's uncle. Sam."

"Uncle Sam?"

He shrugged. "I'm your great-uncle Sam."

"What's with the stage makeup? You thought I gave your description out and you'd be arrested on the spot, didn't you?" Actually, I *had* done precisely that last night, but I didn't want to tell him so.

"I just wanted to apologize. And warn you to be careful. You've been getting in the way, Erin. Of all the wrong people."

"Why did you do this to me, Jerry? Why did you try to kill me?"

"*Sam*," he corrected. "I just . . . wanted to get your attention, not put you in the hospital. Or worse."

"Next time you want to get my attention, tap me on the shoulder. Don't slip me poison."

He hung his head and nodded.

"Thank you for saving my life, though. Even if you're the one who nearly killed me in the first place."

"That deed won't exactly earn me the keys to the city."

"It'll get you leniency from the judge, though." I sighed. "I gave your name to the police. If you killed Laura, you deserve whatever happens to you."

"I *didn't* kill her. I'd never kill *anyone*."

"But you know who did?"

He nodded and tamped the perspiration off his forehead. "Probably too late for me to run."

"Then go to the police. Tell them everything. They'll protect you."

He looked at the door. "I've got to get out now, while I still can."

"You're going home to Detroit?" I asked, pulling a location out of the air in an attempt to trip him up.

"Yeah. Maybe."

"You never said you were actually *from* Detroit, Jerry."

"Didn't I? I can't remember. I say a lot of things. Too many things to keep track of . . . get my stories all messed up that way." He released a sad chuckle and shook his head. "You'd have figured I'd have learned more about how to pull off cons from Laura than I did."

"Were the two of you partners?"

He let out a guffaw. "Me? Partners with *Laura*? No chance in hell."

"Who have you been conning? Is this whole bit about your being homeless a lie, just like it was about your not having a car?"

"No, Erin. I *live* in my car. Have for the past couple of months. And I really do want Americans to get a better grip on what's important in life. I just made a huge mistake in saying yes to something that looked too good to be true. Be real careful of who you agree to work for, Erin. You're making the same mistake I did. Believe me."

"Who are you talking about? Henry Toben?"

He started to leave, and I pushed the button for the nurse, calling to Jerry, "Wait. You *did* put those photographs under my door, didn't you? Are you working for someone as a private investigator?"

"You've been warned, Erin. If I say another word, it'll probably be my last."

"*Who* are you trying to warn me about?"

He gave no answer.

Audrey was insufferable after she picked me up from the hospital and brought me home. By midday, word had spread through the Crestview rumor mill that I'd been hospitalized for poisoning, but Audrey was a regular pit bull of a watchdog, refusing to let anyone visit. She ruthlessly screened my calls—keeping the cordless phone in the pocket of her caftan and answering the instant it rang. She tried to deny both John and Steve phone access to me. Her plan was foiled when I happened to come downstairs for some tea and was standing right next to her as she answered the phone and told the caller that I was "still asleep." She then tried to draw me into a discussion about table linens, but finally—when I threatened to move out—admitted the caller was John and that she'd done the same thing to Steve half an hour before. Her entire defense for her actions was to point at the sheet of paper on the refrigerator and cry, "But they're on the list!"

Livid with Audrey, I snatched the phone away from her and returned their calls—John first and then Sullivan— and both times regretted it. John was unable to focus on the fact that I was perfectly fine now, instead pointing out that I shouldn't have taken the risk of working alone at a house that I'd already known to be booby-trapped. I made some remark about his point being well taken, but that it was too late to get the proverbial spilled milk back into the carton.

By the time Sullivan started harping on the exact same point, I shouted at him, "Enough already! It was stupid of me. I realize that! And as helpful and healing as it is to have you insult me and yell at me, I promised Audrey that I'd spend the day resting in bed. So goodbye!" I hung up on him, but the problem with cordless phones is that they can't be slammed down. Although I pressed the off button with extra force, it just wasn't as satisfying.

The next morning, something felt wrong as I unlocked the door to my office building and stepped inside the small area in front of the stairs. An instant later, I realized that the feeling was caused by the very air I was breathing; the place didn't smell quite right.

"Hello?" I asked cautiously, my heart pounding. "Is anybody here?"

Silence. I could hear only the pounding of my own heart. The door had been locked. I had to be hallucinating about the foul odor, and yet even as I told myself that it must be my imagination, the scent grew stronger as I started to ascend the stairs.

I spotted the back of a man's head first, and for a moment felt a measure of relief when I recognized Jerry Stone. No doubt he had been breaking into my office and sleeping here at night. "Jerry?"

No answer. He was seated in my beloved Sheraton chair—the one with my mother's cross-stitching.

"Jerry?"

Frightened, I rounded the chair to look at his face. He was slumped slightly, his legs at an unnatural-looking angle. I sent up a quick prayer that he was merely asleep. Then I saw the blood.

He'd been stabbed in the chest. The black-handled knife looked like the twin of the one that had been jammed into Audrey's door.

Chapter 18

Anything else you can tell me that can maybe help us find the killer?"

Linda Delgardio's eyes were full of concern. We were seated on the bottom step of the flight of stairs that led up to my office. We had to rise to get out of the path of one of a myriad of investigators or coroner's office personnel, but I'd insisted on staying on the staircase because the macabre scene was out of sight, and yet I hadn't allowed myself to be driven out of my office entirely. My emotions were in a complete jumble: I felt like throwing a furious tantrum and simultaneously curling into the fetal position in a corner.

Linda continued, "You said that you detected some cigarette smoke as you climbed the stairs?"

"The odor was so subtle, I'm not sure anyone actually lit up in my office. It could just have been the odor from Jerry's clothing. He was such a heavy smoker that he always reeked." I paused, thinking. "And yet he *wasn't* smoking that time he was waiting outside Paprika's for Hannah Garrison . . . even though he was waiting outside in the cold. He lived in his car, apparently, so it's not like he had a lot of disposable cash. He must've been out of cigarettes at the time." My mind seemed to be wandering of its own volition.

"He had a lot of money in his wallet."

"Really?"

"A thousand dollars. All in newly issued fifties."

"Huh. He told me he was going to skip town. He probably pawned something to get the cash he needed." *Or he'd recently gotten paid for services rendered as a private investigator.* "There wasn't much blood. I was thinking that his body had to have been moved here afterward. Which had to have taken place late last night, when Chestnut Street is relatively deserted."

"You'd think so," Linda replied.

I studied her placid features, but there was little point in asking her outright if Jerry had been killed elsewhere or here; she would not divulge key information and possibly had already stretched the rules by telling me about the money in his wallet. She'd already made a huge concession by coming to my office when she was off duty. She'd warned me that she could take only a peripheral role in this investigation, because of our friendship.

The Powers That Be considered me a murder suspect now.

"As far as I know, the only smoker besides Jerry who's in

any way connected with both me and Laura Smith is Henry Toben," I told Linda. "But Dave Holland might smoke, too. That information came from Laura, who lied to me about everything."

Linda made no reply.

I sighed. "I wonder if it was just a coincidence that his body was in my favorite chair in the whole world . . . if the person who did this could have known how much sentimental value my chair has. My mother and I refinished it together."

"Who else knows about the chair's significance?"

Steve Sullivan. John Norton. With feigned nonchalance, I answered, "No one who would have done this. I'm being paranoid, come to think of it. That was just the closest chair to the entrance."

Linda raised an eyebrow. "Okay, but who knows about the chair who *wouldn't* have done this?"

I frowned, but then buried Steve's and John's names within a list of a half dozen friends who'd never as much as met Laura Smith.

Linda shut her notepad, implying that this was the end of the interview. I was about to rise, and barely managed to stifle a groan, when Detective O'Reilly arrived, our eyes locking before he'd even opened my glass door. *There have to be dozens of detectives in Crestview, and he has to be the one on call today?* When a client's murder had shaken me to the core last winter, his cruel accusations had nearly been the final straw. Physically, he was a nondescript—beige—man: average height and weight, fortyish, brown hair, mustache, not handsome but not ugly. He always seemed to wear cheap and ill-fitting clothes on the job, and today was no exception. He had on a five-dollar black, red, and white diagonal-striped tie to augment his brown gabardine suit.

"Ms. Gilbert," he growled. "We meet again." He shifted his gaze to Linda and raised an eyebrow. "Del? Aren't you on swing shift?"

"We're friends," I interjected. "I was badly shaken and called her at home after dialing nine-one-one."

He narrowed his eyes at me. "Oh, really."

I gritted my teeth. Linda had once confided to me that Detective O'Reilly's nickname at the department was "Oh, really!?" because he interrogated all witnesses with such hostile incredulity. He was probably good at his job, but his methods were miserable to endure when on the receiving end of one of his interrogations.

Long after Linda had gone, O'Reilly voiced his final snide remark to me and allowed me to leave as well. My workday was in shambles with missed appointments, but my head was reeling. I drove away without calling a single customer and with no clear destination in mind.

There had to be a link—a single connection that could make sense of this madness. My instincts warned that all of the hideous events of the past week were related, but it felt as though I were color-blind and incapable of seeing the pattern in the fabric right in front of my eyes.

One possible link did occur to me—Dave Holland had, at the very least, set the fire at the storage facility. By the sounds of our last conversation, Jerry had apparently been working as a private investigator and could have been hired by a victim of one of Laura's scams. Dave Holland fit that bill. Dave could have hired Jerry not only to trail Laura but to harass his ex-wife, Hannah, at the same time. Then, in a jealous rage, he could have killed Laura and then murdered Jerry to cover his crime.

Even while I inwardly screamed at myself not to do this—to instead drive straight home and cuddle up with Hildi on my favorite sofa, under my angora afghan—I turned south, toward Dave's office.

Dave Holland's business offices occupied the top floor in a building on the southwest city boundary of Crestview. The three-story concrete structure—the double arches of its façade on all four sides forming what looked like enormous lowercase *m*'s—was painted a dusty rose, which, over time, had deteriorated into *dirty* rose. I walked past the badly smudged stainless-steel doors of the elevator in favor of the stairs, to give myself an extra minute to sift through my thoughts.

I'd visited Dave's office only once before, when meeting Laura and him midway through their job. That had only been three months ago, yet it felt as though everything had changed so drastically in that length of time that I'd acquired a decade's worth of wisdom and cynicism about the human condition. Laura had proven to be nothing like the person I'd believed her to be. Now she was dead, perhaps at the hand of Dave Holland.

There was one big problem with my theory, however; I just couldn't believe Dave was capable of murder. The man *was* an enigma, though. His ex-wife insisted he was this lamblike man, and that had been my overall impression. Yet he'd been livid and confrontational toward Steve Sullivan both times the two men had spoken, so much so that it was easy to see why Steve had once believed Laura's story that Dave had beaten her.

I exited the stairwell on the third floor. Visually, this space overemphasized bold, geometric lines—a bad

Frank Lloyd Wright imitation. The furniture had obviously been selected to give visitors the impression that this company was modern and edgy, but to me, all it said was: George Jetson. When Dave left his gorgeous eighteenth- and nineteenth-century furnishings to come to work here each day, it must have felt as though he'd stepped into a time machine.

Dave's personal secretary, an attractive African American, took my name and asked if I had an appointment. "No," I replied, so emotionally drained that my sarcasm kicked in and I continued, "but does it count in my favor at all that I wish I did?"

She stared at me blankly.

I sighed. "I have some business of a personal nature to discuss with Mr. Holland. A mutual acquaintance of ours has died recently."

"You don't mean Laura Smith, do you? He already knows about her."

"Right, but I don't mean Laura. This is someone else."

"Oh, dear. *Another* person Dave knows has died?"

"I'm afraid so."

"That's terrible! He's had such a rough go of it lately."

"Yes, we both have. Laura Smith and I were friends." Or at least she'd given me an excellent forgery of a friendship.

The woman nodded. "Let me see if he's available. Why don't you take a seat?"

I thanked her and tried to get comfortable in an oversized, padded eggcup centered along one wall. A minute or two later, Dave emerged and said in a somber voice, "Erin. Come on in." We exchanged a few words of meaningless chatter as he closed the door behind us. With his dirty-looking dark hair in need of a trim, his thick glasses, rumpled white shirt, and gray corduroys, he looked the very definition of a computer nerd; his shirt was even buttoned wrong.

His office was enormous, each corner of the room containing large, short-legged tables with pillows on the floor. Unusual that someone more than six feet tall would opt for so much floor seating, but my hunch was that he had a lot of Asian associates. Those low tables, along with virtually every horizontal surface, were blanketed with cyan-blue ink drawings of electronic circuits. Dave's imposing ebony desk was centered in the room. His view of the Front Range through the plate-glass window on the west wall was marred by a hideous parking structure directly across the street.

He took a seat in the enormous leather office chair behind his desk, and I sat down in the nearest of two smaller, but otherwise identical, chairs across from him. His black eye was mostly back to a healthy color; now it looked as though he might be wearing a bit of mustard-colored eye shadow. "What brings you here, Erin?"

"I had a horrible ordeal this morning. Someone I met recently was murdered in my office."

He reseated his glasses on his nose. "Jeez. That sucks. Another murder? What the hell's going on in this town?"

"This death was related to Laura's."

"It was? How do you know?"

"They'd had an altercation at Paprika's. The night before Laura died."

"What do you mean?"

"He'd followed the two of us from Rusty's to the store for a presentation Audrey Munroe was giving. They argued, and Laura wound up flipping him onto the floor."

Dave sprang to his feet, glaring at me, his face instantly so red that I half expected his eyeglasses to steam up. "And you didn't *tell* me this? Christ! Maybe *he* killed her!"

"I told the police at the time. Meanwhile, *you* nearly ran me down, fleeing the scene the night of Laura's murder."

He shook his head adamantly. "That was my brother, not me. I told you that already, at Laura's funeral. I went through this whole story with the police." He pointed with his chin at the door, as if signaling for me to leave. "I'm not going to go back over it with my interior designer." He dropped heavily back into his chair.

"Even if your brother was behind the wheel, it was *your* car." I leaned forward to capture his gaze. "Dave, my life has become enmeshed in all of this. I need to know if what I told you about the antiques being swapped with reproductions led directly to murder. Maybe then I can figure out if there's something I can do to protect myself and my friends."

He balled his fists on top of his desk. "All I know is, *I* didn't do it."

"Meaning you didn't kill anyone, right? But you set fire to the unit, didn't you? You were angry because you realized she had ripped you off, probably for the second time, and you found out where she'd been hiding all the stuff she'd stolen from you, so you set fire to it."

"My brother, not me, was going to monitor the blaze, make sure no one else's stuff got damaged. . . . I just wanted *him* to do a small enough fire that the antiques would get ruined. I didn't want the warehouse to go up in flames."

"And you hired Jerry Stone to track down Laura?"

"Who?"

"The private investigator. That's the name of the man who was murdered this morning."

Dave rotated his seat a quarter of the way around so

that he could stare out the window. He said nothing at all for so long that I worried he wasn't going to say another word to me. Finally, he muttered, "I didn't use an investigator . . . didn't need one. I came home from the bogus errand she'd sent me on and caught her packing. She clobbered me. Said if I followed her, she'd put the car in reverse and bump us both off the road. After you told me about the furniture, I found the bill for her cell phone, called the numbers. Didn't take an Einstein to put a call to U-Store together with a house full of missing furniture. I got the unit number from the manager . . . told him she was my wife and that it was my stuff and that I'd sue his ass if he didn't tell me where her unit was."

"So it *was* you, not your brother."

He snorted. "I'll deny it if I'm forced to repeat it in court or to an officer. I was practically insane with anger and started the fire, even though I was the one who'd bought and paid for those antiques. But I didn't know she was there until I found . . . until I nearly tripped over her." His words became more forceful as he grimaced and continued, now looking straight into my eyes, "It was such a shock, finding her there like that. I've never been so scared in my life. I knew I'd look guilty as hell. There she was, dead on the floor . . . and there *I* was, burning the place down. Shit! I figured the killer might still be around and would kill me, too. I panicked. So I left as fast as I could."

"You nearly ran me down in the process."

He scoffed, "I could have driven through a stampede, for all I know. I just wanted to get the hell out of there and pretend none of it ever happened."

"The killer's made a couple of threats on my life, Dave. A knife was stabbed into my door. And I got poison injected into me from a jerry-rigged picture frame."

Even though he'd poisoned me himself, Jerry Stone had

saved my life by getting me to the hospital. Now he was dead.

"I don't know anything about that, Erin. You can ask anyone. I'm just your basic Joe Schmoe. I would never hurt anyone."

The receptionist knocked, then cracked open Dave's door. Her expression revealing deep concern, she said, "There's a detective here to see you. He says it's urgent."

Damn. If it was O'Reilly, he was going to be furious with me for butting in.

The receptionist shifted her gaze to me. "Sorry to—"

"I was just leaving," I said, heading toward her. "Thanks for your time, Dave."

There was no escape; Detective O'Reilly was standing right outside Dave's door. His eyes bored holes into me as I strolled past. "We meet yet again, Miss Gilbert."

"Yes. Like two carrot peels going down the same drain." I trotted down the stairs, got into my van, and started the engine. I believed Dave, at least as much as my newfound skepticism would allow me.

Not two minutes into my drive, a news announcer spouted from my radio: "*A man's body was discovered in a downtown Crestview office this morning.*" Too agitated to drive, I immediately signaled and pulled over as the reporter continued, "*The business owner, Erin Gilbert, an interior decorator, made the gruesome discovery this morning when she climbed the stairs to her office. Crestview police are not releasing any names or details at this time, but have said that the death was a probable homicide. . . .*"

I smacked the steering wheel with the heel of my hand, cursing under my breath. Nobody would want to drop in on a designer whose recent visitor was murdered at her office. At the same time, my thoughts made me feel all the worse, at how egocentric it was of me to consider my own, relatively petty, issues when two people had been brutally murdered.

For reasons I didn't feel like examining closely, I drove straight to Steve's house. I parked at the foot of his driveway, headed up the slate walkway, and used his door knocker. A few moments later, he opened the door. One look at his face told me he'd heard the news. It was probably fortunate, in a way, that Sullivan had a broken leg. Otherwise I might have given in to my temptation to do something really stupid, like throw myself into his arms, which would, of course, have been a disaster.

Leaning heavily on a cane, he hobbled aside to let me pass. "I was listening to my radio just now, Erin. Who was it? Did you know him?"

"Jerry Stone." *What am I doing here? I should have driven to John's office instead.*

Sullivan said sadly, "The guy Laura had the altercation with. I knew this would happen. You're a target. That's why I . . . We've got to get you out of this. Maybe you should go away for a few days—"

"I don't want to. Not unless I have no choice. That's what the killer wants me to do. I can't run forever, and I if I'm truly a target, I won't be safe anywhere till the killer's under arrest. I'm better off helping to find out who it is, while the police are at least still keeping an eye on me." I tried to collect my nerves. "We were right about Dave, by the way. He admitted to me in private that he set the fire, but says he discovered Laura's body, panicked, and ran."

Sullivan limped across the room and eased himself onto his chaise. "I never should have dragged you into this mess."

I remained standing near the door. "You *didn't*. I made my own choices."

"Still."

I sighed, thinking: *In for a penny, in for a pound.* I sat down in the Windsor chair, as distant a seat from Sullivan's as was available. "I'm pretty sure it was Jerry Stone who slipped the photographs under my office door. That he was working as a private investigator for someone he came to believe was the killer. He slipped me those photographs to help me along."

"You're thinking he gave you the photos because he had a guilty conscience?"

"Essentially. He admitted he tried to poison me by rigging the picture frame, and no doubt the stairs. He could have had an attack of conscience. Maybe Henry Toben or Robert Pembrook . . . or George Wong . . . one of them was behind this and knew that Jerry had become a weak link, so he killed him."

Steve said slowly, "Henry paid Laura off once, years ago, to save his marriage. He hated her, but . . . bad enough to kill twice?"

"The embarrassing photographs could have been just the tip of the iceberg, Steve. Maybe she was currently blackmailing him for something incriminating that would wreck his life." I glanced at my watch and grabbed my cell phone. "Linda's back on shift by now. I want to run all this past her." *And then call John to tell him what's happened.* I'd left my boyfriend in the dark too many times already.

Linda came to Steve's house, arriving less than an hour after I'd called her. After I finished telling her my theory, she looked at me with weary eyes. "All very interesting, Erin. Thanks. Now, do me a favor. Go home and stay there. For the next few days, at least. Let things cool off for you, and let *us* do our job."

"I can't just stay home and not work, Linda. That's one

of the problems with owning a one-woman business—no paychecks during days off."

"Listen to me, Erin. I'm warning you, not as a cop, but as a friend. Whether the killer is Henry Toben or someone else, the person's vicious. And on the loose."

Chapter 19

I had called John's work number shortly after calling Linda, but he wasn't in, and he called me back on my cell phone just as Linda was leaving Sullivan's place. "I just got your message," he said, sounding slightly out of breath. "I found someone to cover for me and left, but you're not at your house."

"I'm at Sullivan's."

"Office?"

"House."

"Tell him to come over, too," Steve said.

"Why don't you come here? Steve said to invite you."

His voice testy, John said, "I don't want to be a third wheel."

Through a tight jaw, I said, "The *police* have just left. Sullivan and I are kind of focused right now on anything we might have missed that could help *get the murderer arrested*, if you get my drift." I added in silence: *Enough with the jealousy, already!*

"Okay. I'll be there in fifteen or so." He hung up.

Guilt was shading my mood darker by the moment. John had already told me he was jealous of my relationship with Sullivan. If John's and my situations were the exact reverse, I wouldn't like this any better than he did.

"He'll be here in a few minutes," I said to Steve, slipping my phone back into my purse and reclaiming my seat on the Windsor chair on the far side of the room from him.

It's so much easier to fix a home's interior than one's own interior, I mused as I scanned my surroundings. This one-bedroom bungalow in the foothills of the Rockies was a mouthwatering space. Sullivan's architectural elements were extraordinary—a wraparound deck, vaulted ceilings, a picture window with a fabulous view, oak floors. "Your walls are still bare. Haven't you been painting lately?"

"You mean *wall* paint?"

"No, oils. You once told me that was your major hobby."

"It was, but I got a good price on my art supplies . . . so I sold them, too. I've gotten to like the place this way. Easy maintenance. Hardly anything to collect dust. Plus, it comes in handy when you're trying to get around in a leg cast . . . less stuff to bump into." He gave me a darting glance. "You know, Gilbert, when I found out about the sabotaged picture frame, it hit me that we're not doing a good job at keeping each other informed. We need to compare notes."

"Okay," I muttered, thinking he wasn't going to be

happy to hear for the first time about the knife in Audrey's front door. "You go first."

"I've been slowed down a bit"—he tapped his leg cast—"but I made some calls to Chicago and South Bend, and I found out that everything Pembrook says is legit. He was a head honcho for a retail clothing company at one point, but served eighteen months at a low-security prison for a cooking-the-books conviction. Also, Laura's birth name was Montgomery, like he said, and it *was* a murder-suicide that took her parents' and younger brother's life."

I nodded. "I verified that, too. I talked to the Smiths at the reception. Her adoptive father thinks *you're* guilty, by the way."

He grimaced. "I know. I spoke to him, too, after the service. It's no easy feat to find 'Mr. and Mrs. Smith' in a hotel, but we finally hooked up. Didn't do much good. He still thinks I did it. Cleared *my* conscience a little, though. I shouldn't have taken off like that from the service. I'd intended to do what I'd said . . . sit in the back . . . but I just couldn't take it all of a sudden. Anyway. I also checked into Hammerin' Hank's background, but didn't uncover anything we don't already know. He's your basic sleazeball womanizer, who married a nice, sweet woman he unfortunately outlived." He gestured at me. "That's it for me. Your turn."

He certainly hadn't gotten any earth-shattering revelations. Neither had I, but I seemed to have had more personal contact with the people in Laura's life. "Um, did I tell you about George Wong visiting my house the day after I spoke to him at his workshop?"

Sullivan peered at me. "No," he said, dragging out the word. "Nor that you went to his workshop."

"He was angry that I'd given his name to the police, and he told me to mind my own business. Then, after that, there was a knife stabbed into the front door at home."

Sullivan paled and sat up straight. "Wait. You mean, Wong got so mad at you, he stabbed a knife into your door?"

"It was an . . . anonymous door stabbing. I found the knife there when I got back from Laura's service on Saturday. It had a black wooden handle, just like the murder weapon used on Jerry Stone."

Sullivan uttered a very colorful four-letter word. "You're going to get yourself killed, Erin. And it's going to be my fault."

"No, I'm not, and nothing that happens to me is *your* fault. I'm in charge of making my own decisions and dealing with the consequences."

He shook his head. "You wouldn't be forced to make these kinds of decisions if I hadn't dragged you into my screwed-up life in the first place."

I said firmly, "For one thing, you *didn't* drag me, and for another, your life's no more screwed up than anyone else's."

But Sullivan wasn't listening. He grumbled, "If it hadn't been for the damned broken leg . . . Shit! I knew this was going to happen! I tried to get you uninvolved clear back when I found that ashtray in Toben's storage unit. I *knew* you'd flip out. But then I fell, and now—"

"You already knew about the gorilla's paw?"

"They delivered it Saturday afternoon, right before Laura's service, along with the exchanges. That's part of why I was so . . . weirded out at the time. I had to sign for the ashtray. How *else* did you think it wound up in the delivery truck?"

Stunned, I stammered, "I . . . couldn't figure that out at the time, then I forgot all about it." I searched his flushed features. "*That's* why you made the crack about

sewing the paw back on the gorilla's leg? You were trying
to get rid of me?"

He clenched his teeth. "I didn't want you to get hurt,
Gilbert. This is *my* mess, damn it all, not yours."

Someone knocked, and Steve hollered, "Come on in,
Norton," without leaving his seat.

I was still too shocked by Sullivan's latest revelation to
assess my feelings. Numb, I automatically rose and started
toward the door as John opened it. He pulled me into a
hug and whispered into my ear, "I'm so sorry you're going
through all of this."

"Thanks. It's been a messy couple of weeks, I've got to
admit." *And getting messier by the minute.*

With his arms still around me, John muttered, "Hey,"
in Steve's direction, then said to me, "This is insane. It's
too dangerous for you to stay here, Erin. Let me take you
away for a few days."

"I already suggested that," Steve interjected, "but she
said no."

"Did you?" He was looking at Steve over my shoulder,
and though John didn't push me away, every muscle in his
body grew tense. "You suggested that she go away with
me? Or with *you*?"

"Give me a break," Steve retorted in a smoldering
voice as I pulled away from John.

"Hey. No problem, dude. You want me to take out your
other leg?"

"Stop this right now!" I scolded. "Both of you!" I knew
I was sounding like their mother, but then, *they* were acting like children.

Steve held up his palms as he looked at me.
"Hey, Gilbert, this is all due to loverboy's ego trip. Don't
blame me."

"Like hell!" John grumbled.

I turned to him and said, "Of *course* Steve didn't ask

me to leave town with him, John! Sullivan and I are just friends!"

"And barely even that," Sullivan added.

That stung. I'd made similar comments, but this wasn't the time for sarcasm or rudeness. John, apparently, begged to differ, for he taunted, "Steve Sullivan always gets the girl. It's carved in stone someplace."

"What the hell *is* this, Norton? Sour grapes? Almost two years after the fact?"

"There you go again. You don't seem to have learned a damned thing from what happened between you and Laura."

"What exactly was I supposed to have *learned*? You two were past history. She was already with Dave Holland, for Christ's sake!"

John ticked off on his fingers. "She wasn't available, she was my ex, and the three of us still traveled in the same crowd! You broke the code by chasing after her."

"What code? And, anyway, what's it to you now? You're lucky you got away when you did. That woman destroyed me! *And* Holland."

"Maybe you deserved it. Bad karma."

"Come on, guys." I tried to step between them. Sullivan was now sitting up on the chaise, gripping his cane in both hands as though it were a baseball bat. "This isn't—"

"I deserved it for falling for the same woman as *you*, you mean?" Sullivan retorted, speaking straight through me as if I were invisible. "Did you kill her?"

"Jesus, Sullivan! Of course not! If you'd get your brain back in your skull where it belongs, you'd realize that!"

"You hated Laura for dumping you, didn't you?" Steve said, rising. "Why *else* would you be bringing it up, after all this time!"

"*You're* the one who hated her, not me! I'm starting to

think *you* killed her and are trying to get me to take the rap!"

I hollered at the top of my lungs, "Stop it! Now! Both of you!"

They gaped at me, dumbfounded.

"I discovered a *murdered* man today! I'm not going to stay here and listen to you two shout horrible accusations at each other!"

I stormed out of the house and marched to my van. While fumbling for my car keys, I hesitated. *Wait a minute!* Sullivan wasn't so callous as to say that we were "barely even friends" unless he intentionally wanted to hurt me. I whirled around. Sullivan had just done it again; he'd duped me into walking out on him. The man had manipulated me twice.

John followed me. "Erin, wait. We need to talk."

Sullivan had staged his part of their confrontation. But what was John's excuse? He *was the one who'd actually cast the first stone.* Unwilling to look at him, I growled, "Now's not a good time, John. Call me tonight, after I've had some time to cool down, if you want."

"Steve's just pissed about his life getting so out of control. He was just lashing out at me, you know. He knows I didn't kill anyone, for God's sake."

I looked at John's handsome face, realizing that I didn't know the man at all. He went on, "I said some stupid things just now that I didn't mean. Truth is, it bugs me that he's always the first one you turn to, rather than me. The bottom line is, Laura meant nothing to me."

"*That's* your 'bottom line'? Is it supposed to make me feel better about you? Laura meant nothing to you, so I'm supposed to be impressed?"

He sighed. "No, Erin. That just . . . came out all wrong. I don't even know what I'm saying. I care about you . . . a lot. I don't want you to leave like this." He tried to give me a sheepish smile and said gently, "Come on, Erin." He grabbed my hand. "Let's get a fresh start on things, okay? We've got a good thing going."

I yanked my hand free from his. "No, we don't, John. We almost did . . . if none of this had happened with Laura. But I just don't think we can bounce back. I'm sorry, but I think we need to end things."

"You're breaking up with me?"

"Yes."

His face went slack, from shock to anger, then he pivoted and started to walk away—to my surprise and confusion, heading back toward Sullivan's house. "Fine. I'll . . . see you around."

"I really *am* sorry, John."

"Me too."

"If you're going back inside, please give Sullivan a message. Tell him he's fired."

I got into my car and drove away, too numbed by the day's events to cry, too confused and disgusted by Sullivan's manipulations and his shouting match with John to feel much sense of loss.

After a full hour at home by myself, Audrey still hadn't arrived, and I waited impatiently for her. I'd decided to vent by throwing myself into a home-improvement project. There was nothing I could do about the ever-present wall-to-wall furniture in the parlor, so I'd gone straight to my notebook computer and had scoured the Internet sites till I found the perfect armchairs for Audrey's old-world Italian den. Though I'd shown Hildi the chairs on my screen, the experience hadn't been fulfilling for either of us.

The doorbell rang. I checked the sidelight. *Sullivan*. I

threw open the door, ready and eager to go on the offensive. "I'm really not in the mood to—"

"Whoa." He held up his palm. "I need a woman's perspective on something, Gilbert. I just want to ask you one question, then I'll go. Promise. Okay?"

I sighed. "Go ahead."

"How long should a guy wait before he apologizes to a woman for acting like a total ass?"

I looked at him in surprise.

"I mean, I gotta figure I'm the last person you want to see right about now, but then, the longer I wait, the more opportunity there is for you to think about what a jerk I am. So, tell me . . . what's your advice here?"

"First off, I'd need to know *which* asinine behavior you're referring to. When you were deliberately egging John into fighting with you? When you were pretending not to care about Henry's buying goods from poachers? Either way, I don't need or want you to shove me out of the way and take the bullet for me, Sullivan. And, besides, don't you think you owe *John* the bigger apology? *He's* the one you wound up accusing of murder, for crying out loud!"

"Ah, I already took care of that last part. He came back inside after you took off. We'd both let some things explode in us, but in another month or two, we'll go grab a beer and shoot some pool, and it'll be fine. But . . . what about you?"

I crossed my arms and quipped, "You mean, do *I* want to grab a beer and shoot some pool?"

"*Do* you?"

I tried not to look at him, and fought back a smile. My resolve was already breaking. Did the man *have* to be so freaking gorgeous? "Actually, that doesn't sound half bad. But I'd rather wait till you've got two good legs, so you can't blame your defeat on a measly broken bone."

"Does this mean you're accepting my apology?"

"*What* apology? You haven't actually said you're sorry yet. Or even that you'll quit treating me like your weak little underling who needs your protection."

"True." He gave me a cheerful shrug. "Ah, well. That'll give you something to look forward to in the future." He turned and started to limp back down the walkway toward his car.

"So that's *it*? You're leaving?"

He paused, then turned back. "I *said* I just wanted to ask you a question."

"You're incredibly annoying, Sullivan!"

He grinned at me.

"You know, sooner or later you're going to have to accept that Laura was what she was. *She* determined her own fate. She cheated and stole from the men she duped into becoming her lovers. You've got to get past it . . . quit letting it louse up your life."

His smile faded completely, and just as quickly, I felt like a heel for kicking a man with a broken leg. "That's exactly what I *am* doing, Gilbert. But right now, I need justice. I need to know that her killer is going to rot in jail."

Chagrined, I replied, "I understand how you feel. I'm sorry I carped at you."

He snorted. "Okay. Then we're even. And I accept *your* apology."

I groaned in exasperation and started to shut the door, saying, "Go home, Sullivan."

"Sure, but I'll see you tomorrow afternoon. We've got a meeting with Pembrook and Toben at Toben's house."

At that, I swung the door fully open again. "No! *We* don't. *I* do." Although it would be safest if *neither* of us went, I needed to get Robert to sign off on the work, or I wouldn't get paid. "This is *my* project. You wouldn't even accept payment, and all you've got to show for it is a broken leg!"

"Whatever. I'm still *your* assistant on Toben's job."

"No, you're not. You were fired. Didn't you get my message?"

He turned toward his van and said over his shoulder, "I called Toben a few minutes ago. He told me he finished installing the interiors himself . . . that he even replaced the booby-trapped picture frame that the police confiscated. All that's left to do is to get Pembrook to sign off on everything."

"Even so, you're *not* coming with me."

"Yeah, I am. See you tomorrow." Limping, he rounded his van and got in, giving me a mocking wave in the process.

The next afternoon, I drove to Henry's home. Sullivan sat in the passenger seat. After all, there was safety in numbers, and my decision soon seemed prudent: a spring-green VW Beetle was parked in Henry's driveway.

"Oh, my God. George Wong's here!" I cried as I parked behind the Bug.

"How would *they* know each other?"

"Other than via a nefarious connection?" I asked rhetorically, opening my door. "Henry's expecting us, so he obviously isn't trying to hide the relationship. That's got to be a good sign."

"Maybe. In any case, it'll be interesting to hear their explanation," Steve replied as he got out, already sounding a bit out of breath, as he had to balance his weight awkwardly on his good leg to rise and shut the door behind him.

Predictably, he became grouchy when I tried to carry his briefcase for him. Interior designer or not, the man truly was insufferably macho. We reached the front door, and I pushed the doorbell and could hear the regal gong inside. My prediction was that Henry would soon swap that classy bell with one that sounded like a trumpeting elephant. Or screaming monkeys.

Henry's eyes widened as he threw open the carved hardwood door. "Hi, Erin. Steve. I . . . forgot you were coming, or I'd have told you sooner: there's no need for you to come out. I love what you've done with the house, so thanks. It's been a pleasure."

"I'm glad you're pleased, Henry, but I have to get Robert to sign off on my work. It's in our contract. If all goes well, we can be out of here in five minutes."

"Oh, jeez. That's right. Pembrook's coming, too." He glanced behind him. "I guess there's nothing to do, then, but have you come in. I'm in the middle of an important business meeting right now, and I—"

"Miss Gilbert," came a voice from deeper inside the house. George Wong stepped behind Henry, towering over the stocky little man. "Good afternoon." He patted Henry on the shoulder and said, "Why not let Miss Gilbert and her companion join our discussion? I would like to hear her opinion of our business venture."

Henry hesitated for just a moment, then muttered, "Come on in," and ushered us inside.

The reason for Henry's reluctance to invite us into his home was instantly apparent. He'd made the living room—the first room visitors entered after the foyer—into the safari room that Sullivan had envisioned for the den in a *back* room. The décor was every bit as ghastly as I'd expected it to be. The sectional sofa was blood red, a perfect counterpoint to the leopard-skin ottoman and the zebra hide splatted spread-eagle on the wall behind the sofa.

As though his speaking louder could somehow deprive

me of my eyesight, Henry said in a near shout, "Mr. Wong here told me about how you know him through his furniture-manufacturing company." He gestured at Steve. "This is Steve Sullivan, Erin's right-hand man. Which is better than being her right-*leg* man, now that it's broken."

No one joined him in laughter at his joke . . . though I did smile a little at my own silent pun in thinking how *lame* it had been.

"How did your accident happen?" Wong asked.

"A stair to the storage space above the garage had been sabotaged," Sullivan explained as he sat.

"You broke your leg in Mr. Toben's house?" Wong was all innocence, but I, for one, was permanently leery in the huge man's presence.

"I'm afraid so." Although Sullivan was far too good at exuding charm to make this obvious to anyone else in the room, I could tell that he didn't like George Wong one bit.

"I shall remember to take great care when climbing your steps," George said to Henry with a wink.

Still feeling immensely ill at ease, I took a seat near Steve on the garish red sectional and asked, "What's this business venture you mentioned?"

"Ah, yes. That should be of some interest to you both. Henry and I are going to invest in the home-design retail business. We hope to start one store here in Crestview, but we'll rapidly expand across the nation."

"Bulk sales. That's the name of the game," Henry interjected. He tapped on his white toupee as if to indicate that he was a deep thinker. "Quantity allows you to undercut other stores."

"So . . . you envision this as the next Pottery Barn?" I forced my voice to sound pleasant.

"In a manner of speaking," Wong replied.

Nodding enthusiastically, Henry added, "We're going

to be the Far East version. Pottery *Pagoda*, more like."
Again, he alone laughed at his joke. "We already worked
out a plan of one of the storefronts. Show Steve our plans,
George. He's the one I was telling you about, who I was
thinking we could hire as a consultant."

I couldn't help but flinch, and Henry said, "No offense, honey. You do great work, but I think Steve, being a
guy, could better help us to appeal to both sexes. You gals
flock to furniture stores like moths to a bonfire, so we already don't need to worry there."

Henry's logic was severely flawed. Maybe he was delu-
sional and heard voices in his head saying: *If you build it,
women will come.*

"Erin and I are partners," Sullivan said firmly, "so you
can't hire just me alone."

I was surprised by Steve's reply, but reasoned that he
probably felt I'd clobber him for cutting me out of the picture, so I nodded.

Henry furrowed his brow. "Really? You said when we
first met that you were her assistant temporarily, but had
your own business."

"We've adjusted our plans since then," I lied, thinking
the stakes here were low. If either man had been involved
with the murders, it hardly mattered whether they hired
Sullivan or me; they'd soon be in jail, and their assets
would be seized by the government.

Sullivan's cell phone rang, and he grabbed it and
showed me the number on the display. The caller was at
the Crestview police station. My blood pressure went up
several notches. Why would the police be calling Steve?
Were they checking alibis—seeing if I could have been
murdering Jerry Stone in my office the other morning?

"I'd better take this in private," Sullivan said with a wan
smile. Henry gestured to the doorway to the kitchen, and

Sullivan said, "Thanks," then answered the phone as he left the room.

Henry turned to George and said quietly, "We may as well show Erin our plans for the store, since we're in for the package deal with the both of them."

The remark made me feel like the throwaway gift that patrons at banks were given for starting up a new savings account. The doorbell rang before they could unfurl the plans. Henry gave a quick glance at his Swiss Army watch. "This has got to be Pembrook." He shook his head as he rose for the door. "Crap! It never occurred to me when I first got to thinking I needed an image consultant that I'd be hiring a light-in-the-loafers Jewish mother to nag me to death."

It was remarkable how Henry had such a way with words as to insult diverse groups of people all at once.

Robert swept into the room and was instantly taken aback by our safari surroundings. He caught his breath and began to turn toward Henry, obviously on the verge of giving him a tongue-lashing, but then he spotted George Wong in the recliner and froze.

"Robert Pembrook," Wong said with a chuckle. "Of course you're here. Only *you* could be behind two sudden murders in this sleepy little town near my home."

Robert had recovered from his initial surprise and was now pretending to be nonchalant. "My, my, Georgie." Robert took his act so far as to study his cuticles. "Still carrying a grudge, are we?"

Henry had been listening in silence, standing beside Robert. Now, as the hostile conversation paused, Henry said, "I take it you two know each other," with no hint of sarcasm.

Wong nodded to Henry and, with that chillingly serene smile of his, stated, "We are old friends. We were once roommates."

"*Roommates?* That's what we're calling it these days?" Robert sneered at George. "How very P.C. of you. Of course, that was before you let yourself go. Too much fast food, American style, Wong."

Wong maintained his smile and patted his sizable stomach. "Too much pampering, from too many lady friends, Pembrook."

Robert fidgeted with his glasses. "Ah. Well, good for you. You always were a switch-hitter."

"So, what's new with you, Robert? Are you still cheating nice people out of their savings in the garment business?"

Robert fixed a magnanimous smile on him. "My business is still going strong, if that's what you mean, though I'm now a consultant."

"Ah, that's right. I heard about your being an image consultant and working with a decorator." He glanced at me. "So, you two have been working together for three or four years now, yes?"

I shook my head. "No, this—"

"You're thinking of my previous designer, Evan Collins," Robert interrupted. He hesitated and corrected, "*Cambridge*, rather. How about you? Are you still passing off cheap imitations as ancient Chinese treasures?"

Wong maintained his smile. "My business is going strong. Thank you."

"Speaking of Chinese treasures . . ." Robert looked at me. "You should ask George to tell you how he was transported to the country when he was ten or eleven. His parents hid him inside a drawer in a chest that they shipped to the United States. A harrowing journey, to say the least."

I widened my eyes, thinking such a journey must have been much more than "harrowing." Wong, however, showed absolutely no emotion at the memory. It hit me then that this entire inscrutable-Asian-man routine of his was a put-on; George Wong had lived in the United States since he was a child. He was simply playing on that stereotype to serve his own purposes—to control others through intimidation.

In what I realized was a ludicrous attempt to make my intense curiosity seem casual, I asked Robert, "How long ago was it that you knew George?"

"Clear back in college at the University of Chicago. More than thirty years ago."

"Quite a coincidence," Henry mused aloud. "Here I hook up with a new partner out of the blue, and he turns out to be your former significant other."

I very much doubted that it was pure coincidence.

Sullivan returned to the room. Either his conversation with the police had been of little consequence or he was masking his reaction well. He greeted Robert and reclaimed his seat.

"George and Robert are old friends, as it turns out," I told him.

"Small world," Sullivan replied mildly.

"It sure is. They haven't seen each other in thirty years. Yet they know about each other's business ventures." I tried to make the remark sound like a bland comment. Sullivan eyed me, obviously picking up on the significance.

"Yes." Wong again gave me his Cheshire cat grin. "As I advised you before, Miss Gilbert, it is best to know many people."

"As proof of that theory, George once saved my life," Robert contributed. "That was how we met. I'm indebted to him forever."

"An exaggeration." Wong made a dismissive gesture. "Those men were probably not going to kill you. Merely beat you and maybe leave you with some very bad scars."

"I was at the wrong type of bar in the wrong section of Chicago," Robert explained to Sullivan and me, "the type of place where macho patrons take personal offense to men of my persuasion. Three beer-drinking men saw fit to try to convince me to change my sexual orientation by beating the crap out of me. George, however, happened onto the scene in the nick of time."

"You fought off three men . . . single-handedly?" Henry asked, his eyes widening in obvious newfound admiration for his would-be business partner.

Robert smirked at George as he replied, "Our Mr. Wong is very skillful with a knife."

Chapter 20

At that remark, George Wong finally lost his smile. A palpable tension filled the wretched room. It grew so quiet that I could hear the grandfather clock in the hallway tick. Unlike the furnishings in my current setting, that clock was a thing of beauty—Windsor cherry cabinet with holly-and-ebony inlays, beveled glass, every inch classic and top of the line. Henry began to nervously jingle the coins in his pockets.

Robert rubbed his hands and said, "Erin, Steve, I have a second appointment this afternoon that's clear down in Denver." Grimacing at the zebra skin behind us, he continued, "I'm suitably familiar with your floor plans and have already seen enough to know you're not responsible for the final results of my client's home. You did a fine job, under the circumstances."

"Thank you," I said, which was echoed a moment later by Sullivan.

"We'll have to do this again sometime. Next time I'm working in the Denver region; I promise you'll be the first designer I call, Erin. And you'll be the second, Steve, if Erin declines."

Despite the tension, I felt cheered by the compliment as I rose to say goodbye. "It's been a pleasure working with you, Robert."

"You, too, darling. A pleasure. A pleasure indeed." He spread his arms. "Come, come. Give us a hug." He squeezed me in a bear hug, then held out his hand toward Sullivan, who was attempting to rise on his one good leg. "Don't get up, you poor thing." They shook hands, then Robert turned to the two other men. "Henry, we still have one more session, so I'll see you here on Monday at three." He hesitated, then looked at me. "Erin, you or Steve should stop in then, too. Have your revised bill ready, and we'll go over everything, and I'll pay you before I leave town."

Mentally checking my calendar and realizing my Monday schedule was light, I answered, "All right. See you then."

"Wonderful." Robert gave George Wong a long, appraising look. "George, do stay out of trouble, won't you?"

"I always do, Pemmie."

Robert smirked, then replied, "Not really." He let himself out, and a second awkward silence fell over us.

George Wong's proximity still made me uneasy. If ever there was a person who struck me as being capable of a double murder, this was the guy. I had a disturbing urge to huddle closer to Sullivan for protection.

Henry started noisily rifling through the papers in a rectangular safari basket that had been converted into a coffee table. Stupidly, a sleek, smoked-glass oval table that I'd purchased on his behalf had been swapped for this basket, which had an uneven surface, unsuitable for supporting cups or drinking glasses. The basket gave him extra storage space, however. *Large enough to hide a body,* I thought anxiously.

"Let me show you my ideas for the showroom," Henry said, looking at Steve and then me.

"*Our* ideas," Wong corrected.

"Right, right," Henry replied, a trifle nervously. He unrolled a large blue-line plan, and I moved a seat cushion closer to Sullivan as we surveyed the drawings together.

"The furniture placement needs to be rethought," I blurted out. "It looks like you've got your chairs in one section, your case furniture—cabinets, et cetera—in another, tables in yet another, and so forth."

"What's wrong with that?" Henry asked.

"Furniture showrooms should be set up to resemble rooms in the house whenever possible," I replied.

Sullivan translated, "You need to give your customers ideas for how each piece might go together."

"That way they can visualize, say, the store's sofa in their own living room. That's infinitely more appealing than simply comparing this new sofa to that new sofa."

Henry began to pace in front of the coffee table, his arms tightly crossed on his chest. In contrast, Wong looked totally at home and relaxed. He had put his feet on the leopard-skin ottoman. "We'll feature the fundamentals of feng shui in the showroom itself," Henry announced.

He had mispronounced it as "feng shoe," bungling not just the second word but with a soft *e* in *feng*, instead of *fung*. Not a good indication that he was an accomplished disciple.

"Have you studied feng shui?" I asked Wong.

"No. However, that will never arise as a question, with my ancestry."

"But *you* know all about it, I'm sure. Right, Steve?" Henry asked.

"Both Erin and I do. It's impossible to be a designer in a place as New Age as Crestview without at least a working knowledge of feng shui."

"When did you get the idea for this partnership of yours?" I asked Henry.

"That's what they call serendipity, sweetheart." He stopped his pacing long enough to rock on his heels. "I met George here when he came and bought a used VW Beetle from me, just two weeks ago. We got to talking about showrooms and everything, and I told him about how I'd wound up acquiring a storefront over at the downtown mall but hadn't decided how to best utilize the space . . . and he was saying how *he* didn't have a storefront at all for his furniture business. Next thing you know, I made a little joke about two wongs not making a white, then how *white* rhymed with *Dwight*, which is my actual first name, and viola! Dwight and Wong was born. That's going to be the name for our new store."

"I see," I said, battling a smile at how Henry had named a musical instrument when he'd meant to say "voilà."

I eyed George Wong, who gave me a knowing grin. There was little "serendipity" involved, of that I was certain. George could have learned that Robert was working with Henry and then arranged to meet Henry at the dealership. Though I didn't know what his motive for doing so might have been, I did know that their having met "two weeks ago" meant that George had met Henry Toben *before* Henry's stair had been tampered with. That in turn meant that George could have been the one to saw through the stair while Henry was holed up in the hotel.

Sullivan and I exchanged glances. I knew from his expression that he was drawing similar conclusions.

We left a minute or two later. We both knew better than to give too much free advice before we'd actually been hired. Sullivan winced a little as he climbed into my passenger seat. As I drove away from Henry's, I asked, "How's the leg?"

"Still hurts."

"What did the police want?"

"It was your friend calling."

"Linda Delgardio?"

"Yeah. She was returning *my* call, from this morning."

"What about?"

"When you were being so stubborn and thickheaded about my not coming here with you, I wanted to let her know you might be walking into an ambush."

"Gosh. All this flattery could go to my head . . . if it weren't so *thick*, that is."

He cleared his throat but didn't reply. Frustrated and embarrassed, I yammered about how something extremely fishy was going on with those three men — Henry, George, and Robert. When he didn't respond, rather than demanding to know what in heaven's name was going on in that handsome-but-ever-inharmonious head of his, I found myself blathering about the scenery. April *is* a ravishingly beautiful month in Crestview. The flowers and greenery gleam against the purple-and-white-peaked backdrop of the mountains. The town itself is a lovely cross between Old West and modern, with liberal use of red brick for office buildings. The homes are virtually always meticulously maintained, and range from the fabulous historic mansions in Audrey's neighborhood to the charming little bungalows that we now drove past.

We were at a red light halfway to our offices by the time Sullivan finally spoke up. "So . . . you broke up with Norton yesterday?"

I looked at him in surprise. "Yeah, when he followed me out the door at your house. I assumed John told you at the time."

Sullivan scoffed, "I'm the last person he'd tell something like that to."

"Why? You said you two already managed to . . . Oh, wait. I get it. You mean he wouldn't tell you about our ending things because of that macho jealous dance you two are doing."

Sullivan grumbled, "I sure wouldn't call it a 'dance,' Gilbert."

"Boxing match, then," I replied.

"Whatever. Anyway, he's not good enough for you. He's no one I'd want to depend on when the chips were down."

I didn't feel like talking about John and, as the light changed, quickly said, "To my eye, it's George Wong who's looking guilty as hell."

"He does to mine, too. But if this Jerry Stone character was trying to warn you by slipping you those photos, *Henry's* actually the villain in all of this. Plus, don't forget, *Pembrook's* tied to both Toben *and* Wong. Not to mention his ties to Evan and Laura."

"Just like you and I are tied to those same people."

He made no reply.

"We should tell Linda about all of this."

"Your cop friend?"

"Yes," I said tersely, annoyed. *He called Linda just*

today! Why is he yanking my chain? I stopped in front of his office to let him out. "I'll call her myself. Later today."

At home that evening, Hildi was showering me with attention—cuddling onto my lap affectionately when I sat down, and shadowing me wherever I went. I soon rewarded her with a flake of the salmon I found in the fridge. Isn't it nice how our pets train us into trading them treats for affection?

Audrey, on the other hand, was far harder to train. Though she'd had a week to get rid of the excess furniture, she'd merely stacked the overflow coffee tables in one corner of the parlor and had balanced the smaller, lighter sofas upside down on the larger ones. We now had more space to walk through the room, along with a possible concussion in the offing if her stack of tables were to topple over on someone. The way my luck had been going of late, I had no doubt which one of us would be victimized. At least the staff in the emergency room would get a chuckle when I explained that I'd been hit on the head by a falling coffee table.

With Hildi wrapped around my ankles, I checked my voice mail and discovered a message from Hannah, asking me to call her at home. She'd never called me for anything other than work-related issues, so I anticipated that she must need me to host a presentation at Paprika's.

She answered on the first ring, her voice bubbly as she said, "Erin! I'm so glad you called! Can you please come to the store tomorrow at ten? That's my official break time. I'll brew us a fresh pot of coffee this time. We need to talk."

We do? "You're working on a Saturday?"

"I almost always do. It's one of our busiest days. At least they give me Sundays off . . . and a couple of half days.

I'm trying to toe the line, now that I'm in so much hot water with the owners."

"Is everything all right?"

"Oh, sure. More or less. I just feel like venting a little with someone, face-to-face. Can you make it? Please?"

"Yes."

"Great. I'll see you then."

I puzzled over the call after we'd hung up. Justifiably or not, my instincts were on red alert. Hannah's voice had seemed unnatural—breathy—as though she was nervous. Or lying about something.

As promised, at ten on Saturday morning I arrived at Paprika's, still a little apprehensive. I found Hannah right away, setting up a new display of bold, primary-colored linen place mats. Working at a leisurely pace, she said, "Oh, hi, Erin. Glad you could make it. I need just a couple of minutes to finish up what I'm doing, if you don't mind."

"No problem," I replied. "I'll just look around the store."

She nodded and glanced at her watch. "I'll be with you soon."

Like a lemming, I went straight to the salad bowl section. That magnificent mahogany set was still unsold. I decided to play it coy and focus my attention on the other, less compelling bowl sets first.

As I did so, however, Dave Holland stormed through the door. When he made a beeline for Hannah, I ducked out of sight. "I'm here," he growled at his ex-wife as he crossed the floor. "Exactly when I said I'd be."

"Good for you, David. But I'm busy. Exactly like *I* said I'd be. Sorry."

"Let's get this over with. We can't just leave everything hanging like this."

"David, this isn't the time nor the place. I'm at *work* now, in case you failed to notice."

"Of *course* I noticed. *You're* the one who said to come to Paprika's at ten o'clock. Let's go to your office. Come on."

She set this up deliberately so that I'd witness Dave's combative behavior. Why?

"Take your hands off me!" she shrilled. "I've told you this before. If you so much as touch me again, I'm calling the cops!"

Setup or not, I couldn't stand by if Dave was manhandling her. I walked out from behind the high shelf and said innocently, "Hannah? Dave? Is everything all right?"

Dave instantly wore a cat-that-swallowed-the-canary expression. He released his grip on his ex-wife's upper arm. Hannah, meanwhile, forced a weak smile. "Absolutely. *Dave* was just *leaving.*"

Peering at him, she announced, "For your information, David, I've been dating someone really special for the past month who treats me like royalty. Why should I waste my time talking to you? Ever!"

"Just so *you* know, you're not going to get away with any of this, Hannah! You hear me? None of it!"

"Get out of my store!"

He started to leave, then stopped, picked up a large duck-shaped soup tureen, and hurled it onto the floor. The porcelain smashed into pieces. "Put that on my Visa account! Just like you have all your other freaking purchases, you bitch!" As he pushed out the door, he called over his shoulder, "Now at least *one* 'purchase' was worth every penny!"

A salesclerk promptly appeared with a broom and dustpan, asking Hannah if she was all right. A second one rushed over. Hannah replied, "Yes, I'm fine." She gestured at me. "But my friend is here now, and I'm going to need to take a longer break than usual." The two women went on to discuss their horror at Dave's actions, but the glint in their eyes indicated they were inwardly delighted to have some excitement.

As Hannah led me to her desk in the storage room, she gave my elbow a squeeze. "I'm sorry you had to see that, Erin," she said with a dramatic sigh.

I was too annoyed with her routine to play dumb. "It sounded to me as though you knew in advance that we were both coming to see you at exactly the same time."

Her cheeks reddened. She hesitated by the coffee station, where, as promised, a full, fresh pot of coffee was on the warmer. "Well, that's kind of true. I *did* want to chat with you this morning, but I also wanted to make sure I had a witness, just in case things with Dave got out of hand."

I took a seat—the same uncomfortable slat-back wood chair as before. "I thought you said Dave didn't have a violent temper."

"He doesn't. He just . . ." She let her voice fade. "Okay. I fibbed when I said that. He kind of *does* have a bad temper. But I know he didn't kill Laura."

"How can you be so sure?"

She poured us both cups of coffee and handed me one. "I've known him for twenty years, back since we were in grade school together. This is the worst I've ever seen him act in all that time. He's just . . . under a lot of stress right now."

I blew on the surface of my coffee and took a tentative sip. I almost laughed; once again, the flavor was dreadful, and it was ironic that with all of the state-of-the-art coffeemakers Paprika sold, the employees were apparently forced to use bargain-basement grinds and a thirty-year-old machine.

She released another overly theatrical sigh. "He's trying to reconcile with me again, now that he's single once more."

"Are you considering it?" I asked to be polite, but feeling as though I was playing an awkward role in a vengeful scene entirely of Hannah's making.

"Not on your life." She frowned. "Dave's the type of guy who can't be without a partner, but also can't be bothered to go searching for the right one. I'm sure, though, with all his money, women will throw themselves at him." Her bitterness eclipsed that of the coffee.

She set her cup down, brightened a little, and, while opening the top drawer in her desk, said, "Come to think of it, now that I accidentally spilled the beans about the new man in my life in front of everyone at Paprika's, there's no sense in keeping *this* under wraps."

She removed a framed photograph and set it on the corner of her desk. I stared at it in disbelief. It was a picture of Hannah locked in the arms of John Norton.

Chapter 21

Feeling Hannah's eyes on me, I tried to cover my reaction but came up short. "What's wrong, Erin? Do you know John Norton?"

"We met a few months ago."

She held her hands to her lips in a reaction that still felt well rehearsed to me. "Oh, God. Did the two of you used to be an *item*?"

"We're no longer together."

"Obviously not." There was a haughty edge to Hannah's voice. "Since he's with *me* now."

The remark made me bristle. John and I had broken up less than forty-eight hours ago. "How did you meet?"

She smiled as she stirred the sludge in her cup. "He

came into the store one day a couple months ago, and we started flirting with each other." Her voice was as full of artificial sweetener as her coffee. "He was buying a gift for his sister's birthday."

I nodded and said nothing, but I was smoldering. John had two brothers but no sisters. The gift for "his sister" could only have been the platter that he'd bought for me on my birthday, after we'd been dating for a few weeks.

Eager to end this conversation, I cried, "Oh, shoot!" and set my cup down. "I just remembered . . . I've got an appointment in Longmont at eleven-thirty."

"You'd better get going, then."

"Yeah. So, what was it you wanted to talk to me about?"

She shrugged. "That can wait."

"But you made it sound important in your phone message—"

"Well . . . it's just that I was so rude the last time you were here. I wanted to apologize in person."

Strange that she'd felt no burning need to apologize a week ago, when we went out for coffee after Laura's service. "That's really not necessary."

"It is to *me*. What you were saying at the time . . . about Dave's possible connection to Jerry Stone . . . pushed a button, I guess. See, not long before Jerry started showing up and hassling me, I warned Dave that I was thinking of suing him for more alimony. I started to think maybe that was something Dave would do . . . hire somebody to make my life miserable so that he'd have some leverage against me." She gazed wistfully at the picture of herself and John. "Now that I've got a new man in my life, I've begun to realize that it's time to let go of past hurts." She reached over and patted my hand. "And also, not to take my minor troubles out on my friends."

I forced a smile and rose. "We all get brusque from time to time, and I truly didn't need an apology."

"Good. Thanks." She ran her finger along the edge of her desk. I was rooting for a sudden splinter to jab her, but no such luck. "And . . . there's one more thing."

"Oh?"

She nodded and gestured for me to sit down again. Reluctantly, I did.

"A couple of business owners came into the store yesterday. They're scouting the downtown area for space to put in their new furniture store. They were curious about pedestrian traffic and customer bases in the immediate area. I happened to ask if they were consulting with any interior designers, and your name came up." She paused for my reaction, but I deliberately remained impassive. "You're working with Hammerin' Hank? And George Wong?"

"Yes. Why?"

"I was . . . wondering if you'd mind putting in a good word for me, whenever they get around to hiring and are looking for store managers."

I rose again and said with a fake smile, "I'll be sure to mention your name."

She beamed at me. "That'd be great! Thanks, Erin."

The moment I left the store, my pace slowed. That photograph of Hannah and John had been taken very recently, at the annual Cottonwood Creek Spring Festival just two weekends ago; I recognized the sign on an artisan's tent in the background. John had asked me to go to that event with him, but I'd had to work. Later, he told me that he'd gone with friends.

Maybe she'd orchestrated the whole scene between herself and Dave so that, afterward, she could call my attention to the photograph, just to let me know that John was now hers. In fact, she could have lied about John's saying my birthday gift was intended for his sister. If he'd instead said that it was for his girlfriend who was an interior designer, she might have asked and learned my name. It was even possible that she'd trapped him into posing for that photo with her. For my peace of mind, if nothing else, I had to learn the truth.

Unable to rid my mind of the hideous image of Jerry's body, I still wasn't up for going to my office, so I let myself into my parked car and impulsively called John on my cell phone. He greeted me coolly and asked, "What's up?"

"There's a framed photograph of you and Hannah Garrison on her desk at Paprika's. She told me you two have been going out for a couple of months."

"What?!" He made a noise of disgust at the back of his throat. "That's bullshit, Erin. We've gone out on *one* date, last night. And I doubt there'll be a second date, now that I know she's this wacky."

"Yet the two of you had your picture taken together?"

"Yeah, but not by *my* choice. I was at the festival a couple weeks back with my friends Mark and Julie and bumped into Hannah there. I'm a regular customer at Paprika's, and she's gone out of her way to be friendly. She latched on to me at the festival, said she happened to have her camera with her, and asked Mark to take a picture of us. So . . . what was I supposed to do? Tell her to shove it?"

I ignored the understandable rancor in John's voice and said gently, "That's precisely what I was starting to suspect had happened. I was getting strange vibes from her. She's probably just staking out her territory."

He snorted. "I am *not* her territory, Erin, believe me."

Thinking aloud, I muttered, "It's just . . . all so strange. It seems as though everyone even remotely connected to Laura Smith has been . . . comingling, let's say. You and Sullivan both used to date Laura. Dave Holland was liv-

ing with her, after divorcing Hannah. Now it turns out
that you're dating Hannah, after me."

He said testily, "What are you saying? That my going
out on *one* date with Hannah Garrison makes me a *murder suspect*?"

"No, just that it all feels so weird to me. Even George
Wong and Robert Pembrook were apparently once a couple."

"Robert who?"

"Oh, that's the image consultant who hired me as a
subcontractor. To work for Hammerin' Hank Toben, who
keeps asking Audrey Munroe out. So there's yet another
prospective couple. This is like a soap opera. It boggles
the mind."

"Yeah," he snorted, then added sadly, "meanwhile, the
only two people who *belong* together just broke up."

I said nothing, and the silence grew heavy.

"Anyway," John said, "thanks for the heads-up. Hannah's got to be manipulative as hell to have put our picture on her desk at work after just one date. What a
weirdo."

"You're welcome."

We said our goodbyes and hung up.

Though I detested the fact that my suspicions were still
running wild, I couldn't seem to keep them at bay. It was
vaguely possible that John was in league with Hannah in
some evil plot hatched back before I'd ever arrived on the
scene. Maybe Hannah was a homicidal maniac who
killed her rival Laura and now had her sights set on me.

Much more likely, though, maybe I'd dumped the one
decent guy who'd come into my life in months.

Already out of the house and on the go on what, for me,
was a rare Saturday off, I decided to call a couple of

friends and suggest a matinee. We wound up going on a leisurely late lunch as well, and the afternoon proved to be wonderfully restorative. Even better, when I arrived home, I discovered that the parlor had been restored to its pre-centerpiece, pre–coffee-table-sofa-arrangement condition. I felt like singing the Hallelujah Chorus at the top of my lungs.

Audrey was chatting on the phone as I entered through the French doors, and she gave me a wink as she completed her conversation. The moment she hung up, I enthused, "I love what you've done with this room."

"You mean what *you've* done with it. All I did was put everything back the way you had the room originally."

"True, and I love it. This is a first, isn't it? The first time you've restored a room to exactly how it was, prior to a Dom Bliss experiment?"

"Maybe so. Well, *that* can't be good. My creativity must be slipping."

"*Or,* maybe my taste in interior design is starting to rub off on you." Hildi pranced over to me, and I swept her into my arms. "See, Hildi? Isn't this nice? Our favorite sofa is just where it should be." I carried her over to said sofa and sank triumphantly into its plush down cushions, feeling immensely better than I had this morning.

"By the way, Erin, that was your and my least-favorite pseudo-Texan on the phone just now."

"Hammerin' Hank? Asking you out again?"

She grimaced. "For a late dinner tonight. He was so persistent . . . just will *not* take no for an answer. But eventually he'll learn that even when he extracts a maybe out of me, it's *still* just a no."

I grinned at her. "How can you say 'maybe' to a date that's supposed to take place in just a couple of hours? Is he going to arrive tonight and see if you're willing to get into his car?"

"Essentially." She fluffed up her ash-blond hair. "He's going to be attending a business meeting over cocktails this evening, where I'm invited to join him, should I change my mind. Which, of course, is never going to happen. Do *you* have any plans tonight?"

"None. So I was thinking that—" I broke off as the phone rang, the double ring indicating that the call was for me. I'd been on the verge of proposing that Audrey join me for a marathon evening of watching the home designing shows on cable, during which I loved to play armchair quarterback. "Let me get this. Just a sec." I picked up and said hello.

"Hi, Gilbert."

Sullivan, I realized, and my pulse quickened at the surprise of his calling me on a Saturday evening.

"It's me," he continued before I could respond. "I'm meeting with Henry and George for drinks at Rusty's in an hour. Can you make it? They want to negotiate the conditions of our contract as their consultants."

A little disappointed that he was calling for mere business reasons and even more annoyed that Henry had obviously contacted Sullivan alone in an attempt to cut me out, I snapped, "*Our* contract?"

"Yeah, Gilbert. No way am I accepting money from those yahoos unless it turns out they're both innocent *and* that you get half of everything." He let that settle in for a moment, then asked, "So, are we in or out?"

Sullivan was acting the complete gentleman, so I quickly softened my tone. And my attitude. "It certainly won't hurt to see what they're offering. I'm not going to sign up for some sort of commission deal where they'll expect us to work as salesmen on the floor."

"Me neither. But I think I made that clear enough. This is consulting work on the initial setup of their showroom only."

"Sounds promising. Maybe we can teach them about feng shoe, while we're at it," I joked, poking fun at Henry.

Sullivan laughed, then asked, "So, can you make it at seven?"

"I guess. Sure. See you then."

"See ya, Gil." He hung up. I glowered at the earpiece for a moment before returning the phone to its stand. I'd come to rather enjoy how he called me Gilbert, but there was no way I would let him nickname me after a fish part.

Audrey was studying me with a cocked eyebrow. I said to her sadly, "Guess I'm not home yet for the night, after all."

"Oh, dear. Where are you headed?"

"Ironically, I'm meeting *your* Henry Toben, plus Sullivan and George Wong, for drinks at Rusty's in an hour. Turns out *I'm* one of the parties of Henry's business meeting tonight. Albeit as your basic tagalong little sister. The men are cooking up a deal and actually want to just hire Sullivan, but he's dragging me along as a conditional clause: 'You want me, you're stuck with her, too.' Really makes me feel ten feet tall."

Audrey furrowed her brow. "Aren't all three of those men suspects in these murders? Every *one* of those names is on the list on the refrigerator that we drew up after that knife was hurled into our door."

"Actually, only two of them are. At the time, I hadn't realized Henry Toben knew Laura, too."

She put her hand on her hip. "I added Henry's name in big red letters after you were poisoned at his house. Don't you *read* my notes on the fridge?"

Wanting to sidestep the issue that I had a personal policy of *not* reading refrigerator bulletin boards, I said, "This is just an innocuous business meeting."

"With possible double murderers." She crossed her arms. I suddenly realized that we were seeing nearly eye to eye, and looked down to see that, uncharacteristically, she was wearing significant heels.

"Rusty's is always crowded. There's going to be a ton of possible witnesses to any . . . funny stuff. Besides, I *know* Steve Sullivan is innocent. He can be my bodyguard."

"Doesn't he have a broken leg?"

"Well, yes, but—"

"What good is a bodyguard in a leg cast?"

"He's not going to need to do any running or chasing," I said brusquely. Audrey continued to look worried as she studied my face. "It's just a *business* meeting, Audrey. At a downtown *restaurant*. It's not like I'm suddenly going *skydiving*."

"Obviously not," she fired back. "Skydiving is *fun*."

Ninety minutes later, I was nursing a margarita and attempting to read over a contract in the dim lighting, Sullivan on my left, Henry on my right, and George Wong straight across from me.

"You know, I just realized something," I announced to Sullivan. "It's in my contract with Robert Pembrook that I won't accept any additional design work from Henry on his house for a period of twelve months, or I have to pay a finder's fee to Robert." Looking at Henry, I continued, "This isn't your *house*, so I'm probably in the clear, but I'm going to have to check with Robert before I sign anything. We'll be seeing him Monday afternoon. I can discuss it with him then."

Steve pushed back from the table. "We're a team on this one, so I'll hold off signing, as well."

A melodic voice behind me sang, "Well, look who's here!"

I swiveled in my seat and couldn't believe my eyes. "Audrey! What are you doing here?"

"Just felt like stopping in to see if there were any familiar faces." She gestured regally at our table in a way that included the four of us, and gave a friendly wink to George Wong, whom she'd never met. "And here are two and a half." She bestowed a magnanimous smile upon Sullivan. "Please don't be offended at being accused of having just half of a face, Mr. Sullivan. I merely mean that we've only met once, and quite briefly." They'd happened to cross paths at my office, before my semi–ill-fated introduction to John Norton.

"Not at all." Sullivan rose on his good leg and said, "Good to see you again, Ms. Munroe. Why don't you join us?"

Puffing out his chest like an oversized cookie jar, Henry boomed, "George, this here's my new lady friend, Audrey Munroe." Making the introduction in the reverse order for proper etiquette, he continued, "Audrey, this here is my new business partner, George Wong."

Though Audrey was sure to have noticed the breach, she replied politely, "How do you do, Mr. Wong?"

He not only rose but bowed, deeply. "Just fine, thank you, ma'am."

She gave him a small curtsy, obviously delighted. "Please call me Audrey."

"Audrey," he agreed with a nod. He grabbed an empty chair from the adjacent table and held it for her as she sat down, then reclaimed his own seat. Henry, meanwhile, remained seated, guzzling his beer. *Yet another area where sessions with Robert hadn't done much good. Henry might as well slip himself into the nearest toaster where Audrey was concerned.*

Sullivan slowly angled himself back down into his chair. Audrey looked at Steve's cast and, feigning surprise, said, "My goodness. What happened to your leg?"

"Crashed through my staircase," Henry answered for

him, and shook his head. "Y'all sure have been goin' through hell on this earth, ever since y'all started working for me. Steve's only got the one good leg now. Two people y'all once knew have croaked. It's just downright eerie. Makes you wonder if you two are cursed, doesn't it?" He seemed to think his insulting observations were humorous and laughed heartily.

At the thought that I might now be trapped into prolonged socializing with the man, I sprang to my feet. "Audrey, can I have a word with you?"

"Certainly, dear." She stood up and grabbed my elbow, saying to the men, "We're going to the powder room. We'll be right back."

"Typical," Henry remarked, waggling his thumb in our direction. "Notice how womenfolk always got to go to the toilet together? Like they're 'fraid to go anyplace by themselves."

Although a couple of choice comebacks occurred to me, I waited to allow Audrey to do the honors. When she not only held her tongue but patted Henry benevolently on the shoulder, I knew for certain she was, once again, feeling that she needed to protect me.

The moment the restroom door swung shut behind us, I exclaimed, "Okay, Audrey. What are you trying to pull?"

She gazed at herself in the mirror and began to reapply her blusher before answering, "Well, my dear, if *you* can play amateur sleuth, so can I. I plan to watch how he handles his steak knife."

"You're not serious! You're going to accuse him of *murder* if he cuts his meat with too much flourish?"

She snapped her cosmetic case shut. "I want to see how he behaves around you. It occurred to me that if Henry's the killer, *you're* the one who's in jeopardy. When it comes to women my age—sixty-five and subtracting—

he's used to his late wife's behavior. She was apparently of the cater-to-your-husband's-enormous-ego ilk. Henry hasn't figured out yet that men his age need wives more than women my age need husbands."

"What if the knife in the door was actually meant for *you*?"

She arched her eyebrow. "We have the sabotaged stair and the poisoned picture frame to indicate that *you* were the target."

"True. And not especially comforting, I might add."

"Come along, Erin. Let's see how the broth is coming along, once we stir the pot."

"Stir the pot?" I echoed in alarm, but she was not to be delayed as she sailed across the room, back to our table.

The moment we sat down, she announced, "Crestview is all abuzz with talk of these murders." She fixed her eyes on Henry. "Henry, you knew Laura Smith a decade ago, from what I understand."

He squared his shoulders and shot me a withering glare.

Audrey reached over and patted his hand. "Erin and I do talk to each other, after all, dear."

He shrugged, chuckled, and replied, "I had some real unpleasant dealings with Miss Smith when she set me up for blackmail that would have destroyed my poor, poor late wife." Interesting: he'd dropped the phony Texan accent. "I paid her off to spare my dear wife any pain. But that's all long past, Audrey. I never heard from Miss Smith again, and she had nothing on me, now that I'm a widower." He wiggled his eyebrows at Audrey, leaning closer. "Besides, I'm a changed man," he said. "Laura taught me a valuable lesson. I've never cheated since and never will."

Perhaps to move the spotlight off himself, Henry shifted his attention to his new partner and asked, "She didn't try anything like that on you and *Robert*, did she, George?"

"Pardon?" Wong said, not successfully hiding his alarm—a very rare show of emotion from the large, unflappable man.

Henry continued, "Robert Pembrook said the three of you knew one another . . . you, Robert, and Laura. When you were all in Chicago, ten-plus years ago."

George said evenly, "You must have misunderstood. Till the other day, Robert and I had barely spoken in thirty years."

"But Robert told me privately that he'd fixed you and Laura up on a practice date, back when he was teaching her how to relate to men," Henry persisted, frowning.

Wong gave him his patented teeth-baring attack-dog smile. "Robert was pulling your leg."

"But *you* also told me you started your business in Chicago and . . ." He let his voice fade as he studied George's expression. "My mistake. *You* would know, after all." Donning his Texan accent once more, he said, "As I was tellin' y'all earlier, Audrey, I got us a prime slice of real estate, just a block down from Paprika's."

"And as *I* was about to mention," Wong interjected, "I have been thinking that Wong Furnishings might be a better name than Dwight and Wong. It would be more dignified."

"But . . . you lose the pun that way."

"Yes?"

Henry gaped at him, then began in a firm voice, "I'm your full partner, and I really prefer—"

"I have the option of making you my silent partner. I think that would be best, for the sake of the business."

"But . . . Hammerin' Hank *isn't* the silent type," he

protested. "*I'm* the big man around town. I got the name recognition. I got the connections."

George said, "We'll continue the discussion sometime when we won't be boring your lady friend." He rose and bowed graciously to my landlady. "It was nice meeting you, Audrey. I will leave you all to your evening now. Good night."

The waitress arrived moments later and asked if we wanted a second round. Henry quickly replied, "Audrey and me were fixin' to rassle up a nice, thick steak and have dinner. Lemme buy you all dinner, too. It's the least I owe you, after all the challenges you've been through fixin' up my place. What do you say?"

Sullivan looked at me and said, "It's up to Erin."

"Actually, I'm pretty tired and would like to"— I got a swift kick in the shin from Audrey's direction—"call it a night, just as soon as I've had dinner."

It did seem ungracious of me to leave her stuck alone with Yammerin' Yank like this. Even though she'd brought it on herself.

By wolfing down my dinner and leaving at the earliest opportunity, I managed to beat Audrey home. Though she'd shot me a glare as I made my excuses for having to eat and run, she didn't kick me again. Sullivan, obviously every bit as eager to leave Henry's company, had scarfed down the last of his steak and offered to walk me to my car, and we actually had a good laugh at Henry's expense about our hasty exit.

But just as I headed for Audrey's yummy sofa to await her return, the phone rang with the two double-short rings that indicated it was a call placed after hours to my office. I answered, "Interiors by Gilbert. Erin speaking."

"Erin, hi. It's Dave Holland."

I instantly tensed. Dave hadn't contacted me before. When working on his house, it had always been Laura who called. "Hi, Dave."

"Hey. I wanted to touch base . . . and to tell you I'm sorry about that nonsense at Paprika's. It's just a lot of bad blood between Hannah and me, and I let her get under my skin every time."

"I understand, Dave. It's okay."

"Good. I was wondering. When all this first started, you said you'd appraise the junk in my house for me. Are you still willing to do that? I've decided I'm probably just going to try to sell it back to the guy who made it. I don't want to get ripped off completely, though."

I shut my eyes and cursed in silence. I really did *not* want to put myself into an adversarial role with George Wong. "Did you find out who made the furniture?"

"Yeah. The name showed up on my Visa statement. Guy's name is Wong. I already talked to him. He's coming Monday afternoon to make me a formal offer. Says it's only going to be twenty cents on the dollar, but I'm willing to take a big loss to get everything out of here."

"I can imagine how you feel." *Talk about owning furniture that carried negative associations.*

"Yeah. I've got the salvaged furniture from the storage unit, too, and some of it's fine. I was hoping you'd take a look at everything, help me get a handle on what it's worth . . . what I should keep and what I should maybe sell to Mr. Wong."

"Okay."

"But there's this one chest that's new. I mean, new to me. It wasn't here when I left for Atlanta. And it's kind of nice. Did you order a chest for Laura just before she . . ."

He hesitated and amended the question to ". . . after I left town?"

"No, I didn't."

"Huh. It looks to me like it's a nice piece, and I think it's old."

"Can you describe it to me?"

"It's got all these, like, carvings and little pieces of wood in it, like a parquet floor?"

"An inlay?"

"Yeah. And it looks like a big ol' cedar chest except for that. And there's all these Chinese symbols. Then there's this hidden drawer. I wouldn't have even found the drawer, except it was left open an inch."

"Sounds like a Chinese wedding chest." Something was tugging at my memory.

"It's in the back bedroom. I can't figure out why Laura would have hidden something that nice in a room where nobody's likely to ever see the thing."

"That's puzzling, all right. She might have stashed it in an underutilized room if she wasn't sure she wanted to keep it." As soon as the statement left my lips, I knew it was nonsense. Although that was generally true of furniture buyers, Laura hadn't been like most people; the woman had been utterly certain about every little stick of furniture she bought.

Curious to see the chest and thinking that I could make an excuse and have Linda accompany me for protection, I made arrangements with Dave to arrive early on Monday afternoon, an hour before George Wong was scheduled to meet with him.

The moment I hung up the phone, it hit me—a Chinese wedding chest. That was how George Wong had been smuggled into this country as a child. The unfaded rectangle on Wong's wallpaper had been the right size for a chest.

But what would Laura Smith want with a chest that resembled something George Wong had once been a stowaway inside?

After mulling over the question, I snatched up the phone and called Linda Delgardio.

Chapter 22

DOMESTIC BLISS

"So, *there* you are." Audrey peered into my eyes as she waltzed through the kitchen door. I'd been pacing in the kitchen ever since ending my conversation with Linda. "I, too, finally escaped from that obnoxious windbag. That was a less than enjoyable evening, but we're both still alive and well. If older. Much, much older. But alive and well." She arched an eyebrow. "I was impressed with how quickly you can eat and how fast your Mr. Sullivan can walk in his cast when bolting from a blowhard dinner companion."

"I apologize, Audrey. That *was* rude of me."

"Oh, I don't blame you in the least. But you can make it up to me in the future by having a nice evening out with me. One that *doesn't* end in your making a hundred-yard dash out the door."

"So long as we ensure that Henry Toben won't be your date, no problem." I swept up the printout I'd made yesterday, which had since gotten misplaced but had resurfaced during my fumbling for a scratch pad while on the phone. "Would you like to see a chair that will look amazing in the den?"

"Is it an eighteenth-century Italian love seat?"

"No, a twenty-first-century High Point, North Carolina, one-seater."

"Close enough."

She gushed over the chair, then said, "But let's consider furnishing that room entirely in period pieces instead. In fact, I'm thinking about doing a show on antiques . . . or maybe even a week's worth of shows during next sweeps period."

"That'd be a great idea."

"Wonderful! What can you tell me about identifying fakes and frauds?"

"Nothing."

"Oh, now, we both know that isn't true." She headed for the kitchen drawer where she kept her note-taking materials for the show. "What about the work you did for Laura?"

I shuddered. "Please! Don't remind me."

Even while I was voicing my refusal, out came the Dom Bliss notebook and pen.

"Seriously, Audrey. This isn't my area of expertise . . . which is probably one of the reasons Laura made me her mark. I've taken all of *one* course in antiques. I'm looking forward to watching your shows so I can learn more about them. You'll want to consult with an expert— with an antiques dealer."

"And I *will*. But for now, I'm just looking for a place to start . . . the absolute basics." She looked at me expectantly.

Reasoning that giving her this information was the very least I owed her for abandoning her to Hammerin' Hank, I pulled out one of the bar stools and took a seat. "Okay. All I can do at this point is give you a hodge-podge of information."

"Fine. Hodge this podge however you like. We'll sort through it all later."

"Start by learning your time periods. That's a whole— and, frankly, dry—lecture in itself. You need to know what types of wood were used, when and where, and the types of construction methods used. And the dimensions of furnishings that were popular at that time. For example, during some eras, sofas were made to be almost too long . . . especially the Hepplewhites and Sheratons."

She peered up at me from her notes. "I'm assuming Mr. Hepplewhite and Mr. Sheraton were British?"

"Yes, that's right. You based that on the derivations of their last names?"

"No, on the prototypical Brit's reserved, formal mannerisms. Let's face it, if a Frenchman, such as Maurice Chevalier, were to have designed a sofa, would *he* have opted for a 'too long' couch or for a nice, cuddly love seat?"

At a loss for a suitable response, I could only laugh. "I'll lend you my class notes and charts on furniture history."

"That's great, Erin. Thank you," she said with a smile. "Go on, dear."

"In general, you want to remember that antiques have lasted this long because they were handcrafted with great care . . . made one at a time. Nothing handcrafted can be as precise and symmetrical as machined pieces. Even so, you should be able to put a drawer upside down and still be able to slide it in or out; otherwise, I get suspicious that the drawer, at least, has been replaced with much newer wood.

"As for signs of fakery, circular saw marks are a dead giveaway. Round nails didn't come onto the scene until the eighteen twenties. You watch for silly stuff . . . like the size and curvature of multiple dents on a supposed antique. If they're exactly the same size, that can be a sign that someone deliberately aged the wood by smacking it with a heavy chain. Always examine a piece of furniture in bright lighting . . . preferably sunlight. Look at the wood's patina—the reddish-brown of eighteenth-century walnut, the honey-yellow of aged maple, or the deep brown-red of mahogany. Meanwhile, the backings of pieces were almost always made with *soft* woods, so they will have turned dark with a hundred-such years of dirt and dust. Look for the grayness of tabletops from washings with harsh soap and water. Expect edges and corners to be a little rounded with age."

On a roll now, I gave her a minute to catch up with her note-taking, then continued, "You have to always consider the way life was back when this potential purchase was made. The craftsmen didn't waste time staining the backs of dressers or the undersides of drawers. You should be able to see the grooves of the jack planes . . . the lack of machine-tool precision. Authenticating labels and stamps on pieces should be viewed with extra suspicion. It's just too easy to stick, say, the label 'Paul Revere' on something, because everyone knows about Revere and his pewter.

"So. That's a quick rundown on what I know. Like I said, I'll give you my notes. Also, it's really a good idea to establish a relationship with a trustworthy antiques dealer. By the time you hear from a couple of different sources that a particular antiques shop owner is knowledgeable . . ." Discouraged at the thought of what would face me when I had to appraise Dave Holland's antiques on Monday, I let my voice fade.

Audrey frowned. "I have to admit, Erin, you suddenly don't sound all that convincing."

"It's good advice, though. Dealers spend years examining antiques. They can amass so much more knowledge than anyone who simply dabbles in antiquing. I guess I got so thoroughly conned by Laura that it's difficult for me to talk about trusting others on this one subject. But I'll get over it eventually."

Audrey gave a sympathetic cluck. "I know you're going through a really rough time right now, Erin. I'm sorry if I made it even worse."

"Your heart was in the right place."

"Well, I can tell you one thing I already know about recognizing fakes and frauds. *You're* the real McCoy, Erin Gilbert."

I beamed at her, knowing that this was about as sentimental and mushy as my landlady ever got. "Thank you, Audrey. So are you."

Chapter **23**

Monday morning, I worked with a couple of new clients out in Lafayette, then drove once more to the Crestview police station. Though I had almost an hour free, eating lunch was out of the question. My stomach was as knotted as an elaborate macramé.

The day before, I'd met Linda Delgardio at the station house. I'd told her about the Chinese chest, which I suspected had been removed from George Wong's store, and gave her my theory that Laura had stolen the chest as some kind of trophy, not realizing how dangerous Wong was and how swift and total his retribution would be. To my surprise, Linda agreed with me and began to put a surveillance operation into motion.

For my one P.M. appointment with George at Dave Holland's house, I would be wearing a wire. Now, even after more than twenty-four hours to get accustomed to the idea, my mind balked at the surreal concept. *Wearing a wire? Me?* It felt as though I'd suddenly slid into an episode of *Law & Order*.

"Okay," Linda said as she and her partner, Mansfield, accompanied me into the inner sanctum of the police station, "here's the deal. You're going to be wired for sound, like we discussed yesterday. Manny and I are going to be in the back of your van, listening in. If there's any sign that you're even slightly getting into some possible danger, we'll bust in and make the arrest."

"Like Del said, we're taking no chances here," Mansfield added. "You get nervous, just say, 'Help,' and we'll be there before you've reached the letter *p*."

I nodded, thinking that would make the word *hell*, which was chillingly appropriate. "I can draw you a floor plan of the house right now. That way, you'll know exactly where I'll be and how to get there quickly."

"Good idea," Mansfield said. He grinned at Linda. "Having a designer as our front man has some advantages."

With Linda and Mansfield out of sight in my van, which I'd parked as close to the front door as possible— even having backed into the driveway so the van's back door was a straight shot into the house—I rang Dave's doorbell. To hide the contraption taped to my abdomen, this morning I'd deliberately chosen to wear a three-quarter-sleeve burgundy button-down blouse that was slightly too big for me, flatteringly tight black slacks, and the one pair of Jimmy Choo shoes I own—black sling-back sandals. I'd also given myself a pedicure and painted my toenails to match my blouse. My reasoning was that, on the off chance that Dave or George was into women's feet, I needed to do everything I could to draw their eyes away from my midsection.

Dave opened the door. He was wearing his om-nipresent gray corduroys and a black T-shirt under an un-buttoned pin-striped collared shirt. He'd used some sort of product that only succeeded in making his messy hair look shiny. I felt a hideous pang, as my memory flashed back to the fateful time when he'd let me in to check on Laura, only to discover that her antiques—and she her-self—were frauds. Now that he'd replaced his glasses, he recognized me at once and said, "Come on in, Erin."

I felt like I was walking into a lion's den. My stomach lurched at the sight of the mirror that had been the first spark of the conflagration to follow. A moment later, I spotted the original—the antique—mirror, propped against the wall. I immediately knelt to inspect it, forget-ting for the moment the real purpose behind my visit. "This is gorgeous. You can not only sell it for what you paid for it, but at a profit, so if George wants to bid on it, don't let him have it for anything less than twenty K."

"Whatever," Dave said. "I already decided to take Mr. Wong up on his offer to haul all the crap he made for Laura out of here at a fifth of what she paid. So I just need you to appraise the old stuff again, now that they're dam-aged, to keep him honest when he makes his offer to buy them from me. We still have all the paperwork that shows exactly how much I paid for each piece, so it shouldn't take you long. Right?"

"Right." I still felt ungodly nervous, so it was good news that I wasn't going to be in an adversarial role with Wong regarding his offer on the furniture Laura had commissioned him to build.

"Let's get to it, then. The sooner we're done, the sooner I can get back to my office. I've kind of got a lot going on today . . . set my computer up in the kitchen so I can work at home. That's the one room Laura didn't touch, since we went with state-of-the-art modern appliances to begin with."

"I remember."

"Yeah. So. Where do you want to start?"

"I'd like to see that chest you were describing." If my allegations proved baseless—if it was obvious at a glance that this chest was in no way related to George Wong—I needed to alert Linda and her partner as soon as possible.

We made the journey through the foyer and up the stairs. About half of Dave's antiques intended for the living room had survived the warehouse fire. He'd placed each original beside its vastly inferior clone. A faint charred-wood scent hung in the air.

"The only room that Laura didn't provide duplicates for was the master bedroom." Dave sighed. "Guess the princess wasn't willing to sleep on the pea even for the short time it would have taken to get her plan into effect." His voice was more sad than bitter.

"You're selling your bedroom furniture, as well?"

"Yeah. But it was never in the fire, so it's not damaged, and I don't need you to reappraise it." He swung open the six-panel door to the guest bedroom. "Here we are. These were toward the back of the warehouse, so almost all of 'em were burned beyond recognition."

Indeed, all that remained of Laura's glorious antiques was a Boston rocking chair in the corner. The condition of this room I'd designed staggered me. This had once been a beautiful, serene retreat for houseguests. Now the bureau, nightstands, and bed were garage-sale items—not even of the quality of the fast knockoffs that George had supplied her for the main level. That only made the Chinese chest stand out all the more in contrast. She'd placed it dead center. There were six carved panels on the front. The wood inlays were hand-carved and had a natural red sheen.

I knelt, opened the hidden drawer, and ran my fingertips along the surface of what would have formed the ceiling of this tiny chamber for a young George Wong. I could feel markings—shallow impressions in the wood—perhaps carved there by his fingernails. I reached deeper inside to feel the entire surface with my palm. Every inch was covered; it felt as though there was an elaborate carving there, turning the rough-wood underside into a private piece of art. My throat clenched, and I jerked away and shut the drawer. Whatever horrors George Wong had absorbed as a child didn't excuse him from being a murderer as an adult.

I turned away and saw that Dave was watching me from the doorway. He donned a wan smile. "How much is it worth?"

Ironically, even though it was on the underside of a drawer, George's carving he'd made as a child would drive up the price. "Six, seven thousand. Minimum."

"That's something, anyway."

"Did you mention this chest to Mr. Wong already?"

Dave nodded. "He said he'd like to take a look at it."

No surprise there. Linda and I hadn't discussed my handling of this subject matter with Dave, but I decided to treat him as I would if I weren't wired for sound. "I have to warn you, Dave, it's likely that Laura stole this chest."

He gaped at me. "Pardon?"

"I think that she stole this chest from Mr. Wong. In which case, of course, you won't get anything at all for it."

"Oh, my God." He rubbed his forehead. "Well. I guess

I shouldn't be so surprised. You know, at this point, Erin, I'd believe anything anyone told me about Laura."

"I'm sorry," I replied, and meant it.

Frowning, Dave glanced at his watch. "I should really get to my teleconference call. You remember where everything is, I'm sure. Mind showing yourself around?"

"Not at all."

Dave returned to the kitchen as I pulled out my notes on the original antiques. I was still so nervous about my upcoming meeting with Wong that I needed to talk and kept up a running monologue to my wire as I inspected the one-time prized antiques. In addition to the nearly total loss of this bedroom's furnishings, I was heartsick about some exquisite pieces downstairs that were gone—the cherry console, the mahogany hutch, the fabulous early-Victorian walnut salon chair. The finish on many of the pieces had been badly charred. Because Dave was guilty of arson, he surely wasn't getting any insurance money for the damage to his possessions.

After I'd made all of my calculations and tallies, I sat down with Dave in the kitchen and went over the figures with him. For the damaged pieces, all I could do was give him a reasonable range of the prices that the antiques *should* still fetch on the open market. I explained that my final tally was going to be cut to one fourth or so if he sold the entire lot to a dealer—his easiest solution, but one that would cost him dearly. He was pondering the decision when the doorbell rang. Dave promptly rose and announced, "That's got to be Mr. Wong now."

Lagging several steps behind him, I said quietly, for the benefit of the wire, "I hope the butterflies in my stomach aren't making such a racket that they drown out everyone's words."

Dave swept open the door. With his large frame filling

the doorway, George gave his usual slight bow of greeting and murmured, "Good afternoon. I'm Mr. Wong."

Dave said, "Hey. Okay. George Wong. You're here."

Dave must have been staring at him wide-eyed, because George gave him his placid smile. "Is something wrong. Mr. Holland? You were expecting perhaps a smaller man?"

He gave a nervous laugh. "I guess so."

Even though Dave was six foot two himself, he was intimidated by Wong. I smirked and thought: *Try wearing a wire and suckering the behemoth into confessing to a murder.* Dave's phone rang, and he waggled his thumb and said, "I should get that. You won't need me for a while anyway. Erin, do you mind being in charge?"

"Not at all." I wish I *were* in charge; if things had gone my way, Laura would have seen the error in her ways, turned Evan in to the authorities, and none of this would have happened.

George shifted his attention to me. "Miss Gilbert. You are an antiques expert, yes?"

"No, but I do know the basics of what was made when and where." Trying to embolden my vocal cords, I brayed, "There's a Chinese wedding chest upstairs that I think you'll find of particular interest."

"Yes?" George said as though utterly disinterested. He gestured for me to lead the way.

"Dave tells me you're buying back the furniture Laura commissioned from you."

"At a fair price, yes."

As we climbed the stairs, it was nerve-racking to have my back turned to him. I kept anticipating the agony of a knife stabbed between my shoulder blades. I rotated enough to keep an eye on him, which meant I had to sidestep somewhat. "This chest that I wanted to show you looks to me like it was made thirty to fifty years ago. Not an antique, obviously, but with excellent craftsmanship."

"Yes?" He was feigning sheer boredom.

My heart pounding, I showed him into the room. He kept his features inscrutable as he walked straight to the chest. "You believe this is a valuable piece, Miss Gilbert? But not an antique?"

"I'm estimating it was made about fifty years ago, not a hundred. I think it's probably a reproduction of the craftsmanship from the Qing Dynasty."

"You are indeed correct. This particular chest was made forty-three years ago. By my father." He arched his brow. "How much did you tell Mr. Holland it was worth?"

"More than six thousand."

He snorted. "It could sell for more than ten thousand dollars."

"That much?" I didn't agree, but wasn't about to argue. "I'm sure Dave will be happy to hear that."

George rocked on his heels and crossed his arms. "Mr. Holland will not get one penny for it. I can prove to the authorities that this chest already belongs to me, and I will take it back." He gave a solemn bow. His classic Oriental mannerisms continued to unnerve me, even though I knew them to be a calculated act; he'd been living in this country considerably longer than I'd been alive. "You should go ahead and open the hidden drawer now, Miss Gilbert."

I hesitated, wondering if my familiarity with the drawer's location would tip my hand to the fact that I'd already surmised his lifelong connection with this chest.

He chuckled. "Go ahead. There is nothing to harm you. It is simply an empty drawer. You have my word of honor on that."

I already knew the drawer was empty, of course, and couldn't help but wonder how much the "word of honor" from a probable double murderer was really worth. Nevertheless, I knelt and slid open the drawer underneath the unit.

He chuckled. "Empty, yes? How big would you say that drawer is, Miss Gilbert?"

"I don't know. It's maybe two feet by three feet."

"And how deep?"

"Nine, ten inches."

"That is how I came to your country . . . on my back so that my shoulders were flat, my legs curled, my face turned to the side because the drawer was too shallow otherwise. For nearly six days, this small wooden box was my home."

"That must have been terrifying for you."

"Yes, but it was either endure or die. My father had died the year before, and my mother couldn't keep his furniture business going. I never saw her or my younger sibling again."

I needed to keep him talking, get this dangerous, enigmatic man to trust me. "I'm really sorry, George. That must have been a horrendous ordeal, the likes of which I can't even begin to imagine."

"Yes."

"So how did *Laura* come to own this chest?"

"She stole it from me. Your friend Laura needed her trophies, it seems."

"Trophies?"

"She collected the very best. Of everything. I kept this chest in the front room of my shop. She saw it there and tried extremely hard to purchase it. I told her its history, why she couldn't have it. Even so, she paid off some of my own workers to remove it from the premises without my knowledge. Needless to say, they no longer work for me."

That was indeed "needless to say," I thought, but wondered if his former "workers" were still breathing. Had he killed them for their treachery the way he murdered Laura? "You must have suspected Laura the moment it disappeared. Did you confront her right away?"

"Of course. She protested her innocence and showed me her entire house, but my chest wasn't here at the time. She had concealed it in the storage unit, I'm quite sure, and she probably brought it back here after I left."

"So you *knew* about her storage unit and where it was?"

He bared his teeth. "No, Miss Gilbert, I did *not* know where it was until I heard the news of her death. Had I known where the chest was, I'd have claimed it then, I assure you."

"Why would she steal something that obviously meant so much to you? I mean, why would she want something of yours as a trophy?"

"She was quite angry with me over our fiduciary arrangement." His expression remained inscrutable. "I had insisted on a fair price for my work, and she felt forced to comply. Admittedly, my fee was much more than she had expected to pay." He sighed. "And so, she couldn't sell my chest, for she knew I would only prove it was stolen and would get it back. Instead, she wanted to burn it along with the house, as her vengeance."

"She told you that?"

"She didn't need to. Laura and I understood each other."

"So, you two *did* know each other, after all?"

He chortled softly. "As Robert said the other day, I knew Laura from the old days, when I was with Robert and her parents had hired him to assist their daughter."

And yet during our conversation at the restaurant when Henry asked about those "old days" back in Chicago, George had been disconcerted. He wasn't telling the whole story. "If you two understood each other, why would Laura be willing to risk crossing you like that?"

"Yes." He grinned at me. "I was also surprised. To steal something so important from me. My mother sacrificed every cent she possessed to place me in this chest and ship it to America. Several years ago, I paid many times its worth to get it back."

He knelt, saying, "I made a modification to the piece after I bought it. I dissolved the glue that keeps the false bottom of the chest in place." He slowly pulled the piece out from its slot, then turned it over, so that I could see the underside.

The relief carving that George had crafted was breathtaking—six individual scenes from an Asian village. "That's astounding," I said honestly. "You did this as a *child*?"

He nodded. "I had a small knife with a one-inch blade in my pocket. That was how I passed the time."

I continued to stare at the work. Although the craftsmanship was crude and the renditions simplistic, that was part of its stylistic charm. One section depicted some houses by a river, with a boat that resembled a gondola near a bridge. Another showed three women with parasols. A third showed a gnarled, windblown bonsai tree. A fourth, with the most detail, showed a family. Awed, I said, "You carved these intricate scenes in the dark, when you could barely move, and you were just a ten-year-old boy."

He said impassively, "It is my home, my village." He pointed. "My family, there. My grandparents, parents, my sister." He picked up the board and slid it into place, his carving once again hidden from view.

"Once you get this back from Dave, are you going to at least keep your carving face-out, so people can admire it?"

He shook his head. "My father would have been angry at me for defacing his honorable work. A braver child would not have needed such diversions."

My eyes filled with tears. I knew more about George

Wong than I had several minutes ago, but nothing incriminating, aside from establishing a possible motive for Laura's murder. This could be my only chance to trick him into making a slip of the tongue. I had to provoke him. "And yet Laura stole this from you, intending to destroy it, along with her household of fakes."

He gave me another of his teeth-baring grins. "Laura would not have done so. I would never have allowed her to do so."

"So you killed her?"

He chuckled. "You Americans. You pretend not to know that there are times when killing is necessary. You look the other way, pretend to be horrified."

"In other words, Laura Smith needed to die?"

He held my gaze and said only, "You have too narrow a mind, Miss Gilbert."

"Jerry Stone was killed, too. Was he *also* a necessary death?"

All traces of his smile vanished. Evenly, he replied, "Unless you are trying to anger me, Miss Gilbert, I advise you to stop asking me these ill-advised questions."

"Or else *what*? You'll find *me* a necessary killing as well?"

His expression remained impassive.

I wasn't getting anywhere. This could be the police's only chance to get a confession from him. I needed to provoke him further. "Robert told us how you broke up a fight once by waving your knife around. Are you armed right now?"

He held my gaze. "I never travel without my knife, Miss Gilbert."

Though I said nothing, an instant later, Linda and Mansfield burst into the room, their weapons drawn, Mansfield saying, "Don't move. Police."

I was surprised and disappointed that they'd burst in

prematurely. They must have assumed that George had pulled out his knife during his last statement to me. I felt as though I'd let everyone down. George hadn't confessed; he'd been too cagey.

While reading him his rights, Mansfield put handcuffs on George, frisked him, and, to my horror, found only a tiny, well-used pocketknife. At a glance, I knew it was the one-inch blade he'd had since he was a boy. My cheeks were blazing, and I avoided George's gaze. Linda put her gun back into its holster and said, "We need you to come with us to the station house, Mr. Wong."

Just then Dave bolted into the room, his face white when he saw the police. "What the hell's going on?"

"Stand back," Mansfield demanded. "We're bringing this man in for questioning."

George, closely followed by Mansfield, brushed past Dave and me. "My lawyer will have to be called." He looked back at me, shook his head in disgust, and said, "Miss Gilbert, we'll meet again. Too soon for you, I suspect."

His threat chilled me to the bone.

Linda followed George and Mansfield down the stairs, and Dave and I trailed several steps behind. George and Mansfield went out the still-wide-open front door.

Linda gave me a thumbs-up to indicate I'd done a good job, but I didn't agree. "Did you get enough to arrest him?" I asked quietly.

"To arrest him on suspicion of murder, yes. To convict him, no. But he may talk yet. We'll see."

I wanted to get rid of my wire as soon as possible and started tugging on the tape through the fabric of my blouse. "Let me get this thing off me. It makes my skin itch."

"That's fine. We'll have another patrol officer up here

in a couple of minutes who can collect it. Again, thanks for your help, Erin."

Without asking Dave's permission, I ducked into the quarter bath, ripped the tape off my skin, which smarted, then splashed water on my face. I looked awful, as though I hadn't slept in days, which was partly true. I realized that in the excitement I'd left my notepad and purse someplace, so I retraced my steps and collected them.

I can leave this house now. And never come back.

I almost broke into a full sprint as I charged out the front door. The police car had arrived, and I thrust the wire I'd been wearing at Linda and thanked her for taking my allegations about George seriously. Standing in the driveway, I watched as the police car drove away, George giving me his evil grin all the while.

Dave came out onto the front porch. "Is *that* the bastard who killed Laura?" he asked. "They caught him?"

"I hope so. It's not like he confessed, though." Now, suddenly, I was nervous about being alone with Dave. Sullivan's paranoia had officially taken root.

"I guess this means he's not going to be buying back my furniture. I might have to ask you to appraise the reproductions, too, after all."

So much for my never returning to this house, I thought glumly. "Let's let this go awhile, Dave. We'll touch base in a couple of days."

He nodded, thanked me, and, to my relief, I was finally able to leave. Partway down the mountain I realized that my work wasn't quite done for the day. I glanced at my watch. I was going to be a few minutes late to meet for the final wrap-up at Henry's house to get paid. I was looking forward, though, to telling Steve about the events at Dave's house.

Suddenly it occurred to me that Steve and I hadn't discussed yesterday whether or not he needed to come to

Henry's, too. Sullivan went out of his way not to miss meetings involving Henry and Robert, but for all I knew, he could have another appointment elsewhere. In any case, with any luck, Sullivan wouldn't have to be so careful from here on out; Wong would give a full confession, and all this would be over.

That realization—that this whole terrible ordeal was finally behind me—didn't give me the sense of satisfaction and relief that it should have. John and I were through. Sullivan and I habitually fought like cats and dogs. Evan still had Steve's money and was living high on the hog in Paris or some other exotic locale.

There was a silver Jaguar in Henry's driveway—Robert's rental, I was certain—but no van marked "Sullivan Designs." I felt a touch of disappointment. I was late, so if Sullivan wasn't here by now, he wasn't coming at all.

I rang the doorbell. Robert opened the door and gave me his usual delightful "Come in, come in. I'm afraid it's probably just going to be the two of us. Henry is upstairs, but says he isn't feeling well, and that yummy partner of yours called and is tied up with legal negotiations."

" 'Legal negotiations'?"

He reseated his glasses. "My fault, I fear. I put the bug in Henry's ear that he needed to get his lawyer to take a look at the contract that he and George were working up for you to sign, and, next thing you know, Henry's insisting that the lawyer speak with Mr. Sullivan in advance of our little meeting here. When he called, I told him not to bother coming . . . that by the time he could drive out here, we'd be wrapping things up. I cut you a very generous check."

"That's always nice to hear. Thank you."

He studied my features. "You look a bit out of sorts. Is everything all right?"

"Yes. Fine, thanks." He continued to stare into my eyes with obvious skepticism, so I finally admitted, "I just had a run-in with your former associate George Wong."

"Oh, dear, dear! What happened?"

"The police have arrested him. It appears that he killed Laura. They had me wear a wire, so they have our exchange on tape, and he all but confessed."

"I am totally . . . flabbergasted, Erin! Why in heaven's name would *George* kill Laura?"

"She had stolen something from him that he treasured . . . that chest his mother had used to smuggle him into this country. Laura was going to destroy it in the fire she intended to set at her house . . . just to be cruel."

Robert sank into the nearest chair and rested his elbows on his knees, as though needing a chance to make sense of my words. I took this as an invitation and took a seat myself, in the beige upholstered side chair that was one of my few original selections for the room.

After a long pause, Robert squared his shoulders and rose. "That's too dreadful to think about. Let's just focus on the positives. The killer's been arrested, your work here is finished, and you did a splendid job."

"Still. It's just . . . so painful. Two people have died. People can be so cruel to one another."

He patted my shoulder. "I know just the thing to shore up your spirits. Let's break out my housewarming present to Henry. It's one of the finest cognacs on the market."

"Oh, no thanks. I never drink during the day."

"I'll pour one for myself, then."

"At least I'll get to tell Steve the good news soon. He's had nothing but misery ever since Evan Cambridge first wormed his way into his life."

There was just the slightest hitch in Robert's motions at

Evan Cambridge's name. The reaction reminded me of how he'd accidentally called him Evan Collins the last time we spoke. We'd been standing here in this ghastly room at the time. Something was suddenly ringing a bell . . . a past comment of Steve's.

Robert turned with his drink in hand—he'd used one of the hand-blown brandy snifters from Paprika's that I'd helped Henry select. Robert was watching me, swirling the amber liquid in his glass. "I promise you, it's the best-tasting alcohol you'll ever consume. You're sure you don't want this?"

"I'm sure. But thank you. Henry no doubt greatly appreciated the gift. He once told me how much he loves a good cognac. That's why I helped him select the brandy snifters. I knew he'd be putting them to good use."

Suddenly the ringing bell of my memory turned into a warning siren. *Evan Collins. That was one of Evan's aliases. Steve had mentioned the name to Laura during their argument on her front porch. How could Robert have known it?* If Evan had hidden his sordid past from Robert as Robert had claimed, he should have known Evan only as Evan Cambridge!

I swallowed hard but tried to quell my rising anxiousness. This could all be perfectly innocent; Robert probably read about the alias in some newspaper article.

Even so, I needed to make a hasty but inconspicuous exit and call Linda at the police station to discuss this with her. She could be interrogating the wrong man even now.

I forced a smile and rose. "It's been a traumatic day for me. Would you mind terribly if I just grab my check and run?"

"Not at all, Erin. Not at all. And I know just how you feel. George Wong once saved my life. Now it turns out he's a cold-blooded killer." He continued to swirl the contents of his glass, not sipping any of it. He was also not making any moves to actually retrieve the supposedly generous check he'd made out to me.

All of a sudden, my instincts were screaming at me to run.

I took a step toward the door. "Why don't you just mail the check to me?"

"Nonsense. I'll get it for you right now. I put it right here in this little table, just before you arrived. I had this specially made for Henry. A second housewarming present. Do you like it?"

I couldn't answer. I was too terrified. Robert now stood directly in my path toward the door. *Had I already missed my only chance to run?*

"I've got a bonus for you in the table too. A special surprise for you."

My heart was pounding so hard I could barely breathe.

Robert was saying, "I brought the table over to him today."

I slipped my hand inside my purse.

"You're going to want to put the phone down, Erin," he said, all traces of gentility gone.

He pulled a knife out from the drawer. "I was so hoping it wouldn't come to this."

I swallowed hard.

"Sit down, dear. I can strike you dead on the spot, with a knife in the center of your heart. George taught me everything he knew about knives. I can throw them with uncanny accuracy."

Chapter 24

Not needing to be told twice, I dropped into the side chair. As had been the case with Laura, I'd been fooled by Robert's charm and attractive appearance. I couldn't stop myself from asking, "*Why,* Robert?"

"It was business, darling. I've worked too hard to get where I am today to let my employees cheat me. Let alone to steal my money, like Laura did. In my line of work, if I had let her get away with that kind of thing, I may as well have started digging my own grave."

My mouth was dry. I struggled to swallow. "You were the mastermind behind Evan's and Laura's scams?"

"Indeed, indeed." He pursed his lips. "They'd been my

star employees for more than ten years, till Laura became greedy and decided she could become a free agent. When she skipped out on Evan with all the profits, it was *my* money she was taking. And, alas, Jerry Stone was a mistake from the start. He kept bungling all my assignments. I should have realized he lacked the street smarts to work for me. That's what led us here today."

My thoughts raced. *Jerry was a* hit*man*? He must have bungled my would-be death on the garage stairs and later with the poisoned picture frame. But why had he made such a nuisance of himself at Paprika's? Was that a strange attempt to establish a cover for himself—a homeless-but-harmless dreadlocked person who hung out at the Crestview Mall? Or had he used that persona to glean information from Hannah and locate Laura?

"I *did* try hard to warn you to mind your own business, Erin. You sealed your own fate by ignoring my warnings."

"You killed Jerry for bungling your assignments?" I asked.

"Not for that, no." Pembrook smirked. "Jerry, too, was turning traitor. He told you about the poison. Slipped you the photographs I'd kept of Henry and Laura. Jerry left me no choice. I had hoped, though, that finding his body in your office would frighten you off for good." He chuckled. "You could say that I tried to kill two birds with one Jerry Stone."

"Jerry killed Laura on your orders?"

He laughed at the question. "No, no. I would never have hired Jerry for something of that magnitude. As if *that* sorry sap could take anyone's life. He didn't have the backbone. Which, unfortunately for you, is not a weakness I share."

"Did you kill Henry, too?"

"Sound asleep upstairs, darling. I need Henry alive. The poor man's going to take the blame for all three murders."

I fought against the cowardly urge to start sobbing. "But . . . why didn't you just go back to Hollywood, Robert? Nobody suspected you of the murders. There was no reason to involve me."

"Bad luck there, my dear. I made a slip of the tongue the other day . . . mentioning Evan's real last name to you. I knew you'd put it together sooner or later." He held out his brandy snifter. "Take it, my dear. Drink up. You've always been loyal to me, so I've done you a favor and put a nice strong sedative in the brandy. Worked wonders on Hammerin' Hank. It'll be much more pleasant for you to simply drift off to sleep. You won't feel a thing."

With a trembling hand, I accepted the glass.

The doorbell rang.

"Damn it," Robert said under his breath. In a flash, he moved behind me. "That's got to be Sullivan. You have that man wrapped around your finger so tight, he can barely breathe." He dug his fingers into my shoulder and pressed the knife to my throat.

My van was parked in the driveway. If this *was* Steve, there was no way he was going to simply assume nobody was home and leave.

A conversation I'd once had with Laura about judo came back to me with such clarity, I could hear her voice: "The whole key is balance and leverage. You get your weight balanced so that you can use your leverage, then you throw the attacker *off* balance by using his own momentum against him."

The bell rang again.

I could see the door from here, could see the position of the dead bolt. The door had been left unlocked.

Robert leaned his face next to mine and whispered, "Stay put. Make a noise, and it'll be your last."

I grabbed Robert's knife hand with my free hand and simultaneously smashed the snifter into his face with as much force as I could muster. The glass shattered, cutting into him.

He cried out in pain and released his grip on me, the frame of his glasses snapping in two and falling off his face.

I rose and whirled around. Pembrook was clutching at his bleeding face with one hand, the knife in his other hand.

Behind me, the door banged open. Sullivan called, "Erin?"

"Help!" I yelled. My hand was bleeding profusely. Only the stubby stem of the brandy snifter remained in my fist. I dropped that, grabbed the side table by the legs, and swung it at Pembrook's head with all my might. A corner caught him in the temple. He dropped to his knees.

Despite his cast, Sullivan raced toward us. He dived at Pembrook and flattened him on the floor. Within seconds, he had wrenched the knife away from him.

"Call nine-one-one," Sullivan shouted.

I struggled to catch my breath and to get my mind around the fact that Sullivan had immobilized Pembrook, that he couldn't possibly attack either of us now. Then I grabbed the phone and dialed.

Chapter 25

Whenever you're faced with a hopelessly complex task, concentrate exclusively on performing the first few steps to absolute perfection, and the rest will follow.

—Audrey Munroe

Audrey didn't acknowledge me as I entered the kitchen, apparently too focused on the recipe cards she was thumbing through. Much as I adored every square inch of this room, tonight not even the sweet, tantalizing aromas emanating from the oven could cheer me. I chucked my drawing pad onto the counter and dropped onto a wooden bar stool in front of her. These caned seats were a new purchase and were wonderful; painted the same snow white as the cabinets and trim, they brought the casual elegance of the classic country kitchen chair into the space.

Audrey swept back her bangs. "You're looking a little down, Erin. Are your injuries still bothering you?"

"No, just the bandages." Pembrook's knife had nicked my neck at the shoulder. The wound was, thankfully, shallow, and had only required a butterfly adhesive. It was the cuts from the glass shards in my right hand that had required stitches and splints and would take longer to heal. With Audrey at last granting me a willing audience, I whined, "They're driving me nuts! It's been two days now! I can't draw . . . I can't grip a pencil or a brush. And the worst thing is, I'm going to be like this for at least a week or two, and that's *assuming* everything heals properly. In the meantime, I'm going to be unable to work."

"I thought John Norton was helping you."

"He is." To my surprise, John Norton had insisted upon taking time off work and serving as my "right-hand man." Furthermore, last night he announced that he'd decided he wasn't giving up so easily, that he'd fight even his good friend Steve Sullivan for my affections. "But by next Monday, he has to get back to his own job, and I'll be completely on my own."

"In that case, this will be an excellent opportunity for you to concentrate on all the other aspects of your job," Audrey said with a one-shoulder shrug. "Surely the first few steps to designing interiors have nothing whatsoever to do with putting your plans down on paper. Don't you visualize, plan, find creative solutions to your clients' problems, all in your head before you begin to draw?"

"Yes, of course," I retorted, a little annoyed at how she'd dismissed my troubles as though they were mere specks of lint on a velvet pillow. "And *then* I draw the design. With this!" I held up my useless, bandaged hand.

"So you'll have to adjust your schedule such that, by the time you need to put pencil to paper, your bandages will have been removed." The timer on the stove dinged. She donned her poppy-patterned oven mitts and opened the oven. "In the meantime, you'll have been forced to put all your energy into those ultra-important initial steps of design. I'm telling you from experience, Erin, your end results will only be the better for all of this."

"From *experience*?" I mocked; the woman hadn't worked a single day as a professional interior designer. Instantly I felt a pang for taking out my frustrations on her. Noting the splendid dessert she was removing from the oven, I said, "Your lemon meringue pie looks like something off the cover of a recipe book! I'm thoroughly impressed. I can make a delicious lemon pie, and my meringue looks great with its fluffy white peaks as it's going *into* the oven. But it always comes *out* all sunken and runny and pathetic."

"This is what I'm saying, Erin." She removed her oven mitts and wagged her index finger in my face. "You've got to concentrate on getting the initial steps absolutely flawless. To make meringue, for example, you have to chill the bowl first. You have to get fresh eggs, straight from the farm."

I frowned and sighed, certain that even if I did

those things, my pie would still look nothing like Audrey's.

"You're obviously not convinced." She arched her brow and crossed her arms, regarding me for a moment. "How old do you think I was when I had my first dance lesson?"

I leaned my elbows on the cool, glassy surface of the counter, anticipating a story, which, truth be told, I yearned to hear; I was so sad about how things had ended with Robert Pembrook that I was sorely in need of some old-fashioned, home-and-hearth family connections at the moment. "I don't know. Five or six?"

"I was sixteen."

I sat up. "You're kidding me!"

"No, I'm perfectly serious, Erin. I was sixteen years old and fully grown." She grinned and gestured at herself in her slinky gold-and-indigo silk caftan. "That is, if you consider five foot two as fully grown. In any case, I was the same height then that I am now."

"That's . . . amazing, Audrey. Aren't many dancers already starting to realize by sixteen that they don't have the talent to make it professionally?"

"Oh, absolutely. In fact, George himself used to comment about that very point. He would—"

"George?" I asked, thinking this was probably some ex-husband that I hadn't yet heard her mention.

"Balanchine. He used to—"

"Wait. You knew George Balanchine?"

"Of course. There's only one New York City Ballet company, and George was its prominent figure."

I furrowed my brow, worried that she was pulling my leg. "So you were on a first-name basis with George Balanchine? With the greatest choreographer of the twentieth century?"

She clicked her tongue. "You're really interfering with the flow of this story, Erin, and I *do* have a point."

"Sorry. Go ahead." I tightened my one good fist under the table to force myself to concentrate on not blurting out a host of questions that had popped into my head about her days of hobnobbing with such a famous person.

"Mr. *Balanchine* used to ask me, 'How did you do it, Audrey? How did you get so accomplished at dance when you started so late in life?' I had to tell him that I honestly didn't know, but that it probably all boiled down to the fact that, by the time I finally began to learn dance, I knew that I simply did *not* have the time to unlearn any bad habits. So you know what I did?"

Not wanting to again be accused of interrupting her, I waited a beat and then said cautiously, "No. What?"

"At the dance school, they tried to enroll me in a class with beginning adults, and I said, 'Absolutely not. Put me in with the youngest students. *Those* are the ones who are going to be getting the best instruction on all the basics.' After all, at age five or six, virtually every student has a chance at becoming a prima ballerina. Not so in an adult-beginners class. Granted, the teachers and the little students would give me funny looks . . . . this young woman in a class with girls ten years younger than she. But I went into that class determined to learn the fundamental steps of ballet to absolute perfection. I knew that then, and only then, could I get to where I needed to be."

"Huh," I muttered, impressed and surprised by her tale. I thought a moment about the very design that I was working on now and realized that she was right. Half of those clients' problems stemmed from a slight flaw in the foundation in their house, which then led to a crack in the wall. I was now working on a furniture plan for the very room with the cracked wall, but what really needed to be done was to rebuild that wall with a new foundation. I could do that by extending the dimensions of the room a little—and thereby give them that reading nook that the wife so craved.

"That is truly unbelievable, Audrey. So, you somehow managed to—" I glanced at my watch as I was speaking and leapt to my feet when I saw that it was already a couple of minutes past six P.M. "Oh, shoot! I'm late for a meeting!"

"With a client?"

"No, with Steve Sullivan."

"Oh, good. I'm glad you won't be alone tonight. I'm going to an old friend's house for dinner. And by 'old friend,' I mean both literally and figuratively. You'd be bored out of your mind." She nodded at her perfect pie. "I'm bringing dessert."

I retrieved my purse from where I'd dropped it, gingerly angling the strap onto my right shoulder with my left hand, and headed for the door. "I'll see you in the morning, then, Audrey."

"Take care. And I mean *that* literally, Erin. Do *not* get into trouble!"

"I'll be fine." I smiled at her as I snatched my keys, again in my left hand, resisting an urge to hug the dear woman.

"I hope so." She narrowed her eyes at me, apparently not confident that I was not charging off to once again confront a murderer. "Between Sullivan's broken leg and your bandaged hand and neck, all you'll need now is a fife and a drummer boy with a bandaged head."

I chuckled and said goodbye, then made the short drive downtown, deciding I'd be better off parking at my office and walking than looking for a space at this hour. Ever since the arrest two days ago, I'd barely spoken to Sullivan. He'd suddenly dropped by my office early this afternoon and insisted that I join him at Rusty's this evening. Frankly, though, I was a little hurt that it had taken him that long to get in touch with me.

I waited for the pedestrian light to change and hurried across the street. Rusty's was now within sight.

Someone's cell phone went off nearby, and I glanced to either side of me. Nobody seemed close enough for the tune to be playing quite so loudly. I slowed my pace, puzzled. The phone continued to ring, and I realized that the sound was emanating from my own purse. That was bizarre, because, with my right hand out of commission, I had stashed my cell phone in my left jacket pocket, and *this* phone was literally playing a different tune—a familiar one that I couldn't quite place.

As I struggled to sort through my purse with my good hand, I realized just as I located the silver phone that it was playing a Gilbert and Sullivan song. *A joke from Sullivan?*

"Hello?" I said tentatively, coming to a standstill. If this was Sullivan calling to say he'd be late, there was little reason for me to race to Rusty's.

"You found the present, I see." *Sullivan's voice.* "Good."

"You got me a cell phone? I already have one, you know."

"It's just a loaner. I borrowed it from someone I know. That's not the gift, just the wrapping. Did you recognize the song?"

To my annoyance, I had butterflies in my stomach and my pulse was racing. Was this his way of suggesting more emphatically that we become partners? If so, I might need to point out to him that the collaboration between the original Gilbert and Sullivan had been very stormy; supposedly the two men were constantly at each other's throat. Sir *Sullivan's* fault, no doubt.

Besides, ever since Pembrook's arrest, John had

been treating me like a queen. In addition to waiting on me hand and foot at work, he had sent me a gorgeous bouquet, with a touching get-well card urging me to give him a second chance. I longed to accept the offer and choose an easier path, for once in my life.

"Gilbert?" Sullivan prompted. "Do you know the song?"

"Yes. It's a Gilbert and Sullivan tune. From *The Mikado*."

"Right you are, little lady," he said in a game-show-host voice. "And now, for the bonus question, Miss Gilbert, what is the *title* of that song?"

I had to think for a moment, but was able to replay the notes in my head until the words came back to me. "'Let the Punishment Fit the Crime.'"

"Ladies and gentleman, we have a winner!"

I grinned and peered at Rusty's storefront, just a block away. I wondered if that's where he was calling from. "I don't get it, Sullivan."

"It means I'm hereby going to stop punishing myself and everyone who tries to get close to me because of what Laura did to me."

I smiled, delighted and very surprised at this anti-Sullivan-like pronouncement. "Good for you. I'm really glad to hear that."

"Thanks. And one more thing before we hang up. I'm really sorry I've been such a jerk."

"Hey! Wait a minute, buster!" I said with a chuckle. "Is *that* my long-overdue apology?"

"Yep."

"Over the *phone*? Jeez, Sullivan! I'm, like, two seconds

away from Rusty's! You couldn't wait and do this face-to-face?"

"Turn around, and I'll repeat myself."

I whirled around. He was behind me, standing a block or so away. I must have passed him moments ago.

He stuck his phone back in his pocket, cupped his hands around his mouth like a megaphone, and shouted, "I'm sorry, Gilbert."

I laughed, but then held my hand behind my ear and called, "What did you say? I can't quite hear you."

He limped toward me. When he reached me, he announced, "I said, 'I'm starving, Gilbert.' Let me take you to dinner."

He looked positively scrumptious in his preppy baby-blue polo shirt and khakis, that Hollywood smile on his handsome features. Maybe he'd truly changed. Maybe this was a new start for us. Just as Audrey had advised, we could now concentrate on getting our initial, fundamental steps right, and we'd be able to proceed from there—to get along, to quit bickering over every inanity that arose. "It's a deal," I said, beaming at him. "But I'd like to choose the restaurant."

"I made reservations at a sushi bar."

"I hate sushi," I blurted out.

"You'll like this place."

"Fine. Just so long as it's not Jimmy Sum's. I got food poisoning there."

He scoffed, "No way did you get food poisoning from Jimmy Sum's. I've eaten there at least a dozen times, and I'm telling you, the food is great. You probably got the stomach flu and jumped to the conclusion that it was the restaurant's fault."

I gritted my teeth, but was determined not to leap down his throat at the implication that he knew more than I did about my own health history. "Let's just go to Rusty's. All right?"

"Can't. It's packed. And you were late. They made me relinquish the reservations, so that's why I made new ones at Jimmy Sum's."

"Let's get Mexican."

He shook his head and snapped, "I had that for lunch."

"Jeez, Sullivan!"

"Hey! You're the one who was late and made me blow off the reservations!"

"You didn't tell me we had reservations! I'd have been on time if I'd known!"

"In other words, you could be on time for a free meal, but can't be bothered to be on time for me otherwise. Thanks, Gilbert. That makes me feel great."

"Oh, whereas you're making me feel just peachy, Sullivan!"

He flung his hands aloft. "Then we're stuck with keeping our reservations at the sushi bar. And if you get food poisoning, I hereby vow to act as your indentured servant for a period of one full month, or until one of us kills the other, whichever comes first."

"Deal," I said with a sigh. As he began to limp toward Jimmy Sum's and I struggled to match my stride with his, it was yet another lesson learned today: Gilbert and Sullivan would never, *ever,* be mistaken for Rogers and Astaire.

about the author

Leslie Caine was once taken hostage at gunpoint and finds that writing about crimes is infinitely more enjoyable than taking part in them. Leslie is a certified interior decorator and lives in Colorado with her husband, two teenage children, and a cocker spaniel, where she is at work on her next Domestic Bliss mystery, *Manor of Death*.

If you enjoyed the latest Domestic Bliss mystery, **FALSE PREMISES**, you won't want to miss any in Leslie Caine's charming series.

Look for the first Domestic Bliss mystery, **DEATH BY INFERIOR DESIGN**, at your favorite bookseller.

And read on for a tantalizing early look at Leslie Caine's next mystery, **MANOR OF DEATH,** in which Eric Gilbert redecorates a home rich with history . . . and reveals old unsolved crimes, unexamined truths of the past . . . and new complications in Gilbert and Sullivan's budding relationship!

MANOR OF DEATH

a domestic bliss mystery

by

Leslie Caine

Coming in Spring 2006 from Dell

MANOR OF DEATH

Coming in Spring 2006

A ghost was on Francine Findley's roof! That was my first thought at spotting the figure in white—almost luminescent in the moonlight outside my bedroom window.

My second thought was that the stress I'd been under lately was getting to me. Not a ghost. Just a girl wearing a white nightgown, her long red tresses blowing in the breeze. Could that be *Lisa*, up on her mother's roof at this hour? Who else had long red hair? No, this girl was taller and older than the twelve-year-old Lisa. It was too dark and too distant for me to be certain, but she looked a lot like Willow

McAndrews, the college coed who was renting a room in the house next door to Francine's. Willow had short blond hair, though.

Still staring out the window, I brushed aside the sheets, swung my legs off the bed, and struggled to rouse myself from my brain fog. Why would Willow McAndrews don a red wig and climb out onto her neighbor's roof? And how could she or anyone else get onto the roof of the third-floor "tower room" in the first place?

As an interior designer, I was intimately familiar with Francine Findley's octagonal-shaped room. She had hired me recently to renovate her Victorian mansion in preparation for Crestview, Colorado's, annual tour of historic homes. Contrary to my advice, Francine had insisted on keeping the wall intact that sealed off the only staircase to the roof. Decades ago, previous owners had built that wall after their daughter had fallen to her death, a tragedy that later inspired the rumor that the ghost of "Abby" haunted the widow's walk—the flat banister roof modeled after homes along New England shores where wives of fishermen could watch for their husbands' boats.

That afternoon Francine had mentioned that she, too, was exhausted and planned to "have an early dinner and collapse in bed tonight." She could have been forced to leave home suddenly and had asked Willow to stay overnight to watch Lisa. That would at least explain Willow's presence *in* the house, just not *on* it. The windows were all dark. Should I call Francine's cell phone? I looked at my radio alarm clock on my nightstand. The red digital numbers read 1:06 A.M.—a horrid hour to call a single mother probably in the midst of a real emergency merely to report that her sitter was walking around on the roof.

I looked outside again, but just like that, the girl was gone. She couldn't possibly have climbed down a ladder or even eased herself over the railing that fast. She must have dashed down the stairs and was now in the three-by-ten-foot walled-off space. That meant she was getting in and out through the window near the staircase. The glass had been boarded up, though, last time I'd looked. Yawning, I rubbed at my eyes as I lay back down, cursing this insomnia that had left me so addled for the past month. In desperation, I'd poured a small fortune into my bed: Egyptian sheets that felt like the finest silk, a goose-down comforter, which—

Wait! I bolted upright. There was a second—and horrible—means for someone to vanish from a rooftop in an instant!

I gasped as my door creaked farther open. I could make out my black cat's silhouette in the doorway and see her yellow eyes. My heart pounding, I looked out the window again. No one was on the roof. "Oh, Hildi, I have to go check my neighbor's yard!"

I flicked on the small vintage table lamp atop my nightstand, sprang from my bed, jammed my arms into the sleeves of my dusty-rose bathrobe, and grabbed the first shoes I could find—black sandals. I hoped I wouldn't trip on the two-inch heels if I had to run to assist some badly injured girl. I started for the door, then remembered I had a small flashlight by my bed and doubled back. I snatched that up and raced down the stairs, my confused cat darting out of my path. I threw open the back door, crammed my feet into my shoes, and tore across the lawn. My leather soles slipped with my every step on the wet grass, but, thankfully, I was able to maintain my balance and didn't slow my pace until I reached the landscape rocks among the row of rosebushes that rimmed our property line. It hit me then that I absolutely did not want to go traipsing around my neighbor's property at that hour.

With the stones crunching beneath my feet, I stopped at the short decorative wrought-iron fence and swept my dim beam across Francine's back lawn. "Hello? Is anybody out here?" I asked the silent darkness, my voice barely above a whisper.

No groans. No crumpled bodies clad in white nightgowns. No maniacal cackles, either. My presence did, however, set off Francine's next-door-neighbor's dog to barking—Hillary Durst's beagle. Hillary's attic window was aglow with a yellow light. Was that lamp on earlier, or had I wakened her? Or could that be the room that Willow McAndrews was renting from Hillary? If so, Willow had the closest view available of Francine's widow's walk. Hillary had once told me that her new renter was a rock climber; maybe pretending to be the red-haired ghost of some unfortunate, long-dead soul was Willow's idea of humor.

Hildi joined me, her soft fur now brushing against

my bare shins. One reassuring thought occurred to me as I turned around: if anyone had fallen off Francine's roof, Bugle would *already* be barking.

Come to think of it, his shrill barks were what had originally awakened me.

Crestview, Colorado, was doing its best impression of Seattle on the mid-June afternoon as I walked to Francine's home. I held my London Fog overcoat closed with my free hand, careful not to crush the rolled-up four-foot lengths of wallpaper that I'd angled into my inner pockets. The steady patter of raindrops on my umbrella was a soothing sound, which was helpful to me. When I'd called Francine that morning and reported what I'd seen last night, Francine assured me she'd been home all night and that "it is absolutely impossible that there was a prowler on my roof." She sounded as though she thought I was as flaky as old paint on a picnic table.

Could I have dreamed the whole thing? I'd never had such a vivid dream, if so. Maybe my current struggles with the neighborhood association and with my beloved landlady, Audrey Munroe, were wreaking havoc with me, even during my sleep.

While stepping over a puddle, I silently repeated my personal mantra: confidence and optimism. In so many ways, this was my all-time dream assignment—an interior-design job within my own astonishingly lovely neighborhood of Maplewood Hill, at the Victorian mansion that I'd lusted over for two years now, ever since I'd first moved to Crestview. Granted, I'd hit nothing but snags and roadblocks so far, but that goes with the territory—the better the job, the bigger the challenges.

And, after all, Audrey had already told me she understood and supported my decision to accept this assignment at Francine's—that I couldn't very well damage my career without as much as knowing *why* Audrey didn't "wish to associate with Francine. Ever." (Nor was Audery willing to elaborate on the matter, even so.)

Furthermore, soon enough the neighborhood association would approve of our plans to install three picture windows within the tower room. If not, I would plead with Francine on bended knee till she allowed me to go with my plan A: remove the blasted inner wall that made the room all lopsided. Her sole argument was that she had "a severe fear of heights" and didn't want Lisa to be able to get onto the roof. But, for the life of me, I couldn't understand why she refused to let us simply remove both the wall *and* the staircase to the roof. Be that as it may, when it comes to interior design, the customer is always right; after all, the customer, not the designer, is the one who will live with the final results. However, some customers need more nudges than others to discover their own good taste and sound decision-making skills. Francine Findley required a nice, firm shove in the back, and fortunately for her, she'd hired just the right designer to give her one.

Speaking of shoves, a chilly blast of wind encouraged me to step up my pace a little. Francine's and

Audrey's backyards bordered each other, so when the lawns weren't drenched and muddy, it was a thirty-second walk between our back doors. Even as I picked my way across a veritable river forming along-side Francine's walkway, I was so taken by the looming presence of the tower room that I tilted my umbrella to look up. The curtains were quivering, as though someone had spotted me and ducked out of sight—Lisa Findley, no doubt, Francine's daughter.

Protected by the roof over the Findley's stoop, I shook off my umbrella and closed it. I rang the old-fashioned twist-key doorbell, and after a brief wait, Francine, a pretty woman in her late forties with auburn hair like mine, threw open the door and greeted me with a gusty "Good afternoon, Erin."

"Hi, Francine. We're having quite the shower to-day."

"We sure are. Let me take your coat for you."

I thanked her, wondering once again what could possibly have caused such a deep rift between my landlady and Francine in the three short years since Francine had moved to Crestview. She had always been nice to me. "I've got the wallpaper samples in my coat pockets," I explained as I extracted the samples and some heavy-duty double-sided sticky tape.

"I *thought* you looked a little stiff—and wide—around the waistline," she teased. As she grabbed a hanger out of the coat closet, I noticed a Halloween costume. It was a cheap department-store purchase—a skeleton painted on thin polyster black fabric and a plastic mask for the skull, its elastic cord looped over the hanger hook.

"Oh, look, Francine," I said with a grin, "it seems as though you've got a skeleton in your closet."

Francine followed my gaze, chuckled, and said, "Well, I suppose we *all* have skeletons in our closets. But this one in particular must be Lisa's doing." Francine clicked her tongue and said with a sigh, "She must be trying to give us a message about the lack of closet space in her bedroom."

Along with my landlady and the homeowners' association, Lisa was a third source of contention for me on this particular job. Francine's twelve-year-old had been on very friendly terms with me—up until she'd learned that I had been hired to turn her would-be bedroom into a studio for her mom. It was my job to insure that *all* members of the family were satisfied—and preferably thrilled—with the transformation of their living spaces. "I can design a wonderful, spacious closet for her."

Francine scoffed, "Oh, that won't do the trick. Believe me."

"She's still hinting that she wants to have the third-floor room as her bedroom, then?"

"Yes. But I've told her all along that I was eventually going to convert that room into my music studio." Francine was a musician who played some kind of modern-day electronic harp that she'd yet to demonstrate for me. "But now, after we've lived here for almost three years, she seems to think—"

Francine broke off as a door above us slammed, followed by the sound of tromping footsteps down the stairs. Lisa, Francine's only child, sneered at me as she descended the final step. Today she wore a black camisole underneath a demin jacket. She was a freckle-faced redhead, and I couldn't help but study her now to see if that could have been Lisa on the roof, after all. I was certain, though, that the girl I saw was a young woman and not Lisa. She lowered the headphones on her Walkman as she returned my steady gaze and grumbled, "Oh. *You're* here."

"Yes, Erin just arrived," her mother replied breezily. "Which you would have realized if you weren't always pumping rock music into your ears."

Despite Francine's pleasant tone of voice, Lisa rolled her eyes.

Francine smiled at me and, while Lisa grabbed a backpack out of the closet and slung a strap over one shoulder, explained, "Lisa here is off on a sleepover before her best friend leaves town for three weeks."

Lisa shrugged off her mother's attempt to hug her, muttering, "You don't need to tell the whole world my private business, Mom."

"I'm only mentioning it because, at some point soon, the three of us need to sit down together and discuss what we want done with your bedroom."

"Jeez! I already *told* you! I *want* the tower room as my bedroom! If I can't have that, you might as well do whatever *you* want to *my* room!"

It was now Francine's turn to roll her eyes in response to her daughter's words. In a huff, Lisa proceeded to step into a pair of black flip-flops on the closet floor.

"We noticed your Halloween costume, by the way, dear."

"*What* costume?"

"This skeleton." Francine removed the costume on its hanger to show Lisa.

Lisa clicked her tongue and replied in a voice rancid with disdain, "That's not mine. I've never seen it before."

"Well, it certainly isn't *mine*. It's six sizes too small, for one thing."

Francine examined the tag inside the costume neckline as she stashed it back in the closet and added, "It must be one of your friend's costumes, then."

"Nope. Not possible. I'd've remembered. Bet it's Abby's."

"Lisa!" her mother admonished.

"Abby's a ghost," Lisa explained, one hand on her hip, which was jutted out in my general direction. "Our house has been haunted ever since a teenage girl jumped off the roof fifty years ago. Abby lives in the room that you're remodeling. And, I can tell you right now, she is *not* going to approve of the way you plan to destroy her bedroom."

"Lisa! That's enough!"

Whether Lisa felt the same way about me or not, I liked her immensely and understood her frustration at losing out on her favorite space. I smiled at her and said, "Then we'll just have to put all our heads together to come up with a fabulous room that we *all* approve of."

"Yeah. Like *that's* gonna happen." She made a derisive noise and returned her headphones to her ears. "I gotta go, Mom. We're riding our bikes and meeting halfway."

"But . . . it's pouring outside."

"I know," Lisa said. "That's why we're riding our bikes." Lisa headed out the door, letting the screen door slam in her wake.

"Wait!" Francine followed her out to the stoop. Lisa was rolling a bike across the lawn that must have been leaning upright against the west side of the house. "You shouldn't be wearing sandals while you're riding your bike. And take your headphones off!"

The flip-flops stayed put, but Francine managed to pantomime the removal of her headphones and, although Lisa grumbled something to herself in the process, she pushed the headphones down to her neck. Francine sighed and watched her daughter, holding up a hand and calling, "See you tomorrow," as Lisa rode off.

Francine shut the door. "Sorry about that, Erin. Lisa's social skills have been taking a nosedive, ever since her father's and my divorce."

"Oh, hey, it's truly not a problem. Lisa's a total sweetheart most of the time. My half sister's roughly Lisa's age, and she's equally moody." The fact that I rarely got the chance to see my sister, who lived in California with my semi-estranged father, brought a lump to my throat.

Again Francine rolled her eyes. "I'm just hoping she grows out of this soon."

I decided to give the matter of last night's nocturnal visit one last mention. If Willow was climbing up the tower on a lark to fool people into thinking she was a ghost, Francine might want to reconsider hiring her as Lisa's baby-sitter. "It's funny that Lisa happened to mention Abby. Last night when I saw someone on—"

Francine guffawed, interrupting me. "Oh, heavens! Is this about the 'prowler' you think you saw? Erin, you don't actually believe that ghost nonsense, do you?"

"No, of course not. I was going to suggest that Willow McAndrews might be doing this as a practical joke, making people think that they'd seen Abby."

Her jaw dropped. "What possible reason would Willow have to pull something like that? Honestly, Erin! You must have been dreaming last night. That's all." She spread her arms for dramatic effect. "That's the only rational explanation."

Truth be told, I'd rather believe that I saw a ghost than worry that I was losing my mind. Which is what it would take for me to be unable to distinguish my dreams from reality. I forced a smile as I searched her green eyes, curious as to why she was so resolute; from her second-floor bedroom she wouldn't necessarily have heard someone on the tower roof.

The doorbell rang. Francine shook her head and chuckled. "Watch. This'll be Lisa's friend. They'll have taken different routes and missed each other."

She swung the door open, but it was Hillary Durst who'd rung the bell. Hillary, a real estate agent who ran the historic homes tour, was in her late thirties, plump but attractive, with dark brown hair and eyes.

She wore one of her customary pastel skirt-suits and her ever-present broad smile.

"Come in, Hillary."

"Brrr," she exclaimed to Francine. "Goodness! It's raining cats and dogs out there!" She craned her neck a little to smile at me. "Hello, Erin. I spotted you on the sidewalk a minute ago and hoped you'd be here."

"Hi, Hillary." I couldn't help but return her smile. The woman was always so upbeat that anything else would feel like scowling at a puppy. Which reminded me: should I admit that I caused her dog to bark at one in the morning?

She touched Francine's arm. "Did you hear any strange noises last night, Francine? Coming from the tower room, maybe?"

"Oh, *no!*" Putting her hands on her hips to emulate her daughter, she clicked her tongue. "You, *too?*"

"Pardon?"

"Erin told me on the phone this morning that she thought she saw someone on my roof."

"Oh! Oh!" Hillary was actually bouncing up and down as she turned away from Francine to look at me. She'd once told me she was a former cheerleader, and right now it was easy to envision her with pom-poms. "This is so exciting! I knew you and Audrey would have had a good view. Did you see her?"

"The girl on the roof, you mean?"

Hillary giggled and put a hand to her chest. "Oh, thank goodness! Someone other than just me saw her! Did you show Audrey, too, by any chance?"

"No, I didn't want to wake her, but—"

"This is amazing!" In her excitement, Hillary grabbed Francine's wrist. "We'll be able to sell twice as many tickets now, once the word gets out."

"*What* word?" Francine asked, in no way sharing Hillary's perky attitude.